PENGUIN BOOKS

...ıs Year's for Me and You

Emily Bell is an *Irish Times* bestselling author who grew up in Dublin and moved to London after university. She has had various jobs including tour guide, bookseller and pub singer, and now writes full time. She lives in north London with her husband and daughter.

By the same author

Baby It's Cold Outside

This Year's for Me and You

EMILY BELL

PENGUIN BOOKS

PENGUIN BOOKS

UK | USA | Canada | Ireland | Australia
India | New Zealand | South Africa

Penguin Books is part of the Penguin Random House group of companies
whose addresses can be found at global.penguinrandomhouse.com

First published 2022
001

Set in 12.5/14.75pt Garamond MT Std
Typeset by Jouve (UK), Milton Keynes
Printed and bound in Great Britain by Clays Ltd, Elcograf S.p.A.

The authorized representative in the EEA is Penguin Random House Ireland,
Morrison Chambers, 32 Nassau Street, Dublin DO2 YH68

A CIP catalogue record for this book is available from the British Library

ISBN: 978–1–405–95269–9

www.greenpenguin.co.uk

Penguin Random House is committed to a
sustainable future for our business, our readers
and our planet. This book is made from Forest
Stewardship Council® certified paper.

To my nieces Giulia and Marianne
With love

Prologue

New Year's Eve

'Celeste! I'm here! Quick, quick – only four hours till midnight!'

It's Hannah, right on time, which is early for her. I'm halfway through applying cat's-eye liner, a rare and risky manoeuvre for me, so I call 'Hang on' as loudly as I can through the edge of my mouth. But Hannah, not hearing me, continues to bang cheerfully on the door until I run out to let her in.

'You have a key, don't you?' I ask, laughing and giving her a hug.

'Of course I do, but where's the fun if I just let myself in? Oooh, I love the eye make-up. Asymmetrical! That's going to be the next trend, I'd say.'

Hannah hangs up her coat, zips up my silver dress and puts the Prosecco and cheesecake she's brought in the fridge, all in the time it takes me to finish doing my left eye. I've bought the cassis liqueur that she likes, so she pours herself a Kir royale and me a glass of plain fizz, moving swiftly as she knows where everything is.

'Cheers! That really suits you,' she says when I'm done.

'I know it's a bit mad putting on make-up when it's just us two, but I felt like dressing up.' I close the eyeliner and put it away carefully in my 'fancy make-up' drawer, full of

1

intimidating implements and palettes; all purchased aspirationally and rarely used.

'Well, if it's just us, that's even more of an occasion. When's the last time it was just the two of us? I've even made a special New Year's playlist! May I, madam?'

She connects her phone with my speaker; soon 'Celebration' by Kool and the Gang is playing and we start to bop around my tiny galley kitchen, from which most of my one-bedroom flat is visible, including the sofa bed where Hannah will sleep later.

It *is* a bit odd to be having a slumber party for New Year's Eve at the ripe old age of thirty-five. But our friends are all increasingly coupled up and unlikely to want to spend New Year's Eve at a crowded bar or even at a party. Sibéal and Rishi are exhausted with two children under five; Mel and her boyfriend Pablo are having a cosy evening together. Of course, Hannah is part of a couple herself, but Vikram, her boyfriend, isn't bothered about New Year's. So she's journeyed from their place in Hackney to my flat in Finsbury Park to continue our tradition, unbroken since that first one we shared in Dublin when we were eighteen; we always spend New Year's Eve together.

It's fashionable to hate on New Year's, but Hannah and I both love it with its particular mix of nostalgia and novelty. Hannah loves the dressing up, partying and new beginnings – three of her favourite things. I love the sense of occasion, the chance to say a proper goodbye to the year that's been, however good or bad. And we've always agreed that if Christmas is for family and Valentine's is for couples, New Year's should be for friends. I didn't really expect our tradition to last after Hannah and Vikram got so serious – but so far it has, which makes me feel a bit guilty tonight.

'Are you sure Vik doesn't mind spending the evening alone?' I ask. 'He could have come too.'

'Not at all . . . He knows this is our thing. And he'll be delighted to have a night in alone to play *Super Mario* in his pants. Anyway.' She holds out her drink for another toast. 'Cheers! Happy New Year!'

We both clink, take a sip, and I beam at her while admiring her outfit. She's also dressed up: her tawny hair is scraped up in an artlessly messy bun and she's wearing a navy printed jacket with a black-and-red silk camisole peeping out from underneath and no make-up except red lipstick. Wide black trousers and flat shoes that would look like granny slippers on me. Very Hackney, very Hannah.

'So . . . it's all going ahead, with the house?' I ask.

'It should be.' She holds up crossed fingers. 'The whole probate thing has finally concluded, and we've signed the paperwork so . . . yep. We need to get a date for the keys, but we're hoping February.'

In a bizarre accident of family history, Hannah's boyfriend Vik has inherited a house in Suffolk – not just a house but a literal manor, complete with a pond and resident swan. I can't imagine Hannah, an urban creature to her bones, really living there. It's not that I don't think it will happen – Hannah always does what she says she will. And she and Vik are solid, four years in. I'm just worried that she will miss her countless friends and the urban buzz here, not to mention her Deliveroos and Ubers. Mostly I'm worried about how much I will miss her.

Reading my mind, as ever, she says, 'It won't change

anything, Celeste. I mean, it will, but you'll just have to come and stay. We'll have a big house party for next New Year's – it will be like something out of Agatha Christie but without the murder. And I'll come here whenever I need an urban plunge. It'll be great.'

I smile at her, marvelling at how she's got it all worked out. 'Of course you will. It's just . . . how do you know? I mean, how do you know that it's the right thing for both of you?'

She shrugs. 'I don't really. But there's only one way to find out, isn't there? Sometimes you just have to hold your nose and jump.'

I clink my glass against hers. 'Well, here's to the move. I can't wait to see you and Vik – lord and lady of the manor.'

'Thanks, hon. It's going to be a bit of a scramble – I'll just be back from skiing with my mum when I have to pack for the manor move.' She throws her head back and laughs. 'It's a hard life, isn't it?'

'The worst,' I agree. 'Is your mum looking forward to skiing? Has she been before?'

'Nope,' says Hannah. 'I mean . . . am I proud that she's taking up adrenaline sports at the age of sixty-two? Yes. Am I a bit nervous she'll bust her ankle on day two and we'll have to airlift her back to Dublin? Also yes.'

'Well, she's earned the right to take a few risks, hasn't she?' I say. Hannah's mum was successfully treated for breast cancer three years ago.

'She sure has,' Hannah says soberly. 'No, it will be great. I'm looking forward to it.'

'Here's to Dervla,' I say, and we clink glasses – again.

Hannah continues, 'She does love the idea of me and

Vik living in a manor house. Though the number of bedrooms is giving her some ammunition on the whole grandchild thing. "You need to get busy filling those", etc.' She rolls her eyes.

'You'd like that too some day – right?' I ask, not because I want to pry but to make sure I haven't misunderstood her feelings on the subject.

'Sure, some day, but not now. We've enough on our plate with the move . . . Ooh, I nearly forgot.' Hannah digs in her bag. 'I have a present for you.'

She pulls out a tiny package, exquisitely wrapped, a skill honed during her long stints working in various retail places while building her illustration work on the side. I open it and gasp. It's a necklace, but not just any necklace; it's a silver version of her precious golden bee necklace. Bees are Hannah's personal symbol – she's always had a thing for them and she has a ton of bee-themed items, from mugs to writing paper.

'I can see why you like them,' I said once. 'They're sort of like you.'

'Loud and annoying, you mean?'

I had grinned. 'Buzzy – and hard-working – and good at networking.'

Now I thank her profusely and put the necklace on, admiring how it looks with my black hair and paper-white skin. To make room for it I start to take off the other necklace that I always wear – the one with the emerald pendant, which I bought for myself after I gave back my engagement ring.

As she watches me take it off, she says, 'Hey, you can wear them both!'

I look at her, knowing, as ever with Hannah, that she understands the significance of my necklace – a kind of promise to myself that I would make a great life on my own. She nods and continues, 'Layering. You may have heard of it.'

'I have . . . but I've never really got the hang of it. I can only cope with one necklace at a time. But this is so gorgeous – thank you.' I feel bad that she spent all this money on me, especially as she's presumably saving for the house move, but that's Hannah: generous to a fault and also fairly free with the old credit card.

'I love that I'm in bee club now. And I love that it's silver . . . I've been paranoid ever since reading that article that said silver is out. As are heels, apparently.'

Hannah rolls her eyes, dismissing the idea of trends, as trendy people often do. 'Whatever. I suppose, yes, gold and flats are more – modern. But silver is you. You're silver and heels, and you always will be. Never change, Celeste.' She gives me a hug.

'I won't,' I tell her, hugging her back. 'OK, now I have something for you . . .' I skip the three steps to my bedroom, excited to show her what I have.

Hannah unwraps the small package and then shrieks out loud. 'Celeste,' she says, 'I can't believe this. Where did you get it?'

'It was in my old room at home. You know I've been meaning to clear it out for donkey's years . . . anyway, I found it among a whole load of Leaving Cert notes on oxbow lakes.'

It's a framed photo of the first New Year's Eve we ever spent together, when we were eighteen: New Year's Eve,

1999, the Millennium. Me, Hannah and some others in the drawing room of her beautiful old house in Dalkey, County Dublin. What a night. All sorts of people came, we danced till 3 a.m. and then fell asleep in various heaps around the house. Until the next morning, most magical of all, we took a boat out to Dalkey Island and lit a fire there as the sun was rising.

'I love it. I can't even remember anyone taking it – who was it?'

'It might have been your mum,' I say. 'Don't you remember, she came home and you thought she was going to throw everyone out, but she stayed for a drink? Look, there's Deirdre Fogarty there and John Ryan . . .'

'Oh, and look, there's Patrick! We just saw him last week.'

'Oh yeah.' This is Hannah's old family friend, who has just moved to London on a short-term IT contract. He works in Canary Wharf, like Vik, and the two have struck up quite the bromance. 'How is he?' I ask.

'He's fine. We had dinner with him and his girlfriend Ivana in Seoul Bird recently. She does my head in, to be quite honest. First she was an hour late, then she spent the whole dinner practising her American accent – she's an actor, don't you know. I shouldn't make fun of her, though, she has a drinking problem. God love her, it's very sad.' Hannah adds thoughtfully, 'That reminds me – there's another Irish guy who's just joined Vik's company, very nice. Maybe I should set you two up.'

'Oh, please no, Hannah. You know I don't date Irish guys.'

'Why not?' she objects, though I've told her many times.

'You know why. They all have drink problems or mammy issues or both. Or else I feel like they could be related to me? I dunno. I just never fancy them. The gene pool is too small, I think.'

'Celeste! You can't say things like that!' But Hannah's laughing. 'Irish guys are the best!'

'Says the girl dating the British guy.'

'OK, fine. I won't try setting you up.' She gazes at the photo again. 'Look at the state of me. The fake tan, those low-rise jeans – ouch. You look just the same, though. Even the hair – and, look, you're wearing silver there as well!'

'God, you're right,' I say, startled. I suppose I'm not the greatest fashion innovator.

'Do you realize, except for that year when I had flu, we've kept up our New Year's thing for – what is it? Oh, God, is it seventeen years? It can't be!'

We stare at each other in horror. Seventeen *years*? This is like when people ask me when I moved to London; I don't like how 'thirteen years ago' sounds so I've started saying 'around ten years'.

Hannah recovers first. 'Right,' she says, 'do you want to hear my resolutions?'

'Definitely.' I love hearing Hannah's resolutions, in the same way I love reading travel articles about places I will never go to or trends I will never wear. They're generally lists of new things to do – like 'Try ombre nail paint' or 'Run with the bulls in Pamplona'. Whereas I tend to make the same ones every year, generally along the lines of 'Lose half a stone' and 'Declutter wardrobe'. But she loves hearing mine too, so it's win-win.

Hannah takes out one of her little doodle-filled Moleskine notebooks in which she always writes her resolutions. She's about to read them out when she's distracted by the music. 'Hey, listen!' she says. 'It's our song.'

And indeed, 'Fairytale of New York' has just started, which is the signal to drop everything and serenade each other. I don't know when this became our New Year's anthem: a song about drunken derelicts who've fallen on hard times and are blaming each other for their woes. But we always cheer when it comes on and belt it at each other in a tuneless duet, with the high point being the line about this year being for me and you. Then the song ends and Hannah hugs me, sighs in happiness and looks at her photo again.

'I hope you made a copy for yourself,' she says.

I wave my hand over towards my desk/dining table, where my copy has pride of place among my framed photos: me and my parents and my younger brother, a few of some old college friends, and some more recent ones of me and Hannah. It's a small collection but that's OK. One thing I've learned in my thirty-five years is that you don't need a huge group of friends: a few good ones – one good one, even – and you're golden. Or silver, as the case may be.

'Say cheese! . . . Happy New Year!' Hannah says, pulling me in beside her for a photo. We smile at the screen, our two faces side by side, silver and gold bees glinting. Not knowing that this will be our last New Year's together, or that Hannah won't be around to see the next one in.

I

Six months later

You can get used to almost anything. This can be good and bad, of course.

Take this place. I can remember the first time I came to Leadenhall Market, soon after moving to London. I was so charmed by it, with its vaulted ceilings, antique lamps and red-and-gold fluted columns; not even the real Diagon Alley could have felt more magical. Now it's just a convenient place to meet Vik for lunch, at a little place that does sandwiches and coffee. I don't normally take a lunch break like this, but he particularly wanted to meet me, and he's the one person I will always make time for these days.

'Celeste!' There he is, loping along and waving one hand, his cycling helmet clasped in the other. His shorts and T-shirt suggest he's been working from home, which his IT job seems to allow more often than not. It's convenient, but I don't know if it's good for him to spend so much time alone. I notice how thin he's got, and I make a mental note to make sure he has a proper lunch.

'Sorry I'm a bit late.' He gives me a quick kiss on the cheek and sits down opposite me. 'How's things?'

That's another strange thing I've got used to – meeting Vik on a regular basis without Hannah present. We've leaned on each other so much recently: from the first nightmarish day when Hannah's mother called from their skiing holiday in France, to the funeral in Dublin and the coroner's report. In the initial aftermath, when I met up with him I couldn't wrap my mind around the fact that it would be just us two. I was honestly certain that Hannah was about to walk into the room, or that she would text me to tell me she was running late – again. I thought I was going out of my mind until I confided in Vik about it and he told me he was experiencing the same thing.

That initial sense of disbelief has faded, but each month seems to bring a horrible new milestone. Just last week, I went to their place in London Fields to pick up a few of Hannah's things, including a photo album of our walking holiday in Spain and her precious golden bee necklace. Seeing that in the box just broke me all over again. 'Didn't her mum want that?' I asked Vik, who shook his head. I took the 106 bus back home afterwards, cardboard box on my lap. I thought my tears were discreet until a woman opposite me leaned forward and said, 'He's not worth it, love.'

'What's up?' I ask once we've ordered our food. 'You said you had something to tell me.'

'Well. Just a bit of news. I wanted to tell you in person . . .'

I tense, because any news that has to be delivered in person – or over the phone – now makes me nervous. For a mad minute my mind spirals. Vik's ill. Or . . . he's met someone? It's not that, but what he says comes almost as a bigger shock.

'It's about the house.'

'Oh yes?' I ask, realizing that by 'the house' he means the one in Suffolk that he's inherited, not the flat in Hackney where he and Hannah lived.

'I've decided I'm going to move there.'

'You are?' I try to hide my dismay, with difficulty because this seems like a *terrible* idea. It was one thing for the two of them to move there together but quite another for Vik to live there completely on his own, away from all his friends and family.

'But I thought the plan was to sell it?'

'It's been on the market for three months now, though, with no offers. The feedback seems to be there's too much work to do. So I'm going to live there while it's being done . . . I can still work remotely, so that's a big help.'

'What about your place here?'

'I'm going to rent it out.'

'Oh, I see,' I say, filled with relief. It sounds as though it's going to be a temporary project, and before long he should be back where he belongs, a bus ride away in Hackney.

'It's just going to be easier to supervise everything on site. And some of it I can do myself.' He makes a comical face. 'I was pricing electrical sanding machines this morning.'

'Really?' I ask, trying not to show my amazement. I don't think of Vik as the most practical person ever; I don't know if he's ever even put up a shelf or used a drill.

'Yes, really!' He laughs. 'I'm not completely softhanded, you know.'

'I know! Well, let me know if you need help with any of it,' I say. 'Like, dealing with tenants. Or . . .' I don't conclude my sentence because I can't really think what else I can help with. I'm not exactly going to be much use on the DIY front.

He smiles. 'Thanks, Celeste, but you're a busy lady. I don't think you want to be woken up at three a.m. to fix a leaky roof.'

'Oh, I could be handy with a bucket,' I say valiantly. 'But seriously – let me know if I can help with anything. Packing up, etc. When are you leaving?'

'I'm thinking the first of July.'

'So soon?'

'You'll have to come and visit,' he says. 'The place is really special. It needs a bit of love, but I think it could be beautiful. The garden too. It's a wilderness, but it's gorgeous as well – especially this time of year.'

I nod, not wanting to say that it won't be so nice when winter descends and he's stuck indoors on his own, a ten-minute drive from the nearest village.

'And my grandfather would be pleased,' he adds. 'I hope. It's quite special, you know, the way it came to him. So I do feel some responsibility for making sure the place doesn't tumble to the ground on my watch.'

'Of course.' I only know the gist of the story but it's quite an extraordinary one. The short version is that Vik's late grandfather saved the life of a British officer in Italy during the Second World War and that Vik has inherited the officer's family house as a result. I can see why he feels a sense of family obligation; I just hope he knows what he's getting into.

'There is something else actually, which I was going to run by you . . .'

'Yes?' I ask. Vik is a great one for schemes and I'm half expecting him to say he plans to open an alpaca farm or something like that.

'I was thinking about New Year's . . .'

I look down, thinking that this will somehow be the most painful celebration of all. Worse than her birthday or Christmas.

'I was thinking of doing something at the house. A party.'

Another gut punch, as I remember the house party that Hannah planned.

As if he's reading my mind, Vikram says gently, 'It's going to be a rough one. But I thought a few of us could get together and raise a glass to her. What do you think?'

I let out my breath, which I realize I've been holding. There's every reason to say yes; it would obviously make Vik happy, and it would be a way to honour Hannah's memory. So why does the prospect fill me with dread?

'But do you think you'll still be there, Vik?' I ask. 'If it's just a temporary move?'

'Oh yeah,' he says, laughing. 'There's at least six months' work there. Easily.'

'Right.' I notice that he has managed to eat his sandwich, even though he's been doing most of the talking. Maybe this bodes well, and the project of doing up the house, and selling it, will give him a much-needed boost or distraction.

'Thanks for inviting me. It would be nice,' I say, trying to sound positive. 'I'll definitely think about it . . . But it's a way away, isn't it?'

'It is. But you know how people get booked up – and

the time will fly by.' He shrugs. 'As much as time can fly by these days.'

'Oh, Vik,' I say, putting down my half-eaten sandwich. 'Won't you be lonely?'

'I'm always lonely,' he says simply. 'So maybe a change of scene would help. Doing up the house was what she wanted, so . . .'

I nod, feeling a lump in my throat, and squeeze his hand across the table. Part of me almost envies Vik this temporary project, because at least he can feel as if he's doing something for Hannah. I sometimes wish I were religious, or that she had been, so that I could do a novena, or have Mass said for her, or set off on a pilgrimage, but there's nothing I can think of that would be appropriate to her memory. There's the party, of course, but I can't face that; anyway, it's a group event, and I'd prefer a solo mission.

We chat about more general things, as we finish our lunch, and then I give him a brief hug before hurrying back to the office. I take the short cut through the back of Leadenhall Market, which is now filled with summer tourists taking photos of the 'magic shop' – which is actually an optician's. I can't believe that Vik is leaving London. I hadn't realized how much I'd been leaning on him – more than I have on my family, or Sibéal or any of our other mutual friends. But it's only temporary, I remind myself. He will come back. Unlike Hannah.

This brutal thought hits me like a sledgehammer, and I have to place a hand on the window ledge of a nearby shop while I catch my breath. Gone, gone, gone. Never coming back. It can't be true, but somehow it is. There was a time when this realization would fell me, almost like a panic attack, and at times it made me physically sick. But I'm better able to cope now, and it's only a few minutes before I'm able to stand up and make my way back to the office, looking for all the world like a normal person. I almost envy the Victorians, with their black mourning clothes that showed everyone what they were enduring. Most of my work clothes are dark, of course, but it's not quite the same.

Back in the office, I take the lift fifteen flights to our floor, where I head to one of the meeting rooms to prepare for a call. I'm exhausted from having woken up at 5 a.m., a frequent occurrence these days. I wish I'd thought to grab a coffee on my way back.

'Celeste?' There's a knock at the door; it's Swati, one of the junior analysts. She pushes her glasses nervously up her nose and says, 'I'm doing a Pret run and I just wanted to check if you'd like anything?'

'You're a mind reader.' I reach for my bag and hand her a tenner from my purse. 'Could I please have a flat white – and a brownie? Thanks, Swati.'

'Not at all,' she says and trots off. Swati is amazing: she's able to grasp the big strategic picture, but she's also across all the details – including coffee. I know that my friend Gemma, who manages Swati, is a bit worried that she'll burn out; she certainly works even harder than I did at her age. But I don't have the brain space to worry about her right now, or about anyone but myself and Vik.

As I put back my wallet, I notice my personal diary for the year hiding at the bottom of my bag. It's pretty blank, unlike my work calendar, which I know is crammed to capacity. I'm a management consultant, which means I do pitches for work, and then hopefully get the work, which means meetings, reports and spreadsheets, then billing, then pitching and off again. I used to find it really rewarding – intense but just challenging enough in the right way – but lately the thrill has faded, and I can't tell if that's because of Hannah or because I've plateaued.

I flick through the remaining months of the year. There's a christening in August and a wedding in September, but otherwise it's not exactly jam-packed. December has my work Christmas party, and my trip home to Dublin for a week. I flip to the thirty-first, get a pencil and write, very lightly, *House party at Vik's?*

But even as I write it, I know that it's not going to happen. I want to support Vik, and I'll do anything I can to help him with the move. But a party at New Year's? No. Maybe some time in the future, but this year, the first New Year's without Hannah, is too soon. Togetherness, emotion, showing it in public: I can't deal with any of that right now.

Though the glass partition, I see Swati heading off down to Pret with Dasha, another junior whom I manage. A bubbly party-going blonde, she's quite different from the solid, serious Swati, but in the last few months they've become joined at the hip. I feel a wistful pang as I see them together, giggling over nothing, in the honeymoon flush of their friendship. And I remember when Hannah and I first became friends, and how a text from her transformed my world, a lifetime ago in 1999 – the worst New Year's of my life, which turned out to be the best.

2

New Year's Eve, 1999

'Guys, I was wondering. Shouldn't we be doing something – for the Millennium?'

It was December 1999, and I was sitting with my best friends Bronagh Clarke and Fiona Leahy at our adjoining desks in the front row of the classroom in St Brigid's, waiting for our first lesson of the day: Maths with Mrs O'Connor. I felt very grown-up as I posed them both the question, as if expecting them to consult their Filofaxes, instead of looking blankly back at me.

New Year's had never mattered much in my world before, but lately everyone was talking about it, because this was the big one: the Millennium. The headline news was, of course, the impending Y2K crash, which was causing consternation among my friends, all of whom were expecting global computer systems to grind to a halt, ushering in a Mad Max-style era of chaos.

'I really don't think it's wise,' Bronagh said. 'Haven't you been reading the news? The whole world could be falling apart. Aeroplanes falling out of the sky, the whole nine yards. The buses might not even be running.'

'Well, we could use our bikes,' I said tentatively. 'How about a sleepover at my place?'

Fiona, sounding evasive, said, 'I don't know. I think it's

probably wiser if we all stay at home. I want to be with my parents if there are major issues.'

I said nothing but I was disappointed. Something was definitely up with them – they had been acting oddly lately and I'd felt, several times, as if they had changed their topic of conversation when I arrived. I put it down to stress over the Leaving Certificate, which we would all sit the following June and which would decide where we went to university and therefore our entire future – assuming we weren't all scrabbling around in a post-Y2K apocalypse.

The next morning, I found out the truth. I was sitting on the 46A bus which would take me from my home in Mount Merrion to school in Stephen's Green, when I received a text on my Nokia phone. I had just got it that year, amid protests from my parents who didn't see why I needed one. I mostly used it to play Snake. The text was from Bronagh and said: Heya Fiona. OK so new yrs: c u 8pm 31st at my place? I'll say it 2 Laura n Roisin but DO NOT tell Celeste.

It was my first experience of a very twenty-first-century phenomenon: receiving a text that was about you, not for you. Seconds later, I got the equally 2000s follow-up: SORRY that text not meant 4 u. I reread both texts ten more times on the way to school, trying to think of a reply that was suitably cutting and dignified all at once. I just couldn't believe it. Ours wasn't the only group that was fraying at the edge, but there was also an unspoken agreement that however annoyed people got at each other, we only had six months left together and then we'd all go our separate ways. Surely I wasn't so awful that they had to dump me ahead of that? But these two texts – and the fact that Bronagh had gone to the effort of locating the all-caps button for 'DO NOT tell Celeste' – told me I was wrong. She had mustered up some caps for her apology, but that was cold comfort at this point.

I delayed going into class until the last minute so I didn't have to face my so-called friends. But Bronagh and Fiona had obviously decided that some confrontation was needed, and during Maths I received a handwritten note – *Meet us in back fields at break* – which I took as a hopeful sign. We had all been best friends since the third year, and even if things had been a bit rocky recently, surely it could be resolved.

However, it was clear within minutes that this wasn't going to be a good chat in which we all learned something and hugged it out; this was, though I didn't know the term then, an exit interview.

'We've just all been really upset by the way you've been acting lately. And by some of the things you've said,' Bronagh began, when I was sitting on our usual bench with the two of them on either side of me, arms folded like guards.

'What things?' I was honestly baffled.

'Well, for a start it was really out of order for you to complain about losing weight – when you know how Laura's been struggling.'

I knew of Laura Hannigan's struggles to lose five pounds but I honestly couldn't remember complaining about my own recent stress-induced weight loss. 'I didn't!'

'You asked if you could use the home ec. sewing machine to alter your uniform skirt in front of her – did you not? And then you said why?'

'Oh yeah. But Miss Cotter asked me why! I didn't know Laura was listening!'

'And you've generally been quite a know-it-all. For example, telling us we're all losers for wanting to go to college in Dublin.'

'What? But I didn't mean it that way, I just meant that we should *consider* places outside Dublin. I didn't mean you guys were losers!'

'It was implied,' said Fiona. 'But the icing on the cake for me – I don't know about you, Bronagh – was the Y2K lectures. I think our fears are very valid and it didn't make me feel good to have you just dismiss them.'

'But I didn't! I was trying to reassure you! My dad says –'

'We know what your dad says,' Bronagh said. 'You've told us about a billion times. I think Y2K is going to be a big deal. I just hope you don't regret being so –' she paused to search for the right word – 'complacent about it.'

I had heard enough. I stood up, and said, 'So if there really is going to be a global meltdown, why are you planning a sleepover?'

That left them lost for words, and I had a feeling of satisfaction, swiftly followed by shame and remorse. They were right. I was obnoxious, too big for my boots, a know-it-all. I deserved to be cut off. But I couldn't say that, so instead I mumbled something about how I was late for class and dashed off before they could see the tears in my eyes.

I got through the day somehow, until it was finally time to go home on the bus, thankful for once that I was the only one of my friends who took that particular bus home. I let myself into the door of 31 Clonmore Park, grateful that my parents were still at work and that my younger brother Hugh was at band practice. That was just another of my afflictions; having a younger brother who was already cooler than me, playing in a band that had actual gigs in pubs he was too young to drink in.

I took off my maroon uniform and got into my tracksuit bottoms, curling up on my bed as I contemplated the wreck my life had become. It was all well and good to think that I only had six months left with these girls. Without them to support me through exams and college applications – without friends, in short, and with a public pariah status – it would be a long six months. I wondered if break-ups were this painful, and then decided they couldn't be. If you were dumped by a boy, you were guaranteed endless sympathy and almost star status among your female friends. If your friends dumped you, you were untouchable and rightly so.

I was wondering whether I could actually ask my parents whether I could somehow transfer to another school for the next six months, when I heard the buzz of another text from my phone. I sat up, terrified that it was another text from the girls outlining my crimes.

But it wasn't. It was a text from a new friend I'd made at summer camp, Hannah Golden. **Hi Celeste! What RU doin new years eve? Having a party @ mine – want 2 come? xxxH** I stared at it as if it was a message from outer space, which, considering the social stratosphere Hannah occupied, it could very well have been.

I had met Hannah the previous August, at summer camp in Connemara, in the Gaeltacht – one of the Irish-speaking regions in the west of the country. Irish college, as it was known, was a rite of passage for almost all Irish teens. We did wholesome activities like basketball and Irish dancing, but the camp's purpose was to teach the Irish language through total immersion. Hannah and I were both quite old to be there – most people stopped at sixteen – but my parents had thought my Irish could do with another top-up, and Hannah wanted to get out of the house.

Our mornings were spent in Irish language lessons at a local school, and we stayed with local families who lived within walking distance, most of them in bungalows spread along the road behind low drystone walls. Hannah and I were in different houses, but we were both *ceannairí* – leaders of our houses – and therefore we met at weekly 'leader meetings'. I socialized mainly with people from my house and the small number from my school, but Hannah was one of those people whose name was known by the whole of the college.

In our second week a major scandal erupted when Hannah was rumoured to have kissed another house leader, Colm O Ríordán, who had a girlfriend back home; typically Hannah was blamed for it and it was the talk of the college. Her friends were standing by her, but there was another large faction all gossiping about her behind her back, as I found out one Friday evening when I was brushing my hair in the girls' toilets during the weekly cei-lidh dance.

'Is there no shame on her?' I heard one of the friends, a Mean Girl type, say as she fluffed out her long blonde mane and applied sticky lip gloss. She spoke in Irish as we all did; if you were heard speaking a single sentence of English you got a warning, and a second got you sent home. They continued talking about Hannah in very unflattering terms. I made a mental note to remember the word she used for shame but also thought the girl could have asked herself the same question; she was supposed to be Hannah's friend.

'*Tusa*,' the other girl said to me, quite rudely I thought – you. 'Are you not a leader? Is there any story at the meetings – about Hannah and Colm?'

I turned to face them. I knew what I wanted to say – 'if I knew I wouldn't tell you' – but in the heat of the moment I couldn't remember the right conditional tense. Instead I said, 'There is no story at all. It's all made upwards.'

I wasn't even sure if that was true, any more than I knew the right word for 'made up', but it didn't matter; I hated that kind of gossip. The girl raised her eyebrows, and muttered, 'Take it easy', before they all filed out, talking under their breath and then laughing loudly.

Minutes later one of the cubicles opened and – just like in a movie – Hannah herself came out. 'Hi,' she said, nodding to me. She didn't look embarrassed, or indignant; she looked as calm and confident as ever, though I was shocked as I realized she must have overheard everything. She wasn't gorgeous exactly, but she was very attractive, with long honey-blonde curls and a triangular, almost foxy face.

'Hi!' I replied. I stowed my hairbrush in my trusty Jan-Sport backpack and was walking out, when behind me Hannah said, 'Excuse me? Celeste?'

I turned round, surprised that she knew my name.

Hannah said, 'I'm trying to write a new song for the concert. Would you give me a hand with it?'

'I would,' I said, intrigued and also a little bit flattered.

It was a big challenge to write a new comic song for your house to perform at the end-of-camp concert; if it was any good, it would be passed down and sung by other students for years to come. I wasn't sure what made Hannah think I would be any good at it, but I was happy to give it a try.

On Saturday we all went to the beach after lunch; Hannah came and found me and we went off to sit on a little rise of grass overlooking the breakers. There were teachers there, and I wasn't expected to supervise the students in my house, but I found my eyes straying to them anyway out of habit.

'Do you like being a house leader?' Hannah asked me, following my gaze.

I hesitated, wondering if it was safe to admit that the answer was yes. It was no exaggeration to say that it had been the making of me: transforming me from a shy, mousy fifteen-year-old to a more confident, articulate Celeste. I loved the responsibility – teaching the younger kids the college songs, refereeing squabbles and helping with homesickness. I also loved the sense of being in the know, meeting the other leaders and hearing all the gossip first-hand, sometimes from the teachers themselves.

'I do,' I said. 'Do you not?'

'I used to, long ago, but not now. I had to report on someone last year for speaking English, and she was sent home. It was awful.'

I shivered at the idea. I had never had to do that, but I knew that I would have to if it came to it.

'Why did you come back so?' I asked curiously.

Hannah sighed. 'I wanted to get out of the house, and this was the only trip that my parents would pay for.' She added, 'I'm taking French and Spanish for the Leaving. I thought maybe I could get a summer job in Paris or Madrid. But where did I end up? The Cuan.' She laughed suddenly, and I joined in.

'Hm,' I said. 'Maybe we could put that in the song.'

'What do you mean?'

I sang her last words to the tune of an old song, 'Only You' by The Flying Pickets. 'You won't know it, I'm sure,' I added, slightly embarrassed since 1980s music was very uncool. I only knew these songs because my older cousins had the original tapes of *Now That's What I Call Music*, and I had played them over and over while staying at their house in Sligo one summer.

'Yes, I know it! I have that tape! With "Radio Ga Ga" – and "Girls Just Want to Have Fun"!' Hannah said. 'I love it!'

So that was how we became friends. Not only did we discover a shared love of 1980s music, we also found a shared sense of humour, writing a song that we both thought was pure genius. It was set to the tune of 'Only You' and was a lament about being stuck in the rainy west of Ireland instead of sunny Europe. The chorus translated as: 'All I wanted was to go to France/All I wanted was to go to Spain/But where did I end up? The Cuan.' By the time we'd finished writing the whole thing, we had laughed so hard we could barely speak and we knew that we had a mega hit on our hands.

'I did kiss him by the way,' she said casually, as we were packing away our notebooks. 'But I didn't know he had a girlfriend.'

'That's fine,' I said, not knowing quite what to say in either language. I added, 'I'm not a gossip.'

She repeated the word I'd used for gossip – *cúlchainteoir*, literally 'behind-talker' – and asked me how you spelled it, before writing it down in her notebook. I noticed that she was left-handed and wrote with a beautiful slanting script. Her notebook was also covered with intricate drawings, flowers and leaves and stars, a cut above the usual doodles that most people did. Something else occurred to me, as I watched her write. I said, 'He's the one who has the girl-friend. Why is the blame not all on him?'

Hannah looked at me with an expression that I thought I would best describe as 'interested'. She looked as if this hadn't occurred to her – as indeed it had only just occurred to me.

'Your Irish is very good,' she said. 'Are you from Dublin?'

'Yes, I live in Mount Merrion. But my parents are from Sligo.' I didn't bother explaining that my dad was from just over the border in Mayo, knowing that the distinction would be lost on her, like on most Dubliners.

'Ah,' she said. 'I live in Dalkey, so not too far from you. Would you like to meet, when we have returned to Dublin?'

'Of course,' I said, though I couldn't really imagine such a thing happening. But it had. We had met up twice for a mooch around the Stephen's Green Shopping Centre and now I was staring at a text inviting me to her party.

Hearing my mother's key in the door, I slipped down-stairs, wanting her company and to tell her about the invitation. She was taking off her smart camel coat and washing her hands thoroughly. Mum taught science in a girls' school, thankfully not mine, and she was fanatical about not catching colds; she hated calling in sick and letting a substitute mess up her carefully laid lesson plans.

I stood for a minute to watch her, dressed in her brass-buttoned navy blazer and jeans, stepping into her Donegal-tweed slippers. One of her students had told me she was one of the most stylish teachers at her school, working a late Princess Diana look with lots of blazers and houndstooth, plus jeans, extremely daring at forty-eight. I felt a rush of affection and ran to give her a hug – something I rarely did any more.

'What's all this, pet?' she asked mildly, as she hugged me back.

I hadn't intended on telling her about the row with the girls, but it all came out and I wiped away a few tears as I told her what had happened. Mum shook her head. 'I've always said that one would buy and sell you,' she pronounced, referring to Bronagh. 'And Fiona, she's as bad. Those tight ponytails. Listen, Celeste. You're about to start a whole new chapter in your life. You'll meet dozens of new friends at university. Leave them to do what they want, and you do what you want. This way you can put in a few more hours on your study plan, and beat them in the long run. You can take New Year's off – we'll watch the TV together, they're showing celebrations all over the world.'

'Well, that's the thing,' I said, and explained about Hannah's party.

'That's probably fine . . . Will her parents be there?'

'I'm not sure,' I said, thinking that from everything I

knew about Hannah and her family, it sounded pretty unlikely.

I showed Mum the invitation on the screen of my phone, first translating it from text speak into English. Looking at her peer dubiously I realized, with a sinking heart, that she and my dad might well say they didn't want me to go. They had never met Hannah and knew nothing about her, except that she lived on Ulverton Road in Dalkey. That was only a few miles as the crow flew, though it would be a bus and DART ride.

'How would you get home? It's such an awkward journey.'

'I'm sure I could stay the night there,' I said. I hadn't asked Hannah about this but I couldn't see her objecting; from what I understood it was mostly just her and her mum, who kept a bohemian open house. Which was very different from my parents. Sometimes I felt that they had used up their last ounce of adventure moving to Dublin in the 1980s. They had faced some terrible times when my dad's travel company went bust and he was out of work for three years. Now they were new citizens of the Celtic Tiger age, with its spiralling house prices and luxuries such as Tropicana orange juice and CK One perfume. My teen years were so different to theirs; it was as if there were three generations between us instead of one. No wonder they wanted to be cautious with me. But Mum also had a fine sense of pride and I knew that the antics of Bronagh and Fiona would have got her back up. She didn't want me to have to go back into school tamely in January saying that I had stayed in on my own, when I could boast about going to a party in my new friend's house.

'Go to the party, Celeste,' she said. 'And I tell you what, you can use my appointment at the Hair Box, on the thirtieth. You don't want to be going to a New Year's party looking streelish.'

I smiled at the word; one of those untranslatable ones that meant unkept, loose, messy. 'Thanks, Mum,' I said, giving her another hug.

'Not at all. Put on the kettle there now and tell me. What are you going to wear?'

I did so, feeling madly excited; not just at the party but at the fact that Mum was talking to me more or less the way she would talk to one of her friends. I glanced back at the text, feeling that my real adult life, with college and jobs and independence, was about to begin. I could picture myself, years in the future, striding into a glossy office in a tower building, wearing a business suit and talking into my mobile. And it was all going to start with this party.

3

Some dreams do come true, and I do work in a glossy office in a tower building. Though my dreams didn't include arriving in the dark or sitting all day at my desk with a sandwich for lunch. It's 8 a.m. on the day of our Christmas party when I arrive at the offices of WBH Consulting, which is the third name it's had since I joined as a graduate. So, even though I've worked for the same company for fourteen years, at least I've *technically* worked in three different places. And the location has changed too – from our original offices in St James, where we each had our own desks, to this glass tower in Liverpool Street. And I've changed too: from starry-eyed junior analyst to associate director, and hopefully, soon, to director.

I flash my lift pass and get the lift fifteen flights up to our floor, where I make a beeline for my usual desk. Hot-desking was introduced three years ago, but I outwit the system by booking the same desk a week in advance every Sunday evening. I have a morning full of meetings, so I put my earphones on to make the most of my hour-long lull to look over a report for a client that's been drafted by Ahmed, one of the juniors. It has to go out by the end of the day, but he hasn't done a proper job and it's in a complete state. I'm very tempted to rewrite it for him, which would be quicker, but one of my targets for this year is to be better at delegating, so instead I write up areas for him to improve.

I want to check on Ahmed's progress with the report but first I have a call with some clients, for which I use one of the meeting rooms. It takes less time than I'd scheduled, for once, leaving me with a few minutes to stare out of the window at the winter sunrise, illuminating everything with gold and red. I used to love the view from up here, but now it's like I don't even see it any more.

Suddenly I'm startled by the sound of my mobile, ringing loudly in the quiet room. Who on earth is calling me at this hour? I check the screen.

'Hi, Vik,' I say, answering it immediately. 'How's it going?'

I've seen him a few times since he moved to Suffolk back in the summer; I haven't been to visit yet, but I've caught him on a few brief trips to London. The New Year's party is still going ahead but I've told him I won't be coming; I'll be in Dublin instead. I feel a bit bad about this, but I know that I simply can't face it. I've rarely dreaded anything more than this first New Year's without Hannah, and the only way I can cope is just to ignore it. Maybe in a few years I'll change my mind, but for now New Year's is something that I no longer want to celebrate.

'I'm very well,' says Vik, sounding pretty cheerful, as he mostly does. 'Can you talk?'

'I mean, sure.' I look at my watch. It's 9.35 a.m., not exactly a great time for personal calls, but I'll always make time for him.

'So, I was just doing my big supermarket shop for New Year's,' he says, 'and I thought I'd make one more attempt to persuade you to join us.'

I sigh, feeling desperately guilty. 'I . . . I'm sorry. You've got lots of people coming, though, don't you?'

'Sure,' he says. 'But it won't be the same without you.'

'Who have you got confirmed?' I ask, hoping nobody else has let him down.

'Just a select few. Sibéal and Rishi – just them, not the kids. And Mel. With no Pablo obviously.'

'What do you mean, no Pablo obviously?' I ask.

I'm stunned when he replies, 'They broke up – like, two months ago. Didn't you hear?'

I had no idea. It's true that I haven't been in touch with Mel all that much since she moved to Cambridge with Pablo, but still. I feel terrible that I didn't know.

'And Patrick and his lady friend Angelika. And that's it. Did you know Shib is expecting by the way?'

I did know that at least. I got the news via text recently and I texted back many heart emojis, though, I realize now, I haven't actually spoken to her about it. I've avoided her in recent months because the last time we met I felt as if I'd been strong-armed into an unwilling therapy session. A party animal turned earth mother, with a sideline in sage healing, Sibéal is big on drunken 3 a.m. heart-to-hearts. 'You're so closed, Celeste,' she slurred, before suggesting I try Reiki healing. I am really fond of Shib, who's been our friend since university days, but I can't handle stuff like that: another reason for staying away.

'Anyway,' says Vik, 'I would really like you to be there. Is there any way we can persuade you? We'll have board games. And walks.' He clears his throat. 'And we'll make Kir royales,' he adds, referring to Hannah's favourite drink. 'Come on. Join us?'

Suddenly I hear a loud buzzing above my head: it must be a fly. One of my quirks is that I can't be in a room with a fly; it drives me nuts. I have to drop everything to get rid of it. I don't want to leave Vik hanging but I also don't have an answer for him; I want a minute to think before I can give him a proper excuse – or reason.

'Vik, I'm so sorry. I have to dash, but I promise I will think about it. I'll call you back, OK? Thanks for phoning.' I hang up and focus on the source of the noise – way up high at the top of the floor-to-ceiling window. How on earth did it get here anyway? It's at least ten floors to the nearest open window; it must have got the lift.

Wait a second. It's not a fly, it's a *bee*. I can hear the hum and see the stripes. It's banging itself against the window hopelessly, as if it's expecting the glass to melt into an escape hatch. Casting around for something, I grab an empty paper cup and a printout of a report. I hop up on my desk and reach as high as I can, which is quite high, as I'm five foot ten in heels.

Gemma, one of my colleagues, picks this moment to walk into the room. 'Hey, Celeste, how is your diary? Do you think you could join in on the . . .' Her voice trails off as she sees me towering two metres above her. 'What are you doing?'

'Just saving a bee. Wait a sec. Yes!' I trap it between cup and paper with shaking hands, and feel the buzz reverberate in my hands, before it goes quiet. 'Can you hold the door open? Thanks.' I slip past her, knowing that she wants me to help her with a pitch or a new project.

A bee in the office. It's pure coincidence, of course, but

my heart is pounding and my hands are sweaty. Because bees are – were – Hannah's thing.

Carrying my buzzing cargo carefully, I hurry to the lift and press the button with my elbow. Luckily it's empty, and I reach the ground floor without stinging anyone to death. Luis, on reception, buzzes me through without asking any questions. I rush through the revolving doors and cautiously lift the cup, hoping my little passenger will still be alive.

It is. After a few seconds, it achieves lift-off and weaves drunkenly upwards. Soon it's a speck high in the air, buzzing towards its unknown destination, oblivious to the passing cars, bikes, the human drones going in and out of their office buildings. I take a deep breath, wondering how on earth it got here, and where it's going now. Shouldn't bees be hibernating?

I'm not a superstitious person – at all. Star signs, psychics, none of it even interests me, let alone convinces me. I don't even believe in life after death, despite my Catholic upbringing. But this appearance of the bee, and the timing, while I was on the phone to Vikram, is so bizarre, it's given me pause.

'Was that you, Hannah? Were you the bee?' I whisper, gazing after it.

A woman smoking beside me gives me a very odd look and I blush crimson as I step away slightly. I don't know where the impulse to whisper mad questions to myself came from, any more than where the bee did. I'm probably just tired from being up since 5 a.m. And from the insomnia that's been driving me crazy for the past year. I've been to the doctor, who said it was stress and suggested cutting down on work and coffee – which I haven't done.

Obviously I don't believe that that was Hannah appearing to tell me I should work less hard or go and spend New Year's with Vik and the others. But could it be a little reminder that I need to – shake things up somehow? Take a risk or something?

The woman beside me stubs out her cigarette and goes inside. I check my watch and see that I'm late for our weekly senior team meeting. There's no more time to ponder the mystery of the bee, so I rush inside and get into the lift.

The meeting goes on for so long that I barely have time to grab a quick sandwich in Pret. It's nice and festive inside; they're playing Christmas music – the Waitresses, 'Christmas Wrapping'– and the red cups are out. I'm making a beeline for the fridge when one of the Pret staff, who is restocking it, hands me a sandwich and calls 'Flat white, please!' to his colleague behind the register. I look down at the Pret Christmas sandwich he's just handed me: exactly what I was reaching for.

'Oh, thank you. How did you know?'

'Every day you have the same – flat white and chicken and avocado sandwich, except when it's Christmas when you have the Christmas sandwich. Today it's on the house!'

'Well, thanks.'

'No problem. See you tomorrow!'

I go to the counter for my free coffee, feeling uneasy. Surely everyone has the same sandwich every day? That isn't so freakish, is it?

Back at the office, I return to my email to see that Ahmed has not only not done everything I've told him to do but he's skipped off on annual leave, leaving the report in a state which means that it definitely can't go out to the client. I'll have to rewrite it after all. With a glance at the time on my screen, I see that I'm going to miss the Christmas party but it doesn't matter. I went last year, and no doubt I'll go next year as well. The office is quiet as most of the teams have gone for a pre-party lunch out.

After about an hour, I get up to stretch my legs and go to get some water. The whole place is deserted; the party will be just getting started and soon they'll all be dancing to Slade.

Not completely deserted, though. I notice Swati, my diligent junior colleague, sitting alone in a bank of empty desks, typing away. It's a poignant picture, and I go over to check on her.

'Hi, Swati.' I pause beside her. 'Not going to the Christmas party?'

She looks up at me, her eyes tiny and exhausted behind her glasses. 'No, no . . . I've got to get this finished for Gemma.'

'Sure, but you'll work better with a break. Have you even had lunch today?'

She shakes her head, and I think of my free lunch; I wish I'd brought her something.

'You know . . . I really admire your work ethic,' Swati says, pushing her glasses up her nose. 'I mean, even the fact that you'll work through the party if you have to . . . You're sort of my role model here.'

I smile uneasily, a horrifying idea taking root. Swati, who is killing herself with work, considers *me* to be her role model? Me, the person with an unofficial Pret loyalty badge and the only other person who's skipping the Christmas party?

'You know, I didn't always skip the Christmas party,' I tell her. 'When I started – when I was doing your job – I was the first to arrive and the last to leave.'

'At the office? I know.'

'No! At the party!'

She nods, but I can tell she doesn't believe me; either that or she wants to fast-forward to being the Celeste of now, who avoids all socializing and eats the same lunch at her desk every day. I want to explain: I wasn't always like this! I have been the one stumbling home from the party at 3 a.m. and swigging from my Garnier micellar water having mistaken it for a bottle of Evian. But I don't think she would believe me.

'What's keeping you anyway? Are you stuck on something?' I ask.

'Yes, it's so silly but I'm getting mixed up with the OKRs and KPIs.'

I offer to take a look at her Key Performance Indicators and Objectives and Key Results. While she opens it up, I look at my paper-bag lunch and wonder how many of these I've consumed in the past year while sitting at my desk. Hundreds, probably. And then I go to work, and go home and eat dinner in four minutes, while scrolling through social media, and go to bed and do it all over again. I help Swati with her issue, which I could do in my sleep, and I realize I haven't just fallen into a rut. It's a trough, a crevasse so deep I don't know how I'll ever climb out of it.

I realize something else too. The bee, wherever it came from, wasn't Hannah. Trapped in the office, banging fruitlessly against the glass, buzzing in the same circles over and over – it was me. Which means that I have to do something. There has to be more to life than this. I don't quite know what I need to do, but I can start by raising a glass to honour the one person who got more out of life than anyone I've ever known.

'Good luck with it all. And make sure you get something to eat,' I tell Swati. I walk back to my desk, take out my personal phone and text Vikram, telling him that if it's not too late, I would love to join him and the others for New Year's.

4

New Year's Eve, 1999

31 December 1999. A date from science fiction; it felt like the whole world was holding its breath. But nobody could have been more nervous than me when I set off for Hannah's house in Dalkey. My dad had said he could give me a lift to the DART as long as he could be back home by eight; he and my mum were having our neighbours the O'Flahertys round for a poker night. Mum and Dad had originally met in a poker club in Dad's small town in Mayo. Dad used to say that the luckiest day of his life was the day that Mum agreed to join his poker night. 'Followed by the day when she agreed to come with me to Dublin.'

We got deep in our chatting, as we always did – he was trying to explain the plot of a new film he'd just seen called *The Matrix* – and he ended up driving me all the way to Dalkey.

'Thanks, Dad,' I said, as soon as I'd realized that we'd passed the DART station.

'No bother, miss,' he said. 'It's quiet enough out tonight.' This was one of his comedy bits; he liked pretending to be a kindly old taxi driver who expected a big tip.

'I'll get a good fare back here,' he said, when we arrived at Ulverton Road, looking at the beautiful street of old red-brick houses.

'I know,' I said, peering out. 'Dad.' I turned back to him. 'If anything happens – I mean, if all the systems go down – don't worry. I can always walk back.'

He smiled. 'You're staying the night, aren't you?'

'That's the plan,' I said, feeling a bit out of my depth. What if the party turned into an illegal rave and I had to share a bed with a load of strangers or something?

Dad obviously saw my worries. 'I tell you what,' he said. 'I have my phone now, and I'm on the text. So you can send me a message any time you want. Just put an X – that's all, just an X – and as soon as I see that, I'll jump in the car and come and get you.'

'Thanks, Dad.' I put my arms around him and hugged him, breathing in the smell of Paco Rabanne that Mum always got him for Christmas. 'I'll see you next year.'

'See you next century,' he said with a grin.

I stepped out of the car and walked up the drive, my feet crunching on the gravel. The house was beautiful, a classic Georgian red-brick, with a short flight of granite steps up to the red front door with its fanlight. I was quaking in my knee-high boots; I liked Hannah, but how well did I know her really, and what on earth would this party be like?

Before I could ring the bell, the front door swung open and revealed a blonde woman dressed in a short black dress with a pink pashmina draped around her. Backlit against the hall light, she looked like Hannah and I was about to greet her when she said, 'Are you looking for Hannah?'

'Oh gosh, I thought you were Hannah!' I said artlessly.

A slow smile spread over her face; I had obviously said the right thing.

'No, I'm Dervla. Hannah's in her room. Come on in, my sweet.' She beckoned me in and waved vaguely in the direction of the stairs, before grabbing her car keys from a side table and her coat from the bottom of the stairs. 'Have a lovely evening.' She paused beside me for a moment, and under the chandelier I could see the fine lines that had been invisible a second ago. She was actually even more beautiful than Hannah, her face a classic oval with perfect high cheekbones. 'Will you keep an eye on her for me, though? I told her no spirits and no red wine. That's a new carpet in the drawing room. Happy New Year. Bye, darling, have fun,' she called up the stairs. Then, without waiting for a reply, she swept out of the house, banging the front door behind her. I noticed it hadn't closed properly, and I stepped forward to shut it all the way. Then I stood uncertainly in the hall, until Hannah appeared at the top of the stairs.

'Celeste!' she said. 'You made it! I'm so glad you're here early.' She ran down the stairs and gave me a hug. 'Let me hang up your coat. Did Mom go out? Grand. We can get ready in peace.'

I hugged her back, smiling at the 'mom', which seemed to be unique to the deep Southside of Dublin; the rest of the city said 'mum', 'mam' or 'ma'. We went upstairs, chatting as easily as ever, and my nerves began to calm down. Hannah's room was up not one but two flights of steps – an attic with a stunning view over Dublin Bay. 'This is a fabulous bedroom ... Your house is gorgeous,' I said, looking around. Posters and framed drawings covered every surface, including artwork that I thought must be Hannah's. Macy Grey was playing from her CD player and her little dressing table had about a hundred products on it, including items from MAC which I had seen in magazines but never in someone's bedroom.

'I love your outfit!' Hannah said, which made me feel very relieved; I had made a respectable effort in a sleeveless silver top with sequins and some bootcut jeans. She herself was in a pair of low-rise jeans with a jewelled belt through them, and a clinging tie-dyed long-sleeved top that revealed her fake-tanned midriff; she looked amazing.

'Do you want me to help you do your make-up?' Hannah asked, and I started to laugh.

'I've already done it,' I said, when I could speak again.

'Oh, God, sorry. You have a great sense of humour, Celeste – I'm glad you're not pissed off. Thousands would be,' she added.

I shook my head. 'I'd love you to do my make-up. I'm desperate at it.'

'Great! Sit here.' She pulled up a stool, giving me the chair in front of her mirror. 'My mom sent me on a modelling course . . . Cringe, I know . . . I learned it there. I'd actually like to do make-up professionally, but you can imagine what my folks said to that.'

I nodded, remembering from our previous conversations that Hannah's parents were opposed to her even studying art at third level, let alone becoming a make-up artist. 'Where are your parents tonight?' I asked curiously.

'Mom's at some dinner party,' Hannah said. 'And my dad is off on some golfing trip in Mount Juliet.' She put down her brush and reached for another one, dabbing it in a dark grey shade. 'So what happened with your friends? I didn't really understand from the text.'

I told her briefly, and she said nothing at first, instead blending my eyeshadow about a dozen times. Macy had ended now and Dido was playing. Then she said, 'I don't think you did anything wrong. They were just jealous maybe.'

'Maybe,' I said, after thinking for a minute. 'Oh well,' I added, not feeling as devastated as I had. 'Whatever.'

'Exactly.' After a minute, she said, 'My dad's not really at a golf trip. He is in Mount Juliet, but it's not golf. But if anyone asks, can you say golf?'

I was completely baffled by this – what did she mean, golf but not golf? But then the penny dropped. Mount Juliet was a famous hotel, and her dad must have gone there with a woman – not her mum. I had never come across such a situation outside of books or films, and I was shocked, but my answer was as prompt as if I saw this every day.

'Of course I will,' I said.

Hannah nodded silently. 'Now. Have a look-see . . .' She spun me round to face the mirror. 'Good so far?'

'Oh my God,' I said. 'That's incredible.' My grey eyes were twice their original size, my lashes looked false: the effect was mesmerizing. 'Thanks so much,' I said, making to stand up.

'Hang on, I haven't finished yet!' She reached for a small iridescent pot, whose purpose I couldn't even guess at. 'Let's go all out . . . It is the Millennium after all. Might be our last night on Earth.'

Our preparations finally over, we went downstairs where Hannah, ignoring her mum's prohibitions on spirits, mixed us both two strong gin and tonics; I nearly gagged on mine so she remixed it with more tonic.

'We'll be grand as long as nobody spills it on the rug,' she said, when I mentioned her Mum's warnings about red wine. 'It's a new Persian thing, kind of pale pink – a mental colour for a rug really.'

'Why don't we roll it up?' I suggested.

'Genius!' she said. 'I can't believe I didn't think of that. Roll it there, Celeste.' She grinned, and we set to, rolling the thing up into a sausage and hiding it behind the sofa. I glanced at the antique clock ticking serenely on the mantlepiece: it was already eight thirty.

'So who's coming?' I asked, feeling the butterflies build in my stomach.

'Oh, just people,' she said vaguely. 'Some from school, some local . . . My neighbour Clodagh Lacey, you'll like her, and her brother Paddy . . . just various heads. Everyone's cool. Oh, here's our first guest!' She jumped up at the sound of the doorbell.

I hesitated, not wanting to follow her like a puppy, and wondering who it would be. It sounded like it was going to be an older, cooler crowd, and I was worried that the talk would all be of people I didn't know, or parties I hadn't been to. But the first arrival, a tiny redhead in a fake-fur coat, couldn't have been less intimidating. 'Oh, hi,' she said as soon as she came in. 'You must be Celeste. I'm so scared about this evening, I feel like it could be my last night on Earth! At least I'd get out of doing the Leaving Cert, is the only thing.'

'This is Clodagh,' said Hannah, laughing. 'Don't worry, Clo, the world won't end, I'm sure.'

46

'Are you sure, because my friend made me watch this really terrible film called *The Matrix* – it freaked me out. It was all about how everything is an illusion or we're all living in a video game, I'm not even sure, and if it is a game, what if someone just presses stop or whatever?'

'Oh, my dad just saw that,' I said.

'Your *dad* saw it?' said Clodagh. 'My dad hasn't seen a film since *The Mission*. That's literally the only film he's ever liked and that was only because it had Jesuit priests in it. God, you must have a really cool dad.'

'I suppose,' I said, thinking that actually she wasn't far off; Dad did have his cool moments. The doorbell went again and Clodagh, still talking, dragged me into kitchen where she poured herself a gin and tonic with an expert hand, obviously knowing where everything lived. Did nobody in Dalkey drink Heineken? Clodagh turned down my offer of lemon slices, saying lime was much better with G & Ts. I stared at her covertly, thinking that this was a whole new world.

But as the room filled up, and became louder and smokier, I started to relax. I didn't know if it was the threat of impending apocalypse, or the rapidly multiplying gin and tonics, but the atmosphere was fantastic. It became clear that Hannah had invited people from every kind of social group. There were rugger buggers and blonde socialites, but also indie kids and arty kids and people of no particular tribe. Hannah introduced me to everyone as her friend, which seemed to be an instant ticket to social success. Three girls from her school immediately took me under their wing, and we spent a long time dancing and chatting, with them pointing out various guests and explaining their backstories in terms so entertaining that it was like watching a play or a soap opera. The time flew by so fast that I was amazed when I saw, on the clock on the mantlepiece, that it was already a quarter to eleven.

We were having an earnest discussion about whether we would ever get tattoos and where we would have them, when one of them said, 'Did you see who just arrived? Patrick Lacey.'

For once I didn't have to ask who that was because I knew. He was just one of those people whose names everyone knew, a bit like Hannah herself, in fact. Two years older than me, he went to the same school as my brother, where he'd played on the senior rugby team, and he had also dated one of the most popular girls in our school. I also knew, though I couldn't have said how, that his uncle was the attorney general and that he was related to one of the country's first presidents. This must be Hannah's neighbour Paddy, whom she'd referred to so casually.

At this point Hannah joined us and we all started dancing to 'Groove is in the Heart', one of my favourite songs of recent years. I was less keen on the next song, 'Blue (Da Ba Dee)', so I went off to the kitchen to get a drink of water. The air was so thick with smoke in there that it was a minute before I even saw where the sink was. Then I noticed that among the group standing opposite the sink was Patrick Lacey himself, drinking from a can of Heineken. I went past him to get my water; there were no clean glasses so I decided to wash a few up, before filling my own. The others were talking about the film *Titanic*.

'I'm telling you,' one of the girls was saying, 'there was plenty of room on that plank! All she had to do was budge up!'

One of the guys then made a crack about Kate Winslet's weight. The rest of them all laughed, including the girl, while Patrick just swigged from his can, looking deadpan. I was quite surprised at his lack of reaction – not that I thought it was funny, but it was the kind of thing guys said all the time. But then he said, 'Kenny, if you'd got on to the ball half as well as she hung on to that raft, we might've had a chance last Saturday.' The rest of them hooted and laughed.

Kenny gave Patrick a sideways mock-punch, trying not to look too bothered, though I could tell he was. 'Anyway,' Kenny continued, 'I read that the whole women-and-children-first thing was a myth. Makes sense. Survival of the fittest.'

M People started playing 'Search for the Hero' and the rest of them all ran off to dance. Patrick said, 'Be there in a sec,' and lit a cigarette.

I had decided to wash up the rest of the sink, which was filled with crumpled Heineken cans, and I glanced covertly at Patrick as I did. His blond hair was cut in the curtains style that was still beloved of guys at that time, and he was wearing the usual uniform of Ralph Lauren polo shirt and Diesel jeans; I didn't even have to look down to know that he would be wearing Dubarry deck shoes. He was leaning back against the kitchen counter with his arms spread wide; it was hard to imagine a more confident posture. I knew he was considered a major heart-throb, but I preferred the edgy appeal of Johnny Depp or Jared Leto from 'My So-Called Life'.

'Um, women and children first wasn't a myth. Not on the *Titanic* anyway. Lots of men gave up their places in the lifeboats. Like Benjamin Guggenheim, the millionaire . . .'

Patrick looked back at me silently and I felt the internal panic rising; what on earth was he going to think of this weird girl who eavesdropped on his conversations and then busted in with a know-it-all fact?

'I know,' he said. 'He put a rose in his buttonhole and said he would die like a gentleman. I've often wondered if I'd be able to do the same.'

I looked at him in surprise; I hadn't thought that he would know about this.

'I mean, he was with his mistress, so he wasn't perfect,' I said nervously.

'Was he? I didn't know that. Where were you when I did my *Titanic* project in sixth class?' He smiled at me, and suddenly I saw the reason why everyone was so enamoured of him; it was one of those smiles that made you feel as if you were the only person in the room.

'Paddy!' a voice said behind us. A girl with dyed mahogany hair was advancing towards us. 'It's nearly midnight! They're going to do the countdown in a sec.'

'Oh yeah,' he said. 'Coming.' He lifted his can of beer to me and said, 'See you on the other side.'

'Come on, you don't want to miss it!' The girl beckoned me too, smiling.

I was alone in the kitchen now; Hannah was waving at me from the door to the drawing room.

I looked at my watch: five minutes to midnight. I was thrilled and terrified; what if something dreadful *was* about to happen? What if the lights all went off, or the music stopped playing or – worst-case scenario – all our bank accounts were simultaneously attacked by the mysterious 'hackers' my dad had told me about?

'Where've you been, I was looking for you?' Hannah asked, running to grab me.

'Just getting some water,' I said, almost forgetting my encounter with Patrick.

'Oh my God, there's only five minutes to go! Do you think the world's going to end?' she said to me.

'I hope not. I haven't done anything yet,' I said.

I hadn't really been joking, but she laughed out loud and swept me into the drawing room. 'I'm so glad you came!' she said into my ear over the din of music and hugged me. 'And your make-up still looks amazing!'

'Thank you! So does yours!' I said fervently, hugging her back and thinking that if the world *was* about to end, at least we had given it a great send-off.

5

I'm just back from the airport, after my trip to Dublin for Christmas, when Vikram calls and tells me that Patrick Lacey is driving to Suffolk the next day and can give me a lift.

'That's kind,' I say. 'But tell him I can get the train.'

'It's no problem. He lives near you in – Haggerston? Haringey? One of those areas that sound like someone clearing their throat.' Vik gives the hearty laugh of someone born and raised in leafy Surrey.

'Hey, mister,' I say. 'Remember you used to live in Hackney.'

'True. Cough! Anyway, he can pick you up tomorrow at six, he says. He's bringing some stuff down for the garden, but he'll have room for you. It just makes sense – Rishi and Shib are coming from his parents in Harrow, and I'm picking up Mel from the Cambridge train an hour before yours would get in . . .'

'But there's a taxi company at the station, I checked. And I'd rather get the train. Honestly, it just suits me better.' I actually love long train journeys: looking out of the window, eating Minstrels and reading magazines. Plus, I feel a bit awkward about sitting in a car for hours making small talk with someone I barely know.

'OK, suit yourself. I'll tell him.'

'Thanks. Can I bring you anything, Vik?'

'No, no, I've ordered a big shop online.' Vik sounds

excited. We chat some more and then we hang up, while I wonder why he keeps calling instead of sending texts like a normal person. I really hope he's not too lonely. Suddenly the dream I had last night comes back to me in all its disturbing vividness. Vik was in the house and it was burning. I was doing my best to pour water on the fire, but to no avail. It's obviously a manifestation of my general reservations about this project; probably best not to mention it to Vik.

Despite Vik's assurances that I don't need to make anything, I've decided to whip him up a batch of my home-made Baileys Irish liqueur, which I know he loves. I'm carefully pouring it into my special decanters, complete with home-made labels, when I hear my phone buzz and pick it up, thinking it will be my mum.

It's a text from an unknown number. Hi Celeste. Patrick Lacey here. I just got your details from V and I'll pick you up tomorrow at 6 p.m. sharp. It's no trouble. See you then.

'What the hell?' I say, staring at the text. Does he not know a polite brush-off when he hears it? Unless Vik didn't relay my thanks-but-no-thanks – though the 'It's no trouble' implies he did. 'Please respect my no, Patrick,' I say aloud to the phone.

'I didn't hear you,' my phone says. 'Please can you repeat that?'

This makes me laugh, and I wonder if I'm being a bit contrary. Maybe this is less alpha-male pushiness on his part and more Irish hospitality Mrs Doyle-style: 'You will, you will.' 'Six sharp', though. That's annoying. He obviously doesn't know I'm never late. I reply to say thank you and that I'll see him tomorrow.

It's funny because in one sense I've known Patrick

forever – peripherally as Hannah's neighbour and family friend, along with his sister Clodagh; someone to say hi to in passing at Christmas parties or at Hannah's mum's house. But in another sense I don't think I know him any better than I did after that first encounter in Hannah's kitchen. He's had some kind of IT career that's taken him all over – South Africa, Switzerland, Canada. There was also a longish stint in Dublin, which coincided with the two years that Hannah and Vikram spent there, while Hannah's mother was being treated for cancer. He and Patrick really bonded while they were all in Dublin, to the extent that he's still friends with him independently now that Hannah is gone. Unless maybe it's the connection to Hannah that Vikram values. I remember that Patrick came to the funeral. I remember everyone who came to the funeral, and everyone who didn't.

I line up my bottles, shaking my head. It seems so wrong that the world even still celebrates New Year's. I realize I still have a chance to get out of this. I could say no, tell them I'm sick or something. But the reality is that this is the closest thing I've got to celebrating with Hannah – and supporting Vik. If there are glasses being raised to her, I want mine to be one of them.

At 6 p.m. exactly the next day my buzzer rings. I'm checking over my electricals cube bag to make sure I have the chargers for everything, including my electric toothbrush; there's nothing worse than being stuck with a grubby mouth on a weekend away, and I'm guessing Vik's place doesn't have a twenty-four-hour shop across the road like mine does. I go to answer it.

'Celeste? I'm double-parked outside so I can't come up – can you manage your bag?'

'Sure thing. See you in a sec.'

I take a last look at my flat – my nest – patiently decorated over the years in a sort of girly boudoir look, courtesy of B&Q and eBay: dusky pink velvet accent chairs; palm-print wallpaper; marble-effect quartz kitchen counter; copper accent lighting. Is it a litany of millennial decor clichés? Yes. Do I love it more than anything on earth? Also yes. After I complete my triple-lock ritual and set my security alarm, I give it a wave and whisper 'Goodbye' under my breath, glad nobody can see me.

Outside, Patrick is adjusting something in the boot of his car, a white Fiat 500. I have a memory of him always in neatly pressed jeans and Ralph Lauren shirts, or dark wool coats with the collar turned up, blond hair immaculate. Today he's got a navy wool coat, collar turned up also, but it looks like something a fisherman would wear. Underneath is a sweater that looks like it's been hand-knitted by shepherds, and his boots are dusty. His fair hair, which I remember being close-cropped, is shaggy, and golden stubble is glinting on his jawline.

I approach his car and take a step back, saying, 'Whoa!' The back seat has been flattened and both it and the boot are crammed with bundles of dead twigs and leaves, and some kind of bushes, their bases wrapped in sacking.

'Is this . . .?' I wonder how to phrase it. 'Is there actually room for me in here? You seem to have quite a . . . load. What is all this stuff?'

'It's just bare-root roses and fruit trees for Vik. For his

garden. Do you mind having your bag in the front seat? Great. Hop in.'

It's not ideal. It's pretty awkward with my long legs, but there's clearly no room in the back, so I throw in my canvas bag and fold myself in as best I can. I remembered Vik saying Patrick was helping him with the garden, but I wasn't expecting him to be transporting a forest.

'Watch out! The roses!' he says sharply, as I feel something jab into my hair. He has them all lying flat on the back seat but they're thrusting out all over the place.

'It's OK – nothing broken,' he says, moving a branch slightly away from me. 'Sorry. I've two dozen David Austin rose bushes in here, and three cherries – it's going to be a squeeze but we should get them there in one piece.'

'Lucky Vik, getting roses,' I remark.

'Indeed. That's all you've brought? Good woman. Off we go.'

Did he think I'd pack like Reese in *Legally Blonde*, with twenty pink suitcases and a miniature dog? I've just clipped my seat belt in and straightened up, when I feel a sharp pull on my hair and let out an undignified yelp.

'Oh, sorry, it's caught in your hair. Want some help?'

'No, I can do it.' I'm soon forced to let him, though, as I just can't see. I stay as still as I can, feeling my cheeks redden as Patrick leans in to untangle my hair from his blasted twigs. His fingers move carefully among the strands and leaves, and I'm almost touched at how gentle he's being, until he says, 'Not to worry. No damage done, you didn't actually break any fronds.'

We set off, with me trying to ignore the ongoing jabbing of branches in my hair; I feel as if I'm in a woodland grotto. I'm already regretting the peaceful two hours I could have spent on the train.

I've always thought you could tell a lot about a person by the way they drive. Patrick drives confidently and smoothly but in an almost aggressively courteous way, yielding to other cars at every opportunity and staying precisely within the speed limit. The car is immaculate as well – the front of it at least; the back is going to take a lot of hoovering.

'Thanks for the lift,' I say.

'No problem,' he says. 'You'd have to be a right eejit to get the train when I'm driving. Especially with train fares the way they are.'

I don't know if 'eejit' is exactly the word I'd choose, but I make a non-committal noise before adding, 'I must give you something for the petrol.'

'No, no, you're grand.' Patrick continues, 'I actually live really near you, which I hadn't realized till Vik told me. I'm right across the park, near the reservoir at Clissold? Near the climbing centre. Have you been there?'

'Not yet,' I say, not wanting to admit I didn't know that such a place existed.

'Seriously? You're missing out,' he says. 'Anyway, I can give you a lift back too if you want. I'm leaving on the second – what about you?'

'Unfortunately I have to leave on New Year's Day. Thanks, though.'

'Right. Angelika – my girlfriend – has to work too,' he adds. 'She can't make it at all, though.'

'Oh, that's a shame. What does she do?'

'Angelika? She's a medical researcher. Cancer research.'

'Oh, wow. Good for her.' She sounds as perfect as him.

I feel momentarily confused – I thought his girlfriend's name was Ivana? But then I realize that must be an ex: it was a whole year ago, or a whole girlfriend ago, that I had that conversation with Hannah. I'm losing track of time.

'How was your Christmas?' he asks.

'It was OK. Quiet, you know?' This is true as far as it goes. It was nice enough: me, Mum, Dad, my younger brother Hugh and his wife Nessa, all sitting in exactly the same places, having the same turkey and pulling crackers with, it seemed, the same jokes inside them. Everything was the same, except, of course, for Hannah. I missed her more acutely in Dublin even than in London; I still half expected my phone to buzz with her suggesting a walk on the pier or a drink in town.

He says, 'It was a tough one for you I'd say . . . The first one without Hannah.'

I shift uncomfortably in my seat, not willing to get into this right now. 'Thanks . . . I mean, yes, but what can you do?' Which sounds both banal and heartless, but what am I supposed to say?

'Did you see Dervla at all, when you were back?'

'Yes. I called over there for a cup of tea.' Hannah's mother's grief is something I can't bear to look at directly, can't think about. Not that she wears her emotions on her sleeve any more than Hannah's dad does – though I can't be sure, given that he now lives in Australia. Our conversation mainly revolved around my work and her upcoming travel plans. But I know she feels it, despite the brittle smile she puts on every morning.

'It's pretty cruel, isn't it?' says Patrick, and I say, 'Yes.'

Cruel is the word. Because in what world does a woman

have successful cancer treatment and celebrate her recovery with a skiing holiday with her only daughter, only for said daughter to die in a senseless accident on the nursery slopes? There was no other skier involved; Hannah just slipped off the edge of the slope and hit her head on packed snow. She seemed fine initially but complained of a headache that evening. She was airlifted to hospital that night and died the next morning, on what would have been the third day of their holiday: 19 January.

'I saw her as well,' he says, meaning Dervla. 'I was just home for a week, but you know my mom lives across the road from her.'

'Of course,' I say. I clear my throat, trying to think of something to steer us away from this topic before I start choking up. 'How long have you lived in London now, Patrick?'

'It's been about fourteen months. I was originally meant to be here on a six-month contract, but I've extended it for various reasons.' He glances at me. 'You've been here forever, though, haven't you?'

'Fourteen years.'

'Wow. You must really like it.' He says this as if I've just signed up to a second mission to Mars.

'You sound surprised,' I say, smiling.

He laughs. 'I suppose I am. I'm mainly still here because the money is good to be perfectly honest. And my girlfriend is here, and it's been great to go and visit Vik. But London itself I could take or leave. The sprawl, the pollution . . . I mean, what do you like about it?'

I've had people ask me this before, and it always amazes me. I mean, if I went to Vik's parents in Surrey or my cousins in Sligo and asked them how they could stand it, it wouldn't go down well; and yet people say it about London all the time.

'It's the whole world in one city,' I say, my standard reply.

He laughs. 'It's a pity they didn't leave some bits out.' We're driving through some of the featureless north-eastern suburbs right now, which admittedly aren't the loveliest.

'So I take it you'll heading back to Ireland before too long?'

'Yes. I'm planning to leave at the end of this year. That's the beauty of contract work, isn't it? You can just pilot in, do your bit and then ride off into the sunset. My plan is to buy a little plot somewhere, maybe in Wicklow. That's the dream, though I've got some competition. Everyone dreams of a cottage in Wicklow, don't they?'

I don't, but I make a polite noise. 'You must be pretty into gardening? Hence the roses.'

'Hence the roses.'

I'm starting to feel like I'm interviewing him, but I don't want to talk about myself either, so I ask him if he wants the radio on, and he nods. I switch it on – Radio 2 – and take out my magazines. One of my New Year's resolutions is to reduce my screen time, so at the airport I impulse-bought copies of the *Economist* and *Vogue*. I decide to start with *Vogue* – but the thought of New Year's resolutions makes me think of Hannah. My mind keeps going back to that list she made last New Year's, of things she wanted to do. I don't know if she managed to do a single one, given that she died in January. It's a small thing, compared to the whole life she'll never have, but the thought of her planning those little adventures for herself pierces me to the heart, and the *Vogue* lies unread on my lap.

Patrick is driving fast, and the car is eating up the miles; before I had expected, we're in the proper countryside.

'Do you want to stop anywhere, or just bust straight on through?' Patrick asks.

'I'm fine to bust if you are.' I look out at the view, which is just fields and hedges, with a crescent moon now chasing us on our left. 'It doesn't look like there's anywhere to stop, does there? It's the middle of nowhere.'

'It's Suffolk, not the South Pole,' says Patrick, sounding reproachful. 'You haven't been to the house yet?'

'No,' I admit.

'Wait till you see it. It's a bit shabby at the moment, but it will be beautiful. And so will the garden. You'll see.'

I'm suddenly distracted by a well-known song on the radio. Piano chords and Shane McGowan's voice. It's 'Fairytale of New York' – the song Hannah and I always sang at New Year's. I reach forward to turn it off as quickly as I can.

'Not a Pogues fan?' Patrick asks.

I'm not even sure if I can speak without sounding wobbly, so I just shake my head.

Patrick gives me a curious look but says nothing, and we drive on in silence.

'What's that clanking?' he asks, after we round a sharp corner.

I clear my throat and take a steadying breath until the danger has passed and I can speak normally. 'Oh, I brought some of my home-made Baileys ... Vik really likes it. You'll have to try some.'

'That's very sweet,' he says. 'I brought a case of champagne.'

Of course you did, I think. 'So do you know everyone who's coming? Sibéal and Rishi . . .'

'Shib and Rishi? Sure,' he says. 'He's a great guy. And Shib – she's hilarious.'

'Yes,' I say, taken aback at the 'Shib' – I thought it was just her oldest friends who call her that. 'And Mel?' I'm sure he won't have met her. Mel used to work with Vik in London, back in the day, until she went off travelling to Argentina, which is where she met her boyfriend – or rather her ex-boyfriend.

'Of course! Such a pity about her and Pablo, huh? But it sounds like he never adjusted to living in the UK really.'

'Well, yeah.' I give him a sidelong look, wondering how he's become everyone's best friend like this, while I haven't seen any of them in months. But it must my fault for declining so many nights out.

'Look, there's a sign for Bury St Edmunds,' he says. 'We should be there in the next half-hour or so. Would you text Vik and let him know? The electric gates don't work, so he'll have to open up or we'll be walking up the farm track in the mud.'

'Sure,' I say, wondering for the hundredth time what I've let myself in for.

6

We've entered deeper countryside: flat and featureless at first and then turning woody, with winding roads and hedgerows. We pass a village, impossibly storybook-looking with fairy lights everywhere and Christmas trees glimpsed in the windows of cottages and pubs. But soon we leave the village behind and the woods grow deeper and darker. I shiver as I think how remote it is.

'Not this one . . . not this one . . . Here.' As we take the final turning uphill towards the house, it's as if we're going into a tunnel, with hedges and trees rising higher on either side, then we pass through tall pillars and on to the gravelled drive.

'Here we are . . . Cotwin Manor,' says Patrick.

Although I've seen pictures, I'm still surprised at the size of the house. It's a rambling old pile, with dark wooden beams patchworked all over it and windows with tiny leaded panes. I see trees clumped behind it and lawns spreading out towards more high hedges; to the left of where we've parked there seems to be a lake or pond of some kind. I get out of the car – taking care to avoid the roses this time – and inhale the smell of the night air, which is fresh and damp and lovely with a tinge of woodsmoke. Patrick is busy checking his bundles of sticks have survived the trip, so I take a minute to absorb my surroundings.

I look up at the sky and almost gasp. There's no moon, just star after star, limitless and remote; endless galaxies and constellations so thickly splattered across the firmament there's barely any darkness. I stare at it for a moment, and breathe in again, scenting woodsmoke and earth and dead leaves, that particular smell of death and regrowth all at once. Despite my reservations about this move being the right thing for Vik, I can see that it's beautiful. I'm already glad I came.

Then, out of nowhere, a vicious jab in my backside makes me shriek. I whirl around, seeing something white and floaty hissing three feet below me – a swan! It hisses at me again and I lunge at it with my handbag.

Patrick appears at my side, brandishing his spade until it retreats. He's trying to keep a straight face, but I can tell he thinks it's very funny, which it isn't. Swans are dangerous! It's well known that they can break a man's arm with their wing.

'That's Sigmund,' Patrick says. 'He's a bit territorial. Probably just checking you weren't an enemy.'

'Checking *I'm* not an enemy?' I say. 'He's the enemy! What's so funny?'

'Sorry, I shouldn't laugh.' He looks serious. 'You really should be careful. Swans are dangerous, you know. They can break a man's arm with their wing.'

I'm trying to formulate a suitably tart reply, but Patrick is already striding towards the front door, which is intricately carved out of dark wood with a worn stone step. There's a huge round metal knocker which he lifts and bashes; I also notice a rusty iron bell with a chain.

Remembering Vik and Hannah's place in Hackney, I feel oddly disoriented, as if I've stepped into some parallel universe. Then the door opens with a fairy-tale creak.

'Celeste! Patrick!' Vik says. 'You made it.'

We both step inside for hugs and greetings all round, while Patrick says, 'Celeste's just met Sigmund. He got snippy.'

'Oh dear, I'm sorry. Are you OK?' Vik asks, all concern.

'I'm fine,' I say, not wanting a fuss. 'How are you, Vik? You look well.'

He's very smart in a new shirt and jeans; the hollows under his eyes seem a bit lighter too. 'I'm doing well, thanks. So, welcome to my humble abode,' he says with a wave of his hand. 'Cotwin Manor. What do you think?'

'It's beautiful,' I say, looking around.

The hall looks just as ancient as the outside: half panelled in dark wood, with oak beams high overhead, and flagstone floors covered with worn red rugs. The overall effect, on such a frosty night, is cosy and welcoming, especially with the greenery Vik has hung everywhere: holly bursting with red berries and branches of fir. Patrick's carrying in his crate of champagne; I hand Vik my own little offering, hoping it doesn't look too measly. But Vik, like the sweet guy he is, makes a big fuss of it.

'Celeste's home-made Baileys! Wait till you try this, Pat. It is . . .' He makes a chef's kiss. 'Right. Let's get you both a drink – or do you want to dump your bags first?'

'I can show Celeste her room, if you want,' Patrick offers. 'She's in the little blue room, right?'

This seems a bit presumptuous to me. Who's hosting

here, Vik or Patrick? I'm relieved when Vik says, 'No, I'll take you both.'

Vik leads us to our rooms: up the big staircase and then up and down several smaller flights of steps, and along a wood-panelled passage that seems as if it should have minstrels strumming or at least a brace of Victorian urchins playing hide-and-seek. The ceilings are lower up here, and the men have to duck their heads to avoid the low beams. The wooden floor is as uneven as a wave of the sea, and the door to my room is cut out of the wood-panelling. It opens up into a little room with exposed beams and a tiny, high four-poster bed. A leaded window overlooks the garden. It really is like something out of a storybook.

'This is gorgeous, Vik,' I tell him. 'Did that bed come with the house?'

'No, Facebook marketplace,' Vik says, looking proud. 'All the antiques are things I've bought – then the hideous eighties stuff is from the previous tenants. Pat, you're next door in your usual room – the Cheese Room,' he adds with a flourish; and, indeed, I notice a neat gilt-lettered sign announcing it. Patrick flashes us an appropriately cheesy smile and disappears inside, looking very smug indeed.

'Why the Cheese Room?' I ask.

'Presumably for keeping cheese cold? It's from the nineteen thirties. I know that's when a lot of the work was done – including the electricity,' Vikram says, as we head downstairs. 'There's so much I still don't know, though. It'll take me a lifetime to find out probably.'

I'm about to point out that he's not going to spend the

rest of his life here, but we're already in the drawing room, where the others are gathered.

It's a vast rambling space with a higher ceiling and a dozen oak beams overhead. Melanie is perched on Vik's leather sofa from their old flat, which looks distinctly out of place here. Rishi is lounging on a more old-fashioned-looking upright sofa that looks as though it came with the house. A fire is roaring in a fireplace big enough to cook an ox in, with a giant crooked beam. The flock wallpaper strikes an off note, with its hideous design that looks as if it's from the 1980s, but there's a six-foot Christmas tree covered with fairy lights and red ribbons, more holly everywhere, and candles burning on every available surface. It's gorgeous, though I suddenly remember my nightmare about the place going up in flames. I make a mental note to make sure I help blow them all out before we go to bed.

'Champagne, Celeste?' Vik asks, while I greet the others.

Melanie is looking very pretty with her hair in long braids over one shoulder, and wearing a cool red sweater dress and boots.

'Hi, Celeste!' she says, getting up to greet me. 'How are you? It's been ages.' She adds in a lower voice, 'Thanks for your text.'

For me Melanie has always been the one who got away. I've always really liked her and wished we could be better friends, but circumstances have kept us apart. She used to work with Vikram as an IT writer, before giving up her job and travelling around the world. She met Pablo in Buenos Aires while she was doing tango classes and they moved to Cambridge together, though now, of course, they've broken up. I don't even know if he's still in the country. Maybe I should ask Patrick, who seems to be all up to speed. Suddenly I realize they must have all been here together for some previous weekend that I declined. Which is my own fault, I suppose.

'Thanks . . . cheers, everyone,' I say, taking the glass Vik pours me.

I'm beginning to relax. This is nice. I don't know why I've resisted coming here, except for the obvious reason that I felt it would be too sad without Hannah. But it's good to be with old friends, and I'm realizing how much I've missed seeing them, especially Vik.

I'm about to ask where Sibéal is when a stir behind me tells me she's arrived.

'CELESTE.' I turn around to see all six foot of her, rippling auburn waves held back by a fifties-style hairband. She's wearing jeans and some kind of dark silk maternity top, which I think I just saw in my *Vogue*, but I can't really register her clothes before she steps forward and embraces me – not just a quick hug but full body contact head to knee.

'YOU CAME,' she breathes into my ear.

I try to move away after a second, but she keeps me pinioned to her, bump and all. I breathe in the familiar sweetly spicy scent of whatever perfume it is she wears. Knowing her it will be either something ruinously expensive or something dirt cheap she picks up twice a year in the local pharmacy on her trips home to her parents in their tiny town in County Leitrim. This hug is going on far longer than is reasonable, but it's nice to be hugged, and I know that she's genuinely pleased to see me, as I am to see her.

'Drink, darling?' Rishi asks her. 'I made you a pomegranate spritzer.' He's wearing a tight-sleeved T-shirt with a sweater vest, showing that he hasn't used the Christmas holidays as an excuse to slack off at the gym. Like Vik, he's very into health trends like Peloton and turmeric lattes, but without Vik's sparkle of eccentricity or enthusiasm. He makes Shib happy, though – or, as she put it on Instagram on his birthday, he's her 'soulmate who I've loved in so many lifetimes, my hero from beyond the stars, my man in a million getting better each year like a fine wine xoxo'. Understatement is not her thing.

'How was your Christmas and everything? How are Lorcan and Síofra?' I ask. 'Who are they with?' I brought their two kids, who are three and six, some little presents, though no doubt they got given half of Hamleys last week.

'It was great, really magical. They're amazing. They are right now bonding with their Dada and Dadi in Harrow; it's so beautiful to see,' Shib explains.

'We dumped them on my parents,' Rishi translates.

Shib throws back her head and laughs. 'Can't argue with that.' She lowers her voice, as much as she can at least. 'Rishi said we should have a child-free weekend before the baby arrives.' She puts a hand on her bump.

I smile at her. 'Yes, how are you feeling? You look blooming.'

'Totally grand. Twenty weeks down – not a bother.' She turns to Rishi. 'You know, I was thinking, we should have brought the kids after all. They're no trouble.'

'Oh my God, love, what are you on? They're so much trouble,' Rishi says. 'For the others if not for us.'

'There's all that open water here and the blazing log fires,' I suggest. 'You'd need eyes in the back of your head.'

'Tell me about it,' Rishi says. 'Did Shib tell you what Lorcan did while we were staying with her parents?'

'No! What?'

'He called the fire brigade,' says Shib. 'And they came.' She tells the story with great gusto – Lorcan was inspired by watching *Postman Pat* apparently, and used the phone while nobody was watching. 'They were very decent about it, but I was morto. Seriously, he was in so much trouble. Lucky the head brigader, or whatever you call him, was the year behind me in school or we'd be on some kind of watch list.'

'Lorcan should be on a watch list. Honestly, I feel a hundred years old,' Rishi says. 'Christmas with kids is exhausting enough without the emergency services being involved. So I'm looking forward to a nice relaxing stay here.'

'Me too,' says Mel, who's moved over to be closer to us, while Vik's left the room. 'What do you think of the place, Celeste? Isn't it gorgeous?'

'It's amazing,' I say with perfect truth.

'It really is,' says Sibéal. 'I feel like I'm in Wolf Hall or something. But it's not just that; there's a really special vibe. It's like we're all *meant* to be here – like something has brought us all here for a purpose.'

We all look at her, puzzled. 'Of course Hannah,' she says, looking hurt. 'But not just her. Something else,' she clarifies. 'A message of some kind . . .'

'There was a message. A WhatsApp from Vik.' Rishi winks at me, and I laugh, grateful to him for lightening the mood.

'How are you doing, lovely? I'm sorry about the swan,' says Vik, coming back inside.

'It bit me,' I explain briefly to the others, not wanting a massive fuss. 'It's fine, Vik, but has he bitten anyone else?'

'I'm afraid that would be yes,' says Vik. 'He's certainly got some problems. I believe his mate died a few years ago, and according to Dr Google the aggression could just be because he's lonely. So I might look into getting another for him.'

Everyone looks at him, and there's a sudden silence while we're all thinking, obviously, the same thing: if only Vik's problem could be solved so easily.

'Maybe wait a bit first,' says Sibéal with one of her intermittent bursts of common sense. 'I'd say you've enough on your plate without matchmaking swans.'

'Oh, I'm sure I could get one delivered,' says Vik. 'Mail-order bride.'

'How are the neighbours, Vik?' I ask. 'Have you got to know them?'

'I have. There's a really cool older couple down the road; they've sort of taken me under their wing. And then there's the Morrisons, but I haven't completely cracked them yet. They've got horses and I think if I had a horse, or was a horse, we'd be good, but not yet. Oh, and the landlord of the Rose and Crown – he's become kind of a pal. Speaking of which, top-up, anyone?'

I look at him, wondering if I should be worried; his collection of friends here sounds a bit sparse. Vik has seven hundred Facebook friends; in London he could be out almost every night of the week. And is it my imagination, or is he drinking quite a lot as well?

'So what needs to be done to the house? Have you got a plan?' I ask.

'Yes, I've already bored these guys with it,' says Vik. 'So the past six months have all been about rewiring the electricity, and trying to get the place furnished if not quite done up yet . . . The roof is sound, so that's something. But the main thing, really, is outside, with the render on the walls.'

On cue everyone groans loudly.

Melanie says, 'Please, no more about the render.'

'We've already heard about the render,' says Rishi.

'What? It's interesting,' Vik says. 'I'll just explain it briefly to Celeste. So, as you saw, outside the building is whitewashed, or in other words limewashed. Which is a breathable natural surface that lets moisture in and out, like skin really. No problem; redo it once every ten years; sorted. But then some idiot slapped some cement over it –' Vik's expression darkens – 'which smothers it and actually *causes* damp. So it's all got to be redone. But it will be worth it.'

Patrick has come in at the end of this speech and is smiling. 'There's a man with a plan,' he says. 'It's going to be great. I can see it.'

'Me too.' Vik throws a log on the fire. 'This is the life,' he says. 'And it's so great to have you guys all here to see it. Cheers! Here's to a great New Year's.'

We all drink to that, and Vik turns to smile at me. 'I'm glad you came,' he says under his breath, squeezing my arm.

'Thanks, Vik. Me too,' I say, and I'm surprised to find it's the truth. This first New Year's without Hannah is going to be hard, but I'm here. I'm trying. And for all my reservations about whether Vik's going to go mad rattling around here for another six months, it does seem a great place for a party.

7

The next morning when I wake up, I can almost see my breath in the air and I send up thanks for my foresight that made me pack full thermal underwear, and my hot-water bottle, which is still lukewarm even though it's 8 a.m. Out of the leaded window, I see lawns and hedges wreathed with frost and clinging mist, and in the distance a red sun just over the horizon. This is one sunrise I can catch. I pull my jeans and jumper on over my thermals and go out to take a look.

Downstairs, nobody seems to be stirring; unsurprising, as we got to bed quite late. I slip out of the front door, leaving it on the latch, and go outside. The grass is crisp with frost, and there's no sound except my feet crunching on the gravel, the occasional bird and, much further, the faint roar of distant traffic. The gardens look a bit bleak: just a pockmarked lawn surrounded by overgrown hedges and some dishevelled flower beds. But the rising sun is lovely, lighting up a line of leafless trees to the left of the house. To the right I can see the fringes of Vik's lake or pond – though I steer well clear of that to avoid the swan.

I turn back to survey the house, which is looking undoubtedly lovely with its oak beams and whitewash, its diamond-paned windows catching the sun's rosy rays. Would Hannah have been happy here? Yes, I think she would have. She would have made the house her project and filled it with people every weekend; she would have made friends locally, maybe had chickens. She and Vik probably would have started a family too, though I know she wasn't in a hurry. I hope whoever buys it can bring it back to life; it's the kind of house that should be bursting at the seams with a busy household and all its associated activity.

Back inside, I put my head round the door of the sitting room, which is a mess of sticky wine glasses and empty bottles. The daylight is much less kind to the place, with its awful flock wallpaper and lighter patches where pictures presumably used to hang. The threadbare carpets and the dated furniture mingle oddly with Vik and Hannah's modern belongings from London. I stare at the grey velvet sofa again, remembering her buying it on eBay and all the drama surrounding the delivery of it up their three flights of stairs. And here it is now, squatting in this house. How did this sofa outlast her?

I scoop up the dirty glasses and bottles and carry them through to the kitchen, which is at the back of the house, a rambling low-beamed place with an Aga cooker. It looks as though it should have a massive scrubbed pine table in the middle with a cat dozing on it; instead, Vik's there sitting at his white tulip table with his MacBook Air open in front of him. He's drinking coffee and looking at something on the screen.

'Morning! You're up early, lovely. Did you sleep well?'

I smile and nod, thinking how thoughtful he is. 'Like a log. It's so peaceful here.'

'Isn't it?' He looks pleased that I've noticed this. 'I've just made some coffee. Help yourself . . . and there's bread in the bread bin. Sorry, I'm actually just in the last stages of an auction here.'

'Oh yeah? What are you bidding on?' I ask, expecting it's some kind of gadget. Vik loves anything tech-related; Hannah and I used to joke that if they ever had a baby, Vik would be hunting for the manual and checking for upgrades from the very first night.

Vik doesn't reply, pecking frantically at his keyboard; I leave him to get on with it and toast some bread and pour myself some coffee. It's normal Lavazza coffee in a cafe-tière, thank God. As well as being into gadgets, Vik is quite the guy for the latest wellness and foodie trends. A few years ago it was bulletproof coffee (black coffee with protein powder and coconut oil – revolting), then cold brew, which was even worse, and then turmeric lattes to 'boost his immune system'.

'Dammit! Just missed out,' he says. 'What a beauty – look.'

He shows me; it's an antique French mahogany armoire, elaborately carved.

'I didn't know you were into antiques, Vik,' I say, buttering my toast.

'I'm getting into it,' he says. 'I mean, it's hard not to, surrounded by all this. And all our furniture looks wrong here – look at this, for instance.'

He points at the tulip table, and I have to agree; it was perfect in their little galley kitchen in Hackney but it looks really strange in here. I don't know how we're all going to fit around it tonight; we'll have to eat in shifts.

'Let me show you around properly,' he says, once I've finished my toast. 'You can bring your coffee. Wait, first, have you seen the servants' bells? They don't work, but it's very *Downton Abbey*.'

He shows me the board with a dozen bells, with the names of all the rooms on them in neat gilt lettering. I have to admit it's really charming.

'Are you tempted to get them rewired?' I ask, thinking that's the kind of thing that prospective buyers would love.

'And give you lazybones the chance to summon me for your every whim? I don't think so.'

We walk around the house with its warren of passages; I feel lost at every turn. I notice the same state of disrepair everywhere and more hideous wallpaper, but also some lovely details I had overlooked – like all the original wood beams and how many of the windows have their original thick and bubbled glass. Vik shows me the formal dining room downstairs, which seems in slightly better nick, with a proper long table. It has a massive fireplace and wood panelling that he says is eighteenth century.

'And this,' he says, pointing to a photograph over the sideboard, 'is the man himself – my grandfather, Ashok. With the 8th Army, 4th Indian Division. That was taken in Italy – he was one of the soldiers who liberated Italy from the Nazis. He fought at the Battle of Monte Cassino.'

I look silently at the picture of the face, young and gawky under his turban. I don't see the resemblance to Vik really, but it's hard to tell. 'How old was he there, Vik?'

'Oh, he was nineteen there – and just twenty-two at Monte Cassino. They were all around that age, you know. But they were legends in the Eighth, the best fighting force in Italy according to some.' There's no hiding the pride in his voice, and I don't blame him for a minute.

'And remind me: what's the connection with the house exactly?'

'So, all we know is that Ashok – my grandfather – saved this man Roger Davies's life during another battle at San Marino. They stayed in touch and exchanged letters, and years later Davies left a codicil in his will, like a postscript saying that in the event of the family dying out, this place should pass to Ashok or his youngest male descendant. Look, this is Roger Davies.'

He points to a black-and-white photograph on the opposite wall: a solemn-looking young man standing outside – I look closer – this house.

'Wow, Vikram. That's incredible. But how did it happen that the Davies family died out? There's always a relative somewhere, isn't there?' Based on stories of wills in my extended family, it seems like long-lost cousins can always be found when a legacy is in question.

'Yes, but the will specified the degree of relatedness . . . and if they died without issue, which they all did, then enter Ashok. Or rather me – his youngest descendant.'

'And did you know about all this prior to hearing from the solicitors?'

'Not a thing. We knew he had saved someone's life, but we never knew anything of the friendship or the will until about two years ago, when Simon Davies, who was Roger's nephew, died and his solicitors got in touch. It took them a while to find us. And then there's been a whole legal process to go through, as you know. It's quite a story – it's been in the local paper and everything.'

'Did he get a medal, Vik? He should have.'

'Yes, he did, and a mention in dispatches. The medal itself we've never found, though.'

I stare at the photo, thinking of the confluence of history that brought these two men together in Italy for this brief and life-changing encounter that's sent ripples into the next century. I can see why Vik's drawn to the place if only for this reason; it's a hard link to ignore. I just hope it doesn't turn into a massive financial burden for him. Even though he's working remotely, and earning rent from his place in London, the cost of the works must be astronomical – surely in the five figures. How is he going to afford it all without going into debt?

'Didn't your parents want it, Vik?'

He laughs. 'Not a bit. They were so stressed out even by the suggestion. Suffolk's not great for golf, you see. And my mum would miss her book group and her wine club. They've got roots, you see. Unlike me.'

'But you're not putting down roots here, of course,' I say. 'Any idea how long the works will take – or how much it's going to cost?'

He runs his fingers through his glossy hair and leads me back towards the kitchen. 'It's very up in the air,' he says. 'It's all dependent on how long everything takes . . . and I've got to meet the conservation officer and then get various quotes and plans in. Quite complicated. Right! Let's not wait for the others. I'm going to put on some food! Want some eggs? I've got smoked salmon too, and sausages if you want them . . .'

I decide not to ask him any more questions for now; the financials of the whole thing are really not my business.

As I help him set the table, I notice the juicer stuffed in a high cupboard and remember when Vik and Hannah were all about juicing; everything they drank or even ate was blended for a month. This makes me feel slightly worried again. This house, and the project of renovating it, seems to be his current obsession – but it will be a lot more costly than juicing. This house could be worth a fortune if he sells it on, but it could also be an absolute money pit, and a white elephant to boot. I just hope that he can extricate himself soon, and that by next New Year's he'll back in London, where he belongs.

8

We've just finished eating, when a door bangs open and Patrick comes inside, bringing a gust of freezing air with him. He's carrying some muddy boots and wearing an old white Aran sweater, and his hair is ruffled from the wind. An Aran sweater! There's a blast from the past; I haven't seen one of those in years. There's something very old-fashioned and wholesome about him – a bit like Chris O'Donnell in the old movie *Circle of Friends*.

'Ha, typical. Look who appears as soon as breakfast is ready,' Vik says.

Patrick says mildly, 'I did just plant fifty bulbs for you. Irises and daffodils, under your apple trees.'

'Fifty!' I say.

'That barely put a dent in it – we've got five hundred to put in,' Vik says. 'Wait. I have apple trees?'

'Yes, they're hiding under some brambles.' Patrick tops up his thermos flask from the cafetière. 'Do you want to take a look?'

'I should really be a good host and wait for everyone else to appear and give them breakfast,' says Vik. 'Actually, whatever. This I've got to see.'

We all go outside, me pulling my woollen hat over my ears. Part of me feels like I've already seen the garden and I wouldn't mind a shower, but I don't want to be a downer when Vik is so excited.

'Here we go,' Patrick says, stopping beside some bare trees smothered in brambles. 'Three apple trees. I'm not sure what kind.'

'And they've been hidden under these,' Vik marvels. 'I had no idea.'

'It's going to be never-ending with the brambles, I'm afraid,' says Patrick. 'But we'll get rid of these for you. I've got some reinforcements to plant – cherries, as I said, and then I also brought some roses to start the summer beds. Suffolk ground roses, and some others.'

'Check this out, Celeste,' Vik says, and we all walk round the corner to the two dead flower beds I saw earlier. 'These are going to be the summer beds – with all kinds of roses, hollyhocks, foxgloves, delphiniums. A massive burst of colour. And then here are the winter beds; that's going to be dogwood, and camellias and forsythia for winter colour. So in summer you can sit at a bench here, and look at the summer colours – and then in winter, you can sit here and admire the winter beds.' They both look at me with identical excited faces.

'That does sound beautiful.'

'Have you shown her that, Vik?' Patrick points beyond the beds to a scrubby area behind the hedges, where a ditch extends in either direction.

'What am I looking at? That's a ditch.'

'Not a ditch,' says Patrick. 'It's a moat.'

'Can you believe it? A moat,' Vik enthuses. 'I mean, an actual moat. It's all overgrown, and the pond itself is silted up. So at some point we'll have to dredge the pond.'

'Well, careful now,' says Patrick, laughing. 'When you say "we".'

I'm glad to hear him sounding some note of caution, but Vik is well away. He continues, 'And then we clear this ditch – put in a couple of little bridges – bit of dredging and, um, sluicing and, hey presto, here's our moat.'

'How are you going to clear the ditch?' I ask, looking at the six-foot drop choked with brambles and with God knows what lurking at the bottom.

'Diggers,' Vik says, brightening. 'We'll get diggers in.'

'Who's going to drive the diggers?' I ask, and they say, 'I am,' in unison. Then they burst out laughing.

'You're both crazy,' I tell them, but I can't ignore the new lease of life in Vik. Even if it is a lunatic project, I have to admit that it seems to have given him a shot in the arm. He's so different already from the grey-faced figure who I remember shuffling around his flat in the months after the accident, barely able to get out of bed. I have to hand it to Patrick; this garden has done more for Vik than all my attempts to cheer him up ever could.

'Anything else?' I ask, smiling. 'Are you planning a draw-bridge to go with the moat perhaps? A swimming pool?'

Their laughter subsides and they exchange a quick look. 'Actually there is something I'd like to show you,' Vikram says. 'Over this way.'

They lead the way to a sheltered spot, back near the apple trees. Vik seems to take a minute to compose himself, and then he speaks.

'Here's where we're going to make a bee garden. Plantings lots of things that bees will thrive on: lavender, hyssop, asters . . . lots of purple and blues.' Hannah's favourite colours. And bees. He doesn't need to explain the symbolism; I get it.

'That sounds nice, Vik,' I say. I don't trust myself to say more without choking up.

He nods and puts an arm around me briefly. I squeeze him back, and we're having a bit of a moment when Patrick adds, 'And you talked about having something here too – as a memorial. Like a stone bench, or a sundial, with her name or dates engraved.'

'*What?*'

They both look at me. I hadn't intended it to come out like that, but I couldn't help it. How could he possibly think of leaving something so precious – a memorial to Hannah – in a house that will be sold to strangers? It would be totally inappropriate.

I take a breath and say, 'Sorry, it's just . . . that sounds rather permanent. You don't want to put buyers off, do you? Unless . . . are you thinking of something that you could take away with you? When you come back to London?'

They both look at me and I suddenly feel like an absolute idiot, as the penny drops.

'Sorry, Celeste,' Vik says. 'I should have said earlier. Never say never, but for now, yeah, I'm thinking of staying long-term. I'm happy here. Or as happy as I can be anyway.' He tries to smile, and I try to recover from my shock and do the same.

'God, Vik, you don't need to apologize. I'm so glad you're happy. I just didn't realize, that's all. I'm sorry.' I look back at the site of the future bee garden, wishing Patrick wasn't here to witness this conversation. I want to ask Vik tactfully about the financials but I feel I can't do that with Patrick here either. Why didn't I say anything earlier?

At this point we all hear the sound of wheels on gravel.

'That must be my supermarket shop,' says Vik. 'See you in a sec, OK?'

He hurries off, sounding rather relieved to have escaped this awkward conversation. I feel so embarrassed. And Patrick is making it worse – he's gazing at me with an expression that I think is meant to be sympathetic but just looks patronizing.

'You don't think it's a good idea?' he says.

His paternalistic tone makes me react more vehemently than I would have to Vik.

'Not really. It's a six-bedroom house in the middle of nowhere – not exactly ideal for a single grieving person. And he's got no experience of managing a project like this or doing any kind of renovations.'

'He has just had the whole place rewired,' says Patrick mildly.

'OK, but what about all this business with the rendering – and everything else it might turn out to need? And how is he going to afford it all? Don't tell me he's getting into debt.'

'Well, he's put his place on the market,' Patrick says.

'His flat in London? What? When?'

'He's been talking about it for a while – didn't he tell you? He's told the estate agent and they'll start viewings in January, I think.'

'Oh,' I say after a minute. All the fight goes out of me as I realize how blind and oblivious I've been. While I've been hiding in my shell, Vik has been embracing a massive challenge and finding a new purpose in life. And he couldn't even tell me about it because he knew I wouldn't approve, because I didn't want anything else in my life to change. I was worried that he would be lonely here, that this place was going to stop him moving on. But I'm the one who hasn't moved on.

'Are you all right?' Patrick is saying. 'Celeste?'

'I'm fine,' I say. 'It's just cold.' And I walk off inside, not even looking to see if he's following me.

9

Back at the house, we find Vik in the middle of a disaster. It turns out that his big internet shop, including six expensive bottles of wine and a special cut of beef for dinner, was flagged by his credit card company, and even though he confirmed the transaction right away the supermarket have cancelled it and there's nothing he can do. The car was a neighbour dropping off some home-made bread, which is very nice but won't feed us all for two days.

The others have got up by now and everyone is in the kitchen having breakfast. At the news of the crisis everyone gets very involved and has a great time suggesting what to do.

'We can just go to the supermarket. I'll drive into the nearest town,' says Patrick.

'Well, sure, except that I had a million specific things on that list, plus a cut of meat you won't be able to get anywhere,' says Vik, looking despondent.

'Look, just tell us what the basics were,' Patrick says. 'We'll get those and then at least we'll have something.'

'We can cook the swan,' I suggest, earning myself a reproachful look from Vik.

'It's all good,' says Patrick. 'Seriously. I love a good trolley dash.'

'Rishi would drive twenty miles to buy a pack of crisps,' says Sibéal. 'Guys, you won't forget my salt, will you?'

'Oh, God, the salt,' Vik says.

Sibéal says, 'I'm doing sea bream baked in salt for our New Year's Day dinner, so I need three kilos of natural sea salt.'

'Will you still be able to get the fish?' I ask.

'We drove down with it. It's in the freezer,' says Rishi, looking long-suffering.

In the end the men all go off in the car, and Sibéal, Mel and I go for a walk along a path that leads behind the house, through some fields populated by cropped winter grass and two horses in blankets, who look up briefly as we approach before returning to their grazing. The walk makes me feel better, and soon I regain a sense of perspective about this morning's conversation with Vik. It's his business after all. And it's not like he's moving to the moon; I can still come and visit him.

'Isn't this glorious?' Sibéal murmurs beside me. I glance at her, thinking how porcelain her skin looks, with barely a single wrinkle – it's quite incredible given how much partying she did in her youth. When we first met as students, she was out every single night; I don't think I saw her in daylight for the first six months I knew her.

Mel and I talk about work for a while – she's a freelance web editor – but then I change the topic because I don't want Sibéal to feel left out. I know that work is a slightly sensitive topic for her, ever since she left her job in PR when Lorcan was born. She hasn't worked formally since then, though she does do some freelance witchcraft – benign spells and charms for which she gets actual clients, mainly via Instagram.

Sibéal stops to pick some leaves that she says will be

useful in some of her 'spells' and I tell Mel that I'm sorry about her and Pablo.

'You know what?' she says. 'It's the best thing that could have happened, for both of us.'

'Really?' I'm surprised to hear this; they were one of those couples that I thought were madly in love.

'Yeah, I feel ten years younger.' She smiles. 'Not that he wasn't a great guy, but it had run its course. I felt terrible for having dragged him here to the UK. He hated the cold and rain; he missed Argentina . . . Honestly, our relationship was so stressful by the end; it was a relief for both of us when it finally ended.'

'That's good. I mean, not good but I'm glad you're not heartbroken,' I say, turning to let Sibéal catch us up.

It's funny; I often think about Mel's decision to pack in her job and go travelling around the world, and how she met her handsome Argentinean and brought him home. That felt like her happy ending. But now that's over and she's on to a new chapter – without a backward glance it seems. How do people do it?

'I'm not heartbroken at all,' she says. 'I'm even thinking of going on a date.'

'Good for you, darling,' says Sibéal, walking up to join us. 'What about you, Celeste? Any dates on the horizon?'

'Not really.' I gaze off across the fields, wondering if I should be making more effort on that score, but deciding not. The idea of meeting someone romantically, right now, feels like a trip to Australia. It's not that I'm opposed to ever going there. But it's a long way, and it's not a priority. If I was offered a free trip there, then maybe. But I have enough on my plate right now.

'That makes sense,' says Mel when I explain my Australia analogy.

Sibéal doesn't say anything, but I can guess her thoughts. Even before Hannah died, she thought I was too closed off to relationships. Her theory is that what happened with Eddie has put me off men for good, though I've told her that's not true. She also thought I was too quick to break things off with him. *Surely you could work through it, Celeste. It's not the worst thing a guy has ever done.* Vik and Rishi were both on his stag do, which meant they knew what had happened. Everyone had an opinion and I'm sure they still do.

But when I turn around, I see that she's not thinking about my love life but turning her face up to the winter sunshine, arms outstretched. 'Feel the rays of the sun god, girls,' she murmurs. 'He's been standing still for the solstice, while the Oak battles the Holly . . . Soon the Oak will win, and spring will come.' Mel and I glance at each other, not daring to giggle. It's undeniable that Sibéal does look quite impressive, tall and stately with her swelling belly and her red curls flaming in the sun; if anyone can carry off this kind of thing, it's her.

Then Shib opens her eyes, resuming her normal tone. 'Oooh, I've had a thought. Why don't we pick some greenery to decorate the table for this evening? I don't think Vik's given much thought to the tablescape.'

We find some secateurs at the back of the house, and cut great branches of holly studded with red berries, and some ivy. In the dining-room sideboard we find a heavy white linen tablecloth, only slightly mouse-chewed, and throw it over the ten-foot table. There's a full set of surprisingly good china, and some wine glasses, most of which match. We find an old candelabra, and add greenery and pine cones all down the middle of the table. It looks beautiful, despite the mottled mirrors and the peeling wallpaper, which is coming down in festoons in one corner. Exhausted from our labours, we settle down for a sandwich lunch and a cup of tea afterwards beside the fire.

'It feels like a country house hotel, doesn't it?' says Mel, sipping her tea. 'Except for the patches of damp and the general air of everything falling apart.'

This seems a good excuse to bring up the topic that's been preying on my mind.

'Did you both know that Vikram is putting his flat on the market?'

They both nod, and again I feel foolish at the thought that everyone knew about this but me.

'I hope it works out,' says Melanie. 'It is a big place, just for him. Especially with the expense of it. And I hope he won't be too isolated here.'

'That's what I'm worried about too,' I say quietly.

'Well, he's made it through half the winter. He must be happy enough,' says Sibéal, which reassures me somewhat.

'I think Patrick did a lot to persuade him,' says Mel. 'Vik was particularly worried about the garden, because he didn't know where to start – but he says Patrick's given him lots of ideas. So hopefully he knows what he's doing too.'

'Oh, I think he does,' says Sibéal. 'It's already looking way better than when Vik arrived – you could barely see the place for brambles.'

The conversation moves on while I wonder how much

persuasion Patrick has been using exactly. If he's been talking Vikram into this decision, I hope he'll be around to help out if Vik ends up in a financial and practical mess.

Mel goes outside to try to find reception for a phone call, while I ask Sibéal how her kids are doing with their grandparents. 'So far so good,' she says, crossing her fingers. 'No calls to the emergency services at least. Or calls to us.'

'You should bring them next time,' I suggest. 'This would be a magical place for kids, wouldn't it?' Looking around, I find myself imagining hide-and-seek and rocking horses and games in the attics, and dozens of presents under that tree.

'Wouldn't it just?' says Sibéal, sounding sad. 'It's such a pity that Hannah and Vik didn't get lucky, isn't it?'

I look at her, startled. 'I suppose . . . but they weren't trying yet, were they?'

'Oh yes they were,' say Sibéal. 'They were hard at it. She was tracking her cycle and peeing on sticks and the whole nine yards. I gave her some of my fertility tea as well.'

'Are you serious?' I ask, and Shib nods, looking surprised.

I'm completely stunned, because I remember asking Hannah about this at New Year's. *Not now. We've enough on our plate.* Of course it was none of my business. But I can't understand why she couldn't confide in me – was it because I was single? Was it just too stressful for her? And I feel terrible for Vik too, that he has to live with that added disappointment as well.

'That sounds like the guys coming back now,' says Shib, turning her head. 'Oh, God, I hope they got some fizz.

I'm having a glass tonight for New Year's. I've been looking forward to it all week.'

'Patrick brought some,' I say, wondering if there's ever anything he doesn't do perfectly.

We find the guys in the kitchen, bearing bags full of groceries and looking very pleased with themselves at their hunter-gathering, though Vik is apologetic that his fancy dinner plans have gone up in smoke.

'It's going to have to be a beef stew, not beef Wellington,' he says sadly, but we all tell him we don't care.

'Did you get my sea salt, babe?' Sibéal asks, and Rishi says 'Yep, I got salt.'

'Did you get wine?' Mel asks, coming inside, and there's sighs of relief all around when they say yes.

'Don't crack it open yet, though – I have a job for you all, before it gets dark. Very important,' Vik says.

I'm assuming he's going to make us come and peel potatoes, or something, when to my surprise he says, 'Chopping wood. Now I'm going to get going on my stew – it's already late! Pat, will you supervise the chopping? You know where everything is.'

'Can I help you in the kitchen, Vik?' I ask.

'No, no. I need to cook alone. Now hurry up – chop-chop!'

I'm not very keen to take orders from Patrick, but Melanie and Sibéal are already marching ahead, so I follow along. Everyone else seems thrilled with the task, especially when Patrick leads us outside to a back yard beside some outhouses, where there are some huge fallen branches and a sawhorse and some saws. This seems like it could be the start of a horror film, but I line up nervously with the others. Patrick is waxing lyrical about the type of wood he's sourced, which winds me up all over again. Get your own manor, I want to tell him.

'It's an apple tree so Vik will have some lovely fragrant fires when it's ready to burn. There should be saws enough to go around.'

Rishi, Sibéal and Mel all grab small individual saws and get cracking, as if they've been doing this all their lives. I don't see any left over, which seems like the perfect excuse to slip away until Patrick brandishes something at me – a long saw with two handles.

'Want to go halves?' he asks.

I get the feeling this is intended as some sort of peace offering so I say 'Sure' politely, scraping my hair back into a ponytail.

'Here's a branch for us,' he says. 'I'll let you set the pace, and we'll soon get into a rhythm.'

But we don't. He keeps pushing when I'm still pushing, and then vice versa. He's very patient, but I can see the others looking at us and soon everyone's roaring with laughter at our antics.

'Celeste! Where's your killer instinct?' Rishi calls encouragingly.

'No, Patrick's the one messing up!' says Sibéal loyally. I can feel my face getting crimson. Then Melanie offers to swap with me, and within minutes she and Patrick are sawing away smoothly, back and forth. They finish the log within minutes and move on to another and another. I make a half-hearted stab with Melanie's little saw, but my heart's not in it and I'm getting cold.

'I don't have my gloves – I'm going to head back,' I say to the others, who wave cheerfully before going back to their tasks. I pick up an armful of logs and go inside, thinking at least I can make myself useful by stacking them by the fire. I know it doesn't matter. It's just a random bit of DIY – not even gardening. But I can't help wondering if this is saying something about me. I can't even saw a log with someone else; no wonder I don't have a life partner. Or maybe – and this makes more sense – I can just blame the whole debacle, sawing, house and all, on Patrick.

I feel better after a cup of tea and a quick disco nap in my room, and soon it's time to get ready for drinks at seven. The importance of this part of the evening was made very clear earlier by Vik. 'We'll be serving pre-dinner drinks in the drawing room at seven o'clock sharp,' he said. 'Be there and be dressed up, please.'

I love the fact that he's made this rule, which makes me think of Hannah's vision for this New Year's. We're all wearing black tie for dinner, which we think she might have liked. My mum lent me a long silvery-gold vintage number from the seventies, and I'm wearing it tonight. It's not quite sequins but a soft metallic material, with a low V-neck and thin straps. It's lucky there's a fireplace in the dining room; and of course I'll also have my wine gilet, as Hannah used to call them. I've just poured myself into it and I'm sitting down to do my make-up when there's a knock at the door.

'Come in,' I call, thinking it's probably one of the girls wanting to borrow my straighteners or something. But it's Patrick, already in his dinner jacket and black tie. He's smoothed back his shaggy hair and he's even shaved for the occasion. And he's carrying two glasses of champagne, one of which he hands to me.

'Oh. Thank you. I thought drinks were later?'

'I thought the ladies might want a glass now, while you get ready.'

'Thank you,' I say, accepting it. I can imagine the others finding this really charming, but his particular brand of charm is starting to grate on my nerves. And why is he playing host? Vikram should be the one handing out drinks.

'Pat!' calls a voice downstairs. 'Come on – search party.'

'Oh, God,' Patrick says. 'The blasted swan has gone missing, and Vik wants me to check on him.' He steps outside before I can tell him that the swan, in my opinion, is much better left unfound.

'I should get a gong,' says Vikram, as we all gather in the drawing room. 'That's going on my list right now actually. A gong for dinner – how cool would that be?'

I smile at him, picturing that this is going to be his next search on Facebook Marketplace. I suppose a gong is a good idea in such a rambling house. It really does feel as if we're in an Agatha Christie novel. Everyone is looking fabulous: Sibéal in tight plunging black; Melanie in a gorgeous yellow silk dress, revealing her toned arms, with her signature flower tucked behind her ear. The men are all in their dinner jackets – Vik has gone mad with a red bow tie. There's lots of chat about the swan, who is back apparently.

'I'm really glad; he's never been missing for that long

before. Although I'm not sure how he's going to react to the fireworks . . . He won't have seen those before,' Vik says. 'I've got a whole bunch. I went into this special place in Ipswich where they demo them for you.'

My heart is full as I see how nervous and excited Vik looks, and I realize how long this evening has been in the planning for him.

'Should we stick him inside? The swan?' Mel asks, and Vik says, 'God, no, he's not a dog. He'd go nuts.'

The fire's lower now, so Vikram puts a couple of logs on. But they don't emit the same satisfying crackle and flame as the others; instead there's a dull hiss, and the fire goes dark and emits an acrid cloud of smoke.

'Oh, shit,' says Vikram. 'What's happened there? Must have been damp.'

'It was the logs *you* told us to cut,' I say defensively to Patrick.

He laughs. 'They just need to be dried first.'

'But they're bone dry! It hasn't been raining, has it?'

'No, it's not to do with them being wet, it's to do with the sap inside. They need to dry for, like, several months. You didn't know that?'

Vik takes the offending logs out with tongs, while Melanie opens a window to let some of the smoke out. I'm really embarrassed; I hope the place won't reek for weeks. But also, why didn't Patrick say anything when he saw me bring them inside? If he saw me, of course.

'Not to worry,' says Vik. 'Look, it's almost time for dinner. Why don't we let things, um, freshen up in here and we'll go in for dinner?'

'I'm really sorry, Vik,' I say apologetically.

'Don't worry, Celeste. You weren't to know,' says Patrick magnanimously.

I murmur the briefest reply, wishing he would just butt out and leave me alone.

At least the dining room and the table both look wonderful. Dozens of tealights are glowing at the place settings, and in the middle of the table blooms the large many-branched candelabra with dripping red candles. It's gorgeous and we've taken at least twenty photos of each other by the time we've sat down and Vik has poured us all red wine.

'Rishi, can you give me a hand?' he asks. They disappear into the kitchen, and then a few minutes later he and Rishi come back out with a huge casserole filled with beef and red wine stew, served with roast potatoes and salad.

'Hopefully the stew will be OK. I wanted to make something fancier . . .'

Everyone clamours at once that it smells delicious, which it does.

'Listen, you're never going to hear me complain about getting stew,' says Patrick.

'I had to rush it a bit more than I wanted to,' Vik says, as he takes a bite. 'Oh, God. I'm really sorry.'

We all take a bite and exchange glances. 'It's . . . I mean, it's a little chewy, but that's . . . all good. It adds interest,' I offer.

'Yes. What you want in a stew,' says Patrick, 'is a good . . . crunch.'

This makes me laugh; we're all laughing by now, even Vik. He hands out more crusty bread, and we all assure him that this, with the sauce from the stew, and the roast potatoes, is perfect. Melanie also offers around some of her mushroom dish, though we all say we can't take it off her as she's the only vegan here.

'That's one of the things that Pablo won't miss about me,' she remarks. 'He's a typical Argentine – loves his steak.'

'Is that why you guys broke up then?' Rishi asks. 'Ow! Sorry,' he adds, Sibéal having clearly kicked him under the table.

'No, it's fine, honestly,' Mel says, smiling. 'Don't worry, Shib . . . I don't mind talking about it. He just wasn't happy here in the UK, but I didn't want to move either. So it was easier to go our separate ways.' She looks down at her wine glass. 'And also . . . it was devastating, obviously, when Hannah died. And I just felt like I was turning to him for support and he couldn't give it to me. That was the beginning of the end really.'

Vik says, 'I'm sorry, Mel.'

'It's OK. Honestly, it made me realize life's too short. Too short to be unhappy.'

Sibéal nods. 'It really is, isn't it? That was actually part of why we did this.' She puts her hand on her stomach. 'I mean, we thought we were done with two: a boy and a girl, done and done. Rishi was all booked to have the snip and everything.'

'Babe,' Rishi murmurs.

'But then I thought . . . I'm not done, I want more, I want another person to love. And Rishi felt the same, so we went for it.' She looks at Vik. 'I hope you don't mind me saying it, Vik. I just miss her so much.'

He nods. 'No, I get it. You're right: life is short. That's

why I wanted to go for it with the house. I needed a purpose. I want to restore it and hopefully turn it into something the local community can use too. I know she would have liked that.' He looks around the table, smiling, though his eyes are bright with tears. 'It's nice to know, actually, the effect she's had. You were saying something along the same lines, Pat, weren't you?'

Patrick, who's been listening intently, looks startled. 'Me? Well, yeah, I suppose so. I don't want to . . .' He makes a 'this isn't about me' gesture. 'I know a lot of you were closer to Hannah than I was. But I've known her all her life – she was friends with my little sister, and she really was like a little sister to me, or a cousin. So, yeah, it was devastating. And it did make me reassess what I wanted. Hence my career change.'

'What career change?' asks Mel.

'Oh, I'm going to quit my job – and open a garden centre. Back in Dublin. And do some garden contracting on the side.' He looks self-conscious. 'It's going to be a challenge – I'll have a lot to learn, but, like Mel said, life's too short.'

I look at him, feeling my assessment of him shift. He doesn't sound perfect or smug any more; he sounds grief-stricken and confused, just like the rest of us.

Then I realize everyone has turned to look at me. I don't have anything to add. No life changes, no new baby or new career; compared to the others, I feel as if I'm trapped in amber. 'Me? I haven't made any big changes,' I say, clearing my throat. Then I add, 'But everything's changed anyway.' I blink a tear away, as Sibéal leans over to give me a hug. Vik gets up, looking worried, and says, 'I don't want to make you all miserable – let's take a break. Mel, will you help me bring in the pudding? It's a vegan chocolate cake. Hopefully more successful than my stew.'

After we've eaten our pudding, we all go into the drawing room for more wine. The floodgates have opened and we're all feeling emotional; I don't know if I can stand it, but I also just really want to talk about Hannah. And Vik obviously feels the same, suggesting that we each share a memory of her.

We all look at each other, obviously nobody wanting to be the first. The silence goes on a beat too long until Sibéal says, 'Oh, God, I've got so many, but they're totally inappropriate.'

Everyone laughs, the tension broken, and Vikram says, 'That sounds perfect. Seriously, have at it.'

Shib says, 'I do have a nice one. I remember Hannah was the first one on the dance floor at our wedding. Rishi, do you remember that?'

'Yes! We had finished our first dance, and it was that cringey moment when we were standing there wanting people to join in, and nobody wanted to be first.'

'Until Hannah got up,' says Sibéal. 'I remember she was wearing this long red dress, sort of flamenco-looking? I don't know where you were, Vik, probably the bar, but she just dragged someone else up, I forget who, and soon we were all dancing.'

We're all smiling at the memory, which is especially vivid to me, even if the others have forgotten: I was the someone else.

'That was Hannah,' says Vik. 'She was always the first on the dance floor, and the last to leave it. I remember she used to ask me which shoes –' He stops short and I hold my breath, but then he smiles. 'She used to ask me which shoes, and I used to say, it doesn't matter; they'll be off by eight p.m. anyway.'

We all laugh, but it's a bit of a knife edge; I can feel the palpable relief from everyone that he was able to say it without breaking down. 'How about you, Mel?' he asks.

'Sure,' says Mel. 'One random thing I remember is from when Hannah and I were doing our make-up together – on that trip to Barcelona, do you remember, Celeste? She gave me such a good tip, which was when you're doing heavy eye make-up, you should do the eyes first and then do your foundation. That way you can mop up any residue from the eyes and it won't ruin your base. I remember it because Hannah was such an artist in everything she did. She was the same with her drawings – it all looked so effortless but you knew there were dozens of drafts. So now when I do my make-up I always do my eyes first. Sorry, is that really superficial?' She looks worried. 'I know there are so many more important things. But I think of her every time I do my make-up.'

'So do I,' I say.

I have to take a deep breath to compose myself. I remember that trip too. I was engaged to Eddie at the time, and I remember trying on wedding dresses in a shop there. It wasn't my hen party – that was just dinner and drinks in London – but it makes me think of that time with sadness. It's not that I miss Eddie, but I miss that time, when life was so carefree.

'I've got a good one,' Rishi says suddenly. 'I remember we had that pub lunch with you and Hannah in Liverpool

Street, Vik. And we were talking about that girl from Hannah's work, who you had met too, Sibéal. And you were asking how she was.'

'Oh yes, and Hannah got out her phone and texted her right away,' says Sibéal.

'Yes,' Vik says. 'She said that if ever she thought about getting in touch with someone, she would contact them right away, while she thought about it. She said it was better to send one quick text than to spend six months never getting around to the perfect message.'

'That's a good one,' Mel agrees. 'That's how she had so many friends, of course. And it's like the drawing really. It looked effortless, but she really worked at her friendships; they were so important to her.'

'How about you, Celeste?' Vik asks gently. 'You must have lots.'

I do. I was going to tell them about how Hannah and I walked the Camino de Santiago pilgrim trail together in Spain, and had a terrible day where we had nowhere to buy lunch, and Hannah shared her one packet of M&S salt and pepper cashew nuts with me. My overriding memory is not the hunger or exhaustion but how much we laughed. But Mel's words about how important Hannah's friendships were have got me, and I know that if I start speaking I'll burst into tears, and then it will be all about me, which is not what I want. So I just shake my head.

'I've got one actually,' says Patrick. 'I knew Hannah growing up, as I said – we were neighbours. And I remember one summer I decided to have a party while my parents were away . . .'

He continues his story, which is about Hannah and

his sister insisting on joining in, but I can't concentrate on it. I feel so ashamed that I can't contribute one simple story, when even Vik has done it. I don't want to start crying in the middle of Patrick's memory. So I say quietly to Mel, beside me, 'Just getting a drink of water – I'll be back in a sec.'

I walk out of the room, appalled at myself. What is wrong with me? I pause on the stairs at the sound of a voice below.

'Celeste? You OK?' It's Mel.

'Oh, I'm fine. Be back in a sec – don't wait for me,' I manage to say.

Safely in my room, I look at my phone; it's five minutes to midnight. I should hurry downstairs so that I'm there for the count. But I can't; I'm frozen to the spot. I stay sitting on my bed, letting the minutes go by until I hear them shouting loudly downstairs: 'Ten . . . nine . . . eight . . . seven . . .' And shortly after: 'Happy New Year!' This finally breaks me, and I give into a year's worth of tears all at once, as silently as I can. Then I wash my face and come downstairs where they're all getting ready to go outside for fireworks.

The others have presumably noticed my absence, but they don't make any remark, for which I'm grateful. It's time for the fireworks and I'm also thankful for the distraction as we all pull on coats, hats and scarves, with quite a bit of clattering around due to the darkness and alcohol. Outside, the cold air and the stars make me feel a bit better momentarily.

'Has anyone seen Sigmund?' Vik says. 'Oh well, he'll just have to cope. OK. Here we go!'

There's lots of shrieking, as he lights the first one. Then we turn and watch the rocket fire up in the night sky, exploding and shedding its trail of red, yellow and pink, then followed by more: blue, green, white and purple, circles and starbursts and arcs of colour. The smell of cordite and damp earth sets off memories, of Halloween and New Year's parties gone by, and of Bonfire Night in Hannah's shared house in Clapton.

'I'll get the champagne. Wait: there's no more clean glasses!' says Sibéal. I remember that she's allowing herself one glass of champagne at midnight, as a treat.

'I'll wash some up,' I say quickly.

I slip inside and head to the dining room, where all the candles are still burning merrily. I blow them out, then bring in a trayful of glasses to wash. Finding my black sweater in a corner, I pull it on, thinking that at least this way I'll save Mum's dress from washing-up splashes.

I'm rinsing my first pair when I hear footsteps behind me. 'Celeste.'

It's Patrick. He's carrying some empty glasses and dishes from the dining room, obviously having had the same thought as me.

'Are you OK?' he asks.

I'm about to say, 'I'm fine,' but it would be such a patent lie that I just shake my head instead. He says, 'I'm sorry. I've been so concerned for Vik; I hadn't really thought what it must be like for you. I know you were her best friend. And you always had New Year's together.'

I'm shaking my head, because I don't want this to be about me; I don't feel I have any right to be in such a state. I wasn't a relative or a partner like Vik; I was just a friend.

But his tone has pushed me over the edge and the tears are sliding down my face now.

'Hey,' he says. He steps closer and puts his arms around me, drawing me towards him. I can feel the rough wool of his coat under my hands, as I breathe in his outdoorsy smell: woodsmoke and wine, and fireworks. His chin is resting on my head. I give in, for a moment, to the comfort of his presence and I find myself holding him tighter – before I realize this is getting a bit too intimate and disengage myself.

Our faces are close together, under the kitchen lamp. He's looking startled, as if thinking the same as me: *what just happened exactly?*

'Um, do you want to come outside?' he says in an overly bright and friendly tone.

'I'll be out shortly!' I say in the same bright voice. 'You go ahead. Take these!' I hand him some glasses and a bottle of champagne.

After hesitating for a minute, he goes back outside, closing the back door quietly behind him. I'm simultaneously relieved to be alone and achingly lonely. I wonder if everyone is drunk enough that I can go to bed without anyone noticing.

Then I hear a voice. 'Celeste? No wallflowers at this party.' It's Vik, closely followed by Sibéal. He comes up to me and holds out his hand. 'Give me those rubber gloves. And have another drink.' Sibéal hands me a glass of champagne.

'Get that down you, and then come back out. We've got more explosions coming,' says Vik.

Sibéal gives me a huge hug, and murmurs in my ear, 'Out of this darkness will come a great light.'

'What she said,' says Vik.

I start laughing despite myself, deeply touched that he's being so brave – and that they both came for me. It's a timely reminder that I'm not alone in this; I've still got friends. 'I'll grab my coat,' I say, and I follow them both outside.

Later, just before I fall asleep, I find myself thinking back to the aftermath of that first-ever New Year's party – the morning after. I had crashed out on Hannah's bed fully clothed, and I had probably only been asleep for a few hours when she shook me awake.

'Celeste!' she said. 'Me and Clodagh have had a brilliant idea. We're going to take a boat out to Dalkey Island and light a fire there. The first day of the Millennium. Are you in?'

I wasn't even sure if I was fully compos mentis yet, or if this was part of my dream. But it didn't matter. Hannah's excitement was infectious, and I loved the idea of visiting Dalkey Island, which I had glimpsed from the shore so many times.

'I didn't even know you could go there,' I said, as we went downstairs.

Hannah looked at me in surprise. 'Of course you can! You just need a boat. Clodagh's got one . . . She's gone home to get the key. She's just across the road – come on.'

But Clodagh, when she came out of her house, was closely followed by her older brother Patrick and another guy, presumably a friend of theirs who had crashed at their house; nobody had been able to get a taxi anywhere, I remembered now.

'You don't have to come with us,' Hannah told Patrick. 'We can handle the boat.'

Patrick just shook his head with a grin. 'You can do what you like, but Clodagh's not drowning herself on my watch. I'd never hear the end of it.'

We walked down to Bulloch Harbour, where Patrick led us to a small motorboat high up on the slip. We had to push it into the water and then jump in, and my feet were predictably soaked. But it didn't matter. The boat zipped off, and soon we were in another element, bouncing over the waves towards the island, which was lying to the east, its two ruined towers illuminated by the rising sun. We tied the boat up to a long wooden pier and got out; Patrick turned to give me a hand out but I smiled and jumped right past him, feeling too free and independent to need any help at all.

Hannah had already walked up the little beach to greet one of the wild goats that were the island's only inhabitants. 'Sorry I don't have anything for you, kiddo,' she said. 'How about here?' she said, turning to the rest of us.

'Fine,' said the guy who wasn't Patrick, unrolling a bag of firewood. Hannah produced firelighters and matches from her pocket. We all watched the flames take light and I felt a solemn thrill at the idea that this was the first fire of the Millennium to be lit here. Clodagh produced blankets and a thermos flask of coffee and some plastic mugs, and we all drank; I had only just started drinking coffee and had been dubious about it, but now I finally understood why people loved it.

'Isn't this the best?' Hannah said to me later. The others had gone to explore the ruined church up the hill and see if they could see Wales, but she wanted to stay on the beach, watching the city wake up across the water. We huddled together under a blanket, our cheeks as cold as seashells, and watched the sun rise. It was marvellous, filling up the whole eastern horizon and casting a pink and golden wash on the hills and mountains of Dalkey and Killiney, and on Bray Head far off to the south.

'I love this place so much,' she said. 'When I was little, I used to dream of coming here and staying for a few months. I thought I could live off the land or catch fish.'

'Well, maybe you could,' I said – not because I thought it was feasible but because I could imagine Hannah doing anything she wanted to.

She laughed. Then she said, 'Thanks for coming tonight. Last night. It was really, really fun.' She turned to me. 'Let's do it again next year? Not a party but … whatever I'm doing, you can do. If you want?'

'Same,' I said. We clinked our plastic together, and I felt a moment of pure joy as I watched the sun rise, on the first day of the new Millennium, with my new friend.

10

January

New Year's Day. My first without Hannah. I've been dreading this for so long I had almost expected some kind of catastrophe or natural disaster to occur, like the ones we anticipated back in 1999. But, just like then, the world hasn't ended and I've lived to see another dawn. It's a cold grey dawn this time, but I can still see someone moving outside at the edge of the lawn. I wonder for a second if Vikram has a burglar before I recognize Patrick, up even earlier than me.

I pull on my thermal top and trousers, jeans and a jumper, all while sitting up in bed, then pad downstairs. The kitchen is quiet and miraculously tidy considering all our revels last night – someone must have stayed up late cleaning up. I make a pot of coffee and cringe slightly as I remember my odd encounter with Patrick last night. But it wasn't a big deal. We were all in a state. I find some paracetamol and wash it down with some water. I feel a bit better now; hungover, certainly, but calmer somehow.

Patrick still hasn't come in from the garden, so I decide to take him out a cup of coffee. I don't know how he takes it, so I slosh in a bit of milk and call it good.

The air is bitingly cold; it really is so fresh after London it takes me by surprise each time. I walk over to where

Patrick is kneeling over some dark earth and hand him the coffee.

'Cheers,' he says with an unmistakable look of surprise.

'I wasn't sure how you took it – hope this is OK.'

'This is great. Thanks.'

'Happy New Year,' I add, clinking his coffee cup against mine.

'Happy New Year.' He takes a sip and looks at me. 'What do you think?'

I glance at the bushes that he's planted, which look a bit sad and withered. 'Very nice,' I say politely. 'I didn't know you could plant this kind of thing in winter.'

'Like everything in gardens – it depends. These can go in, as long as the ground's not frozen. They're not growing, they're just sort of existing, until it's time for them to flower.' After a minute, he says, 'Are you feeling any better? I don't mean, feeling better exactly. But if you wanted to talk about it . . .'

I shake my head immediately. 'I-I'm sorry. I don't. But thanks, though.'

'Fair enough.' He puts down his coffee. 'Would you like to help with the summer bed? I've got some more bulbs to plant.'

'Sure,' I say, picking up the trowel and following him over.

'Just dig a hole – about five inches should do it – and pop it in, with the twisty part of the bulb facing down. Then just pat a bit of earth on top.' As I put the bulb in, I realize this is a first for me; I don't think I have actually ever planted something before – aside from maybe some cress in biology class.

As I put in the last of the bulbs and straighten up, I have to admit that it's a nice feeling to think that we've completed a concrete task that should lead to a concrete result – flowers.

'Very nice,' Patrick says. 'Now we cover these up with chicken wire, and then breakfast.'

'Don't mention breakfast – I'm starving,' I say, as he unrolls the wire.

'Go back in if you want, I can finish these.'

'What, and let the squirrels get my bulbs? I don't think so,' I say, and hold out my hand for the wire cutters.

We have a quick breakfast together in the quiet kitchen; everyone else must still be sleeping off their hangovers – lucky things. Then Patrick goes off to phone Angelika, and I go upstairs to pack. On the way back to my room I pass Vikram's door, which is open. He's sitting on the bed, looking through a pile of notes and letters.

I knock on his door. 'Hi.'

He looks up. 'Hello, lovely. Happy New Year.'

'Happy New Year. How's the head?' I ask, coming and sitting on the bed.

'It's OK,' he says dully. 'I'm not, though.' After a minute, he continues, 'I suppose I had just been focusing on this all so much. Seeing you all and hosting a big party here like Hannah wanted to. I somehow thought it would be this big cathartic moment that would help me move on – whatever that means. But now I feel just the same. Except hungover.'

We both laugh, and then we sigh in unison.

'I know just what you mean, Vik. I feel the same. I

couldn't even share my memory last night. I'm sorry about that.'

'It's OK. I've got enough memories. Too many really.' He looks down at the notebook in his hand.

'What's that?' I ask.

'Mostly sketches . . . but it's got her resolutions for last year. Do you want to see?'

I pick it up and look at her list. The sight of her handwriting, as familiar as my own, smites me to the heart again. As does this list. *Do hot yoga. Try a climbing wall. Get my astrology chart done* . . . It should have been the fuel for a dozen entertaining anecdotes. Instead it represents all the things she never got to do last year – or in life.

'Do you know if she did any of them?' I ask Vik.

'I don't think so.' He sounds so desolate I can't bear it. 'I was thinking maybe I should do them for her. But I'm not in a place to do it really – geographically or otherwise. And some of them are just a hard no for me, honestly.'

'Hot yoga?' I ask, taking a guess. He nods emphatically, which makes me smile. Despite his love of wellness, Vik hates being too hot, which makes this house perfect for him, I suppose. I look at the rest of the list, imagining Hannah ticking them off in her usual unstoppable style, and read it aloud.

1. Do hot yoga
2. Try a climbing wall
3. Get my astrology chart done
4. Have afternoon tea somewhere fancy
5. Go to the ballet
6. Go c. dancing

7. Have a session with a personal shopper
8. Do a canal boat trip
9. Go jogging in Hyde Park
10. Go outdoor swimming
11. Visit a Christmas market
12. Help someone in need

'Do you know what "c. dancing" is by the way? I meant to ask,' Vik says.

'Oh gosh. No idea. We know it's not country dancing, I suppose.'

Hannah hated country and western music, to the extent of being the only person in the world who didn't love Dolly Parton – or her music at least. Obviously Hannah loved Dolly herself.

'Well,' I say, 'that one's a mystery. But . . .'

I look at Vik, and I think he knows what I'm thinking. I'm just not sure how he will feel about it. 'What if I did it?' I ask him tentatively. 'The list, I mean.'

He smiles. 'I think that's a great idea. Why not? I've got a project – now you can have one too. There's twelve of them – you could do one a month.'

I look down at the list feeling suddenly daunted. 'Oh gosh. Get my astrology chart done . . . I'm not sure about that.'

'Well, at the very least, it might give me a laugh.'

I give him a shove, but we're both smiling now.

'I'm sorry I didn't tell you I was staying on here before by the way,' he says. 'I sort of had the feeling you wouldn't approve.'

'It's OK honestly, Vik. You didn't need my approval.'

'I do see that it's a slightly mad idea from a practical point of view.'

'Maybe. But I suppose life's not just about being practical.'

I look at the list, feeling a sense of possibility and potential for the first time in weeks – months even. Finally here is something I can do for Hannah – not a pilgrimage or a prayer but a little private mission to honour her last wishes and keep her memory alive. I try to imagine what she'd say if she could see me attempting to complete her list; and I can almost hear her laugh.

'All right, Celeste,' says Vik. 'Here you go. Your mission, should you choose to accept it.' He hands me the Moleskine notebook, raising one eyebrow.

'I accept it.' I take the little black book and exhale slowly, as the reality of what I've just committed to sinks in. But I'm energized too at the thought of having something like this to do: a new purpose in life that's not just work or commuting or going to the gym. It's on a modest scale, of course. I'm not having a baby or renovating a house or launching a new career. It's just a list. But it's a start.

11

Vik and I go downstairs to find everyone in the midst of a heated debate. It turns out that there's been another shopping disaster. Rishi has bought three kilos of, not sea salt as Sibéal specified, but ordinary table salt.

'Won't it do?' he's asking helplessly.

'Of course it won't do!' Sibéal sounds beside herself. 'It would impregnate the fish and make it completely inedible. I'm sorry,' she adds, catching sight of me and Vik approaching. 'It's fine. It's fine. I'll bake it in the oven. I just wanted to make us a nice dinner.' Her face crumples, and she starts crying; I've never seen her in such a state.

'No, no,' Rishi says immediately. 'I'll go and get some.'

This sparks off yet another discussion, of what shops in the vicinity might be open on New Year's Day and selling salt. I feel sad that I'm leaving, but it can't be helped: I have work first thing tomorrow.

'Rishi,' I say. 'If you're driving to the village, do you think I could get a lift to the train? I can pop into the shop if you want.'

'OK,' he says, looking distracted at all the suggestions of shops, supermarkets and delis coming at him from all sides. 'Leave in twenty minutes?' I thank him and run upstairs for a slightly shivery shower in Vik's antique bathroom, feeling grateful for modern plumbing and for being single and child-free: poor Rishi and Sibéal are both clearly on a knife edge from years of exhaustion.

I come back down, showered and slightly less hungover, to find that there's been a change of plan. Rishi and Sibéal are going to go to the big supermarket to get the salt together, and Patrick has offered to drive me to the station.

'Are you sure?' I ask him. 'That's very kind – thank you.'

'It's ten minutes,' he says, waving away my objections.

I exchange hugs with everyone, and we all promise to see each other again soon; I've decided I'm going to be better at keeping in touch with people. Especially Vikram.

'Thank you for a brilliant stay, Vik,' I say. 'It was so good to see you.'

'You too. Don't be a stranger, will you? And let me know how it goes – with your mission.' He smiles down at me.

'Of course I will. I'll call you soon.' I give him the biggest hug of all, and then it's time to go. Patrick takes my bag, and hoists it into the back of his car, empty now without all the rose bushes and cherries, though there are a few scattered rose leaves still left on the floor.

As we drive away, I look back once over my shoulder to see the house getting smaller at the end of the wooded lane. I imagine Vikram inside after they've all left, clearing away the last of our mess, maybe stripping beds and tidying – or just sitting by himself, staring into the fire. Or, more likely, he'll just get on with the next phase of his project. I understand his reasons for staying here now, better than I did when I went. I can understand him wanting a feeling of purpose, and I feel as if I have one now too – on a smaller scale, but that's OK.

Patrick says, 'It's a shame you have to leave so early.'

'I know . . . but duty calls.'

'What is it you do again?'

'I work for WBH Consulting,' I say, and he nods. Suddenly I remember about his girlfriend, who also had to work. 'Did, um, Angelina have a good New Year's?'

'Angelika?'

'Oh yes. Sorry.'

'Well, yeah, except she was working – in the lab. I think they stopped at midnight for some Cokes but that was it. She had an experiment going,' he says, sounding admiring. 'She's still working on it, so we'll celebrate next weekend instead. She works so hard but it's in a good cause, you know? She's not just killing herself for some corporation . . .' He tails off, as he seems to realize what he's just said. There's an awkward pause before he adds, 'Sorry. I didn't mean you . . .'

I start laughing again. 'It's really OK, Patrick. We can't *all* be curing cancer.'

He laughs too but he sounds very embarrassed. 'God, I'm sorry.'

'Don't be, it's funny.' It has tickled me for some reason, and I quite like the fact that he can put his foot in it too on occasion.

He says, 'What was Vik saying – about your mission? I'm just being nosy.'

'Oh, it's just a list of New Year's resolutions that Hannah made last year.' I explain my plan and mention a couple of the items.

'Tell me the rest?'

I read them out from the notebook, adding, 'I'm confused by this one though – "try c. dancing". What on earth is "c. dancing"? I would be tempted to say "country" except Hannah hated country music; she really couldn't bear it.'

'*C. dancing*,' Patrick repeats. 'I don't know. Circle dancing? Colour dancing? Crazy dancing? No idea.'

'Well, never mind. The one I'm really dreading is rock climbing.'

'You could do bouldering instead?' he suggests.

This conjures up visions of being squished under a huge rock at the bottom of a canyon. 'What's that?'

'It's just climbing on a lower wall, which is generally more uneven – so it's more like being outdoors, except that obviously there's not a drop underneath you. If that's what bothers you.'

'Really? OK. I appreciate the tip.' I had no idea that such an option existed, and I wonder briefly if it counts before telling myself of course it does. 'Have you done it?'

'Oh yeah. Not for a while, though . . . Hey,' Patrick says suddenly. 'C. dancing. Could that be "ceilidh dancing"?'

'Oh gosh, yes! You're right! Hannah did always want to try that. Isn't there somewhere in north London?'

'Probably. That's good then – that gives you a start.'

We're nearly at the station now; I can see the sign for it. After he turns in and pulls up, Patrick says, 'Well, you should be in plenty of time for your train . . .'

'Yes, that's brilliant. Thank you.' I lean forward to get my bag from the footwell, and as I do so he says, 'You know, there is that climbing centre near my place – and yours. If you ever wanted to check it out, we could go together.'

I look at him, surprised; that's a bold move into definite friend territory. My instinct is to say something non-committal, as it's probably easier to go on my own. But I've realized by now that the point of this list probably isn't just to tick things off it. I could afford to be a little more open to new friends, as well as new experiences.

'OK,' I say. 'That sounds good. I'll send you a text when I'm ready.'

Sitting on the train, I treat myself to one last scroll through my phone, given that my own New Year's resolution is going to be to reduce my screen time. There are various 'Happy New Year' messages that I reply to, before taking a last peek at Instagram. I've garnered about ten likes on the picture I posted of the sunrise the other morning, and a few nice New Year greetings. I flip through, hearting them all, until I come to the last one, left at 9 a.m. this morning. It's from an account called eddie345, and it says, **Beautiful. HNY, Celeste x**

Eddie. I didn't know he was on Instagram. I click through to his profile and see that he's got no stories and only half a dozen pictures up on his grid, arty/ugly shots of street signs and empty beer cans. There's one picture of him, looking a bit older and cuddling a dog. A nice dog too. It looks like a mutt that he's adopted from a rescue place, not a pedigree, which sounds like him. He always did the right thing, except when he didn't.

I didn't want to stay in touch; I told him that it was best that we make a clean break. But that was two years ago and I suppose he thinks enough time has passed that we could be friends. I'm not so sure, so I ignore his comment and put away my phone, opening up my *Economist* instead. But my mind keeps wandering back to the summer when I met him, which seems impossibly distant now, like something glimpsed through the wrong end of a telescope. Am I even the same person still?

12

I had been emailing Eddie for months before I actually found out his real name. We didn't meet on a dating app or even a website, though, but in a much odder way. Eddie wrote a column called Corporate Boy – a bit like the much more scandalous City Boy in the late noughties, except it was less about exposing strip club visits and £3,000 lunches and more about lampooning the kind of corporate speak that was so familiar to me from my job.

'I don't get it,' Hannah said, when I read out one of my favourite bits from my phone. It was a Saturday morning in May, just after my birthday, and we were sitting outside Caravan in Exmouth Market. Inspired by the gorgeous weather, our plan had been to meet for a quick coffee and then go for a run together, but instead it had turned into a three-hour brunch complete with mimosas, which I'd always wanted to try, feeling only slightly disappointed that they were just another word for Buck's Fizz.

I laughed again, reading it. 'It's just funny . . . I suppose it won't make sense if you don't work in that kind of environment. Don't you have any jargon at your work?'

'Not really,' said Hannah. She had an agent now for her illustration work and was doing freelance jobs for various corporate clients as well as her own stuff. 'It's more like mixed messages – like when the client wants it upbeat but moody, or approachable but aspirational. That kind of thing. Oh, and they always want the logo bigger. Sometimes I think I should just draw them a big logo with a tiny illustration in the corner, that would probably go down better.'

I commiserated, before looking back at Corporate Boy's byline photo. It was one of those black silhouettes, so it was impossible to guess what he looked like, but from his writing I thought he was probably around my age: thirty-two. 'Honestly, I could write this column. I have so much material.'

'You should then,' said Hannah immediately. 'Be Corporate Girl.'

I smiled, but there was no way I was going to run the risk of my work finding out about something like that. Plus, I knew my job paid better than any column could.

'You should drop him a line then,' suggested Hannah. 'Tell him you're a fan. He'd love it.'

'I can't email him. What if my work found out?'

'Celeste! That's why God gave you a Hotmail address.'

'Only psychos still use Hotmail,' I said, to tease Hannah, still loyal to the Hotmail account she'd had since the previous century. 'I could set up a new gmail, I suppose.'

Hannah sighed, puffing at her old fringe, which she was trying to grow out. 'This isn't Watergate. Just email him, tell him you love his column, and see what happens.'

So I did. I created a new anonymous gmail and emailed him, and told him how much I loved the column, and mentioned a few funny things from my work. Soon we were messaging regularly – not every day, but enough for Hannah to refer to him as my 'You've Got Mail' guy.

'Wouldn't it be funny if he turned out to be someone

you worked with – like Hugo?' she said. 'Or if he worked in, like, a rival tower.'

'A rival tower?' I laughed at Hannah's extremely hazy picture of my work. 'I don't think so. For a start, Hugo is exactly the kind of person he takes the piss out of in the column. And he's never mentioned anything that's specific to our place . . . not even the bits I've given him.'

'I told you you should write your own column.'

The following week, though, one of my little bits did make it in – my boss's love of the word 'presenteeism', which didn't mean quite what he thought it did. He thought it meant long hours and dedication, whereas I knew it meant putting your coat on your chair and then going to the gym, another solid Hugo move. I was terrified he would read it, but also thrilled that my gem was in print.

'That's fab,' said Hannah when I told her. 'You should email him and tell him you really liked it.'

'And ask him out?' I suggested.

Hannah looked thoughtful. Despite her spirit of adventure, she was surprisingly old-fashioned when it came to dating. She didn't play games, but she always said the less chasing the better. It had certainly worked for her. She could have opted for any one of the hot, arty and unreliable men who stumbled in and out of her circle, but she had chosen Vikram, whom she had met when he did an illustration class that she ran as a one-off for some corporate clients. He was kind, funny and – crucially – reliable. She was very secure in the relationship, never once worrying about how much he loved her. But not all of us were that lucky; I'd been single for over a year, and I rarely met men that I liked.

'Right,' I said, taking out my phone and setting a timer.

'What's that?' she asked, looking amused.

'Let's discuss this for no longer than – let's see – five minutes. Otherwise I'll obsess about him too much.'

'That is genius,' said Hannah. I knew she would love this. We were constantly sharing our little 'life hacks' with each other and telling each other how brilliant they were.

'So, I'll email in a light, flirty way – like, "Hey, don't you owe me a drink for my gag?". What?' I could tell from her face that she was sceptical.

'Honestly? I know it was your gag, strictly speaking, but . . . as a creative person he might not appreciate you actually saying so. I'd be more flattering about it – like, tell him he really nailed it.' She raised her eyebrows, somehow managing to make this sound suggestive and flirty and sincere all at once.

'Really? You think he'd be that sensitive?'

Hannah sighed. 'I don't know what to tell you, babe.' It was one of her favourite phrases. 'Us creative types, we're a nightmare.'

I wasn't completely convinced, but I decided to take her advice and wrote him a flattering message, dutifully including the words 'nailed it'. And I said that if he wanted more intel in person, we could always meet for a drink.

'But that's *it*,' said Hannah. 'Don't do anything else, don't suggest dates, don't look up bar or restaurant reviews. Just leave it all one hundred per cent up to him.'

'What would Gloria Steinem say?'

'I don't know anything about her except she wore cool glasses, but Hannah Golden would say that chasing in a dating situation is emotional labour which you should not be putting in at this point. You've done enough. Now let him do some work.'

'God, that's such a good point. You should write a book,' I said in honest admiration.

'We should have a podcast!'

'I know!'

That was another thing that we loved telling each other: that our conversations were so fascinating that we should have a podcast, though we never got any further than saying so.

So I emailed Corporate Boy. To my delight I got a prompt response: When and where suits? which seemed perfect, until I forwarded it to Hannah. I had recently started using emojis in my email and I accompanied it with a row of heart-eyed faces.

'That's great, but just watch out you don't end up planning the whole evening,' she wrote back. 'Tell him that it's up to him to choose a place. If you let him be lazy now it will never end.'

This was exactly why I hated dating. Why did it have to be so complicated? What did it matter who chose what pub? I realized that I had already made too big a deal of it and involved Hannah too much as well. I closed my eyes and tried to get back in touch with my own inner sense of judgement. What did *I* want? I decided that I was happy to choose the date, but I did want him to choose the place. So I wrote back, Next Thursday or Friday are good. Anywhere central is fine.

After a day's suspense, he wrote back suggesting a bar in Soho the following Thursday. I replied that that sounded great, and put away my phone, feeling as worn out as I did following a five-mile run or an all-nighter before a presentation. And I still had to decide what to wear. Why was dating in your thirties like an exhausting part-time job? It was tempting to give it all up and just tell Corporate Boy that I couldn't make it after all, but if he was half as funny and charming in person as he was on the screen, it would all be worth it.

A week later, I arrived at the bar, which was called the Bar du Marché, on Berwick Street in Soho – where one of the last surviving Soho street markets was still held, though it was more food stalls with takeaway poke and falafel, rather than rolls of fabric and fruit and veg. There were tiny rickety tables outside where people were drinking wine and eating mussels: including one man, sitting alone, with a copy of the *Evening Standard* as we'd arranged.

On seeing him I couldn't help but feel a tiny pang of disappointment. This was him – the nondescript dark-haired guy with the glasses? But when he looked up, he gave me such a charming smile that I knew that whatever happened, it would be a fun evening.

'Would you like a drink?' he said, as I sat down. 'I just ordered a glass of rosé – it seemed like that kind of evening.'

'I'll have the same,' I said, holding up a hand for the waitress.

'My kind of woman. God, sorry. That was cheesy. I meant, my kind of person.' He gestured helplessly. 'I'm a bit nervous. I've never met a reader for a drink before.'

'Really?' I said. 'Well, I've never met a columnist either. I'm a bit nervous too.' I took a deep breath. 'My name is

Celeste by the way.' Such was my paranoia, I hadn't even wanted to reveal that yet, and nor had he told me his name.

'That's pretty. I'm Eddie.'

We smiled at each other, and all the awkwardness vanished, almost as if by magic. Over rosé and *steak frites*, I learned that Eddie did indeed work for one of the Big Four consulting groups and that we had a few acquaintances in common, but that he had decided on a career change and was doing an evening diploma in freelance journalism. This struck me as being quite a modest move, given that he already had a column in a big newspaper, but he said he needed all the help he could get.

'It's a bit mad to go into journalism right now, with all the papers folding. It's like getting a job as a blacksmith or something. But it's what I really love doing, so.' He shrugged apologetically. He was from Sunderland in the north-east, though he told me his accent was much fainter now than it had been when he'd moved to London.

'So is mine,' I said, commiserating. And then, somehow, I found myself telling him my entire life story, for what it was worth – except that somehow, Eddie's skilful questions and reactions made me feel much more interesting than I ever had before on a date. I could see why he would make a great journalist. I also liked that, unlike some men, who were sometimes unsettled by my success at work, Eddie seemed genuinely happy for me. Nor did he consider me a corporate drone or sell-out, as I'd thought.

'No, I think it's great,' he said. 'It's horses for courses, isn't it? That's not very original but you know what I mean. I'm not calling you a horse either.' He smiled and added, 'Quite the reverse. I've just realized who you remind me of . . . Have you seen the film *Labyrinth*?'

'The Jim Henson one? Yes, of course I have. Don't tell me. The Junk Lady?'

'No – Sarah.'

I was thrilled but very self-conscious; I never knew how to react to compliments.

'I should be rocking my waistcoat and peasant blouse!' Too late, I remembered Hannah's tip to 'compliment the compliment'. I added, 'That's a lovely thing to say – thank you.'

'I had a serious crush on her. God, that's embarrassing.'

'Not at all. I know those formative crushes. I had a bit of a thing for Doogie Howser M.D., if you can remember that far back.'

He laughed, and I suddenly realized that although he was no Doogie Howser, I was suddenly finding him madly attractive. In fact, it was just as well I hadn't shaved my legs or I would have been seriously tempted to go home with him that very night in contravention of all my self-imposed rules.

'I should probably get home,' I said reluctantly.

'Of course,' he said immediately, and asked for the bill, which he insisted on paying. I was flattered by that, but even more impressed when he asked the waitress if the service charge went to her.

'Oh yes – thank you for asking, though.'

'That was nice of you to ask. I would have assumed that it would in an independent place like this,' I remarked.

'You can never assume,' he said. 'It's a real scandal. I

want to write a piece on it actually – I'm pitching it to a few places.' He smiled. 'Listen to me – I sound like a real journalist.'

'You are a real journalist,' I told him.

He smiled back at me, and suddenly I could see it all coming at me like a train: our kiss outside the tube, our next date, his first time staying over; our first weekend away together. I knew that it was going to be a thing. And not just a fling or a four-month relationship; it was going to be the real thing, real lasting love. And I was right about that or partially – because, as Eddie said, you could never assume.

13

I don't think I need to follow Hannah's list in the exact order she wrote it, but I decide it makes sense to start with the first one: hot yoga, which is one of the ones I'm dreading most. It's not that I don't enjoy yoga – I used to go quite often – but the 'hot' aspect seems dubious to me; I don't feel like stripping down and getting red-faced and sweaty in front of a mirror, which is what I believe is involved. But it's on the list, so as soon as I'm home I google 'hot yoga near me' and am rewarded with about half a dozen different studios near my office. This is the great thing about London: no matter how bizarre your interests, there's always somewhere that will cater to them for a price.

It's January now, of course. I used to love this time of year, when the discarded Christmas trees litter the pavement, and it's considered OK to stay home and do jigsaw puzzles. Or I used to, before it contained Hannah's anniversary: 19 January. After pondering for a while, I decide to book the yoga for the date itself, as a sort of remembrance. I send Vik a screenshot of my booking, and he sends me back a text that just says 'x'.

When the day comes, I finish work early and head to the yoga class, which is a short bus ride away in Whitechapel, a place I don't really know at all. I'm reminded of how, in London, we're siloed into our little areas, with barely any reason to leave them. It's years since I was in a yoga studio, but nothing has changed much; there's still the same air of smug serenity, the same expensive soy candles and recycled-bamboo workout gear. The air smells of incense and money. Everyone looks floaty and bendy, and happy and bronzed, as if they spent New Year's in Bali or Ibiza. Someone called Sage, with glowing skin and a nose piercing, books me in. She makes sure I have a bottle of water and a towel, as well as a yoga mat, and points me towards the changing rooms, where my adventure begins.

I walk into the changing room to be confronted by a massively pregnant woman, who beams as me as she strips down to a tiny tank top and hot pants. Two simultaneous thoughts occur: one, it can't be that hard if a massively pregnant woman is doing it; and, two, how is it that she looks better in her current condition than I do at my thinnest? Everyone seems to be wearing tiny tank or bra tops and tiny shorts. I'm in a vest top and cropped yoga leggings, which I hope won't get me chucked out of class. But I tell myself to stay calm. It's yoga in a hot room; how hard can that be?

Clutching my extra-large bottle of water, I slip into the studio, to be greeted by a wall of heat. I knew it would be hot, but it really is like stepping into a sauna – though at least it's a dry heat, and the smell is of incense, not sweaty bodies. Terrifyingly the entire far wall is made of mirrors, meaning we will be trapped in front of our reflections for the duration of the class. Some of the students seem totally fine with it, stretching ostentatiously while checking out their gorgeous doubles on the wall opposite. I find myself a spot at the very back, where hopefully I can flail around undetected. I watch the other students filing in and I decide that this is hot yoga in more senses than one. Though I don't know if it's the yoga that's made them hot, or if only those with perfect bodies are willing to spend ninety minutes throwing half-naked shapes in front of a mirror.

The place is very full now and there's a charged atmosphere, like a gig before the main act comes on. When the teacher enters I can almost feel the waves of adulation rippling towards him.

'Namaste, everyone. I'm Ravi. Welcome to class.'

I was expecting a muscle-bound hunk who would be barking orders at us all, but Ravi's an unassuming-looking guy, not tall or especially muscly, wearing a pink T-shirt that says HEART CENTRE. His voice is quiet, but he doesn't have to make any effort to make himself heard; you could hear a pin drop.

'Is anyone new here today?' A handful of us raise our hands. He says, 'Welcome, thank you for coming. You've already done the hardest part – you're here. Copy the moves as best you can, but don't worry about doing the exact same thing as your neighbour. It is hot in here, but that's OK. It's just a hot room; nothing more, nothing less. If you find it too much, you can take child's pose, but please stay in the room. And breathe. Now let's begin.'

We stand together and cup our hands around our mouths expelling air in a 'ha' sound. That's easy enough, and I start to relax a bit. Then we point our arms together overhead and stretch to the side in a bow shape. This is getting harder and I am already really having to push myself. Sweat is pouring down my face and I want to wipe it off but I'm too terrified to break ranks to get my towel; I wish I had worn sweatbands on my wrist, like others have.

'Remember,' Ravi says, 'just focus on your own mat. Don't look at your neighbour to see how they're doing. Don't compare yourself to others . . . Whatever happens is going to happen here on your mat. Everything else is entertainment. Now, eagle pose. Bring your right elbow above your left elbow . . .'

He drops effortlessly into a hideous twisted shape, standing on one leg with both his arms and legs wrapped together. I try to follow suit and instantly topple over. Ravi was right about entertainment; I'm providing it for free. I don't know if my beet-red face in the mirror is down to the heat or the humiliation, but both are proving absolutely crushing. The torture twist ends, and I take a sneaky sip of water, but then straightaway we're on to an even more sadistic challenge – standing on one leg again, but with the other one stretched out in the air in front of us, holding on to our big toe. In theory.

How is anyone doing this? But they are. Looking around the room I can see that most people are managing it, some of them quite effortlessly. I can't do it at all and collapse into a child's pose. The heat is making me crazy. This is torture. Surely it's not meant to be this hot. Surely something has gone wrong, and it's been set to 'kill' mode rather than just 'maim'. I'm going to have to leave. I can't stand it.

They're on to a new thing now, some kind of sideways triangle, but I can't even pretend to attempt it. I'm roadkill on my mat, soaked in sweat; I can taste it on my lips and feel it dripping in my eyes. I hear Ravi's voice through the thudding of my pulse. 'Right about now your mind is probably telling you some very extreme things. Like "I can't do it" or "I have to get out of here" or "This is tor-ture". But what you have to remember is: those are just thoughts. You can observe these thoughts, but you don't have to engage with them. If you can breathe – then it's all good. It's just a hot room.'

I'm not sure what he's on about. Surely my thoughts and me are the same thing – how can I just observe them? Who's doing the observing if it's not me? But then I think I start to get it. It reminds me of mind tricks that Hannah and I played as we walked the Camino. I remember her saying, 'It's not pain; it's just a sensation,' which I thought at the time was distinctly dodgy. But it helps now. I join in tentatively with the next thing, which is standing on one leg again with hands in prayer pose. It's still awful. But it's doable. It's just a hot room.

My Zen feeling flags a bit in the next section, though, as we fall into another trough: horrible forward and back bends. I'm soaked through with sweat now; even my water has heated up. I feel humbled and humiliated. This isn't easy; why did I ever think it would be? But then, just as I think I genuinely can't stand it any more and I'll have to leave – we're released. We get to lie flat on our backs. I've done this before, obviously, but I've never known what a completely blissful sensation it can be. I'm floating above my body. All my worries, my sadness over Hannah, are released and I can just be. I feel my eyelids fluttering, and decide to close them just for a second.

I don't know how long elapses before I'm gently woken up by someone shaking my shoulder. It's Sage from reception.

'Oh my God,' I say, sitting up. 'Did I actually fall asleep?'

'It happens,' she says. 'More often than you'd think.'

I crawl out of the studio and into the changing rooms where I barely have the energy to stand up in the shower; I really want to sit down. But the feeling of lukewarm water coursing over my body, and the lavender shower gel, is so exquisite, I feel as if I've died and gone to heaven. I am so exhausted it takes me what seems like hours to get dressed and ready to leave, but eventually I manage it. I float out through the changing rooms and give Sage an equally blissful wave.

'How was your class?' she asks.

I try to think how to describe it. 'It was great when it stopped?'

She laughs. 'I feel you. Well, if you want to try it again, we have an introductory offer – twenty days for twenty pounds.' She looks at her screen. 'Where do you live by the way? We're opening a new studio in Finsbury Park . . .'

'Are you serious?' I yield to the impulse, very uncharacteristically, and sign up, figuring that if I manage to go twice more it will be a good deal.

Stepping out into the night, the cold air hits me with another delicious shock, and I realize how long it's been since I did anything that involved so many new physical sensations. I stand outside for a minute, breathing in and trying to reorient myself for my journey home.

And then I hear a voice. 'Celeste?'

It's Eddie.

I stand and stare at him. To say that I'm dumbfounded is like saying the yoga room was hot. I'm utterly stunned to see him – here on this busy street full of warehouses and pound shops, miles from where he lives or works.

'What are you doing here?' he asks.

'I just went to yoga. What are you doing here?'

'I live here. Right above the yoga studio.' I look up to where he's pointing; there are obviously flats there, though the building looks really run-down; a very different set-up to the pretty Victorian conversion in Kensal Rise where he used to live. I remember now, though, that he had friends in this area and used to come here quite often; he loved the restaurant Tayyabs and used to go there a lot. But this exact building?

'Well, that's a coincidence.' I step aside, as some yogis come out of the studio behind me. Eddie looks at them and then back at me, obviously surprised too to see me do something so out of character.

'So – I – How are you?' he says.

'Yeah, good, thanks,' I say, unable to think of a single follow-up. I consider mentioning that I saw his comment on my Instagram, but things are awkward enough already.

Eddie nods, then says in a rush, 'You probably want to get home right now but . . . would you be free to meet some day? It would be good to talk . . .'

My immediate impulse is to say something vague or even put him off. But then something stops me. He was a big part of my life once. And the fact that he's here – that he lives above the very building where I randomly chose to do yoga – is such an extraordinary coincidence that I think most people would be inclined to call it a sign. And I'm more open to those than I once was.

'Sure,' I say. 'Send me a text.'

14

I wake up the next day feeling as if I've been beaten up. Every extremity aches, especially the fronts of my thighs; I'm so stiff that I genuinely have trouble going down the steps of my building, and I also have a mild but persistent headache which I attribute to dehydration. But at the same time I feel a tiny sense of pride, that at least I've tried something new.

Something new, something old. I can't stop thinking about my encounter with Eddie, and marvelling at the coincidence that brought him back into my orbit. We've had almost no contact in nearly two years – except for his brief email when Hannah died. It's not as if we never had closure, though; we had plenty. Too much, in fact. Even after our official break-up, we still had to work together for weeks afterwards on the dreary task of cancelling venues and suppliers, not to mention telling guests: it was like the Fyre Festival of the wedding season. Time has done its work, and I'm not resentful any more, but I'm still glad that there's a yoga studio near me and that I don't have to visit his building every week to maintain my new hobby.

Soon it's time to limp off to the senior team meeting, where we start by discussing time sheets, a tedious bit of admin that's only worth doing because it makes the lives of those in charge of our client billing easier. My colleagues Marcus and Hugo are both of the view that we shouldn't have to worry about any of it and the juniors should be able to do it all by combing through our emails and work diaries. This strikes me as unfair, so I decide to say something.

'The thing is, if you keep on top of it, it only takes an hour or two a week. Whereas if we don't do it, it takes the juniors several days.'

'But their time is worth less than mine,' says Hugo.

Hugo, to my shame, is someone I kissed on an office night out about eight years ago. I think we've both been waiting for each other to leave ever since, but neither of us is showing any sign of it, though at least he's married now.

'Yeah, it's easier for them to do it,' says Marcus. Marcus is not my friend either; he joined last November and I congratulated him on his luxuriant moustache, which I thought was for Movember. It wasn't for Movember.

'Let's decide later,' Isobel says, which I know means that she agrees with the men.

'Now, we need to get better at nominating people from our team for our internal awards. Who could we put up for a High Five?'

This is our entry-level internal recognition award; the next level up is a Nailed It, and, for true glory, a Gamechanger. I ask, 'How about Saraswati? She's been making incredible strides.'

'Good point,' says Isobel. 'She could certainly get a High Five. Or a Nailed It even. Lastly . . . we've had a request for a pitch from Footlove. Who'd like to pick up our response to that?'

This innocent-seeming request causes an almost visible shudder to go around the room. Footlove is a family-run footwear empire, which is notorious for in-fighting and for requesting lengthy proposals with endless changes, and then never commissioning work. Everyone starts looking thoughtfully at their screens or at the ceiling, everywhere but at Isobel.

'I'd love to pick it up, but I'm slammed with all that Invision stuff,' says Marcus, naming a random client that is taking up no extra time at all as far as I'm aware.

'I'd love to take part too, but I'm slammed as well . . .' Hugo says. 'Gemma, you were in on the pitch last time, weren't you?'

Gemma looks slightly panicked; I happen to know that her husband is on sick leave due to back problems, and she's coming apart at the seams. I don't want her dropped in it, so I decide it's easier if I just take it on.

'I can do it, Isobel,' I say. It won't be too onerous; I'll just recycle as much as I can from the last pitch we did. And, who knows, they might even say yes.

'Thanks, Celeste,' says Isobel, looking relieved. 'That's just what we need for them. You're such a safe pair of hands.'

'No problem,' I say, adding it to my list. Though I find myself thinking about the phrase she used. Is that what I want to have on my tombstone – HERE LIES CELESTE, WHO WAS A SAFE PAIR OF HANDS? But I suppose it could be worse.

Back at my desk, I see that there's another request in the offing, this time in the form of an email from my senior colleague Ricardo. *Hi Celeste. Can you help out with the Emergen pitch next Thursday? Be great to have your input, and if we get the work, you could lead on it?* I groan inwardly, looking at my diary which is stacked like a house of cards that day. I wouldn't mind, except that Ricardo has a nasty habit of asking you to 'help out' with a pitch but then getting you to do all the work and disappearing on the day. I don't have a specific excuse, though, so it seems easier just to say yes.

I'm about to do so when Dasha, my junior colleague and Swati's bestie, comes over to my desk and asks if she can have a word.

'Sure, have a seat.' I gesture towards the empty chair beside me. 'Did you have a nice ski trip?' I ask; her face is radiantly bronzed under her blonde mane.

'It was OK.' She sighs. 'Except the resort was rubbish and we had to get buses everywhere instead of ski in, ski out . . . I told my dad we should have stuck with Gstaad, but he didn't listen to me.'

'Oh dear,' I say, trying not to smile. Dasha's family is fabulously wealthy; she once expressed surprised that I always flew economy class, and I've also heard her refer to her salary as 'fun money'. 'You said you wanted to talk – is something up?'

'Yes,' she says, and lowers her voice. 'It's Swati.'

'What about her?' I ask, wondering if she's going to voice the same concerns as Gemma, about Swati's burnout.

'Ever since I came back from holidays – ever since Christmas actually – she's been unavailable for coffee, she won't meet me for lunch like we used to . . .' Her pretty face takes on a tragic expression. 'I've tried asking her all week, but she says she wants to focus on work.'

I'm not sure how to respond to this. 'Is your concern that she's working too hard?'

'No! She's regularly having lunch with Adam and Maria and I know she went to Femi's birthday last weekend . . . it's just me. She's ghosted me.'

'Oh dear.' I feel bad for Dasha if that's the case, but what am I meant to do about it? I'm her line manager. I can set her performance targets and help her achieve measurable outcomes. I can't referee her friendships. 'I'm sorry – that sounds tricky. But I don't think there's anything I can do.'

'Could you have a word with her? Or with Gemma?'

I suddenly realize that Dasha needs a major reality check. I've been saying yes all morning. I can and must say no to this. 'I'm afraid not, Dasha. Look, it must be disappointing that she doesn't want to be friends any more . . . but you have to respect it, and just get on with your work. You've got to be professional.'

Dasha looks at me in a deeply disappointed way. 'I'm trying, but it's hard when I'm under so much stress.' Her face changes. 'You don't know what it's like to lose a friend.'

I take a deep breath, though I'm tempted to tell her to pull herself together. 'It must be very hard,' I repeat. 'But just focus on your work, and let all the other stuff go. OK?' I try to think of something else constructive I could give her to keep her busy. 'You said you were interested in pitching, didn't you? Would you like to help me with the Proxima pitch next week?'

'Yes, sure,' she says, looking disappointed, and heads off back to her desk. I feel pretty bad, but, really, what else could I have done? This is not my area of expertise. And it's not as if I ever got help with my social life when I was a junior. When I think of my own manager when I started – an ex-army officer called Gus with a bone-cracking handshake and a propensity to make you lift weights during meetings – I think she's got it pretty easy.

My chat with Dasha has taken so long that a coffee run is out of the question, so I make my painful way over to the kitchen area instead. I'm even stiffer now, after sitting for so long; I'm moving like the Tin Man. Is it really such a good idea for me to go back to yoga? I might never move again.

'Are you all right, Celeste?' says Isobel, who's making herself a green tea. 'You look like you've busted something.'

'Oh, no, I'm fine. I did hot yoga last night,' I explain.

'Ooh!' says Isobel. 'Hot yoga! I used to go to that, back when it was a thing. It was hardcore, but it's so worth it if you stick with it. Unless you're like most people who go once and never go again.' She laughs. 'No shame.'

'Well, actually I've signed up to more classes,' I say.

'Brilliant,' she says, looking distinctly impressed. 'Good for you! It takes a lot of mental strength, doesn't it?'

'Oh, well, you know. Like they say, it's just a hot room.'

'Good for you,' she says, again. And I swear to God, she's showing more reaction than she did when I smashed my sales targets two years in a row or spotted a near-fatal mistake in our biggest client's annual report. Which prompts me to ask her, 'Isobel, Ricardo's asked me for some input on the Emergen pitch next week, but I'm quite committed that day. You don't mind if I pass, do you?'

'Of course not,' she says. 'Just tell him no.'

I return to my desk and email Ricardo telling him that,

though I'm very sorry, I have a diary clash on that day. And nothing happens. It turns out that saying no was as easy as that. Maybe I do need a list of resolutions for work. I take out my jotter and write a list:

1. Say no more often.
2. Delegate – but really.

Number three? I can't think what number three could be, aside from making director, which isn't really an item I can just decide to tick off. I decide that two is plenty; I've already got my hands full with Hannah's list. Speaking of which, I need to get a date in the diary for my indoor climbing session. If Isobel was impressed by hot yoga, what on earth will she say when she hears I've taken up climbing?

15

February

The following evening, I turn up to the new yoga studio which is literally round the corner from my house, and put myself through ninety minutes of torture again. It's a little easier this time, purely because it's less unknown. And it's easier the third time, and the fourth. By the time the fifth session comes round, I am genuinely looking forward to it; what is happening to me? I send Vik a selfie of myself outside the studio and receive a thumbs-up and an unsolicited swan picture as well.

With this confidence boost I decide to book in my February task before I chicken out of it completely. I'm taking a few minutes to do this when I remember Patrick mentioning the climbing centre near us. I could just google 'climbing centre near me' for the name and website, but it might be nice to make contact and get his advice. I throw caution to the wind and send him a text: Hi Patrick. Hope you got back OK from Suffolk, thanks again for the lift to the station. I'm wondering what the rock-climbing place near us was that you mentioned?

After sending my text, my finger goes automatically to the Instagram app, where I flick through and notice a new post from Sibéal. It seems to be just a picture of her sofa with a pink cushion, but the caption is characteristically over the top: I'm so grateful to you for coming into our lives, dear Pan. What a beautiful soul you are – the epitome of a free spirit. You bring us your life force and playful energy. Please stay with us forever xoxoxoxo

Who the hell is Pan? I wonder if she's addressing the unborn baby, but that doesn't seem likely. Or is he, she or they some new spiritual guide or something? Then I see that it's a series of photos and flip through, before I twig that she's talking about their new cat. It makes me laugh out loud, and then I find myself wishing, for the millionth time, that I could laugh about it with Hannah. The pain takes me by surprise, all over again, and I welcome the distraction of an incoming text.

Castle Climbing Centre. They have a taster on Monday evenings at 7.15 p.m. if that suits you – I could come along with you?

It takes me a minute to realize this is Patrick replying about rock climbing. Yikes; that's next week. Before I let myself overthink it, I reply, That would be great.

The climbing centre, which is aptly named, looks like a huge haunted house or Gothic folly built on the edges of Clissold Park. I have been past it quite a few times but never really noticed it; I knew it was a climbing centre but I never felt the need to know more. Climbing seems a very niche interest and I can't imagine that there will be many people there on a chilly Monday evening in February.

I am so wrong. When I go in through the big swing doors, it's like I've entered a parallel universe. The place is immense inside, with walls at least thirty metres tall, dotted all over with coloured dots that look like blobs of giant chewing gum. And it's heaving; there must be at least a hundred people here, or two hundred, scaling the walls attached to ropes, or milling about at the base. I make my way over to the plywood booths where a serene-looking girl with dyed peroxide hair checks me in and hands me about four pages of safety questions and disclaimers to sign. She reminds me a bit of Sage at the yoga place. There's a definite yoga vibe, except for the fact that there are so many men here. I don't think I've ever seen so many men at an extra-curricular event. I see lots of beards and quirky T-shirts and I'm guessing that most of them do something left field and vaguely cerebral, like marine biology or environmental engineering. I've also noticed that everyone seems to be wearing a special kind of climbing shoe with ultra-flat soles. Presumably my trainers will be OK; they'll have to be. I sit down to deal with the form, and sign no to all the conditions it asks about, as well as promising to release them from any liabilities for any injuries. Which isn't worrying at all.

'Hey,' says a voice behind me. I've been so busy reading through all the fine print, I didn't see Patrick approach.

He's wearing shorts over leggings and he's carrying a cycling helmet. In fact, he fits right in – no beard, true, but he has the same rugged look as most of the men here. It's not my thing, but if I meet any outdoorsy single women, I know exactly where to send them.

'Angelika didn't want to come?' I ask, standing up.

'Nope, she's scared of heights. Have you got your climbing shoes?'

'No . . . She didn't say anything about climbing shoes.' I look back helplessly at my Sage-a-like, who is checking someone else in now.

'No panic. You can tell them you're on a course and

they'll let you borrow a pair for the class. You have to leave your shoes with them as ransom.'

'What about you?' I ask, as we go outside.

He points down. 'I've got my own.'

Of course he does. The climbing shop, which doubles as a cafe, does provide me with a pair of shoes, the guy advising that they need to be tight. 'But not medieval-torture tight,' he adds, which I think is meant to be reassuring. Once I'm properly shod, Patrick and I go back to reception, where our instructor Fabrizio is waiting for us. I'm reassured to see that he's a softly spoken guy, not much taller than me and not noticeably muscly, with a long ponytail. 'Welcome, guys. Are you both new to climbing?' he asks us.

'I've done a little bit,' says Patrick.

'I've never done it,' I say, and without meaning to I blurt out my main worry. 'I have no upper-body strength. I mean, I go to the gym, but my main exercise is walking, and I think my legs are OK but my arms are quite weak . . .'

'That's OK,' says Fabrizio. 'Climbing is all in the legs. It's more important to be secure in your foundation than it is to try to get too ambitious with your arms – that's called overreaching.' As he finishes speaking, we're joined by a couple: Sam and Valentina. Sam, who has hugely muscly arms, has done a lot of callisthenics before, what-ever that is, and Valentina, who is tiny and doll-like, is completely new to climbing.

'I am a bit worried because I don't have any upper-body strength,' Valentina says. Fabrizio explains about legs all over again, and Patrick catches my eye with a smile.

'And I have freakishly small hands!' Sam says. We all

look at his hands, which look average to me, though I wonder if maybe they just seem small to him because his arms are so beefy.

'Also, is it harder to climb if you're small, like me?' asks Valentina.

Fabrizio shakes his head. 'Climbing is like life,' he says encouragingly. 'Everyone is different and it's all about working to your advantages. So you're short, that just means you need to look for the holds that suit your reach, and maybe you can get into little spaces that others can't. Your most important body part is . . . ?' We all look blankly at him before he taps his temple. 'Your head,' he says.

Fabrizio then leads us in a series of easy but humiliating warm-ups, and I try not to look at Patrick as we wobble our jaws, rotate our wrists and do huge hip circles. It's all very cringey and I can only imagine what I'm going to look like when it's time to actually climb the walls. I don't relish falling flat on my face in front of this crowd of thrill-seekers. Luckily, of course, we're only bouldering, which I understand involves staying low.

With our warm-up complete, Fabrizio takes us round a corner to a small wall with various blobs on it, some only inches from the ground. He shows us how the different colours make a route, numbered for difficulty, and suggest we start with the yellow route – which is actually a children's course. Sam goes first, and crosses in quite a nifty way in spite of his tiny hands, then Valentina who goes slowly but surely. Next, Patrick scuttles across like a lizard, barely seeming to glance at the holds as he goes.

'Nice, nice,' says Fabrizio. 'You've done this before, right? See how he keeps his arms outstretched – you always want to be reaching in the arms, and flexible in the hips.'

I'm regretting going last, because now they've finished their climb and are free to watch me. I go to the start and put out my hand for the first blob, and straightaway realize how much harder it is than it looks. The blob is barely there; there's nothing to hold on to, and the foothold is similarly tiny. Having got my right foot on the hold, I have no idea where to move the left one to, and try to put them both on the same hold as Valentina did, before getting tangled up and falling off. It was only a few inches, luckily, but obviously if this were a real mountain, I'd be dead.

'That's fine for your first try,' Fabrizio says encouragingly. 'Maybe as you're a little taller, try the pink route. And try reaching a bit further with your arms, instead of being like this.' He mimes T-rex arms, hugged close to his chest, which I feel is less than tactful. My second try is a bit better, though the others are scuttling round at twice the speed. They've done so well, in fact, that it's decided we are ready for the bigger bouldering walls upstairs. This means heading up four flights of stairs – the place is so huge, there's plenty of climbing here without even touching a wall.

'All good?' Patrick asks as we walk up.

'Well, sort of.'

'You just need to relax a bit, maybe.'

I nod, thinking that this is the least helpful advice ever.

The bouldering area, as the name implies, features man-made surfaces that mimic big rocks, complete with overhangs and crevices, all dotted with the same multicoloured rests as downstairs. But the climbers here seem so much more advanced; I see people grappling effortlessly, arm over arm like monkeys, and even hanging upside down like Spider-man. It's also intimidatingly busy, with an audience who watch the climbers as they wait to have their own turn. Even though the walls are shorter up here, I'm sensing this isn't the easy option.

Fabrizio confirms this, crouching down in front of us as we wait. 'So this is bouldering, and this is the most dangerous area in the whole climbing centre,' he says in his mellow hippyish way. 'You're not using harnesses, so if you fall, you can potentially hurt yourself quite badly. Like, if you fall on your knee, or on your ankle or let's say on your head. So if you feel yourself getting tired, definitely take a rest, use your head and study the route, instead of just racing up and grabbing whatever comes to you.'

Words to live by. I am getting worried, though, especially when Sam asks, 'Has anyone ever died up here?'

'No, no . . . at least I don't think so,' says Fabrizio. 'OK, who is first?'

Patrick and Sam go first, clambering to the top via the most advanced grips. Then Valentina, in a left-field move, scuttles up a wall behind us and disappears briefly, before reappearing behind the parapet and waving triumphantly. Beside me Sam and Patrick are deep in conversation with the instructor.

'It's really most of all a challenge for your mind,' Fabrizio is saying. 'It's about looking at your route and assessing it, trying different combinations of holds . . . That route over there with the yellow holds, do you know how many times I tried it before I cracked it?'

'A thousand times?' Sam suggests, which I think is a bit mean.

'Twenty times?' Patrick says.

'One hundred and seventy-five,' says Fabrizio, his eyes gleaming. 'It's like a, what do you call it, one of those box puzzles, with the coloured squares.'

A Rubik's cube. I can do a Rubik's cube. I turn back to the wall that Valentina just scaled and take my time assessing the route. There's a seemingly clear-looking path with blue holds. They're further apart than her holds, but that's good because I am taller. I start climbing and immediately notice that this is easier; the grips are bigger and I get one for each foot instead of having to cram them together awkwardly. And maybe it's my imagination, but I think I'm stronger already from the yoga. Up, up, up I go until I can see the top, reachable with just one more push. Taking a deep breath, I go for it and haul myself over the top, landing ungracefully but triumphantly on the platform above. There's the sound of cheers from below; I peer over to see the other four all clapping and giving me a thumbs-up.

'You did it!' calls Fabrizio. 'Great – let's try some more.'

We go off to another area where more giant grey man-made boulders are waiting, and take turns crawling around them. We're all getting quite tired now and Fabrizio produces some chalk for us to wipe on our sore and sweaty hands. But I'm feeling exhilarated. I'm not hopeless at this new physical challenge. I've scaled the wall; I've conquered a mountain – or at least a boulder.

'That's great,' says Fabrizio, after we've all circumnavigated the last boulder. 'So I know this taster is boulders only but we have some time if you guys wanted to practise the wall as well – that way we could use the harnesses as well and give you a taste of the belays. Are you interested?'

I'm assuming that the others are going to be equally reluctant since we've only signed up for bouldering. But, no, all of them are nodding eagerly. I try to catch Patrick's eye and raise my eyebrows to signal panic, but he just smiles back at me enthusiastically, and we all start marching downstairs. We're going to be roped together, which means that if I don't do it, he won't be able to do it either. Telling myself it will be OK, I follow the others to the bottom of the wall, where Fabrizio helps us into humiliating crotch-bothering harnesses.

'Let's see . . . actually, let's swap partners. You guys can climb together, and you ladies too. Valentina, do you want to go first?'

She nods, and Fabrizio shows me how to stand, legs braced, at the bottom, while grappled to Valentina, and let out a little bit of rope at a time as she shins up.

'If you don't give her enough rope, she could fall down on top of you, so just watch out for that,' he says. 'And too much rope, of course, she could fall also. So just enough. Just stand there, left foot in front and right foot back – be her rock.'

I stand as instructed while Valentina clambers slowly and surely to the very top; by the time she reaches it she's just a dot of sportswear at the summit. Then she bounces down gracefully, legs braced, as I deal out rope. I'm feeling increasingly panicked at the idea of going that high, and I decide that I'll just go halfway.

As Valentina reaches the bottom, though, I realize there's another problem in that I'm twice her size. I could take her weight, but can she really take mine?

I point this out to Fabrizio, hoping he will dismiss my

fears and say we're both the same weight, but instead he says, 'Oh yes. We'll use this.' He lifts up a floor tile and reveals a bracket stapled to the ground. So Valentina has to be stapled to the floor to take my weight. The humiliation almost takes my mind off the panic.

'Where should I look?' I ask, as my last seconds on land tick by.

'Just look at your hands, your feet and the next hold. That's all – nothing else matters.' Fabrizio steps back and gives me a thumbs-up. 'And remember – it's just a tall wall.'

His words remind me of Ravi's at yoga. It's just a hot room. Which is all well and good, except that a tall wall seems a lot more ominous than a hot room.

I start climbing, taking deep breaths to try to conquer my nerves. One hand stretches up, then another and then my foot, as the floor shrinks below me and I climb into unknown territories of holds and heights. The wall seems impossibly flat after the friendly boulders, but the holds are a little more easily placed, and before I know it I've made my way, albeit shakily, halfway up the wall.

I've done it. I have made it to the height I said I would. It's a respectable achievement And if I can inch my way back down, without actually looking down, I'll never have to do it again. I glance down and see that Fabrizio is giving me a thumbs-up and gesturing downwards, I think to say that I've done plenty and I should come back down now.

But the idea fills me with a weird kind of regret. Having come this far, don't I want to be able to say that I've climbed to the top – and back down? But that seems reckless, so I start to climb down, a hold or two at a time.

Then I stop again. Isn't this my whole problem in life – that I always play it safe, always quit while I'm ahead? I never make it to the top of the wall. If I've climbed this high, surely I can make it a bit further? Without giving myself time to think or talk myself out of it, I crawl up one more hold, then another. Then another, and a few more, and then there are only three more between me and the top. The top! I've made it. I grab the last hold, panting, and savour my triumph. *I did it, Hannah*, I tell her silently and joyfully.

And then I look down.

It's a dizzingly horribly distorted and tiny view; the room below looks like a doll's house, and I can only see the tops of people's heads, tiny as they mill around below. A black mist descends in front of my eyes, and I blink frantically until it clears. Phew. I brace myself to come down and manage a few bounces outward before my hands and legs slip from the wall, and I'm windmilling frantically like a cartoon character. Below, I register that Fabrizio has grabbed the rope and is helping Valentina to reel me down like an overgrown fish on a hook. Then I grab the wall again, and half bounce, half kick myself towards the ground, where I collapse and embrace the carpet tiles like a long-lost lover.

'You really didn't hear him say that?' Patrick asks for the fourth time, as we sit over drinks in the Brownswood, opposite the Castle. I've never been so happy to be in a pub. Outside, the wind is howling while inside it's cosy and candlelit – it's all so delightful, especially when I thought I would never make it to a pub again in the middle of that ordeal. Which, it turns out, wasn't even necessary.

'For the tenth time – no. I had no idea we weren't supposed to go all the way up on the first go. You did!'

'Only because I had done it before. And I thought you wanted to push yourself.'

I take another grateful swallow of my gin and tonic before setting him straight. 'No, I didn't! I didn't want to do the wall at all. I sent you a signal to say as much, which you ignored.'

'What signal?'

'You know. This.' I demonstrate the wide-eyed look of panic that I gave him earlier.

'That? I thought you were sneezing. Was that a signal?'

'Obviously!'

'Not obvious at all.' He shakes his head. 'You're a riddle wrapped in a mystery wrapped in a Ted Baker coat.'

I laugh despite myself. 'Wait. How did you know my coat was from Ted Baker?'

'Oh, I noticed the label when you went to the bar. I'm sorry, is that creepy?'

Looking behind me, I see that the label would have been on display where my coat is hanging on the back of the chair, so I tell him he's off the hook. It occurs to me that it's strange to be sitting here with Patrick, for all the world as if we're friends, when I haven't seen him at all since New Year's. I suppose there's nothing like a near-death experience for breaking the ice.

'It's a nice coat,' Patrick says, taking a sip of his pint. 'Looks very good quality.'

I laugh again, and tell him that's such a mammy-ish

thing to say. But I'm glad he appreciates the coat because I love it. It's a classic black wool trench coat, belted at the waist, with a colourful red-and-yellow silk lining. 'It's not the usual style, is it?' Patrick asks. 'I mean, the way it goes in at the waist. Most women's coats are more sort of over-sized these days, aren't they?' He shakes his head. '*These days*. Listen to me. I do sound like my mum. Though she's actually pretty stylish, I have to say.'

'What does she do for a living?' I ask, curious.

'Well, she worked as cabin crew for Aer Lingus for a number of years before she met my dad. Then when they got married she stopped flying. She didn't exactly work as such. What she did was the garden. The garden in our house in Dalkey, and also we have a house in Wexford – they're both pretty special. She could have done it professionally for sure. She has a great eye. That's how I got into it all really.'

'Maybe the two of you could go into business together?' I suggest.

'There's a thought. Although . . . would we kill each other? I'll already be living with her, when I go back to Dublin, so maybe it's a bit much. And Clodagh will be around quite a bit too, so it's going to be a bit of a family reunion slash sitcom.'

'Oh?'

'Yeah, she's going through a marriage break-up un-fortunately.'

'Oh, I'm sorry,' I say, thinking of the bubbly red-headed girl I still remember from New Year's and a few times afterwards, though Hannah saw her less after she married young and moved to Scotland.

'Thanks.' He sips his pint. 'What about you? What's your family like?'

'My family? They're pretty regular.' I don't have anything as eventful to report. 'My parents are recently retired . . . My dad plays golf and reads a lot of sci-fi, and my mum has a book club. The usual. And then I've got a younger brother. He went to your school actually,' I add. 'He was maybe four years behind you – Hugh Healy?'

It's a long shot but I think Patrick is the kind of person who remembers names and, sure enough, he does. 'Healo! Yes, I remember him. Wasn't he in a band? Guitar player?'

'Yeah, he still is, though they mainly do friends' weddings these days. He works for a digital marketing agency. They live in a converted artisan cottage in Stoneybatter, and they do a lot of cycling around tiny festivals in the Aran Islands, and making their own kombucha – that kind of thing.'

'Good man, Healo,' he says. 'He was always a free spirit.'

This reminds me of Sibéal's effusive Instagram post about the new cat, and I chuckle at the thought. I can't resist showing him the post, thinking he will appreciate it, which he does, saying, 'I think that caption needs to be taken with three kilos of natural sea salt.' Which makes me laugh even more. I love Sibéal, but I'm glad she's more down-to-earth in real life than in her social media incarnations.

'So . . . have you decided on your next challenge?' Patrick asks when we've finished laughing.

'I haven't decided what order they should go in. But some options are: ceilidh dancing, get my astrology chart done and the ballet. I'm guessing all those would be your worst nightmare?'

'The astrology and ballet, yes. But ceilidh dancing maybe. Irish or Scottish?'

'Scottish, I think. I've looked them both up and it looks like Scottish ones are easier for first-timers, or if you haven't done it in a while.'

'Good thinking. It's been a few too many years since I tried the Siege of Ennis,' he says. 'I really don't think I'd cope.'

I laugh again. 'Me neither. Well, maybe I'll get a group together to go.' I add, 'Would Angelika like to come? How is she?'

'Um, she's good. Working very hard, though, as ever. And she has a lot going on. She's had a bad day at work actually.'

'Oh, sorry to hear it.'

'It's OK. Though I had a text from her earlier, saying she wanted company. So I might go and meet her now if that's OK.'

'Of course!' I say, feeling bad. 'Gosh, and I've been sitting here yapping away. Why didn't you say?'

'Well, I didn't want to abandon you either, after your troubles on the wall,' he says, standing up.

'I'm totally fine. I'm going to stay here and finish this,' I say, gesturing at my drink. 'You go. I'll see you around.' I watch him hurry off, thinking that it must be hard to be so responsible: torn between traumatized climbers and unhappy girlfriends.

I don't feel traumatized in the least, though: I feel invincible after conquering my wall. Two down, ten to go. *I'm doing it, Hannah*, I think. And I'm not scared of whatever's next. I'm ready for anything.

At that exact moment a text pings on my phone. It's from Eddie. It says, Celeste, was great to bump into you recently. I would love to talk to you. How about the Pain Quotidien in Marylebone High Street this Sunday at 11 a.m.? Would that suit? If not, I can do any other time you like. E.

This seems a random choice, far from where either of us live, but that's fine by me; there are no painful associations. Not that our break-up feels all that painful any more, I realize suddenly. It was tough at the time, so tough, but that was a long time ago. And I've been through worse things since then. I also appreciate that he's suggested a specific place and time, rather than putting me through an endless round of scheduling texts. I'll go along, and see what he has to say, and then I'll get on with my life – and my list.

16

The Circle Line is up to its usual tricks on Sunday, and I'm running slightly late, but I don't hurry as I usually would; if I'm five minutes late, so be it. He's already there when I arrive, and I make my way towards him, past the usual Marylebone mix of ladies-who-brunch and French and American families. He's got the crossword open in front of him, the one we used to do together. He's not making any progress, though, but staring out of the window, his foot jiggling anxiously under the table.

'Celeste!' he says, looking up when I arrive. 'I'm so glad you came.'

'Hi, Eddie,' I say, sitting down opposite him. I am surprised to find myself not feeling any particular emotion: just neutral.

The waiter arrives surprisingly promptly, and I order a tea. Eddie asks for a flat white coffee, which is what we both used to drink; he doesn't comment on the fact that I've changed my order.

'It's really good to see you. How are you?' he asks. 'You look great by the way.'

'Thanks. I'm OK.' I pause, realizing this is true; I'm certainly better than I was. 'How are you?'

'Good, thanks. I don't know if you knew, no reason why you should, but I'm working for a think tank now. We do consultancy work for various government groups and NGOs.'

'Oh, really? So no more writing?' This seems like a sensible decision actually. Too much time in a room on his own wasn't good for him.

'No. The job contains a lot of writing, but I'm not pitching to papers or anything. It was too precarious.' He looks at me, as if hopeful of a reaction, but I just nod and say, 'Sure.'

'And you've moved?' I ask.

'Yeah, I'm sharing with Paul – remember him? He's doing me a favour, mate's rates.'

'Oh yes. What about his wife?'

'They split up sadly. So we're just two sad bachelors living together now.'

I don't know what to say to that, so I murmur that I'm sorry to hear it. There's an awkward pause while the waiter sets down our drinks and we both thank him without looking at each other.

'And you? Is work good with you?' he asks.

'Yeah, it's fine. Same old, really.'

He looks at me compassionately, and I know that he's thinking of the one thing that is no longer the same and never will be.

'I'm so sorry about Hannah,' he says. 'You got my note, I hope.'

'I did, yes. Thank you.' I pause and take a sip of coffee before saying, 'I don't want to be rude, Eddie, but . . . was there a particular reason you wanted to meet? Aside from bumping into each other?'

'Um . . .' He looks briefly miserable, and I do feel sorry

for him. I'm guessing he wants to apologize again, and it doesn't seem easy.

'I know I apologized to you over what happened,' he says. 'Obviously. But . . . I just wanted you to know that I have changed. Like, completely. I've done a full three hundred and sixty.'

I nod, waiting to see what this means.

'What happened . . . what I did . . .' He pauses. 'It's taken me a long time to understand *why* I did it. You said at the time that it was like an addiction and I know now that you were right. I've had professional help basically. Counselling. I mean, I say counselling but more like therapy.'

'Good for you,' I say, meaning it.

'And . . .' He takes a deep breath. 'It's gone. The debt. All of it.'

'God. Well done,' I say. Fourteen thousand pounds repaid in less than two years; that is an achievement.

'I wanted to tell you that, and that I'm so sorry. I'm so sorry for everything I put you through. Having to cancel the wedding. Having to tell your family. Having to tell your friends. It's a horrible thing to do to anyone. And at the time I know I blamed you for it, because I was still in so much denial. And I did feel a bit inadequate when I changed jobs and you were out-earning me. That wasn't your fault, though – obviously. Because the only person to blame, I know now, was me.'

I'm amazed. I thought he would express some kind of remorse, but I never thought he'd be so willing to own what he did. Especially as I have had so many moments of wondering if there was something else I should have done – if I'd been too rigid or penny-pinching myself. Or if I should have helped him work through it to overcome his issues. To hear him take full responsibility, like this, really means something.

'I'm just sorry that it's taken me so long to get my act together. Because it meant losing – sorry if this sounds cheesy – losing the best thing that's ever happened to me.'

He looks straight at me for what seems like the first time, and I see the little details on his face I once knew so well: the scar above his left eyebrow; the freckle on his right cheekbone. Suddenly I remember that weekend in Whitstable, when we stayed up all night together and went for a walk on the beach as the sun was coming up, and he asked me to marry him. I remember him lending me his coat as it started to drizzle, and feeling I could never be happier. And then, two months after we got engaged, I happened to see his credit card statements while I was looking for my gym membership card. I only saw the top statement of the top one; the purchase of my ring. But the sum was so horrifying that I looked at the rest, and that was how it all came out.

'Anyway,' he says. 'There's no pressure at all to have a reaction to it – any of it. I just wanted to tell you again how sorry I am. That's all I wanted to say for now.'

'Well, thank you,' I say finally. 'I appreciate you saying that. But, Eddie, it wasn't even the debt. It was the fact that you lied to me about the stag. We had had all that talk about our finances. We had a plan, and I thought we were back on track. You told me the guys were all paying for themselves. And then I find out that you covered all their train fares, and the Airbnb, *and* the restaurant.' I can't even

164

mention the final sum; it still makes me feel a little sick to think of it.

'I know, and I'm really, really sorry,' he says. 'Again, I can't say how sorry I am. And . . . I can't imagine what you've been through in the past year. Losing Hannah. It's so awful, I couldn't believe it. I'm so sorry – again. It's so horrible.'

'It was. It is.' I can't help but think of how much easier it would have been – or less awful anyway – if I'd had someone to lean on in the aftermath of the funeral. Not someone like Vik, whom I was supporting too, but some-one to look after me. Someone to go with me to the funeral or coax me to get dressed and go out or even make me a cup of tea when I got home. I've never expected life to be fair, but it really isn't fair that I lost my fiancé and my best friend in the space of two years.

He continues, 'Also, I'm sorry it's so late but I want to pay you back for your share of the deposit for the venue. And the cost of your wedding dress. If you'll accept it, of course. With interest.'

Now I feel depressed; I wish he hadn't said it. My share of the venue deposit is water under the bridge as far as I'm concerned. And the dress I donated to Oxfam. It wasn't expensive anyway by wedding dress standards; it was around £150 from Monsoon. I think deep down, even when we were first planning the wedding, I knew that I shouldn't invest too much money in it.

'I don't want that, Eddie – honestly. If you have the money to spare, you should be saving. For a place of your own maybe.'

'Well,' he says, with a slightly twisted smile, 'that's

unlikely. Unless I move back up north, of course . . . which I am considering.'

'That sounds like a great idea,' I tell him.

I think I can detect a trace of disappointment on his face. But, honestly, what did he think I would do – beg him to stay in London and move back in with me? Sunderland, where he's from, is a beautiful seaside town full of red-brick houses surrounding quiet squares. It's got everything you could want, including a fabulous artisan pizza place on the beach. I used to think it would be a great place to take our kids to visit their grandparents.

'How are your folks?' I ask. I really liked his parents. Bernard and Joy, both teachers, both with slightly eccentric hobbies: Bernard, with a white beard, was very into the folk music scene, and Joy did a lot of embroidery and needlework. Their house was warm and messy and welcoming; when I went there, it felt a lot like coming home.

'They're fine,' he says. 'Dad's written a new sea shanty, which was performed as part of some themed evening at the Sage in Gateshead . . . and Mum's walking Hadrian's Wall again. You know. The usual.'

'That's good.'

'Actually, he did another song that night at the Sage. The one he wrote about you. Remember that? He adapted it a bit . . .'

I do remember it. Bernard had written a song about me in lieu of the usual father-of-the-groom speech, to perform at our wedding. Eddie was embarrassed initially; I had to explain that a song at an Irish wedding could never be out of place. It's a nice compliment, of course, but the mention of our wedding is a bit too close to home and my smile fades.

'What do they make of . . . all this?'

'They've been great. I moved back in with them obviously, to help with the repayment. I was there for a year and a half. And we've had some conversations about my school days . . . and how that whole environment might have, you know, played a part.'

This is interesting; it's crossed my mind before that his experience of school can't have helped, and I'm glad he sees it too. Eddie, a bright boy, got a scholarship to a posh school where he was surrounded by the kids of millionaires or those with moneyed connections, who went skiing or to the Caribbean for their holidays, while his own family went camping. His parents were so unworldly, I don't think they ever realized that being academic was only half the story when it came to fitting in there. I think it gave Eddie a feeling of inferiority that he tried to assuage by splashing cash around.

'Not that it's about blaming them,' he adds quickly. 'That's not the idea at all. The responsibility is all mine.'

I nod, liking him for saying this. 'Well, good for you. Honestly. I am impressed.'

'Thanks. Anyway – what's new with you?'

I start to say my usual 'nothing much', but then I realize I do have some news. 'Oh . . . I've just been trying a few new things. Some resolutions.' I don't tell him about the link with Hannah, but I explain that that was why I was doing the yoga – and that I'm going again on Monday.

'So what's next?' he asks, eyes bright with interest.

'An astrologer,' I say.

At this Eddie laughs so much that tears come to his eyes.

'What?' But I'm laughing too.

'It's just . . . I simply cannot picture you consulting an astrologer. I would pay money to see that, I really would.'

I smile at him, thinking how long it's been since I was with someone who knows me so very well. Not since Hannah, in fact.

'I can't wait to hear how it goes.' He pauses. 'If you feel like telling me, obviously. I don't want to assume anything. I'd better go now – I've got football practice in Regent's Park.' He gestures to the waiter to ask for the bill. When it arrives, he insists on paying, as he often did, but he also checks the amount – which I don't think I've ever seen him do before – *and* keeps the receipt. Maybe he really has changed.

'So can I call you some time?' he asks, when we're outside the cafe. 'Another coffee or something?'

I take a deep breath, and say, 'Sure. Why not?'

'That's fantastic.' He gives me a brief kiss on the cheek, and we go our separate ways. That was nice, I think, as I watch him go; surprisingly nice, in fact. Not what I expected. But, then again, nothing is what I expect lately.

17

March

When I thought of an astrologer, I vaguely pictured an older woman in embroidered shawls hunched over a crystal ball – maybe someone like Whoopi Goldberg in *Ghost*, though she's a medium obviously. Or a silver-bearded old sage in long robes and Jesus sandals maybe? I certainly didn't picture Peter Green. A softly spoken, handsome Canadian guy, he's wearing a smart shirt and trousers, and looks more like one of my work colleagues than Whoopi, or Jesus.

'Hi!' he says, opening the door to his flat. 'You must be Celeste. Come on in.'

It's the first Saturday in March and I'm here for our appointment at his flat, which is on one of the back streets east of Upper Street in Islington. I got Peter's details from Sibéal, who said one of her witch friends recommended him.

'He's meant to be really good,' she said. 'The only thing I would say, though, is that astrologers are kind of . . . a bit basic? They're just very by the book, charts, numbers, blah blah. But if you're up for something conventional, then you should be fine.'

The fact that Sibéal considers Peter to be too conventional is a strong recommendation in my book, and he seems very nice and normal so far. I follow him inside his place, which is beautiful, with high ceilings and framed artwork on the walls. There's also evidence of a small child everywhere – a Tripp Trapp chair and various stuffed animals in baskets – which is also not quite what I expected for some reason.

'Our daughter, Juno. She's gone to the park,' he says when I ask. 'So the house is quiet for once! Do you want some tea or coffee?'

He makes me a coffee in a snazzy-looking machine, before leading me to a cosy book-lined study at the back of the house that overlooks the narrow gardens behind the terraces. Peter shows me to a low armchair and sits opposite me in the office chair, but immediately cranks it down so we're on the same level, which I find very charming.

'So is there any particular thing that's bringing you here today – or general interest?'

'Oh. Well . . .' I'm obviously not going to tell him that I'm here on behalf of my late friend. Or that I consider it all to be nonsense. 'I just wanted to try it,' I say in an effort to combine truth and tact.

'Great. So you've seen horoscopes and you probably know you're a Taurus. But there's a bit more to unpack. Shall we begin?'

'Yes, great,' I say, sipping my coffee. This doesn't seem so bad so far.

'The first thing I always say is you are the expert in your life. The second is that the astrology is never wrong but the astrologer can be wrong. So I'll give you some suggestions but if something doesn't sound right to you, then please give that a voice and we can figure it out together.'

I nod and smile, enjoying his soothing voice. He seems so nice but my inner cynic is saying this also sounds like a convenient get-out if he starts saying anything that's completely out of whack.

Peter swivels around and takes a printout from the table behind him. 'Here is your birth chart.'

I take the printout, which looks like three concentric circles with some squiggles like hieroglyphs inside them. Peter explains that these represent the planets and the twelve signs of the zodiac.

'The chart is also divided into twelve different houses. They represent different parts of our lives such as work, family and so on.'

'Um, sure.' I notice that one of the houses is very empty. 'Which is that one?'

'That one? That's the fourth house, which is the house of home and family.'

'Oh.' I can't help but add: 'It looks . . . empty.'

'Don't worry! This chart only shows the main planets. But this house might contain millions of other objects: asteroids, minor planets, other stars. No house is truly empty.'

Great, I think. Some people get Venus in their home house; I get an asteroid.

I don't know why I'm getting so hung up on this – since I don't believe any of it anyway – but I say, 'It just looks a bit unbalanced. Is that normal?'

'There's no such thing as "normal" when we're looking at a birth chart,' he says. 'And I always say the fact that you are here in front of me is testament to these things being in balance.'

'Hm,' I say, trying to hide my scepticism.

'So, the place I like to start is not with a planet but with a point – this point labelled "AC" is the Ascendant and it's the rising sign. That's what was on the eastern horizon when you were born. You were born at seven sixteen a.m. just after the Ascendant moved into the sign of Cancer and that's how we know that Cancer is your rising sign.'

This means nothing to me, but I nod anyway. 'OK.'

'So, Cancer is a water sign and they're all about intuition and the subconscious. Cancer is a sign that I associate a lot with caring for others. It's deeply emotional, and nurturing.'

'Mm,' I say, a little disappointed that he's already got this so wrong. I'm not an emotional person, and I'm certainly not nurturing. I'm scared of babies, and I'm not even keen on pets.

'That doesn't mean that Cancer is often outwardly very emotionally expressive. But if someone were to come to your home, you might have their favourite tea or drink ready. Or if you're visiting someone, you'll take them a special gift of something you know they like.'

This does make me think of all the presents I brought at New Year's, and of having all Hannah's favourite things for her when she arrived. But surely everyone does that?

'Rather than being all huggy and outwardly expressive, Cancer tends to be about protecting and holding in emotions. We can't show who we are unless we feel safe. Safety and security are big issues when it comes to Cancer. You might be very security-conscious. And your home is very important to you, as your protective shell.'

I think suddenly of my triple-locked door and find myself listening more carefully.

'For you Cancer is very important. You have Cancer rising and the moon is on top of the Ascendant, which makes Cancer themes very notable for you.'

'Mm-hm,' I say. 'Is there a downside to that?' Not that I believe it, of course, but just to see what he says.

He smiles. 'With Cancer, as I said, there's often a wall between them and the rest of the world. And Cancer can be a little snippy and nippy. We can retreat within ourselves and pinch out if we don't feel safe. Especially if we feel tired or hungry – those basic physical needs are important to Cancer.'

And to everyone else, I think, but I can't help but think of how hangry I get. Peter continues, 'So it's important to look after yourself physically, make sure you're eating well, getting enough sleep. With the moon in Cancer you have that urge to take care of other people – make sure they're well fed and warm. I'd also urge that you take care of yourself in the same way.'

'OK.' Obviously this could apply to anyone, but it is somehow quite sweet.

'Now there's another planet sitting here in the first house, and that's Mars. Mars is a planet that's very much about striking out into the world. It has a separating energy. It's also the god of war and it can also describe anger and frustration.'

'Ah.' I shift uneasily, trying to look as if I don't know what those are.

'Cancer isn't always the most comfortable place for Mars. The Cancer crab wants to go sideways and Mars wants to thrust forward. Which can mean you don't have an easy time with conflict. Rather than expressing it more directly you can be more . . . subtle.'

'You can say "passive-aggressive",' I say, smiling. Peter grins too, and we both laugh. I ask, 'But isn't everyone passive-aggressive? Isn't it just being Irish or British . . . We don't do outward expression of difficult emotions.'

'Certain cultures do shape how we express things. But Mars is not in Cancer all the time. And I can assure you that this is something that's unique to you. That sense of gusto and energy – it can be a good thing. It probably stands you in good stead in your work? And I'm guessing you're a loyal and protective friend.'

I nod, feeling very sad suddenly.

'So to me it calls up an image of firefighting – of fighting with water to protect people's homes. That's the kind of energy you bring to friendships and possibly even to your work.'

I look up at him sharply, remembering my dream about just that – about Vik's house being on fire. But that's a common nightmare, of course. I try to focus on what he's saying now, about Cancer being just over a degree within Polaris when I was born.

'So, Polaris, as you probably know, is the North Star or the Pole Star. It's a fixed star, which makes it even more significant than the planets – almost divine. It's right around now – in this phase of your life, say, which I see is late thirties – that that Polaris energy will show itself strongly and give you that feeling of wanting to find yourself.'

I nod, feeling cynical again, as I think: *Who doesn't want to find themselves in their late thirties? Or at any age?*

'Polaris has this incredible guiding force. But also – if you are not on track and you're not living in the way that reflects your higher calling – Polaris is not shy about knocking you off course and making you question everything. That could be with an injury or a loss.'

Again I feel myself resist. *He's guessing,* I tell myself.

'What kind of loss?'

'I can't speak to that in specific terms,' he says. 'But since we're talking about loss, one thing I noticed is that you recently had a year in which the twelfth house of your chart was very important. That's the end of the cycle, and it's got the energy of endings and disappearances. Venus is there, so that could suggest a romantic loss – maybe a serious relationship?'

'Yes,' I say, telling myself again that this could apply to anyone.

'And it's in the sign of Gemini – the sign of twins – which could also suggest the loss of someone very close. Like a sister?'

I stare at him, and it's a minute before I can say, 'I lost a friend.'

'I'm so sorry,' he says.

'It's fine. I'm fine. What else?'

'Well, just to say that the twelfth house, where I see that loss, is a deeply spiritual place. It makes sense that following the loss of your friend you might actually end up having a spiritual awakening of sorts.'

This sounds far-fetched, but I say 'I see' just to be polite. Then I realize I'm being a typical Cancer!

'To return to the link with Polaris, that kind of crisis can be painful. But tragedy can also be an opportunity – a calling to connect with your true self. To understand that you are guided and you are a guide.'

'Me? A guide?' I repeat, and he nods. 'OK,' I say, feeling completely torn. Is this all still gobbledygook, or is he actually telling me something incredibly important?'

'So you mentioned you've been in the same career for a while?'

'Yes,' I say. I don't want to mention anything else; let him guess.

'If we look over here, this is the part that's the Midheaven – the highest part of the sky. It can refer to our calling or vocation, or our career. So for you this Midheaven is in the sign of Aquarius and in the eighth house. One kind of thing the eighth house is connected with is finance and banks. Aquarius also has a restructuring energy and it can be associated with technology. So restructuring for the future or corporate restructuring for the future, based on new tech.'

'Yes, that's exactly what I do,' I say. He could have found this out from Google, I think – before remembering that I hadn't given him my surname.

'And Saturn, who's the ruling planet of Aquarius, is also in this eighth house. Saturn is a planet that's about discipline and commitment. It likes solidity and consistency. But it can get a little bit stuck. I can imagine you have a solid reputation, but now you're wondering what else is out there?'

'Yes, I am,' I admit. 'Not just in terms of work, but in . . . life. I'm wondering if I should shake things up, but I don't know how.'

He gives me a sympathetic look. 'That makes sense.

I can't tell you exactly how that's going to look for you. But you're already trying new things by the sounds of it. Another theme in the eighth house is mortality, and people often like to explore all the house themes over the course of their lives. If you go down that path, that might also help you deal with your friend's passing. You might even find yourself guiding others through the processes of grief or death. Guiding a friend maybe, as I said earlier.'

'Really?' I ask, not wanting to admit, even to a kindly astrologer, how unlikely that seems right now.

'Yes. I see friendships being very important here. Your sun sign, as I mentioned, is Taurus, and at your birth Taurus was sitting in the eleventh house. The eleventh house involves friendship, groups, society, hopes and dreams. In your chart it's in the sign of Taurus and that's your sun sign as well. So I can see friendships being very positive for you. Taurus is very grounded, practical, material. When you are connecting with friends, you might enjoy doing this in a material and even artistic way – for example, framing a photograph of you and a friend together . . . Holding on to memory is also a very Cancer characteristic, so that would fit in well with your Cancer Ascendant.'

A shiver runs down my spine as I remember the framed photograph I gave to Hannah.

He continues, 'Taurus loves physical and sensual experiences whether it be food or music or art. Nature and the Earth are also very key. So I think connecting to nature is going to be really good for you too.' He pauses. 'But to return to your question about change, I think when it comes to change, just remember you're a Taurus. With

Taurus energy I always encourage small changes and patience. If you try to change all at once, you might be like a bull in a china shop. Even doing something a little bit different, like coming to see me today, will hopefully open you up to new things.'

It's true that this is all perfectly neutral, sensible advice that would work for anyone, but I can't help it; I feel stunned at everything he's said. How has he done it? Even if it's guesswork, that's still incredible.

'That's a lot, I know. Any questions about what's come up so far?' Peter says, pouring me some water.

'Not really,' I say. 'Except –'

What I want to ask really, is when I will get over the loss of Hannah. But I can't think exactly how to ask that. 'Do you see it getting easier?' I ask instead. 'I mean, when can I move on?'

'It depends what you mean by moving on,' he says. 'Your friend is gone, but the friendship that you had is still here and so you can still enjoy the things that connected you. It's not letting go of the friendship that was – it's just giving you that chance to move on with your life. Like maybe you want to hang a special picture of her, or wear something that reminds you of her. Maybe there was something she gave you, that you're using already?'

'Yes,' I say, my fingers going to the silver bee necklace around my throat. At this point I have to accept it. Either he's been living secretly in my flat for the past year – and he's a tall guy and I would have noticed – or else he really does have some insight into me and my situation.

'Do you want to take a minute?' he asks. 'Or if you prefer, we can move on to what we call your progressed chart:

the events to come. Which I realize for some people is kind of the point.'

This makes me feel apprehensive suddenly. I don't know if I want to know what the future holds, even if it's accurate – especially if it's accurate. What if it's something bad?

'Don't worry,' he says. 'It's nothing sinister. The chart just shows some overall patterns that you can expect to play out this year. Just some suggestions – I don't have a crystal ball.' He smiles, and I give a small smile in return, nodding for him to continue. He produces another print-out, which he explains shows the position of my birth chart 'progressed' for one day a year, until it corresponds to the year to come.

'So right now it's an interesting time astrologically for you – the progressed moon is transiting through Neptune.'

'OK,' I say, nodding away and suddenly wondering what all my work colleagues would think to see me, eagerly waiting to hear about the moon/Neptune transit.

'Neptune's the planet of dreams and fantasies. It's a watery planet obviously, and it doesn't like boundaries, so it's a time when barriers can dissolve and things feel very fluid. People might appear in your life around this time, who are from a distance or from far away . . .'

I feel stunned. *Eddie.*

'Someone has just come back into my life actually. From my past.' I hesitate. 'Do you . . . I mean, is that a good thing or a bad thing?' *Listen to me*, I think, *asking my astrologer's advice*; but I also really want to know.

'Well, it's certainly a time when barriers can come down, and you might be feeling a bit more emotionally open. For

Cancer that can feel challenging. So I would say protect yourself but also stay open to what might come.'

This is so sensible and non-committal, but I'm going to take it on board too. Peter continues, 'This is also a really rich time to feel connections with the other world in the sense of feeling your friend's presence. It doesn't surprise me that you came to see me around this time, because you're more open now than you might have been previously.'

That's an understatement. I try to think of the Celeste of last year even contemplating having her astrology chart done and fail.

'How you do mean, her presence?'

'I don't mean she's sending you messages or anything— just that it's a good time to tap into the kind of things she might want to tell you if she were here now. Because, like I said, she's gone but your friendship is still a big part of your life. It's like throwing a stone in the water – the stone disappears but the ripples will be seen for a long time, probably forever in your case.'

I nod, taking comfort in the thought.

'Lastly, this loss of your friend – that was about a year ago?'

'Yes,' I say, not even bothering to ask how he knew. He starts talking about Mercury being in the third house, and the moon being in Scorpio. 'And in astrology we have what we refer to as the rule of three . . .'

'Wait. Do you mean you see three losses?'

He looks at me strangely, but then says, 'Oh, no. I mean rather that this loss, this significant loss, was showing up in three different ways in your chart . . .'

But for the first time I don't believe him. I think he did see something. Which is terrifying, but also makes sense. Eddie. Hannah. And then something – or someone – else.

'Are you OK, Celeste?' he's asking gently.

'Yeah. I just – Sorry. Go on.' I realize that if he did see me losing someone else, I don't want to know. And he probably wouldn't tell me. *Also*, my former self tries to remind me, *isn't it all nonsense anyway?*

'Lastly you were asking me about when you might be moving on from the loss of your friend . . .'

'Yes.' I sit forward eagerly.

'Well, as I said, "moving on" is a broad term. But there is something that changes at the end of November this year. The progressed moon will be heading into the seventh house, which is about relationships and partnerships.'

'You mean I'm going to get together with someone?' I ask.

I am so totally dazed by everything that he's said that if he gives me a yes here, I'm going to – Well, not buy a wedding dress exactly but certainly get my legs waxed. So I'm thrilled when he says, 'It's possible.'

Peter continues, 'Again, I can't tell you that exactly how your grieving journey will progress.' He smiles again with that kind sympathetic smile. 'But I can say that November this year, or around that time, is when your focus turns to a romantic relationship.'

I let out a deep breath. 'Wow. Thank you.'

He smiles. 'You're welcome.'

'That was genuinely really insightful. I have to admit I was a bit sceptical and . . . I am surprised.'

He laughs. 'Life is surprising. Well, great, I'm so glad it

was good. Let me know if you have any more questions . . . and I will email you both your birth chart, and your progressed chart.'

We walk back out through his beautiful apartment, and I notice little things like the magazine rack stacked with copies of *The New Yorker*, the copy of *The Very Busy Spider* and the little sippy cups and plastic bowls.

'Have you always done astrology, Peter?'

'No, I used to be a lawyer, working for the UN,' he says. 'And then I took sick leave, and started listening to podcasts and reading books all about astrology and . . . here I am.' He smiles down at me and opens up his front door. 'Goodbye, Celeste.'

Of course he was previously an international lawyer. Because everyone I meet recently has radically changed their life. But I don't feel too downcast. I'm a Taurus after all; I'm going to change in my own way with small steps. Who knows how much of it is real and how much is . . . Well, I don't know how to account for any of it, but I loved it; I'm so glad I did it. 'Thanks, Hannah,' I murmur out loud. 'That was surprisingly fun.'

As I walk back down the beautiful street of terraced Georgian houses, I take a deep breath, smelling spring for the first time. The sky is a perfect blue, with tiny scudding clouds; the cherry trees are shedding pale pink blossom. This wasn't a dream; I've just visited my astrologer. And now I am going to get a coffee and maybe go and take some photographs of the cherry blossoms or celebrate them, like they do in Japan.

Suddenly I remember that I still haven't replied to the message Eddie sent me earlier today, just saying hello. I was going to agree to meeting again if he suggested it, but perhaps I shouldn't make any decisions until Neptune has finished transiting. As I walk back towards the tube, I imagine telling Hannah about it, and I smile.

'You know, Hannah,' I say out loud, 'I'll just tell him that my astrologer recommends making no decisions until the moon is heading into my seventh house.' I find myself laughing out loud like a loon as I walk along the pavement, and for the first time in a long time the memory doesn't lead to any tears.

18

The weekend after my astrology appointment, I take up Vik's invitation to visit him at the house, to do some gardening and also just hang out.

'Just a small crew this time,' he says. 'You, me, Patrick and Angelika. I'm sure they could give you a lift, or I'll pick you up at the station if you like?'

'That would be great – thanks, Vik,' I say. It's not that I would mind squeezing into the back seat, playing gooseberry, but who knows what Patrick might be transporting this time – whole oak trees, perhaps, or statues for the garden.

Vik picks me up, as arranged, from the 10.15 train on the Saturday morning in his new car – a fifteen-year-old Land Rover, still smelling richly of dogs from its previous owners.

'I needed the space,' he says. 'I was spending so much time driving around fetching furniture and garden equipment; plus, going through mud – this just seems sensible.'

'Very sensible,' I say, smiling; I can tell he loves his new gadget. 'I like the outfit too.' He's wearing a wax jacket, jeans and Hunter wellies, and looks every inch the country squire.

'Thanks. You don't think I look ridiculous? Toad of Toad Hall?'

'No, you look good. Very appropriate,' I reassure him.

I am wearing a big fleece and jeans; if we're gardening, I don't see the point of being fancy. 'Are the others on their way?'

'They're already at the house actually; they came last night. It's been nice to have a chance to get to know Angelika a bit better.'

I'm about to ask what she's like when I'm distracted by something outside the window. 'Vik! Look at that!' It's a little flock of sheep with lambs who are actually skipping – leaping and bounding across the field. 'Did you see? How adorable!'

'It's sometimes hard to believe you're from Ireland,' says Vik. 'Isn't it wall-to-wall sheep?'

'Not Dublin,' I say, still looking back. 'Sorry, you were saying about Angelika. Have you not met her before?'

'Yes, a couple times. But they got together last summer after I left London, so I haven't spent all that much time with her. But she seems really great.'

'You sound relieved,' I say, amused.

'Well,' Vik says in a confidential tone.

'Go on?' I say, smiling at his cloak-and-dagger air. He seems so much like his old self; one of the things Hannah loved about him was his willingness to gossip.

'The thing about Patrick's girlfriends, is that they are always crazy.'

'Vik, you can't say that! That's really misogynistic.' I think for a minute. 'Is that what *he* says? That's a bad sign if so.'

'No, quite the opposite! He'll never admit that they're crazy. They're always "sensitive", or "highly strung", or "creative" like his ex Ivana. That was the one before

Angelika. She was very messed up, poor thing. Drank too much. And then the one before that was embroiled in some messy legal thing . . . There's always something.'

'So why's he attracted to that?'

'I'm not sure . . . Maybe he thinks he can save them or help them. Or fix them.'

'Yikes.' This sounds complicated. 'But Angelika is different?'

'Yes. She's got her act together. She works in cancer research, as you know; she's very practical and . . . straight-forward. Tells it like it is.' He pauses. 'She's maybe a little serious? But so is he really, so that's all good.'

'I've never met an Angelika before,' I remark. 'Where's she from?'

'Hm. Good question. She moved here quite young and her parents are from . . . I want to say . . . Not Geneva . . . Genovia? That's it. Genovia.'

'Genovia?' I repeat. 'That's not a real place, Vik.'

'No?'

'No! It's the fictional country in *The Princess Diaries*.'

He starts to laugh. 'Oops. My mistake. I could have sworn Pat said Genovia. You'll have to ask her.'

It's a long time since I've laughed so hard; I'm wiping away tears from my eyes. 'Yeah' is all I can say, when I can speak again. 'So what have you got planned for us, gardening-wise?'

'Well, you remember the moat? I thought we might take a little look at that together.'

'Wait, weren't you going to get diggers for that?'

'Ah yes, well. Diggers turn out to be slightly pricey, so I thought it might be fun to have a go at doing it manually.'

'Oh my God. You want us to clear a moat for you? And this is fun?' I'm torn between more laughter and telling him to turn the car around and take me straight back to the station.

'We'll just do a bit,' he says soothingly. 'Nothing too strenuous, I promise.'

We're driving up the lane now, under trees newly touched with a wash of pale green. Vik parks the Land Rover and I get out to see the place transformed from my last visit. The willow trees around the pond are already flush with leaves, the sun is warm on my face and the birds are loud all around us. At the far end of the lawn I see a group of little shrubs with a mist of white blossom hanging over them like a wreath, and I realize these must be the cherry trees that Patrick planted at New Year's.

'It looks beautiful, Vik,' I say. 'Is that Angelika over there?' I see a figure sitting on a camping chair at the other end of the lawn, bundled up in a down coat, and give her a wave. She doesn't wave back, and I see that she's reading something that looks like a hefty textbook.

'Yes it is. Let's dump your bag, and then we'll go and say hello.'

We sling the bag inside the front door and cross the lawn. There are signs of spring everywhere; I see blue flowers that I think might be hyacinths, and all the trees are touched with green, ranging from a pale wash to a deep hue. It's like a different place to the bare landscape I remember.

'Hello,' Vik says to Angelika. 'Meet Celeste. Celeste, meet Angelika.'

'Hi, Celeste,' she says in a husky low voice, keeping a finger in her book as she looks up.

'It's lovely to meet you,' I say, trying not to stare. I'm not surprised that she's pretty, but I hadn't expected her to be quite so stunning, with a perfect oval face, pale olive skin, rippling brown hair and huge brown eyes. She's muffled in a big grey puffa coat, but she looks as though she could be on the prow of a ship. She also has a very slight accent which makes her even more seductive.

'Where's Pat?' says Vik, looking around.

'Down here,' says a voice.

It's Patrick, down in the depths of the moat, hacking at brambles. He looks up, wiping a hand across his face which is streaked with dust and sweat, as is his white T-shirt. He's wearing green utility trousers, the kind with multiple pockets, and a tool belt, gloves and work boots. It's not my personal fantasy – I like a well-cut suit – but I do see why they make calendars of men that look like this.

'How's it going?' I ask, peering down at him.

He smiles back, saying, 'Having the time of my life. Come and join me.'

'Well, let's give you a chance to settle in first,' says Vik. 'Cup of tea maybe?'

'You can have these gloves,' Angelika says, holding up a pair. 'I don't want to do it.'

'Do you have work to do?' I ask, looking at her big textbook.

'Yes. But even if I didn't, it's not my idea of fun.' She looks briefly up at Vik when she says this with a quick smile, and then back down at her book.

'Fair enough,' I say, somewhat surprised. 'I'll do a little bit, and then perhaps I'll join you.'

Vik shows me where to climb down into the moat, via a ladder, and I reflect that it's a good thing that Angelika is still up on dry land, so to speak, just in case the ladder breaks or something and we all get stuck down here, which is not a comedy sketch I want to be in.

'Here,' Patrick says, handing me a pair of secateurs and a bag, presumably to put the brambles in. Vik is already hacking away at the other end of this section of the moat, under the old bridge.

'Where's my hi-vis vest?' I joke, and he smiles.

'Not in the budget.'

The brambles are even worse than I thought; I can clip them all I want, but they seem to regenerate as I do, spiking me right through my fleece. But there's a certain satisfaction in hacking them out, even if it takes me a full quarter of an hour to clear a square metre.

'Do you guys want some water?' asks Angelika, looking over the edge at us. It's astonishing to see that she can even look pretty from below, surely the most unflattering angle known to man. We all say yes please and she brings a jug with iced water and glasses from the house a few minutes later. I take a grateful sip; I'm already sweating in the light spring sun.

Angelika looks down at us, thoughtful. 'You know,' she says to Vik, 'you could just fill in this whole thing with earth, couldn't you? And then plant flowers on top of it. Maybe sunflowers or geraniums.'

'True,' Vik says, nodding. 'And I did consider that, but

then if you think about it, I'd need several tonnes of earth, plus heavy machinery to fill it all in, so.'

'You could pay people to pay to do it by hand. I'm sure there are people around here who need the work.'

'Well, maybe,' says Vik. 'But where's the fun in that?'

'It depends what you consider fun I suppose,' Angelika says and disappears, presumably to her camping chair and book.

Patrick doesn't seem bothered by her pronouncements – he's deep in brambles – but I exchange grins with Vik. I can see why he described her as straight-talking; though maybe 'blunt' would be a better word. I would have expected any girlfriend of Patrick's to be as outdoorsy and gung-ho as he is, but opposites attract, I suppose. I wonder what she thinks of his plans to open a garden centre in Dublin, and I suspect I won't have to wonder very long if I ask her.

We've been hacking away for what seems like hours, and I'm starting to ponder the question of lunch when we hear the honk of a car horn. Vik says, 'Ah. That'll be the bird man.'

'The what now?' I ask.

'He's the guy that you call if you want advice on wild birds,' says Vik, shinning up the ladder. 'He's not actually from the RSPB but he knows his stuff. Come and see.'

'Oh, right. The bird man,' I say, wiping down my face. 'I've got one of those.'

'I've got mine on speed dial,' Patrick says, and I laugh. I had forgotten that he can be funny, or maybe it's just the contrast with Angelika that I'm noticing.

'Shall we?' Patrick says, indicating the ladder. I climb up

while he holds it, getting flashbacks to our climbing session, and we go to meet the new arrival.

The bird man is a balding, round-faced guy in his mid-forties, whose blue van is now parked in the drive. He's holding Sigmund around his body and checking him all over, while Vik and Angelika watch. I approach with Patrick, keeping well back.

'Yep, this is the same swan that lived here before,' the bird man is saying. 'Male mute swan, probably about five years old. I think the previous tenants called him Cyril. He seems in good health, so whatever you're giving him, it's agreeing with him – well done.' He releases Sigmund, who gives an indignant hiss and waddles off towards the water.

'Cheers,' Vik says, looking pleased. 'What I did want to ask you about, was the idea of getting him a mate. I believe he used to have one – and his behaviour went downhill after she, um, passed away?'

'Well,' says the bird man, 'yes, there's a sad story there. He did have a mate, and she did pass away. Unfortunately Cyril, or Sigmund, was involved in that incident.'

'You mean –' Vik says.

The swan man draws a dramatic finger across his throat, and we all make noises of dismay. I glance at Angelika in female solidarity, but she's nodding away as if this doesn't surprise her a bit.

'Oh dear,' says Vik, looking worried. 'What about getting another male, then, to keep him company?'

'A wingman?' Patrick suggests, and we all groan.

The bird man shakes his head. 'No, that would be even worse – a rival. Best thing to do is leave him be. He'll be OK.'

Declining offers of tea, the bird man says he's got to go on to look at some rescue geese in Mendlesham. 'You've got a lovely place here,' he says, looking around. 'It's looking a lot better than it did last time I came.' Which seems to go some way to cheer Vik up, though his face falls again as the bird man drives off.

'Well, that was depressing,' Vik says. 'A cold case reopened, and Sigmund found guilty. Imagine, I might have bought him another victim.'

'Men,' says Angelika, which I have to say I don't disagree with.

'Well, swans,' Patrick says.

'Tell you what,' Vik says. 'I know what will cheer us all up. Why don't we leave the brambles for today – and hop in the car, and go to the beach? Fish and chips for lunch, maybe a cream tea?'

Patrick looks torn, obviously wanting to keep going with his brambles, but I say, 'Great idea, Vik. Can I wash my face and hands first, though?'

'You'd better have a hot shower, darling,' I hear Angelika saying, as we all go inside. I don't hear Patrick's reply, but her muffled giggle a second later tells me a bit more than I want to know about what they see in each other.

I hadn't realized that Vik's house was so close to the beach; we've barely listened to two episodes of *I'm Sorry I Haven't a Clue*, Vik's favourite radio comedy, before we're in the outskirts of the little seaside town of Aldeburgh.

'Thank God for some fresh air; the smell of this car is so terrible,' Angelika says, as we get out.

'Yes, the previous owners had dogs,' Vik says apologetically. 'Never mind, get some sea air down you.'

'I hate dogs,' Angelika says.

'You're a cat person, aren't you?' Patrick says fondly.

I am starting to wonder what he sees in her – besides the obvious – but perhaps all will be revealed now that we're not six feet under her any more.

Aldeburgh is the most adorable town, all clapboard buildings, quaint little signs, and souvenir shops selling tea towels and mugs saying I'D RATHER BE IN SUFFOLK. We buy fish and chips from a place called the Golden Galleon, which has a wooden mermaid sign swinging outside, and go to eat them on the gravel beach, where boats are tied up and seagulls shriek overhead. It's off-season, so we have the place to ourselves, though Vik tells us it will be completely rammed come June.

'So,' I say to Angelika, 'I hear you work in cancer research? That must be very rewarding.'

'Yes, it is,' she says. 'I work with Jane Brewer; she's one of the leading researchers in her area. Though I'm just a lab researcher, nothing fancy.'

'What area is that?' I ask, and Angelika gives me a long explanation about telomeres and analysing their lengths, while Patrick watches her in admiration. I can't grasp all the technical aspects, but it sounds like extremely valuable work, which will ultimately go towards fighting cancers like leukaemia.

'And, you, what do you do?' she asks.

I explain that I'm a management consultant, and she says, 'So it's just about helping companies become richer?'

'Angelika!' Patrick says, while I do a double take.

'I mean, you're not wrong ultimately,' I reply, trying to be fair. 'But we work with all sorts of businesses, large and small. Some of them even sponsor cancer research,' I add slyly.

Angelika nods. 'Yes, you're right. Sorry if I was rude.'

'Not at all,' I say, thinking how odd she is.

'Yup,' says Vik, who's been gazing out to sea with a slight smile on his lips. 'Don't forget I work for evil IT too. And so does Pat.'

'How did you two meet?' I ask quickly, hoping to head off another dispute.

Angelika says, 'Oh, in the pub one Friday night, near my lab in Euston. I was with my work colleagues and he was with his. And he came over to ask me the time.' She gives a smile that's surprisingly mischievous. 'The funny thing is,' she continues, 'I was with my colleague, who's Irish, so I thought that she and Patrick would have lots in common! But it turns out ...' She pauses dramatically while I try to imagine what could possibly be next. 'It turns out that Patrick never dates Irish women.'

'Really?' Vik says. He glances at me with a smile that makes me wonder if Hannah ever told him that I don't really ever date Irish men. Who am I kidding? Of course she did.

Patrick is shaking his head. 'That's ... You're exaggerating. I don't have some kind of blanket ban,' he protests.

'You feel like the gene pool is too small, right?' says Angelika.

'Come on! It's not Iceland,' says Vik, laughing.

I say, 'Well, we do have quite a high incidence of –'

'Coeliac disease!' Patrick and I say at the same time. 'Thank you,' he adds.

We're all laughing, and I'm torn between feeling amused, sympathetic and plain embarrassed. I had been tempted earlier to ask Angelika what she thought of Patrick's plans to move to Dublin, but I'm not going there now; there's no way I'm opening that can of worms. Goodness knows what she would come out with.

Having finished our fish and chips, we decide to stroll along the beach towards the famous Maggi Hambling sculpture, *Scallop*. Vik walks along ahead with Angelika, pointing out landmarks and telling her about the classical music festivals held here and at Snape Maltings in the summer.

Patrick falls into step beside me. 'Sorry about earlier,' he says. 'Angie didn't mean to be rude – she's just straight-talking.'

'Oh! It's totally fine,' I tell him, meaning it. 'I wasn't offended.' I pause, while wondering how to change the subject. 'What do you do, Patrick? I know it's IT, but what is your role exactly?'

'Well, I work for Opencloud,' he says, naming a big tech company. 'I'm a product owner, which means I'm a sort of intermediary between the tech people and the business side. Part interpreter, part peacemaker.' He pauses and adds, 'It's the perfect job for the child of divorced parents, like me.'

'I see.' More oversharing; help! I look out to sea, wondering how we got from my small talk to his parents' divorce in thirty seconds. But then I remember what a friend he's been to Vik, and think that maybe I shouldn't be so closed off just because he's sharing a personal thought. There's something about the crunch of the shingle under our feet, the hiss of the waves and the wind whipping at our cheeks that makes confidences feel a bit more natural.

'When did they split up?' I ask.

'Oh, when I was fifteen. My sister and I lived with my mum after that. And I didn't see my dad for a couple of years. He died five years ago, and I was only just getting to know him. I often wish we'd met as adults – we would have got on better, I think.'

'I'm so sorry,' I tell him, thinking how sad this is.

'Thanks. No, I'm sorry,' he says suddenly. 'I didn't mean to hit you with all that. I suppose, I just thought of it because –' he pauses as a particularly noisy seagull screeches past us, dive-bombing the remains of a box of chips – 'there were a lot of silences in my house growing up. So I appreciate that with Angelika. I never need to guess what she's thinking.'

'I see what you mean,' I agree, smiling. I hadn't thought of that, and it does make sense; he certainly wouldn't have to read between the lines with her. Unlike someone like me, a riddle wrapped in a Ted Baker coat, or whatever he said I was.

'How is Healo by the way?' he asks.

'Hugh? He's fine.' I smile, thinking of the last news I've had of him. 'He and his wife are heading to the Czech Republic in May on holiday. But not to Prague or Český Krumlov or Brno – to some industrial city I'd never heard of, with almost no tourist sites that I can see.'

'Very hip. It will probably be the next big thing,' Patrick suggests.

The sun comes out from behind a cloud at this moment, and we take a moment to pause and enjoy the glory of being on a beach: the sigh of the waves, the rush of the wind, and the sunlight, all the stronger from being under wraps all winter. I have the automatic feeling of wishing Hannah could be here, but I'm used to it now, and the pain doesn't register as much.

'There's nothing like it, is there?' I say, and Patrick nods.

'I'm just turned around a bit, though,' he says. 'Which way is north?'

'Which way is north?' I repeat, laughing. 'Why on earth do you want to know?'

'I just like to know where I am.' He stares off to sea. 'The sea should be east, of course, but the coastline's all twisty around here. Never mind.'

'You could use an app on your phone?'

'I could, but come on. I can be a geek, but there are limits.' He smiles. 'How go the resolutions by the way?'

I'm about to tell him, when there's a shriek from further up the beach. 'Patrick! Paaaaatrick!'

We crunch along the gravel at top speed to investigate; I'm certain from the shrieks that Angelika's twisted an ankle or something. It turns out that she can't find her sunglasses; they might be back at the house, but they might also be where we were sitting earlier, so she wants Patrick to go back and look.

'Were they valuable?' I ask, remembering how pretty they looked on her.

'No, they were just from Primark,' she says. 'But I've got sensitive eyes. Can you go and look, Pat, please?'

He rolls his eyes. 'Only if you come with me. We'll see you at the sculpture,' he tells us, and he takes her hand so they can retrace their steps.

Vik and I stroll on in silence for a minute, neither of us wanting to be the first speak. Then he says, 'OK. So maybe she's not *completely* drama-free.'

I can't help laughing. 'She's a little strange.' I glance back to make sure we're out of earshot. 'But they seem happy enough.'

'She was just telling me her views on him moving to Dublin,' Vik says. 'Bad idea, he has no retail experience and she thinks the garden centre will go bust within six months. Also, long-distance relationships never work, but she'll give it a go.'

'Is she really young, Vik?' I ask, thinking this might explain things. 'How old is she?'

'Thirty-two.'

'Maybe they do things differently in Genovia,' I suggest.

It's the mildest of gags, but it makes us both crack up until I shush him, though the others are far behind us now. I know that it will become a running joke, which makes me think: *How sad to have a running joke without Hannah.*

Vik sighs, obviously thinking along the same lines. 'I wish I could tell Hannah. She'd find it funny, wouldn't she?'

'Oh, Vik. I know it's not the same, but . . . you can always tell me.'

'Thanks, lovely. I know,' says Vik.

It occurs to me that I haven't yet told him that I met up with Eddie, but I decide not to say anything just yet. There's nothing to tell really.

Vik points to a shape on the shingle up ahead: a huge seashell carved in bronze, seemingly fluttering on the horizon. 'Look, there's the sculpture.'

'We made it,' I say, pleased. Looking at Vik, I add, 'We're getting there – aren't we?'

I don't need to explain; he knows what I mean.

'We are,' he says, squeezing my arm.

The rest of the weekend passes off peacefully enough. Angelika makes a couple of other fairly outrageous remarks, but she also cooks a mean moussaka, which we wash down with lots of red wine. I tell the others about my experience with the astrologer, which Angelika says is compete nonsense but probably helpful for 'weak' people – another gem that makes me and Vik giggle. The weather continues bright and sunny the next day, and we clear almost a full third of the ditch before it's time for Vik to drive me to the station.

'See you next time,' I say, giving him a big hug.

'Definitely.' He adds, 'I hope next time it will all be less – *thorny*.'

I give him a groan and he waves me off, standing on the platform until the train has gone.

As the train pulls out, I plug my phone in to charge and I notice that I have a new message. It's from Eddie. It says, How was your weekend? I send him a picture of me wrestling with the brambles, and he sends me back a shocked-face emoji. Then he writes, Also, how was the astrologer? Is Mercury still in retrograde?

We've exchanged a couple of messages recently, but I didn't think he would remember my astrology appointment last weekend, so I'm touched. Smiling, I type out, Not sure about Mercury, but Neptune is in transit. I hesitate, then add recklessly, Can debrief next weekend over a coffee if you are free?

I'm pleased when he replies promptly. I'd love to. Do you want to have brunch on Saturday? I send a thumbs-up emoji back, realizing, to my surprise, that I'm looking forward to it.

19

April

Over the ensuing weeks, as March turns into April, I meet up with Eddie twice – once for brunch and once for dinner. I don't analyse what's happening beyond the fact that we're becoming friends; for once I just go with it and try not to worry about what it 'means' in a larger sense. It's nice to slot back together into our familiar shorthand and easy rapport, while also entertaining him with stories of my weekend at Vik's and my mission with the resolutions – especially the astrology, which he remains very tickled by.

'I can't believe I've just been going about my business like some kind of chump without even knowing that Neptune is transiting,' he remarks, as we sit having dinner in the India Club on the Strand – it's one of our favourite places, a little hole-in-the-wall spot that seems to have survived intact from the 1970s. 'I mean, people go on about Mercury in retrograde; there needs to be more awareness about Neptune for God's sake.'

'Ha, ha,' I say, but I'm smiling as I bite into my masala dosa.

'Although,' he says, 'I will say, I think he was on to something about you being nurturing. I don't mean in a stereotypical cosy way, or a Mother Teresa way, but you are extremely thoughtful – especially when it comes to presents. You give the best presents.'

'Gosh, Ed, you're making me blush,' I say, laughing. But I feel a little guilty, as I remember Dasha's sad story about her friendship break-up with Swati. I wasn't terribly nurturing then; maybe I should have tried harder with her.

'No way,' Eddie says, when I tell him about it. 'It sounds like you did the right thing. You gave her good advice about maintaining boundaries at work – if she can't take it, then it's not your fault. You tried.'

'Maybe,' I say, feeling slightly reassured. 'What's funny?' I ask, seeing that he's smiling to himself.

'Nothing, just . . . I was thinking about him saying you were security-conscious. Remember that time you stayed up all night changing all your internet passwords, because you were convinced you'd been phished?'

'Not all night,' I protest, but I can't help but laugh too. It was probably more like 2 a.m. Then I was so tired I forgot all the new passwords, and now I just have my Safari browser remember them all.

'I think that's OK,' Eddie says when I tell him. 'It's scientifically impossible for one brain to remember all the passwords we're supposed to now. Cut yourself some slack.'

'You might be right,' I say, thinking how Eddie always made me feel better about things.

'So what's next on your list? A fortune teller? Life coach? Not that you need that.'

'I'm not sure,' I say. I've been thinking lately about what Peter said about being intuitive about the list – feeling my way into what I want to do next, instead of charging through it like a bull in a china shop, or a management consultant on a deadline, I suppose. 'I was planning to do the ceilidh dancing this month. But maybe there's something else I want to do first.'

'Well, let me know and maybe I can join,' Eddie says, raising his eyebrows. 'If you want company, that is. Or someone to meet you at the finishing line.'

'I will,' I promise.

The deciding moment comes later that week, when I'm sitting in our team leader meeting discussing yet another upcoming pitch. It's an interesting one this time – an ethical fashion company called Effie. The concept is an app rather like Etsy, but selling clothing and textiles from smaller producers in developing countries, mainly women who aren't online yet. It's far more niche than most clients we deal with – and unlike the footwear company everyone is keen to get involved. It's highly unusual for us to work with a start-up like this. And when I notice that they're based in Dublin my interest is piqued even more.

'I think a good team would be Hugo and . . .' Isobel says, and her eyes roam over my end of the room. And I swear that she clocks my outfit before moving over me to Gemma, who's sitting beside me. 'Gemma? With some support from – Dasha.'

As we move on to the next item on the agenda, I surreptitiously look at the outfits the other women are wearing. Isobel has a skirt, but it's a pleated one that appears to be part of her dress. Gemma has trousers with a side stripe that actually almost look as though they could be joggers, except that she's wearing them with low heels.

Not high heels – I'm the only one wearing high heels. Just like I am the only person wearing a pencil skirt or a shirt. I suddenly feel as though I'm in period costume. It's clear that the next item on my list will have to be: a session with a personal shopper.

Not for the first time I wish I could ask Hannah what was on her mind when she added this one to the list. She was so confident in her fashion choices; I can't imagine her feeling the need to take advice from anyone. Nor was she bothered about 'hiding flaws' or 'accentuating' anything. Everything looked great on her, so for her getting dressed was purely about expressing herself: clothes were 'art that you could wear', as she put it. I remember one trip I made with her to the weird and wonderful Dover Street Market, where I honestly wasn't sure what was clothing for sale and what was conceptual art.

Nonetheless, there it is on the list. Maybe Hannah knew some up-and-coming stylist who wanted to get creative with her? But I don't have any such contacts, and I haven't got the first clue where I'd start finding a personal shopper. So I do what I always do when life is bewildering, and I turn to Google. It's easier than I thought: I just look up my favourite department store and find that they do personal shopping sessions. Yet again an idea that seems impossibly far-fetched – like consulting an astrologer – is just the click of a mouse away.

Unfortunately they're all booked out for what looks like months. Now that I've got the idea in my head, I want to do it now. *Typical Taurus energy*, I think to myself with a chuckle. But then I ask myself, *What would Hannah do?* I don't even have to wonder. I find myself dialling the number, and I speak to a helpful person who says they've just had a cancellation and can fit me in next Friday. I decide to take annual leave and make a day of it.

I realize I'm truly in crisis when Friday morning comes around and I can't even find an outfit to wear to my personal shopping session. I don't seem to own any clothes except workout gear and workwear. I have one pair of jeans to my name, and I don't even like them. But they will have to do, so I put them on with a work shirt, and set off for my session, feeling extremely dowdy.

Having been told to arrive fifteen minutes early for my 10 a.m. session, I arrive to find that the store doesn't actually open until ten. There's already a crowd gathered, eager to be the first inside. But instead of getting all het up, as my mum would say, I decide to get a coffee, finding a Starbucks tucked away on a side street off Oxford Circus that I've never visited. Yet again I'm reminded of how the smallest change to my routine feels like an adventure. In the same way that you read how we only use ten per cent of our brains I feel as if I'm only using ten per cent of London – the route to work and back, via quick trips to the gym. As I glide up the escalators, I feel even more unstylish surrounded by all these gleaming surfaces and brand-new outfits. I hope John Henry – my chosen stylist – is up to the challenge.

The personal shopping area is in the middle of the first floor, and it's a bit like checking into a hotel; there's a reception area with low pink sofas, some potted plants and soft lighting. John Henry – I think, from his photo – is behind the desk waiting for me.

'Celeste? Hi!' he says. 'Great to meet you, thanks for coming in!'

I smile as I say hello, realizing that with that accent he's got to be from Dublin. And he's about the same age as Hannah and I were when we moved to London. I bet he was out reaching for the lasers until 3 a.m. last night, and yet he looks as fresh-faced and beautiful as if he's had nine hours' sleep lathered in Elizabeth Arden.

Declining a coffee, since I've just had one, I follow him into my changing suite. It's a lovely large room, with mirrors everywhere but also some low chairs and magazines, a carafe of water with two glasses and even a box of tissues – which I hope isn't an ominous sign. There are two clothing rails, one of which is already covered in stuff, but I don't know if it's for me or not. Catching sight of myself in the mirror I notice that my work shirt and jeans look truly bizarre together, as if I got dressed in the dark.

'So, Celeste, do you want to tell me what brings you here – do you have a specific occasion in mind, or just a general wardrobe refresh?'

'Oh.' I take a deep breath. 'Well, I suppose a wardrobe refresh. I just realized recently . . .' I pause as I think of all the things I could tell him I've realized recently. 'I feel like I only have gym stuff or work clothes. And I've got like one pair of jeans . . .'

'OK, got it. So you need stuff for going out, which is lunch with friends, dinner date, maybe clubbing . . .?'

'Well, maybe not clubbing. But the first two definitely.' I smile at him. 'And actually, I also think I need some new work clothes. I kind of have a uniform but it's a bit dated.

So . . .' I take a deep breath. 'I'd like to try something different.'

John Henry is nodding intently. 'Grand, grand, got it, got it. I've already got some things for you based on the form you filled in, but this will help me focus.' He asks me dozens more questions – about styles I like, colours, whether I like plain clothes or prints – and then disappears, leaving me to stare at the clothing on the rail and wondering if I've made a terrible mistake.

None of this stuff looks suitable. I see various sweaters with slogans (I hate slogans), wide-legged jeans that I know would make me look like a Womble, and dungarees – actual dungarees. I'm too old for all this. I should have gone with an older, more sensible stylist, who could help me pick out the basics I really need: like a good navy sweater, a good pair of black trousers and some perfect jeans. But then I see a dark green sequin dress with a high neck and puff sleeves and decide to pop it on just in case. I didn't think I'd be lucky with the first thing I tried, but to my surprise it looks good. Actually it looks great.

'I do really like this,' I tell him when he comes back. 'I'm not sure where I'd wear it, though.'

'Dinner date! Or drinks with friends. Or to the theatre, or anywhere really. It looks cute with boots . . .' He pauses, and tactfully doesn't comment on my old knee-high brown boots, scuffed and worn, which I've owned since the Obama administration. 'Or maybe an ankle boot?'

'Just the one?' I ask, joking, although of course I'm familiar with the fashion singular; it would be hard not to be, with Hannah in my life.

'Ha, ha,' he says, beaming. 'No, I was thinking like a

black ankle boot to show off your legs. Because you have a killer figure.'

He's surely just being polite. Looking in the mirror again, though, I see that I do look quite toned – all that yoga has made a difference, though I didn't see it at the time.

'That boot kinds of cuts them off, but with an ankle boot – see? These are vegan . . .'

He passes me a funny-looking pair, black snakeskin with a low block heel. They look way too avant-garde for me, but I try them on, just to show willing more than anything. To my surprise they look, as John Henry says, fabulous. I suddenly picture myself having dinner with Eddie wearing this outfit, then I bat the thought away.

'Now for work,' he says. 'I heard what you said about having a uniform and I thought we could do a uniform like you said, but maybe a more contemporary take . . .'

He shows me some high-waisted trousers which all seem to have that weird paper-bag waist – and silk shirts, which I think look really unflattering on me, all in foresty greens and navy where normally I wear black and grey. These are never going to work; I'm going to look terrible in them, as if I'm dressing up as someone else.

'Thank you,' I say politely, hoping he'll produce something more appropriate, once I've done a token try of them.

'Oh my God,' I say a few minutes later, staring in the mirror. To my astonishment this outfit looks fabulous – still really professional but with an edge; I look more contemporary and more confident. I love the waist and even the shirt, which creates such a sleek silhouette. And it looks great with the ankle boots, though John Henry has also got 'a block heel' for me.

'It looks like I've chosen to drop into the office on the way to somewhere more important,' I say slowly. 'And not like I'm trapped there.' Not that I feel trapped in the office, of course. But somehow, looking at myself, I feel as if my picture of places I could work and things I can do has widened. How is it possible that I'm getting all this from trying on a few new clothes?

Encouraged, John Henry offers me item after item that I would never have chosen in a million years, but which looks amazing on me. A white cotton shirt. A black and yellow floral chiffon midi dress. Wide-legged jeans that are not Womble-ish but incredibly flattering. A pleated black ankle-length skirt – ditto. And even a sweatshirt that says PEACE AND LOVE – in metallic lettering no less. The only item that's a hard no is the pair of denim dungarees.

'Do you remember *Bosco*?' I ask him, referring to the Irish puppet show for kids, whose presenters wore dungarees. John Henry laughs and says he knows what I mean.

'So do you know about high/low dressing?' he asks.

The answer is no, and he explains very patiently, like me when I'm trying to explain how the smart TV works to my mum.

'High/low dressing just means teaming something casual – like your sweatshirt there – with something more elevated.'

'Like this?' I suggest, holding out the pleated ankle length skirt.

'Yes! Perfect.'

I whip the skirt on over my tights – I feel John Henry and I are old friends by now – and I'm stunned at what I see. I've literally never felt myself looking so sharp or so fashion-forward.

Suddenly all my oomph drains away, and instead of feeling sassy I feel weirdly uncomfortable. I can't under-stand why at first but then I get it. I don't look like me; I look like Hannah. And I feel as if I'm copying Hannah. I shake my head slowly. It's not that it doesn't look good, but it's not me.

I don't get into the full details with John Henry, but he is smart enough to pick up on my discomfort and talks to me very kindly about it.

'It really is very personal, isn't it?' he says simply. 'You need to feel like you – not like you're dressing up as some-one else. Can I ask you a question?'

'Sure.'

'When was the last time you wore something that made you feel absolutely amazing? Like, an absolute snack?'

I laugh. 'A snack? Oh gosh. Um . . .' I have to think for a genuinely long minute. Was it while I was dating Eddie? I think I mainly wore pencil skirts back then too, or jeans with nice tops. And I looked nice, sure, but I am not sure I'd call myself an absolute snack. 'Well, in college I had these leather trousers, or pleather obviously, which I used to wear with a sort of sleeveless wool top? It was a bit hot and sweaty, but I loved it. It felt very Studio 54,' I admit.

'I am so happy that you said leather trousers. Because . . .' He produces a pair that look quite different from my last ones; they are matt brown, whereas my old ones were shiny black, and slightly boot leg whereas my old ones were ankle-tight. I try them on with the sweatshirt, as his suggestion.

'I absolutely love them,' I say. 'They're just like the ones I had in college, except a million times nicer.'

'Yes! Great! It's a new style obviously, though, isn't it, because college was – what, five years ago?'

I laugh aloud at his innocence. 'Oh, my gosh, bless you. Not five years, no. More like –' Ouch. 'Like, sixteen years ago.'

I've never seen someone's jaw drop before, but John Henry's does. 'Oh my God. I'm sorry, I know I shouldn't say anything but I can't even. Are you being serious right now?'

I laugh again. 'Yes, I'm thirty-six.'

He clasps both hands to his face. 'You're joking me. I honestly thought you were about twenty-six, twenty-eight tops.'

'You're very kind.' I smile at him. 'I actually feel twenty-eight now to be honest, thanks to you. How old are you if you don't mind me asking?'

It turns out that John Henry is twenty-two. He has 'literally' just graduated from the National College of Art and Design in Dublin, and he tells me all: the flatshare in Peckham, the weekend shifts working in various coffee shops and restaurants before landing this job, the nights working on his own stylist's portfolio. It makes me feel so nostalgic for those early days of arriving in London and grafting at my career, but it makes me remember how hard and precarious it felt, and how lonely at times, even though I had Hannah. I wouldn't go back.

'Let me give you my card,' he says, when I've finished

deciding on all my purchases. 'You can get in touch again when you need summer stuff – or you can book a whole session with denim, that's another option. I hope you enjoy the clothes! It was so nice to meet you!'

'It was lovely to meet you too,' I say, realizing this is true. Peter last month, John Henry this month, not to mention the climbing instructor and the yoga teacher. All these nice people working hard to make my life nicer. Who needs men when I have John Henry? On an impulse I give him a most un-Celeste-like hug, and say, 'Good luck in London too. I really think you're going to love it.'

The next day, I walk into the office wearing my new high-waisted trousers and a silk blouse, plus my new ankle boots. I didn't think it was such a dramatic change, but I receive no less than three compliments before lunchtime.

'You look fabulous,' Dasha says, looking surprised. 'I love the paper-bag waist. It's kind of like Shiv Roy from *Succession*.'

'Well, thank you,' I say, thinking that John Henry must have done a good job if I'm getting compliments from the glamorous Dasha. I'm about to ask her how things are going with her and Swati, but then I decide not to. Swati seems to be keeping more reasonable hours these days, and Dasha is dating the useless Adam and seems more cheerful all round; it's presumably all blown over.

'That's pretty,' Gemma says, seeing me wearing Hannah's necklace. 'Nice to see you wearing gold!'

'Thanks,' I say. I would like to have some kind of layered necklace situation, such as I'm always seeing other people wear, but I think that's a whole other shopping trip. I still haven't mastered the art of layering; one necklace at a time is all I can cope with.

But the best tribute of all comes from Isobel, who approaches me as I'm leaving.

'Celeste!' she says. 'Did you hear we won the ethical fashion pitch – Effie?'

'Oh, yes I did – great news.' I smile. This was the pitch that I missed out on and which prompted me to high-tail it to my own fashion upgrade. Though I'm sure that was just paranoia on my part; obviously my worth as a consultant isn't dependent on what I wear.

'Well, it's all quite new to us and it'll need a lot of research – would you like to join the project?'

'Sure,' I say, feeling very surprised as it's fairly unusual to go on board with a project after the pitch stage. But perhaps somebody dropped out.

'Fab outfit by the way. Have you been shopping?'

'Just a few new bits,' I say. Now I'm even more surprised. Is it possible that my new look has something to do with her asking me on board? Imagine: maybe I could have skipped all those evenings and weekends working and gone shopping instead. Maybe it's just a marginal gain, but, as I'm always telling my clients, you should never underestimate those.

I'm just coming back from my Pret run when I notice a little drama unfolding a few desks down. Swati, Lena and Femi all walk by Dasha's desk, laughing and chatting, all clearly having come back from lunch. My first thought is that it's nice to see Swati taking her lunch break, but then I see Dasha. She doesn't say anything, but from the way she's staring down at her sad desk salad I can see what's happening. I thought she and Swati had patched up their differences, but evidently it's not so simple.

'Dasha,' I say, going over to her, 'have you got a sec?'

She looks up, and I see that her eyes are red.

'Come on,' I say, sounding deliberately brisk so that I don't make her cry. 'Let's go and have a coffee.'

In the Starbucks concession on the ground floor it all comes out; Dasha's pleas for forgiveness or at least to know what she did wrong, Swati's insistence that she doesn't have time for friends at work, and then her new friendships which have left Dasha feeling excluded. I try to establish if there's any kind of actual bullying or exclusion happening, which might need official attention, but it seems not. But it's still obviously very upsetting.

'I'm sorry I didn't realize this was still an issue,' I say.

'It's all right. It probably sounds stupid,' Dasha says, blowing her nose on a recycled napkin. 'It's hard to explain why it's so bad.'

'You don't need to explain actually.' While she sips her skinny oat-milk latte, I tell her about the girls who dumped me in school, and how painful it felt at the time, far worse than any break-up I could imagine. 'And at least they told me why,' I add. 'Whereas it sounds like you haven't had that from Swati at all.'

'Exactly,' Dasha says. 'I just wish I knew why.'

'If I had to guess . . .' I pause, but she looks receptive, so I go on. 'Maybe it just got too intense? Maybe next time you make a new friend, try to focus on having fun together, not just talking about your problems. And try to cut people some slack. Nobody can be everything to you;

214

nobody's perfect. That's why it's good to have lots of different friends.' I finish my little homily, wondering if I'm making any sense or if I just sound like a fortune cookie.

But Dasha seems a bit calmer now, or somewhat reassured that she's not alone. 'Thank you for telling me – about your friends in school. It's good to know that it could even happen to someone like you – who has it all figured out.'

I laugh. 'Oh, I don't have it all figured out. But thanks. I'm working on it.'

As we go back upstairs, I reflect that, as traumatic as Hannah's death has been, to have been ghosted by a close friend is one kind of pain that I've been spared.

20

May

May contains two challenges: have afternoon tea somewhere fancy, and my birthday on the fifteenth. Your birthday is like a barometer of where you are in your life, and I knew this would be a tough one. It's my second birthday without Hannah, and I don't want a repeat of last year, when I just went to work, came home and watched TV with a takeaway. I feel like doing something very small, but I'm not sure who best to ask. It's not that I don't have friends in London; they're just not really the kind of friends I can text to do things at the last minute – or ask to an intimate birthday gathering. I suppose I could go and visit Vik but that seems a bit needy, especially as my birthday is on a weekday. My thoughts veer towards Eddie, but we're not there yet, if we'll ever be.

'What about the girls you were with at New Year's?' Mum asks when I speak to her on the phone.

'Sibéal? Of course . . . but she's literally about to have her baby. And Mel lives in Cambridge, so that's not very convenient for her . . .'

'Well, life's not just about convenience,' Mum says. 'I think if you reach out to them, they'll make the effort too. You're all wanting to support each other at the moment, I'd say.'

I blink at the phone. This is wise advice, but I've never known Mum to use the phrase 'reach out'.

'You can always just come home, you know,' she adds.

I love her for offering, but I don't exactly feel like doing that either.

'Thanks, Mum, but maybe I'll leave it till the summer, and I can come for a week?'

'Great,' says Mum. 'You can meet the new dog.'

'The what?'

'Oh, did I not say? We're adopting a greyhound – a retired one.'

'Seriously?' I'm almost as stunned as if she'd told me they were adopting a new kid. 'Well, congratulations!' I thought Mum was done with dogs when our red setter Rua died, but she said she and Dad have thought this over and have been mulling over breeds for months before swiping right on a retired greyhound currently residing in Arklow in County Wicklow. Feeling inspired, I tell her I'll text the girls and ask them about tea.

'Don't text them! Ring them,' she says. 'And did you say your challenge is afternoon tea? What about a birthday tea? What could be nicer? You should take the day off and make a day of it.'

'I will, Mum, that's a great idea.' I hang up the phone feeling tons better, and inspired by Mum's new attitude with both my birthday and her new dog. Maybe she has some resolutions of her own?

Mel and Sibéal are both are up for tea and can make it on the fifteenth. I'm trying to figure out a location that's going to be equally convenient for Mel, coming from

Cambridge, and Sibéal who's near her due date and understandably doesn't want to schlep around too far, but they tell me they'll look after it and book somewhere between them. I'm very touched by this, and I wake up on the morning of my thirty-seventh birthday feeling optimistic. I open the window and take a minute to feel the sunshine on my face and listen to the birdsong. It's properly spring now, and the chestnut tree behind my window is starting to glow green. It's a good day to be alive. I'm thirty-seven years old, and I'm healthy and wealthy – by most people's standards – and I have friends and family. I count every single one of my blessings, and then I go to my front door. Cards from my parents, from my brother Hugh – quite unusual, probably Mum had a word – from Vik (bless him), and lastly, to my surprise, flowers from Eddie. Yellow roses and freesias, all blowsy and cottagey, just the way he knows I like them. The card says, *Dear Celeste, Thinking of you today and hope you have a great birthday. Love, Eddie.* I look at it for a minute, then I put the bouquet in water, and go to put on one of my new outfits.

Sibéal and Mel are already at Brown's Hotel when I arrive at four o'clock, Mel in a white dress with a red flower tucked behind her ear, and Sibéal massive and glowing in a long yellow dress with a white trim. They both hug me and wish me a happy birthday as I sit down. I notice that Sibéal has a special hard-backed chair, while Mel and I are in comfortable squashy armchairs. I really hope Shib isn't too uncomfortable – she looks ready to pop – but she tells me she's thrilled to be out of the house and let Rishi do the kids' tea.

'Have you been at work today?' Mel asks.

'Nope,' I say. 'I had breakfast out in a cafe, then went for a swim, then had my nails done.' It's an ombre French manicure with lilac tips. I'm not certain how they will go down at work, but if it's anything like my new outfit, they can't hurt.

'Celeste, I have literally never seen you with nails like that in my life,' Sibéal says. 'And the dress! I love it.'

We catch up on our various bits of news, including my resolutions. Sibéal is thrilled that I was happy with the astrologer and says she might do a birth chart for the new baby. Mel says she likes the sound of climbing and possibly the personal stylist, though we both tell her she doesn't need one.

'Are you still doing the hot yoga?' Sibéal asks.

'Not as much,' I admit. 'Not now that it's hotter. I'm doing Couch to 5k instead to train for Hyde Park.' I explain that 'Go jogging in Hyde Park' is another upcoming item on the list. Hannah certainly did like a workout.

'Did you get nice presents?' Mel asks, once we've exhausted the resolutions.

'Not presents as such, just cards. One from my brother, which I think is a first . . . I think my mum possibly had a word.' I pause before adding casually, 'Oh, and I had flowers from Eddie. We're back in touch.'

'Really!' says Mel.

'Hm,' says Sibéal.

The tea arrives at this moment and there's lots of theatre with pouring it – Earl Grey for Mel, camomile for Sibéal and Darjeeling for me, because I want to try something different. I realize how much I've needed this – just this time with female friends, and not just any friends but people who've known me for so many years. I don't have to catch them up on what happened in previous episodes. I can just be.

'So, tell us, what's the story with Eddie?' Sibéal asks.

I take a deep breath. 'I will tell you guys – I'm interested to know what you think – but first I want to make a toast.' I lift my cup. 'To Hannah.'

We all clink cups and again I feel the relief of not having to explain.

The savoury sandwiches are arriving now in cute little tiered trays: perfect little oblongs of white bread with various dainty fillings plus some tiny mini quiches and tarts.

'So,' Sibéal says, 'Eddie?'

I tell them briefly that he's been in touch and how things have changed with him.

'He said he's done counselling?' Mel says, and I nod. 'But it doesn't sound like he has any other kind of issues . . . like any other kind of addiction issues or anything more significant?'

'Not that I know of . . . He did say that he felt really inadequate when his salary became lower than mine. And he was spending to keep up with me. Which was a killer because none of that mattered to me . . .'

'So what does he want now?' Sibéal says, in the blunt way she sometimes has. 'Another chance?'

'Oh, no, nothing like that,' I say. 'We're just friends.'

They exchange glances and Mel says, 'I don't know, honestly, Celeste. You have enough friends, don't you?'

'Well, not really,' I say truthfully, thinking of my agonies over who to invite today.

'Let's be real. I'm guessing he wants to get back together. Would you contemplate that?' Sibéal asks.

I'm about to say of course not, but honesty makes me pause. 'I don't know. Maybe. But would that be wise? What do you guys think?'

'It all depends on what the rest of your relationship was like,' says Sibéal. 'You guys always seemed very solid. Did you feel like you could trust him in other ways?'

I don't even have to think about it; I nod.

'Well, maybe he deserves a second chance,' says Sibéal. 'But it needs to be on your terms, at a pace you're comfortable with. Oof.' She stands up awkwardly. 'I've been dying for the loo; I just didn't want to miss hearing about Eddie. I'll be back.'

She makes her way to the bathroom while Mel and I watch her, and I think how exhausting it looks to be her right now and what a trouper she is for coming out.

'Well, it's good for Eddie that he's in a better place, as they say,' Mel says. 'Regardless of what happens with you both.'

'Definitely,' I agree. 'Anyway, I don't want to go on about Eddie . . . What's new with you?'

'Oh, that's right, you haven't heard,' she says. 'I was just telling Shib before you arrived. I've got a new job – based in London – so I'm moving back here.'

My shriek of joy causes a few heads to turn around, even in the muffled surroundings of this dining room.

'Sorry,' I say immediately. 'But that's great news! I'm so happy you're coming back! What's the job?'

'Thanks!' she says, smiling. 'It's another publisher. I'll be near my family, that's the main reason . . . and also I've kind of done Cambridge. I want a change of scene.'

'Where will you be – north, south, east or west?' I say this with some trepidation, because to be perfectly honest if Mel moves to south London, she might as well still be in Cambridge for all I'll see her.

'I think north because the new company is based in Euston Road.'

'Amazing! So you might be near me! That's great news.' I'm thrilled; having an old friend living nearby will be absolutely life-changing. As the waiter clears away the sandwich dishes, we start discussing the pros and cons of various areas, with me putting in a very strong case for Islington or Hackney.

'No, please come to Queen's Park,' says Shib, who's come back to the table now. 'I'm so lonely now. All my mum friends are leaving London and I'm too tired to make new ones.'

'I'll make sure I'm on the overground,' says Mel, referring to the train that goes to Sibéal's neck of the woods.

'Are you really stuck for company?' I ask, and she nods. 'I'm sorry. I can come and see you any weekend, but I suppose weekdays are when you need it.'

'They are a bit, honestly,' says Shib.

'Well, I can take some Fridays off this summer,' I tell her. 'I'm not really planning any big trips, so I can come and see you.'

'Would you really?' Shib says. 'I'd love that.' She perks up and I feel very pleased. 'Are you sure that will be OK with work?'

'It should be,' I say, thinking of my recent wins. I don't want to blow my own trumpet, but I think the signs are looking good for a promotion this year.

'Are you all right for time, darling?' Mel asks, as Shib checks the time on her phone.

'I'm fine.' Her face contorts briefly, and then she grins. 'I'm great actually – that was a second contraction, so that's exciting. Hang on till I reset the timer properly.'

Mel and I gasp in unison, putting down our teacups.

'Oh my God! Should I call Rishi? Or an ambulance?' I ask.

'Shouldn't we take you to the hospital?' asks Mel.

Sibéal laughs. 'Are you joking? Six minutes apart. They'd sent me home. I always have these stop-start labours. It took three days with Lorcan. Anyway, you know I'm having a home birth. I've texted my doula. Be grand.'

'Have you texted Rishi?' Mel asks.

'I will in a sec. The cakes are coming, look.' The waiter comes and puts them all out, watched by an eagle-eyed Shib. 'Ooh! Fabulous.' She hooks herself a miniature pink-and-yellow Battenberg slice.

Mel and I look at each other, clearly wondering if we should do some kind of intervention. Seeing us, Shib says, 'It's not like the movies, honestly, girls. It will take forever, and I'm not missing these cakes.' She attacks a little chocolate truffle slice. 'This could be the last time I'll get to eat something with both hands in eight weeks.'

There's no point in me or Mel saying anything; she's on baby number three and obviously knows what she's doing. But it would be a lie to say that we're completely relaxed, and we both keep half an eye on Sibéal as we cautiously eat our cakes.

'Oh my gosh,' Mel says. 'I almost forgot. We got you something . . .'

They produce a little gift-wrapped package that contains a jade roller and a silk pillowcase. 'It's great for wrinkles,' Shib says. 'I mean, not that you have any but for preventing them. And great for the hair too.'

'Thank you both very much,' I say. 'I'm so glad we did this. It makes me really happy.'

'Happy birthday, Celeste,' says Mel, lifting her cup.

'Happiest of happy birthdays, darling,' says Shib. 'I hope it's a fabulous year for you. I think it will be, you know. I've got a feeling. Ouch!' She looks down and sets the timer again. 'Sorry, I didn't mean to ruin the moment.'

'You didn't! But maybe we should get you a taxi.' I can't help laughing and we are all laughing now.

'OK, so,' says Sibéal. 'And I will text Rishi. But full labour won't be for be least another forty-eight hours, I can promise you that.'

Sibéal's prediction is only partly true. Baby Iseult Hannah Shah is born at 9.37 p.m. the following evening, weighing 4.4 kilos and measuring 54 centimetres. I look at the squashed little face, feeling all the bittersweet feelings about her middle name, thinking that this is another milestone that Hannah will miss – another marker of how her life is becoming part of the past. But it's also a little miracle, a new life, something from nothing. It's wonderful. I text Shib a row of heart emojis and go online to find something to send her. I'm thinking frozen food or brownies rather than flowers. Although, as I glance at my bouquet from Eddie, I think flowers can also be lovely.

21

'Happy birthday, Celeste!' Gemma says the next day at work, handing me a card. I'm very touched, especially since I don't tend to announce it, but Gemma is one of those people who are good with birthdays and she holds a spreadsheet for everyone's big day.

'Isobel was looking for you – she said she had good news.'

'Oh. Really? Thanks, Gem.' You don't want to keep good news or your boss waiting, so I decide to go and check this out right away. Is it possible that this is the good news I've been hoping for – that this is when I finally get made director? But I won't get my hopes up. I stand up and smooth down my pencil skirt, which I'm wearing with a new sleeveless blouse and – daringly – yesterday's pink flats. It's another beautiful sunny day so the blind is down in her office. She doesn't seem to be here, so I wait for a minute, looking around. It must be nice for Isobel that she has her own desk, with a triangular name bar with Isobel Chan in gold letters, and family photos. It makes me think that, almost more than the money or recognition, what I'd really love would be to have my own office – a room of one's own.

Isobel comes in at this point, carrying a mug of green tea. 'Thanks for waiting! Happy birthday for yesterday. Did you do anything nice?'

'Thank you. Yes, I went for afternoon tea.' Isobel gestures for me to sit.

'Was it a big birthday?' she asks and I reply, 'Not really. Thirty-seven.'

'Oh!' she says. 'I thought you were much younger for some reason.'

I smile a thank you, though somehow this feels like less of a compliment than it was coming from John Henry. Isobel continues, 'You're the same age as me now! I'm thirty-eight in November.'

'Ah!' I say, taken aback. I had assumed she was older, but I can't say that obviously. 'Great age to be!'

'Yes!' says Isobel. It's all feeling a bit awkward so I'm relieved when she continues. 'Anyway. I just wanted to say – we're all so impressed by all your work lately. You've really been going the extra mile with all your clients – even the unconventional ones like Effie. And the less co-operative ones.' She smiles, and I know she's talking about the Footlove people. 'You've built up a really impressive head of steam, so it's time for that to be recognized. So . . .' She pauses.

I'm quiet, not daring to hope for what might be next. *So you are being promoted to director with immediate effect.*

'I'm putting you forward for a Chairman's Award.'

'Oh gosh. Thank you.' I feel a momentary swoop of disappointment before I tell myself: *This is still good. It's great!* They're not awarded that often, and I think you get a glass ornament of some kind with your name engraved on it.

'Of course it needs to be approved by the board. Though between you and me I don't see any obstacles.

You've been with us long enough, haven't you – you're hardly fly-by-night.'

We both laugh, and I agree. 'Not exactly.'

'How long have you been here actually? Remind me.'

'It will be fifteen years next month. I joined on the graduate recruitment scheme.'

'My goodness. Fifteen years! That's incredible. Well, don't forget to claim your gift. It should already be up on your HR portal.'

I make suitable noises, adding, 'Thanks again, Isobel. I appreciate the support.'

'Not at all. And have fun choosing your gift. Fifteen years!' she adds, shaking her head.

I walk out of her office, feeling that this wasn't the complete morale boost I might have hoped for – like a promotion or a raise. The Chairman's Award: what is it but a glorified High Five? Plus, the discovery that Isobel is my age makes me feel even more inadequate. But then I remind myself how fortunate I am comparatively speaking, especially in this age of zero-hours contracts and crappy wages. A promotion will, hopefully, still come; I just have to be patient. Though I hope it won't take another fifteen years.

Back at my desk, I log into my HR portal to investigate my special loyalty prize. It turns out to be a link to a website with a range of gifts to choose from, including a silver watch, a food processor, or – left-field – a chainsaw. I can already claim it, even though my official anniversary isn't until next month; they must be pretty confident that I'm staying.

'Ooh,' says Gemma, appearing behind me. 'Is this for your WBC birthday? Decisions, decisions. What are you going to opt for? You know you can claim cash instead. That's what I would do.'

'I know,' I say. That would be the sensible option, of course. Normally I wouldn't even think twice about it. Except that I'm getting a bit tired of the sensible option. Before I can overthink it, I click on my gift of choice and press 'select'.

'A chainsaw?' says Gemma. 'Did you press that by mistake? I'm sure they'll let you change your mind if you need to.'

'No, it's OK,' I say. 'I'm going to give it to a friend.'

That Friday the good news is confirmed; I got the Chairman's Award. An email goes around and people are very kind, saying congratulations. Dasha buys me a special card that plays Beyoncé when you open it. And I get an email saying my Perspex trophy is being engraved with my name, and asking me to confirm the spelling. I leave work at six on the dot and go to meet Eddie in one of our old haunts: a rooftop bar in one of the hotels near Liverpool Street.

'So are you on a high?' he asks cheerfully, coming back from the bar. 'Are you going to display your trophy on your desk?'

'Well, we hot-desk, as you know, so I don't know what to do with it. I suppose I could keep it in my locker.' This reminds me of my chat with Isobel and how it left me feeling a bit deflated, and I end up telling Eddie about it.

'I know I should be happy but . . . if I'm not being made director after fifteen years, maybe I will never be,' I admit.

'So would you consider leaving?'

'I could, but I think I'd be much better off doing that at director level; it would give me a much wider range of options. Anyway, blah blah. I'll stop going on.' I take a sip of my Prosecco, thinking that life can't be so bad if I'm sitting here on a hot evening with cold fizz in a sunny rooftop bar with a garden.

'No, no. It's important stuff,' Eddie says earnestly. 'Look, why don't you speak to her explicitly about the promotion? Tell her that you'd like to know what you need to do. Then you can give it another year, or whatever you think is reasonable – and then jump ship.'

'You're right, Eddie. I will.'

'But don't discount how far you've come. I mean, to have that kind of longevity and staying power – a steady income and a good pension too – well, it's not nothing.'

'Thanks, Ed.' I smile at him, remembering how much I loved this about him; he was always so supportive.

'Also,' he adds, 'you did go through something very similar to this before being made associate director. You were convinced it was never going to happen. "I've been there forever! I'm part of the furniture!"'

'Oh, God!' I'm mortified but laughing. 'I'm sorry – was I? How boring.'

'It wasn't boring,' he says. 'Never boring. Also, I just want to say you certainly look like a director. Or a boss anyway. I like the nails.'

'Do you really?' I glance down at my manicure. 'It was out of my comfort zone. Not too much?'

'Not at all. When I was back home, I dated a woman who was very into her nails – the whole thing, jewels and art – it was pretty but a bit much for me.'

'Fair enough.' It's funny to hear about him dating other people; though of course I can't expect him to have stayed single for the last two years, like I did.

'Was that weird that I said that? Sorry if it was.'

'Not at all,' I say, echoing his words.

'Anyway,' he says, raising his glass. 'Here's to your Chairman's Award, and your fifteen-year award – and, drum roll, we almost forgot: your birthday! Come on. Life's not so bad.'

'Of course it's not,' I say, clinking his glass. 'Life is good. Life is great.' I smile at him, feeling grateful for the reminder.

22

June

One of the many surprises this year is that Scottish ceilidh dancing, which I thought would be a niche pursuit
like basket weaving, is actually wildly popular, to the
extent that tickets sell out within a few hours of them
being released a fortnight in advance of each event,
which runs monthly. In an attempt to get organized I
create the obligatory WhatsApp group and offer to book
tickets for everyone at the same time. Vik and Mel are
definites, and Vik invites Patrick and Angelika, who also
say yes. After a minute's hesitation, I add Eddie. I am
sure Vik will be surprised to see Eddie's name on the list,
as I never got around to telling him we were back in
touch; but I decide that the best approach is not to make
it a big deal.

'A ceilidh?' says Mum in bewilderment, when I tell her
my plans for the weekend. 'Why on earth would you go to
London for that? You have them down the road in Com-
haltas in Monkstown, every Friday.'

'Maybe we'll go together next time I come back.'

'That would be brilliant, Celeste,' she says. 'And we'll
have the dog by then!'

As I hang up, I realize that I'm enjoying our chats so
much more now that I have things to tell her. Like my

arrangement to see Shib on the first Friday of every month, it's the simplest thing but it's made a big difference.

The evening of the ceilidh is warm and sunny – it's late spring, right on the cusp of summer. Walking from the tube at Chalk Farm, I find myself noticing the soft acid-green leaves of the chestnut and the purple wisteria hanging over the beautiful Regency houses that lead to Cecil Sharp House, the venue, where crowds are already gathering for their ceilidh fix.

The atmosphere reminds me of when I went to the climbing centre back in February. People are maybe less sporty here, but there's the same slightly alternative vibe. Every man here seems to have a T-shirt displaying some niche interest, with an emphasis on real ale and obscure folk bands like the Spooky Men's Chorale. My memories of ceilidhs in Irish college are that you get incredibly hot, almost hot-yoga hot, and so I'm wearing a short red summer dress splashed with daisies and my most comfortable shoes. Plus a sports bra; those springy steps can take their toll.

I soon spot Mel and Vik, who've obviously just met in the foyer too, and we all head down to the cellar bar to get a pre-dance round in. Mel looks as stunning as ever in a white sleeveless top and jeans, her ever-present flower tucked behind her ears. Vik is also looking very smart in a new pink polo shirt and jeans, with a sharp new haircut. He looks healthy and outdoorsy, and there's a new definition in his arms that I'm not sure was there before.

'You look like you've been training to be a new Marvel superhero,' Mel says, squeezing his arm.

'It's all from doing the garden,' he says. 'Speaking of

which, I want to do another weekend there next month. For my birthday. Are you both free – first weekend in July?'

'Oh yes, definitely.' I pull out my handbag and write in my diary, which is looking a lot fuller these days. 'I'll be seeing Shib on the Friday, but I can come straight after that.'

'Or they can drive you down. The garden's looking fabulous – let me show you some pictures.' He gets out his phone.

'By the way,' I say as casually as I can, 'Eddie's coming along.'

Vik raises his eyebrows. 'So it's that Eddie? I couldn't tell from the WhatsApp pic . . . Good stuff.'

'Really?' I say, because I do care what Vik thinks.

'Of course. I always liked him,' says Vik, smiling.

'Hey, is that him now?' says Mel.

It is Eddie, wearing a smart shirt and shorts – I warned him it was going to be really hot, and he's obviously remembered. Most men look like little boys in shorts, but he has pretty good legs, it has to be said.

'Have you celiidhed before?' Eddie asks Mel and Vik, who both shake their heads.

'Let's get up there before we lose our nerve,' suggests Mel.

'What about Patrick, should we wait for him?' I ask.

'No,' says Vik, looking at his phone. 'He's with Angelika and they're having drama apparently.'

'Drama?' I ask.

'Something about a flatmate, or maybe a cat? I'm really not across the details,' says Vik. 'Come on, let's do it.'

The heat hits us like a brick wall as we walk into the

main hall, a huge room with windows a dozen feet high. The windows are open, but the heat is coming from the crowd; about a hundred people, who are already in the midst of a complicated reel of some kind. The ceilidh band are playing on their platform, and their caller, a girl in a short tartan skirt, is calling out instructions over the music, which some groups are following better than others. We mill around, not sure where to go, until Eddie spots some tiered seats to the side and suggests we wait there till the next dance begins. We all follow him, grateful for the leadership.

'Now everyone into groups of eight, please, for Gay Gordons,' says the caller.

I'm very glad I didn't come on my own; it's tricky enough for us to get a quorum for our Gay Gordons. Vik ends up charming two couples off the seating area, and then the caller talks us through the practice dance.

'Couples, join right hands over the lady's shoulder – left hands join in front.' Eddie smiles at me while we loop ourselves together as instructed. 'Thanks for roping me into this,' he says. There's no time to reply, because we're walking through the practice dance; go forward four steps, pivot, pivot, repeat . . . It takes all my concentration to follow the steps, but Eddie seems to know what to do, and keeps us from getting tangled up, much to my relief. It's so much fun to be in a room full of people all moving in unison – or almost in unison. One of our couples keeps on going forward when they're meant to be moving backwards, but no harm is done and we all finish up more or less in one piece, applauding madly when the song ends.

'Hey, there they are. Patrick! Over here,' says Vik.

We all turn round and beckon them over. Angelika is following along behind Patrick, wearing a long black dress and high heels that look like they might do her a damage during the barn dances. Patrick is more casual, in jeans and a T-shirt. They make a stunning couple, but he looks weary.

'I'm sorry we're late,' he says.

'Is everything OK?' Vik asks.

Angelika replies, 'I had an argument with my flatmate. I want to get a cat and he's saying no because we don't have a garden. So I've found an indoor cat we could adopt, but he still won't say yes, so I'm thinking I should just bring the cat home anyway and let him deal with it.'

'Oh dear. I wouldn't do that,' says Vik.

'It is his place,' Patrick points out, possibly not for the first time from his tone.

The caller is shouting out for us all to take our partners for Strip the Willow.

'Are you all right to join or do you want a drink first?' Patrick asks Angelika.

'Do they have apple juice?' she asks.

'I highly doubt it,' says Vik. 'Cider, maybe? Well, I'm doing Strip the Willow – you guys join when you want.' And he takes Mel's hand and leads her on to the floor. She's so graceful; all her years of tango are apparent even in the way she walks. After some negotiation, Angelika agrees to take part so we all form a big group with some others.

'Shall we, madam?' Eddie asks me, and I nod. Strip the Willow is great fun and easy enough; it's one of those ones where you twirl up and down the two lines, taking turns to be 'first lady' and 'top couple'. The beat of the music, the sound of the accordion and the movement are all so exhilarating; I'm smiling at Eddie as we come together and whirl up and down again, and marvelling at how sure-footed he is.

'You're really great at this,' I shout into his ear, and he looks pleased.

Angelika is less into it; she keeps checking her phone and typing furiously, with the result that when it's her turn to be 'first lady', she keeps cannoning into the person opposite and causing a pile-up.

Strip the Willow is followed by a barn dance, which is more like *Chicken Run*, with everybody losing the plot at different moments, though it's still great fun. Then we get ambitious with the Military Two-Step, which is fiendishly difficult for the first eight bars; I almost get tangled up with the couple in front, but, again, Eddie seems to know the steps, I can't think how, and steers me straight. Patrick and Angelika soon give up and head off to the bar. Vik and Melanie are doing very well; she's a natural at any kind of dance. But the star of the show – to my amazement – is Eddie, who doesn't get lost once and keeps us all in line right up to the very last twirl.

'Eddie, you were amazing,' I say, in astonishment. 'Have you been practising or something?'

He just says with a wink, 'Not my first rodeo. Do you want a drink?'

'Yes please,' I say gratefully, and we go downstairs to the cellar bar, leaving Mel and Vik dancing like they're in the *Strictly* quarter-finals. I notice Patrick and Angelika in a corner of the bar having an intense discussion. Angelika looks extremely agitated, presumably over the cat issue, and Patrick seems to be trying to calm her down.

'Should we join them, or . . .?' Eddie looks dubious.

'Oh, God, no. Let's sit at the bar,' I suggest, not wanting to get involved.

Eddie gets me a glass of wine, as requested, and a lemonade – so thoughtful.

'Aaah,' I say. 'So good. So, Eddie, how on earth did you know all those dances?'

He smiles. 'Nothing to it. Just a few private dancing lessons . . .'

'What?' I say, before realizing that he's pulling my leg.

We're still laughing when we're conscious of a commotion in the corner of the pub; Angelika is hurrying outside, closely followed by Patrick.

'I feel like we're in a play,' says Eddie. 'Is this still, um, Catgate?'

'Or Flatgate. Yes, I suppose so. Or maybe there's more to it? It all seems . . . complicated.'

Eddie shakes his head. 'I'm kind of done with complicated. Aren't you?'

'I really am,' I say, realizing how true this is.

Patrick reappears a minute later, looking distinctly ruffled.

Eddie offers to get him a drink and he asks sadly for a pint of lager.

'Everything OK?' I ask.

He tries to smile. 'It's fine. Just a slight difference in views over, you know, adopting a cat without your flatmate's consent.'

'Is she going to do it?' Eddie asks, looking alarmed.

'I've told her not to. But who knows.' He takes a long sip of his pint. 'Thanks, man,' he adds to Eddie. Normally I think he'd be making more effort to get to know Eddie but he seems utterly distracted. 'Sorry about that. She's had a tough week at work. And she's convinced this cat's on death row, though I've told her it's not.'

'Well, if it is on death row . . .' I say.

'It's not on death row.' Patrick sounds as if he's already said this many, many times.

Vik and Mel rejoin us at this point, having conquered something called the Circassian Circle. 'It was harder than it looks,' Mel says. 'You were doing great, though, Eddie. Have you been to one of these before?'

'Yes. My parents used to drag us to this kind of thing all the time,' he says.

'Of course!' I say. 'That's how you knew all the dances! I'm sorry, Eddie. I hope it didn't bring back terrible memories.'

Eddie shivers. 'Just had a flashback,' he says in mock-dramatic tones. 'Sidmouth Festival, 1995. Our campsite was on a slope. It rained so much we ended up at the bottom of the hill in a lake of mud . . .'

'Oh, God, yes – I remember! Tell them about the Appalachian clog dancing!'

Soon Eddie has us all in fits, with stories of his family camping trips and visits to obscure festivals. It's so funny and I'm grateful to him for lifting the mood. Even Patrick seems to forget Angelika and her cat-related troubles, though I notice him checking his phone a few more times, before putting it away with a resigned face that doesn't bode well for their relationship.

We end up staying in the bar until closing time, after which everyone heads in different directions: Patrick to go home alone, Mel to her new place in Finchley Road, and Vik to stay with a friend in Camden.

Eddie walks me to the tube. 'That was fun,' he says, as we say goodbye. 'Thanks for asking me out with your friends. It was nice to see them all again.'

I smile again, thinking of his funny stories. 'Thanks for coming. I'm sorry if it gave you flashbacks.'

'I wouldn't have missed it for the world.'

We walk on in silence for a minute, neither of us sure what to say next. 'Are you going away anywhere this summer?' he asks.

'Just Dublin. It's been a while since I was home. How about you?'

'I'm going walking in the Peak District with some mates,' he says. 'Rich – remember him? – he's going to borrow his auntie's cottage.'

I am impressed; he has changed – no more trips to Ibiza or Paris, all on his credit card.

Eddie continues, 'Maybe we could go for dinner next week? Or the cinema, or something . . . whatever you want.'

'Yeah, sure. Let's do that.'

We're outside the tube now, caught in the stream of the Friday-night crowd of clubbers and pubgoers, so different from the suited and booted crowds I usually commute with. One of them pushes too close to me, and I'm nudged towards Eddie. He catches me and steadies me, and then – I don't know how it happens – my arms are reaching up around his neck and we're kissing.

He leans his forehead against mine, looking down at me questioningly.

I hadn't planned any of this, and I'm about to express some reservations, but then I just kiss him again. It's been so long; it still feels so good. He kisses me back, and his arms around me are as sure and confident as his dancing earlier.

'I've been wanting to do this all evening,' he says after a minute. 'Is this OK? I'm not rushing you?'

'No, no . . . Can we take it slow, though?' I'm breathless and happy but suddenly afraid of taking this next step.

'Of course. I'm not going anywhere,' Eddie says.

23

July

I've learned by now that change doesn't happen over-night; it's a slow process with twists and turns, fits and starts, and sometimes it's only when I look back that I realize it's happened at all. I've seen Vik's place in pictures, since I was here in March – the brambles and weeds being cleared, the fruit trees blossoming, and the roses coming into bloom – but it's only now that I'm actually here that I can see how dramatic the changes have been. The garden, which was so sad and lifeless, is now a riot of colour, the flower beds, shrubs and trees all bursting with life. And the moat has been completely cleared of brambles; Vik and Patrick have spent many weekends working on it.

'It's like a different place,' I say to Mel. We've travelled up together by train, reading magazines and eating Minstrels; Vik picked us up at the station and is now locking up his car.

It's a beautiful day: not too hot and with a light breeze. We walk up to the house, now covered in scaffolding for the famous render. The giant iron knocker, which was previously hanging sadly, has been polished and rehung. Vik opens the door up for us, and I gasp when I see inside; the place looks so different. Gone is the weird old flock wallpaper and the faded floral curtains; it's been stripped down to what I presume is the original plasterwork, and heavy cream linen curtains hang at each window.

'My mum's work,' Vik explains. 'She's very handy with the sewing machine.'

He shows us to our rooms upstairs; we're both in the attic this time, as he's got a full house.

'So you weren't tempted to invite Eddie?' Mel asks me, when she comes to check out my room.

I shake my head. We've seen each other a few times since the ceilidh, and I did consider asking him along, but he had a stag party to attend, which I think is probably for the best. Things have been going so well between us I don't want to spoil them by rushing it.

'Patrick is flying solo too,' Mel says. 'He and Angelika are done apparently.'

'Oh dear. Do you know why?' I ask.

Mel just looks at me, and we both start to laugh.

'Yeah, OK. She was hard work,' I agree. 'I wonder what happened with the cat.'

'Oh, she got him. She's moved flats and got the cat. So a happy ending for everyone.'

'Even Patrick?'

Mel shakes her head. 'I don't know . . . But Vik says all his girlfriends are a bit like that, so who knows.'

We go back downstairs to rejoin Vik in the kitchen. On the way I notice some of Vik and Hannah's old furniture is still in evidence – like Hannah's grey velvet sofa – but the broken old stuff from the tenants has been replaced with handsome antiques that Vik has picked up from auctions and junk shops, including an upholstered chaise longue in the drawing room and some comfortable-looking chintzy armchairs and sofas. Instead of the tulip table, there's a proper old-fashioned kitchen table in the kitchen, and snoozing on top is a little black cat called Meatloaf, who Vik says has recently adopted him – appearing one rainy night like a bat out of hell, hence the name.

'The great thing is that he's scared of the chickens – which is lucky,' Vik says. 'Come on out – meet the girls.'

He opens the door to the back garden, where his hens come clucking to meet us: Boudicca, Victoria, Elizabeth, Mary, Maeve and Grace O'Malley.

'Do you want to feed them?' Vik gives me some seed, and I hold out my hand; they all come over giving such sweet nuzzling, cooing sounds that I find myself asking, 'They're not for dinner, are they?'

'Shh! Cover your ears, Boudicca!' Vik says, picking one up. 'No, of course not. Layers only. Oh, here comes trouble.'

It's Sigmund, obviously, who's spotted the seed; he comes snaking along towards us, stretching out his long serpentine neck. I feel sorry for him and throw him a handful, as far away as possible.

'Hi, Celeste,' says a voice, coming around the side entrance from the drive.

It's Patrick. I haven't seen him since the ceilidh, and my immediate thought is that he looks much more relaxed; hopefully the break-up with Angelika hasn't hit him too hard. He's also very tanned, and his fair hair seems even brighter from the sun. He's not in his gardening gear for once, but smartly dressed in linen trousers and a dark blue shirt that brings out the blue in his eyes.

'Someone looks pleased to see you,' Vik says, coming up behind me. I'm confused for a second before I see he's referring to the swan, who's lingering near me, hoping for more seeds.

'Look at that,' says Patrick. 'You're a regular bird whisperer.'

'I'm still not turning my back on him.' I brush down my hands on my denim shorts and T-shirt, feeling very scruffy in comparison to both men. 'Congrats on the moat by the way. It's looking very clear.'

'We should be able to keep the Saxon raiders out now,' says Patrick.

'Yes!' says Vik. 'The next step will be to fill it, but we have to dredge the pond first. I've just had a meeting with a hydraulics engineer. Which is a life goal I never knew I had.'

I'm about to ask him more about this, when we're distracted by the arrival of Vik's parents, who've just driven all the way from Reigate in Surrey. Shib and Rishi are on their way too, with all three kids. We all split up along predictable lines: Vik's dad immediately wants a good look at the scaffolding, accompanied by Patrick and Vik, while Amrit, Vik's mum, brings in a Victoria sponge that she's made for his birthday. Like Vik, she's a person of many enthusiasms, and baking is one of them lucky for us.

'How are you, darling?' she asks, giving me a hug, and greeting Mel.

'I was just admiring your curtains, Mrs Chandra,' says Mel.

Amrit looks pleased and soon she and Mel are discussing fabrics and dressmaking. Then they move on to tablecloths, and I show both of them the present I got for Vik: a large gong to summon his guests for dinner. We're just discussing what flowers to have for the table, when Shib and Rishi's car arrives. Rishi opens the car and the two kids erupt from it, Lorcan making a beeline for the chickens before Rishi manages to catch him. Síofra, who is four, comes over to me for a high five. She used to be very shy of me but since I've been visiting more regularly, we've become pals.

'Lorcan got very frustrated in the car,' she tells me.

I smile to myself but I'm not surprised; she is a real parrot with an incredible vocabulary. 'Oh dear,' I say. 'How about you?'

'I'm hot,' she says. 'Mummy was encouraging me to wear these long sleeves – what was she thinking?'

'I'll help you find something to change into,' I offer.

We go over to the car where Shib is unpacking little Iseult, the new baby, from the back seat. I know that she's been worried about putting the baby seat in the back with the two bigger kids, but short of having her six-year-old sit up front there's no other option.

'A new top? Yes, sure, try that bag. Thanks, Celeste.' She looks utterly exhausted, but as glamorous as ever in a long green dress that's smarter than most of my wardrobe, her hair in a fishtail side braid that I wouldn't attempt even for a formal occasion. She cradles the baby carefully, carrying her to the table that's been put out for Vik's birthday tea, under the chestnut trees.

'A swan! Look Daddy, a swan!' yells little Lorcan, who's just spotted Sigmund. The swan, scenting danger, flaps off towards the pond. 'Get him! Get him!' Lorcan begs.

'I've got a better idea,' says Vik, appearing and clapping his hands. 'Would you kids like to pick some cherries?'

Síofra seems tempted, and looks to her big brother for confirmation, but Lorcan says, 'No thank you,' and races off around the lawn doing aeroplane noises, before returning to chase the swan.

'Thanks for trying,' Rishi says wearily, heading off to catch him.

'Rishi, where are the muslins?' Shib asks plaintively.

'Argh,' he says, torn between her and the kids.

'Not to worry,' says Vik. 'I'll watch the kids. How about football, guys? They're about my level,' he adds to Rishi.

Mel offers to make tea for everyone and soon we're all sitting down with Vik's parents, watching the men play football with the two kids. Amrit asks Shib all about the baby while Dr Chandra chats to me and Mel about his favourite spots in Suffolk – we still haven't been to Sutton Hoo or Snape Maltings, which sounds very appealing, with a cafe, outdoor sculptures and concerts in the summer. Shib says she'd like to go back to the Latitude Festival, near Southwold, where she heard Ed Sheeran play a surprise set once.

'It's a bit different from their place in Hackney, isn't it?' I ask Vik's dad, smiling.

'Oh, much nicer,' he says immediately. 'And the parking is free.'

We all laugh. Watching the two kids run rings around Patrick and Vik under the chestnut trees with their candles in full bloom, it's hard to imagine a more idyllic scene. Dr Chandra's expression is thoughtful, and I wonder if he's thinking about his own father, and his experiences in the war, and the strange chain of events that has brought his son to live here.

'Do you know what this place really needs?' he says suddenly, gesturing towards the lawn with his teacup. We all turn to him, expecting a dad-like observation about CCTV cameras or a cattle grid.

'What?' says Vik's mum.

'A croquet lawn,' he says, smiling. 'Then it will be perfect.'

Shortly after this, Vik takes his parents inside to view the engineer's plans for the moat, and Shib goes inside with the baby, leaving the rest of us outside with the kids.

'Congratulations,' I hear Síofra tell Rishi. 'You are now the big daddy, who gets to look after *all* the children.'

'Thanks, honey,' Rishi says.

'Let's try another game,' Patrick suggests. 'Kids, have you never played rugby? Rishi, what are you teaching them? Pity we don't have some tags or we could play tag rugby.'

'We can improvise some tags,' I suggest. 'Here, let's use paper napkins.' I thread a few through my belt, with Patrick watching me in surprise.

'I didn't think of you as a tag rugby fan.'

'Why not? I am from Dublin,' I tell him. 'Mel, are you in? Let's do girls against boys.'

What follows is definitely not a classic tag rugby game, but the kids enjoy the chasing and they get the basic idea of grabbing the 'tags', attacking and defending, even if said tags keep ripping to shreds and floating away across the lawn.

'I got a try!' Síofra shrieks and we all high-five her.

'Good woman. You've mastered tag rugby. Next step . . . the tackle!' Without a word of warning Patrick swoops on to me, picks me up and carries me, kicking and yelling, towards the try line. I expect him to drop me any second but he keeps going.

'Put me down! You swine,' I say, convulsed with laughter. 'Kids, this is not in the rules!'

'OK,' he says, obediently tipping me down. I glance at the others, but they're distracted by Lorcan, who's been methodically tearing up his tags and scattering them across the lawn. Looking back up at Patrick, I see that his breath is still coming quick and hard, sweat beading his brow; he's smiling down at me triumphantly. Our faces are close. Without quite knowing that I'm doing it, I put a hand on his chest, and feel its warmth for a second before I push him back.

'Sorry. Very unsporting of me,' he says. His smile is fading to a puzzled then almost an embarrassed look.

'Penalty to us,' I say, to try to dispel any awkwardness. 'Where's the ref?'

But the game seems to have dissolved; Lorcan and Síofra are now chasing butterflies with Mel, and Rishi is on the phone.

'I think that's the game over,' I say. I wipe my hands and untuck my paper napkin tags from my belt, folding them and stowing them in my pocket. Patrick nods and turns around to watch the others. I'm not sure what just happened there, but I feel a sudden urge to hand him an olive branch so he knows I'm not annoyed. 'I might go and get some of those famous wild cherries,' I add casually. 'Any idea where they are?'

248

'I'll show you,' he says. 'Just wait a minute.'

A few minutes later, he comes back from the house with a couple of buckets, a pair of secateurs and two pairs of garden gloves.

'So why wild cherries? Is there something wrong with the cherries we planted?' I ask, as we set off.

'The maidens? Nothing, they just won't fruit for another two years at least. But they're doing so well – remember the blossom back in the spring?'

'Sure.' That seems a lifetime ago, though it was only five months. As we pass the 'maidens' as Patrick calls them, I see that the blossom has faded. They look like ordinary little green bushes now and I feel an obscure sense of disappointment. But then, round another bend, we come to another patch that's humming with life and colour. I stand for a minute, looking at the dazzling display of blues and purples, and watch the tiny furry specks bob from stem to stem. A scent of lavender wafts from the air, almost as if fanned here by the wings of the bees. It's the bee garden.

I look up to find Patrick's eyes on me. 'What do you think?'

'It's lovely,' I tell him. I know I should probably add something else – refer to our disagreement about it before or tell him how right he was to help Vik with it. Or ask about the idea of a memorial. But I don't feel like it, because that would mean talking about Hannah, and for whatever reason I don't want to get into that with him, not at this moment.

As we walk on, I try to identify what, exactly, is stopping me from wanting to talk to him about this. But I can't, except that I know I'm not ready to yet. So we walk on in silence instead, until round the next bend, I see something that makes me gasp.

It's the roses – the ones that we planted in the depths of winter. They've been transformed into a glorious mass of pink, yellow and red, already shedding some of their silky petals on the ground. I bend my head to smell one, and it's heavenly – a scent you never get in a florist's boutique.

'Do you think I can pick some, for the table?'

'Why not?' he says.

I carefully pull a few from the stems, wincing as one scratches me.

'Are you OK?' Patrick says. 'Vik's got some plasters back at the house. We got scratched to ribbons doing the brambles, so he's got half of Boots actually.'

'It's fine.' I put the sore finger in my mouth briefly, and then pull another stem from the branch.

'Why don't you use these?' He holds out the secateurs. 'Or the gloves?'

'Thanks, but I'm nearly done.' I know he means well, but I just want to pick some roses without all this production.

'All right.' He takes a step back.

I finish collecting my little bouquet and take a last look at the roses. They really are a miracle; it's hard to imagine that they have anything to do with the sad sticks that we planted at New Year's. Maybe I could have a rose bush of my own on my balcony – or even at the front of my building? They grow in the city too. I sink my face again into the deep pink blooms I've picked and inhale deeply, closing my eyes as the scent floods my senses.

'You know, Celeste –'

I look up. I don't know if this will be about Hannah, or Vik, or something else, but I feel almost apprehensive at his intense look.

'What?'

'Nothing,' he says, after a minute. It's as if he's come to some sort of decision – about what, I don't know. 'Doesn't matter. Come on. These cherries won't pick themselves.' And he walks off, leaving me to follow him.

Soon it's time for Vik's birthday tea, another idyllic scene: under the chestnut trees, at a long table groaning with cherries, roses and Vik's mum's Victoria sponge. After we've all stuffed ourselves with cake, Shib goes inside again to try to get the baby to nap. I follow her to use the loo and then, hearing distant wails, go upstairs to see if I can offer any moral support. I know that the baby has had tongue tie, and even though that's been fixed, feeding still seems to be an issue.

'She won't sleep,' Shib says, looking at me with haunted eyes. 'She never sleeps, so I don't either. I'm in hell, Celeste. And I did it all to myself. Rishi said, we're fine with two, but I wanted another, and I love her so much but this is so hard.'

I look at her helplessly, wondering what to do. 'Do you want me to get Rishi?'

'No, he needs to deal with the big ones. Anyway, he just winds her up. I'd ask him to walk her around, but I know he'll just be haring up and down like he's running for a bus.'

'Oh dear,' I say. Surely he can't be that incompetent

given this is his third child, but I don't want to wind Shib up either.

'Would you take her, Celeste?' Shib asks suddenly. 'Just while I go to the loo?'

'Really? Won't she think she's been kidnapped?'

'No, no – she doesn't know who's who yet.'

'If you're sure.' Then I add recklessly, 'In that case, why don't I take her for a while and give you a break? I can't guarantee that I can stop her crying, but I could keep her alive while you have ten minutes to yourself.'

I'm expecting Shib to say no, given that she doesn't even trust Rishi to do this, but instead she grabs my arm with a wild look in her eye. 'Would you? Thank you! I've just fed her and winded her, and she probably won't sick up on you, but just have this just in case.' She slings one of her ever-present muslins over my shoulder, and disappears in the direction of her room, before I can think of another question, let alone ask it.

Iseult continues to cry, and I pace awkwardly until I remember seeing an antique rocking chair, two flights of steps and a passage away. I sit down carefully and try to rock in a soothing way, hoping that I'm not making her worse. The crying goes on for a painful five minutes that feel like an eternity – but then, suddenly, she stops.

I look down at her crumpled little face, feeling the weight of her tiny form curled into me like a prawn as she falls asleep, her small red hand clutching my finger. And I don't feel any sudden maternal urge or wish for a baby of my own exactly – it's still not something that keeps me awake at night. But I do feel the forming of a bond, the knowledge that here is someone who's going to be a presence for a long time, hopefully for as long as I live. I'll help look after her, and maybe in years to come she'll help to look after me.

'Will you drive me around, Iseult?' I ask softly, wagging her little hand. 'Will you take Auntie Celeste to her bridge class?'

A floorboard creaks behind me, and I hear a chuckle. 'Have you taken up bridge? That wasn't on the list.'

'Shh, Vik,' I say. 'I finally got her to sleep.'

'Well done.' He comes and sits opposite me, on the window seat. 'Ahhh. Peace at last.'

'I know. I've sent Shib for a nap – poor thing . . . What's Rishi doing?'

'Looking after his other two kids! He's not a total slacker dad, you know.'

'I wasn't implying it.' I grin at him. 'But good that you've clarified.'

We're quiet for a minute, watching the baby sleep. Then Vik says, 'I bought that chair with exactly that in mind, you know. For me and Hannah.'

My heart breaks at the sadness in his eyes. 'I'm so sorry, Vik,' I tell him, thinking what a wonderful dad he would make.

'It's OK. I mean, it's not OK, but thanks. Maybe we should have started trying sooner or something . . . But here we are.'

'Here we are,' I agree.

After a minute, he says, 'You know, I didn't tell you this but I was angry at her for a long time.'

'About what?' I say, startled.

'About her whole objection to getting married. I was

OK with it at the time, I suppose, but it made me angry afterwards. Because then I could have said "My wife died". Instead of my girlfriend, which made me seem less important to her.' He smiles sadly. 'Even the funeral. I had no part in choosing it, planning it – nothing. It was all Dervla. I remember that poem someone read – do you remember that? It was weird . . . I would never have chosen it.'

'Oh, Vik, I remember. I didn't really like it either.' It was a poem called 'Do Not Stand at My Grave and Weep', which is all about how the person is not dead but present in the beauties of nature; I could understand the sentiment but I didn't think it was right for the occasion.

'But then I thought: Getting angry at your dead girlfriend for not marrying you . . . Pretty pointless really. I just wanted to be angry at something.'

'I know what you mean.' In the aftermath of the accident I also looked for someone to blame: the ski resort, the hospital, Hannah's mum for taking her in the first place. Or even Hannah herself; she was wearing a helmet but it wasn't fastened properly and slipped. But, as the coroner's report said, there was nobody to blame, just tragedy and life itself. Vik says, 'Now I'm over anger. So I'm at depression, I suppose. Or not depression but just sadness. I feel sad is all.' He tries to smile. 'Think that means acceptance next. I'm waiting.'

I wish I could give him a big hug, but I can't with the baby, so I just say, as warmly as I can, 'Oh, Vik. I hope so.' I add, 'This is petty but . . . I was upset too, that she never told me you guys were trying for a baby. I didn't know until Shib told me recently.'

'Didn't she? Well. You know Hannah. She didn't like to unveil her work till she had a finished iteration.' He smiles. 'Remember the Abstract One series?'

'Oh, boy – do I ever.' I laugh softly, remembering Hannah's foray into abstract art that had her, and us, tearing out her hair for months. It's so comforting that I'll always have him to share these memories with.

'Anyway,' he says, 'what's going on with you? What's all this about Ed being back on the scene?'

I sigh, and then look down in panic as the baby shifts and mews for a second. We both hold our breath until she settles again. 'We're just . . . reconnecting, I suppose.'

'You didn't want to bring him this weekend?'

'No, no. He had a stag anyway . . . We're taking it slow.'

'That's smart.'

I think I hear a note of caution in Vik's voice, which makes me say, 'He has changed, you know. Had therapy and everything.' Tentatively I add, 'Is that something you've ever tried, Vik? Therapy?'

Vik starts to laugh and I shush him. 'My God, Celeste, of course I have. Hundreds of pounds' worth. You don't think I could sit here celebrating my fortieth birthday in the gigantic house where I was supposed to live with my dead girlfriend, with my parents and everything, without a bucketload of therapy? Have you never tried it?'

'No . . .' I can't exactly say why not except that I would feel self-conscious confiding in a stranger. 'I saw the astrologer, does that count?'

'No.' He stands up and pats me on the shoulder. 'I'll leave you to think about it. I'd better get back to my guests.'

'Your public,' I suggest, smiling.

'Indeed. Will you be OK here?'

I look down at the baby, who is still deeply asleep; my finger has left her clutches and her starfish hands are relaxed. She could wake at any moment, of course, but I'm feeling optimistic.

'Yes,' I say, smiling. 'I think we'll be just fine.'

It's a hot night, and I can't sleep. Around 1 a.m., when everyone's in bed, I give up on sleep and pull on a denim shirt over my night shorts and T-shirt, and slip outside for some fresh air. After Vik's lasagne, several bottles of wine and an epic game of Pictionary, I'm not surprised that I can't sleep. Especially since the little attic room where I'm staying tonight is bakingly warm and airless.

I'm almost glad of it, though, when I get outside and see the stars. If they were spectacular in December, they're even better now, because I don't have to wrap up and shiver to watch them. I find a seat on one of Vik's new sunloungers, and lie back to gaze at the stars and spot what constellations I can. At the centre of the heavens I find Polaris, the North Star. I think of the astrologer's words. *Polaris is not shy about knocking you off course.* I have certainly been knocked off course recently – last year, and also this year. Lately I've been feeling like I'm back on track, but back on track to where?

Just as I'm thinking this, my phone buzzes with a text. It's Eddie. Just thinking of you. Brighton's hotter than Barcelona apparently. How's Suffolk?

I smile, and send him a quick reply. Hot too. But lovely. xxx I attach a picture of the birthday tea and press send.

256

Seconds later a reply arrives: Looks idyllic. Can't wait to hear more. Wednesday maybe?

I'm about to reply when the front door opens, and I hear a voice behind me. 'Oh. Sorry.'

It's Patrick. I haven't really spoken to him properly since we picked the roses and cherries earlier. If I were feeling paranoid, I'd almost think that he was avoiding me.

'I was just getting some air . . . I'll leave you be,' he says.

'You don't have to.' I put away my phone and indicate the sunlounger beside me. 'It's a gorgeous night, isn't it? Is your room really hot too?' I know he's been kicked out of the Cheese Room and replaced by Vik's parents, which is only fair.

He nods, and sits down beside me, stretching out his long legs. Again he seems oddly quiet, but perhaps he's just down, following his break-up from the beautiful Angelika. I wonder whether to mention it, or tell him I'm sorry, but I don't want to be nosy.

'How are the plans going for the gardening centre?' I ask instead.

'Yeah, good, thanks. I've got a spot picked out, just talking to builders and all that stuff.'

'Where is it?'

'Monkstown Crescent.'

'Oh, that's perfect,' I say, picturing the pretty seaside village. 'I'll have to take a look when I'm there in August.'

'You are? I'll be there too, second week.'

'Me too.' I'm about to suggest we could meet when I'm distracted by a white flash bobbing along the lawn, followed by another one. 'Look! What was that?'

'Rabbits.'

'Oh yes!' I see them now, and I'm suddenly reminded of Irish college, when we used to see them hop across the fields on our way home from the Friday-night ceili dances. I glance over at Patrick, wondering if he went to Irish college. If he did, he was definitely a house leader. The hot night and the summer stars put me in the mood for conversation, and I'm about to suggest that we get some cold beers from inside when Patrick stands up.

'I'll leave you to it. Hope you get some sleep.'

'OK.' I'm oddly disappointed. I would have thought he would be just the person to want to stay up late chatting and stargazing on a summer's night. Before he goes, I decide to make another little overture to let him know that I would like to be friends.

'Hey, maybe I'll see you in Dublin if you're not too busy? I'm there for a week, so.'

'Sure. That would be cool.'

Then he disappears inside, leaving me wondering what, if anything, is up with him. I can't figure him out. At times he's an open book – like on the beach back in March, when he started telling me unprompted about his parents' divorce – but not today. And what was he wanting to tell me in the rose garden? Perhaps it was about that bit of horseplay while we were playing rugby, which I had almost forgotten; was he embarrassed or something?

For the first time I consider the idea that he might have some kind of romantic interest in me. Is that possible? But I don't think so; he was going to tell me something specific, I'm sure. Perhaps he was going to say something about putting a memorial there for Hannah. I'm glad he didn't – I'm not ready to talk about that, not yet.

I gaze up at the stars, thinking again of the astrologer's words about Polaris and how it throws us off course with sudden shocks. I think how remarkable it is that I'm back in touch with Eddie, whom I never thought I would see again. And it all started with that chance encounter outside the yoga place – where I would never have gone, had it not been for Hannah's list sending me there. I take out my phone to reply to Eddie and tell him that Wednesday sounds perfect.

24

After Vik's birthday weekend, the days start to fly by as they often seem to do in summer. They feel fuller now – with runs in the park after work, drinks with Mel, Friday visits to Shib and, of course, seeing Eddie. Things at work are going well, with nothing too unusual except the first meeting with Effie, the ethical fashion business, which happens towards the end of July. It's the first time I've ever worked with a start-up, and it's a refreshing novelty that it takes place in a members' club in Shoreditch rather than an office building. Also unprecedented is that the CEO and COO are both women – Kemi McLaughlin and Orla Butler, both Irish.

'I'm so excited to meet you both,' I tell them sincerely, as we set up for the meeting. 'You know, I would have come to Dublin to see you – and I can next time. But I know this makes sense as you're both here for meetings.'

'Yes, we are,' Kemi says. 'But that's good to know. Although we're also trying to do video meetings as often as we can, just for environmental reasons. Plus, it's cheaper.'

'Absolutely,' I say, feeling impressed already; there's nothing worse than a new company that's spending money just because it can. 'So, would you like to ask me anything before I dive in to our presentation?'

'Yes,' says Orla, the COO. 'We were just talking about

recruiting. We want to hire some really top-tier people, but we can't compete with the biggest fashion companies on salary. So how would you suggest we find and retain the best talent?'

'Great question,' I say, and I outline all my ideas on this exact point, from share options to pension plans. It's all so different, and exciting, that I'm still on a high when I return to the office from the meeting.

'How did it go?' Isobel asks me, stopping by my desk.

'They loved it, and it was really interesting. It was fascinating actually.' I pause as I try to articulate exactly why it was so rewarding. 'Just seeing a company's Big Bang moment – when they have a chance to start off on the right foot, with the highest ideals, and without getting into bad habits or falling into that trap of "This is how we've always done it . . ." Oh, sorry.' I realize that I've been rambling.

'Not at all – it's great that it went well!' she says. 'I just wanted to see if I could get your eyes on the annual client report? By end of play if poss?' She hands me a file as thick as a telephone book, compiled by all the juniors and to be checked by a director. It's the deadliest, dullest document known to man, and it should really be her responsibility to look at it rather than mine, but I imagine she's got some good reason for asking, so I say, 'No problem.'

'Thanks, Celeste,' she says, looking grateful. 'I did have a quick look, but I'm terrible on that kind of detail – I feel like that's much more your wheelhouse.'

'No problem,' I say, wondering what makes her think that it's *my* wheelhouse. But somehow, knowing that I have other things in my life makes it bother me less than it would have otherwise.

On the Saturday evening that week, Eddie and I go for drinks at one of the outdoor bars in King's Cross. And that night he stays over for the first time. I thought it might feel strange or too soon, but it didn't. It felt deeply exciting but also happy and familiar – right down to the breakfast tray he brings in the next morning.

'Morning, gorgeous,' he says. The tray contains a steaming mug of coffee, and toasted bagels with smoked salmon, cream cheese and lots of pepper, just how I like them.

'I didn't know I had bagels. Or salmon.'

'You didn't. I snuck out while you were asleep, and went to the Happening Bagel Bakery . . . God, I've missed that place.'

'Oh gosh, it's delicious. Thank you.'

'That's not the only thing I've missed,' he adds, right on cue, and leans in to kiss me. I make a face because we are being very cheesy. But I don't care. It's a beautiful summer's day, and I have someone to enjoy it with.

'You don't have football today, do you?' I ask.

'Of course not. No football in the summer. So I'm all yours. We could go to the park or get a drink somewhere outside . . . It's so hot.' He looks out of the window. 'Can you believe it's August next week?'

'What do you mean, next week?' I say blankly. Then I look at my calendar and see that he's right. I was sure there were two more weekends in July, but this is the last one.

'Oh *no*.' I glance out of the window at the blazing sun in the blue sky, realizing what this means.

Eddie looks at me, in alarm. 'What?'

'Nothing, just . . . I lost track of time. I need to do my resolution for this month. Go for a jog in Hyde Park.' I groan. 'I've been putting it off. I have to do it before the end of July – so I'll have to go today.'

'Really?' He glances out of the window. 'It's as hot as balls. Can't it wait till next week – you could go some evening after work?'

'I won't have time to go after work . . . Next week's really busy. It has to be today.' I stand up and start searching for my running gear, cursing myself for being so forgetful. I was obviously distracted by work and the whole Eddie thing; which makes me feel guilty, though I know that's irrational.

'Does it really?' he says. 'I mean . . . I do understand about the list, but you don't want to get obsessive about it. I mean, does it really matter if you do it next weekend?'

'It matters to me,' I say, from the depths of the wardrobe.

He's quiet for a minute, while I hunt for my lightest possible running vest and shorts.

'Can I come with you?'

'Are you sure?' I ask, pleased; it would be much nicer with company.

'Why not? I've even got my gym bag from yesterday . . . think I've even got a spare T-shirt. If you don't mind me reusing my stinky shorts?'

'Of course I don't mind. But are you sure?' I feel bad,

especially as I've remembered he's not a fan of exertion in the heat.

'I'm positive. I want in on this whole resolution thing.' He smiles and kisses me quickly. 'Let's do it.'

An hour later, we're emerging from Lancaster Gate station after a long sweaty tube journey. It's one o'clock and thirty degrees in the shade, and I'm hoping I haven't made a terrible decision. Especially as I've just realized we could have gone this evening.

'Well, we're here now. I'll just get some water,' he says, buying it from a stall as we go in and offering me some, before chugging it almost in one go. We've come in near the Italian Gardens with their fountains and formal flower beds in full summer bloom, their gravel paths dusty and white under the hot sun. 'This always reminds me of the Luxembourg Gardens in Paris,' he says. 'Remember?'

'Yes, I remember.' I smile. We did have a wonderful time, staying at a fancy hotel and eating out every night; even if it did all go on his credit card.

'Oh, good,' he says, seeing a map. I smile again, remembering again how much he loves a map. 'Let's work out a route . . . how about we jog around the lake? Would that count?'

'That would be perfect,' I say. 'If we get as far as the Lido, then I think we can call that a full jog.'

'She said jogging *in* Hyde Park, right? Not around Hyde Park.' He lifts his hands. 'We're good.'

I laugh, and we start to jog in the direction of the lake, with the Italian Gardens on our right. I'm very glad that I've put in some practice miles and I've soon hit a rhythm.

I notice that Eddie is a bit breathless, though, so I slow down immediately.

'All good?' I ask.

'Yep!' he says shortly. 'Just – been a while – since my football training.'

It seems easier not to talk, so we both jog in silence while the scenery goes by: the lake with its blue boats, manned by tourists crashing into each other; the seagulls dive-bombing bits of hot dogs; the inexhaustible variety of people with their headphones, hot pants, hijabs, horses, roller skates, scooters, buggies, bubble machines and everything else. The heat is punishing and I'm glad I applied several layers of factor 100, as Eddie called it. We jog over the bridge and pass the Serpentine Bar and Kitchen, with its tables overlooking the water, and I look longingly at it, while Eddie promises me a drink there if we can make it all the way to the Lido. 'Which we easily can. We've already done three kilometres.' He seems like he's found a second wind, which is a relief; I was feeling very bad about dragging him here.

'Go, us,' I pant. 'Oh, good, we're nearly there.' I've just had my first glimpse of the Lido. 'Imagine having a dip . . . Doesn't that look heavenly?'

'But we don't have our stuff.'

This is true. But as we jog closer to the Lido, I can almost feel the cool water enveloping my hot sweaty body; it's quivering on the horizon, like a dream or mirage. When we come to the entrance, we high-five each other.

Eddie pants, 'Well done. We did it. Ouch! I've got a stitch.' He leans forward, trying to touch his toes.

I pat his back, then turn around in the direction of the Lido's entrance.

'What are you doing?' he asks.

'I just want to ask about swimming – hang on.'

I'm fully expecting the person behind the reception desk to laugh me out of town when I ask if we can buy swimming costumes, but he doesn't. Instead he says we can 'hire' them, and towels.

'Eddie,' I say, coming back outside, 'guess what? We can hire swimming things. Even towels. Wouldn't that be wonderful?'

'Oof,' he says, straightening up. 'Seriously? I don't know. The water here looks filthy. And putting on some-one's holey old bathers? Doesn't that gross you out?'

'Not much,' I say, laughing. 'Maybe it should, but I just really want a swim.'

'Tell you what,' he says, 'you go ahead, and I'll meet you on the grass over there.'

'Are you sure, Eddie?' I ask, and he nods.

'I'm going to get an ice cream,' he says. 'Enjoy your mucky dip.'

I'm disappointed that he doesn't want to try it, but I give him a quick kiss and tell him I'll see him shortly. I hurry through the rigmarole of showering and changing as soon as I can; I don't want to cool down before I get into the blessed cool, cool water. As soon as I've stashed everything away, and pinned my locker token to the suit, I hurry out to the pebbly shore. I take a minute to feel the baking sun on me, and then I walk into the water.

When the first cold shock hits me, I gasp in delight and then I'm in the new element, swimming further out into the water. I lie on my back and look up at the blue sky, and then across the way to the white skyscrapers rising up above the green chestnut trees. To my right I can see the round terracotta mass of the Royal Albert Hall; further along I see the bridge over the Serpentine with its cars and joggers going by. I'm swimming in the middle of the city; it's the most incredible feeling.

I swim a few lazy strokes, but I'm too exhausted after the run to expend much energy; I am blissfully happy just lying back and floating, letting the water hold me. I tune into the noises, which always sound so soothing over water: people talking, laughing and splashing, distant traffic. And then music. An orchestra. I turn my head left and right trying to locate the source, before I realize that it's drifting towards me from the Royal Albert Hall, where they're rehearsing for the Proms. I can't believe Eddie missed this, but I'm glad I didn't.

When I'm finally ready to come out, I get dressed and dried and limp to the nearest lawn, where Eddie is waiting for me.

'How was it?' he asks. 'Obviously good, you were ages.'

'Eddie, it was incredible.' I try to explain how magical it was – the cool water, the music from the Proms, but he doesn't seem convinced, saying, 'I just hope you didn't get Wiel's disease.'

I feel deflated that he didn't want to share the experience with me but I know I'm being absurd. He came for the run after all, which he didn't have to; I can hardly accuse him of not being a very good sport.

'I hope you weren't bored, waiting around here?' I ask.

'No! I had an ice cream.' He stands up. 'I'll get you one. Vanilla, two scoops?'

I'm about to say yes to this order – my go-to – when I change my mind.

'Surprise me,' I tell him, smiling.

I lie back, enjoying the sun and the feeling of exhaustion and heat, cooling now after my swim. Then it hits me: outdoor swimming! I just did my next resolution without even planning it. I had planned to go to the Ladies' Pond in Hampstead but I ended up here instead, and I'm so glad. I know that it will always be one of my most special London memories. *Thank you, Hannah*, I say silently once again.

'Here you go,' Eddie says, reappearing with an ice cream – vanilla, two scoops. 'What's wrong?' he asks, and then clasps his hand to his head. 'You said to surprise you, didn't you? Sorry. I totally forgot. My brain is fried from the heat . . . I'm used to getting you vanilla.'

I feel childishly disappointed for a minute, but then I give myself a shake and say thank you. You don't look a gift ice cream in the mouth, and vanilla is still my favourite after all.

'When are you headed to Dublin by the way?' he asks.

'The eighth of August, whenever that is . . . Week after next?'

'And I'm going to the Peak District next week. I'll miss you.'

I smile and tell him I'll miss him too.

'You haven't been in ages, have you? I'm sure they'll roll out the red carpet.' He adds casually, 'Have you mentioned to your folks that we've been seeing each other?'

'Oh, no. Not just yet.' I am not sure why this is. Except for the obvious reason. After all the drama of a cancelled wedding, you don't want to march your troops to the top of the hill and then march them back down again if anything goes wrong. But what could go wrong? He's a known quantity. If the debt issue is resolved, which I believe it is, then there's no reason we can't make a go of things again.

'How about you? Have you told your parents?' I ask, and he nods.

'They're pleased,' he says briefly. 'But I've told them it's early days.'

This is nice but also makes me feel somehow anxious, that things are speeding too far ahead while we're still getting to know each other again. But once more I tell myself I'm being silly. I'm the one who's being weird, keeping good news to myself.

'So,' he says, 'what would you like to do this evening? We could get a drink outside somewhere . . . maybe the Scolt Head?'

'Sure.' As I'm saying this, though, I realize that I'm sick of the Scolt Head. It's been lovely going back to our old haunts together in recent months, and I know Eddie loves familiar places, but a change might be nice.

'Or we could try somewhere new?' I suggest.

'Of course,' he says. 'Anywhere you like – you pick.'

'OK,' I say, thinking how easy-going he is. 'Or honestly if you're up for the Scolt, we can do that. I owe you for coming jogging with me.'

Eddie rolls over on to his back and smiles up at me. 'I don't suppose there's a beer garden in your resolutions? That I could do.'

'No. Next is outdoor swimming . . . which I've also just ticked. And then it's going to be the ballet.'

'The ballet,' he repeats. 'I could try the ballet.'

'Could you really?' I ask, pleased and surprised.

'Twist my arm. Leave it to me – I'll book it.'

'Thanks, Ed,' I say, feeling ridiculously pleased. I don't know what I was worried about; Eddie really is wonderful. A man who'll come running with me, and go to the ballet; what more could I possibly ask for?

25

August

It would be a stretch to say that my parents roll out the red carpet every time I come back to Dublin. They haven't produced a handmade WELCOME HOME, CELESTE banner at the airport recently, not since I had my summer job in Nantucket when I was twenty-one. But they definitely like to make a mild fuss, and certainly always come to meet me at the airport, which is why I'm quite surprised when Mum explains that I'll have to get a taxi or the bus this time.

'Just because of Wispa,' Mum explains. 'I can't leave her that long. Well, I could, but I don't want to; it's her first week.'

'The dog? I thought her name was Heroic Adventurer.'

'No, that's her kennel name. Wispa suits her; she's such a shy little thing. She cringes at the drop of a hat. I've had to put a muffler on the letterbox because she was jumping out of her skin.'

'Oh, OK,' I say, taken aback at this level of TLC. 'What about Dad?'

'He has his personal trainer session.'

'His what now?'

'Galina. She walks the O'Mahonys' dogs and she might be able to walk Wispa too, but she's also a personal trainer. She has your father doing squats, Celeste.'

'Yikes. Well, fair play.' I hang up the phone feeling amused and confused in equal measure. Far from being two sad empty-nesters, my parents are obviously living their best lives and turning their little enclave of Dublin into Beverley Hills, complete with dog walkers and personal trainers. I'll fit right in with my astrologer.

When I arrive with my suitcase on the first Thursday in August, the house seems relatively normal. Except for the sign which says PLEASE KNOCK OR TEXT, NO DOOR-BELL. NERVOUS DOG. I knock as instructed and Dad arrives within seconds, enveloping me in a big hug as soon as I come in. He looks hale and hearty but I'm astonished to see that he's wearing shorts along with his normal polo shirt. I don't think I've seen Dad wearing shorts ever – or not since our holiday to Marbella in 1996, never repeated again as it was just too hot.

'Where's your taxi, Celeste? You got the Aircoach? Good girl yourself, come on in.'

Inside, I'm relieved to see everything else looks the same: the biscuit-coloured carpets, hoovered to within an inch of their life; the side table with its carefully preserved takeaway leaflets and Mass cards; the sideboard with my dad's golf trophies and the good Waterford crystal, never used in living memory. You could look at the house and honestly it could still be 1999, which is exactly how it should be. Not like Dad, who tells me he has to pop back outside, as he's just starting his HIIT training with Galina.

'This is my thirty-second rest,' he explains. He pats me on the shoulder before darting back out to garden where Galina, I presume – a strapping blonde woman of about fifty – gives me a cheery wave, before encouraging Dad back on to the mat.

'Now, Kevin, star jumps! Modified star jumps,' she adds, looking at me reassuringly.

I'm terrified that Dad is going to do himself an injury doing his first star jump since he was eight, so I'm relieved to see that he's doing a kind of Bob Fosse-style side tap instead. I can't say that he has abs of steel or anything, but he certainly looks fit and well; he's beaming away as Galina cheers him on.

Just then, I hear footsteps behind me. 'Celeste! Darling,' Mum says, coming from upstairs. 'I didn't know you were here. That's the dreadful thing about this doorbell thing! Welcome home, my pet. Now, have you met Wispa?'

Startled, I look behind me at the kitchen, where a little brown shape is curled up in a basket under the pine table, ears flattened and eyes peering up at me.

I say in a soft voice, 'Hi, Wispa! I'm Celeste.' I crouch down and hold out a hand so she can sniff it, which she does cautiously after a minute.

'She's gorgeous, Mum. Congratulations,' I say. 'Wait, what has she got there?' I've just noticed Wispa's paw curled over a little sausage with bright red-yarn hair. 'Is that my Raggedy Ann doll?'

'Oh, yes it is. I wanted to give her a comfort object, and all the shops were shut. It was out in the garage . . .' Mum looks worried, but I laugh and squeeze her shoulders.

'It's OK, Mum. I mean, now I feel like she's the baby

sister I never had. And look at Dad! Have you seen this?' We look out of the window where Dad is indeed doing squats; not very low or for very long, but squats nonetheless. I wouldn't have believed it had I not seen it for myself.

'Oh yes, that's Galina,' Mum says. 'She's a miracle worker, Celeste. Your dad has already lost two pounds since last month. I'm going to join the sessions too once I have Wispa settled; she'll have me looking like a supermodel by Christmas.'

'You already look like a supermodel, Mum,' I tell her: I certainly hope I've inherited Mum's genes. 'Oh, look. They're stretching. That was quick.'

'It's only fifteen minutes. But it's very effective,' Mum explains.

Galina and Dad come inside, Dad looking worn out but full of endorphins from his brief exertions.

'Ah, the daughter!' Galina says, greeting me enthusiastically. 'I have heard so much about you, your mum and dad have been waiting for this for months! Months and months!' She declines a cup of tea and speeds off to her next client, leaving Mum to put on the kettle. I'm glad to see that they're still drinking tea; I thought they might have swapped the Barry's Tea for green juice, and maybe Sunday Mass for Yoga with Adriene.

Dad goes off to have a shower, and Mum and I have a leisurely chat, catching up on all the little things that take too long over the phone. She has a teacher's memory for names and faces and she wants all the news from my London friends. I tell her all about Shib's new baby, and how Vik is doing with the new house.

'Oh, that reminds me,' says Mum. 'I've seen Hannah's mum a couple of times at Mass. We've said hello, but I might ask her if she would like to come here for a cup of tea. Do you think she would like that?'

'I'm sure she would, Mum. That's funny, though, why is she going to Mass around here and not in Dalkey? Oh wait, don't tell me. Father José.'

Father José came to the parish from Bogotá in Colombia about five years ago and is already a huge hit with the parishioners, leaning more on the love-and-peace angle than on matters of hellfire.

'Now who's this?' Mum says, hearing yet another knock at the door.

'Well, we've had the personal trainer and dog walker – must be the hypnotherapist,' I say, and go to answer it.

But it's not a hypnotherapist; it's my brother Hugh. He's looking as cool as ever in a deep blue chore jacket, fade haircut and moccasins with no socks, which I think is standard office attire in his digital marketing agency.

'Hugo!' I say, using my old nickname for him and giving him a fist bump. 'What are you doing here? Is Nessa with you?'

'Nope, just me,' he says. 'I heard the eagle had landed, so I hopped on a bus from work to see for myself.'

Hugh comes inside and greets Wispa, Mum and Dad in that order, getting a shy wag from Wispa's tail; she's obviously met him already. Mum and Dad are thrilled to see him, and then the excitement reaches a peak as we decide that it's hot enough for a rare once-a-year thrill: eating outside on the small patio that overlooks our garden, with white wine to go with Mum's lasagne.

'The garden looks gorgeous, Mum,' I say, as I always do. It doesn't have the wild beauty of Vik's, of course, but it's neat and lovingly cared for, with beds of colourful dahlias and roses.

'Thank you for noticing!' says Mum, as she always does. We all go outside and sit at the plastic garden table in our usual places – me and Mum opposite Dad and Hugh, just as we all did last Christmas.

'Cheers to you, Celeste,' Dad says.

'Welcome home, pet,' says Mum.

'Thanks, guys.' We all clink glasses in the sunshine. And I don't know if it's the upheaval of the past eighteen months, or seeing Mum and Dad with such a new lease of life, but suddenly I think, *Why don't I do this more often?* Why has it taken me months and months, as Galina said, to make it back here, when they're just an hour's flight away? Despite Galina's best efforts, Mum and Dad won't be here forever, and I want to make the most of this time with them. I'm glad that I'm here for a whole week – I might even make strides with Wispa before I go.

After dinner, I offer to give Hugh a lift back to his place in Stoneybatter.

'Are you sure, sis? We'll have to cross the Liffey, you know,' he says, knowing this is my special terror. I'm a confident enough driver, but the Northside is tricky territory for any Southsider, as Hugh well knows.

'Well, you can navigate me,' I say. I didn't really touch the wine, as I have a headache from the flight, so I can drive; plus, it's a nice chance to chat. Mum and Dad wave us off with many instructions as to the route and offers from Dad to get out his AA map, though we both tell him we'll use our phones.

'So,' Hugh says, as we set off, 'which are you more befuddled by – the new dog or the personal trainer? And which do you think is giving them more life?'

I laugh. 'Probably the dog. She has them wrapped around her paw.'

'Doesn't she just? No, it's good for them, though. Someone to love in the absence of grandchildren.'

I'm not sure how to reply to this. I've always thought that he and Nessa were of the 'chill, no hurry' school of thought when it comes to kids. But I also thought that about Hannah, and it turned out that I was wrong. I don't like to pry. But I also don't want to miss out, again, on the chance of supporting someone I love if they're in a tough spot.

'Is that something that's on the cards for you guys at all?' I ask casually, indicating left on to the Stillorgan dual carriageway. 'You can tell me to mind my own business by the way.'

'Well . . .' Hugh waits until I've got myself into the right lane, knowing I need to concentrate. Then he says, 'We've been through two rounds of IVF, so we're trying.'

'Oh gosh, Hugh, really? I had no idea.' I glance beside me at his handsome profile gazing straight ahead at the string of traffic before us. 'That must be stressful. Is it?'

'You have no idea,' he says. 'The first one we got a positive test, and then a miscarriage three weeks later. The second one, nothing.'

'Oh, Hugh.' I'm lost for words. I can't believe that my little brother – whom I remember believing in Santa and collecting Pokémon cards – is facing such a trial. And poor Nessa too. Because Hugh's my younger brother, I always thought of the two of them as being basically twentysomethings, but of course they're not. I'm thirty-seven and he's thirty-four; we're both squarely in our mid-thirties and this is our life now.

'Thank you for telling me,' I say.

'Yeah, no . . . It's been on my mind to say it to you. For example, those trips to the Czech Republic . . . they weren't holidays, or not primarily. There's a clinic there. It's much cheaper than having treatment here.'

Of course. And I had presumed they were too cool for France or Spain.

'Does it cost a fortune?'

'It's crippling on top of the mortgage. To the point where I'm not sure we can afford many more rolls of the dice. Maybe one more, max, but then we're out, I think.'

I feel so sad for him that I don't know what to say, so I just shake my head. I think of them cycling everywhere, going on camping holidays and making their own bread; all those things that I assumed were hipster affectations are probably a necessity too.

'Thank you for not saying we can adopt,' he adds after a minute.

'No, quite.' I don't know much about adoption, but I understand that it's a service for vulnerable children, rather than an easy fix.

Hugh says, 'Anyway, that's the story with us. What's new with you?'

Seeing that he wants to change the subject, I oblige and

we chat about my work, my resolutions and Vik's house renovation, which Hugh says he'd like to see.

'Oh, you'd be welcome any time, I'm sure,' I say. Hugh and Vik have never met, except possibly briefly at Hannah's funeral, but I think they would get along. 'And . . .' I add as casually as I can, 'I've also been hanging out with . . . Eddie. If you remember him.'

'Yeah, I remember him,' says Hugh, his tone expressing volumes. 'Hanging out or – hanging *out*?'

'Seeing each other again . . . It's early days. I'll keep you posted. He's sorted out his, um, issues anyway. So that's a good thing.'

'That's great,' says Hugh, sounding surprised. 'Good for him. Mind yourself, though.'

'I will,' I say, smiling at my little brother's protective tone. 'But don't say it to Mum and Dad, will you? I can't deal with all that yet.' Hugh says of course, and I add, 'I presume they know about . . .'

'Yeah, they do. They've been sound.'

Poor Hugh and Nessa. I am sure Mum and Dad have been sound, but it's a sad conversation to have to have. I am so glad that he decided to confide in me too, and I resolve to take better care of my relationships and not let things like this slip under my radar again.

We're entering Stoneybatter now, Hugh's hipster enclave, full of sourdough bakeries and microbreweries. Hugh helps me pilot my way through the narrow streets until we reach the turn into his little alley and pull up outside his place.

'Do you want to come in for a drink? Nessa'd love to see you,' Hugh says. I shake my head; it's a school night

279

for them and I'm guessing Nessa has a lot on her plate these days.

'Another time. I'm here for a week so maybe we could get together for a pint or some dinner? And – Hugh?'

He undoes his seat belt and looks expectantly at me.

'Regarding the other thing . . . there's not much I can do obviously, but I do have some savings. So if you wanted a loan, that's definitely something we could do. No problem. I mean it,' I add, over his murmured protests. 'I wouldn't say it if I didn't mean it.'

'Thanks, sis,' he says after a minute. 'I appreciate it.'

'Of course. And obviously, I'm here if you want to chat. Any time.'

He smiles. 'You're a star. Cheers, big ears.' He gives me a brief hug and gets out of the car. 'I'll catch you in the week. We'll grab a pint.'

'Yeah, cool. Say hi to Nessa.' I give him a wave and look around to plan my reverse out of this little alley. It's a tight spot; but I've been in tighter, and I know that if I stay calm and take my time, I can get out in one piece and make it all the way back to Mum and Dad's. I just wish Hugh and Nessa's problems were as easily solved.

26

I'm still pondering Hugh's situation the next morning, as I stand at my bedroom window after my shower. There's a beautiful view of the Dublin Mountains, shimmering purple and blue in the heat haze; it's going to be another gorgeous day – twenty-six degrees, according to the radio. I had floated the idea of a walk in the mountains today but Mum and Dad both have plans: a golf game in his case and a vet appointment for Wispa and Mum. I could call a friend, but everyone's likely to be at work today as it's a Friday. But that's OK. Something about the lack of schedule, and being in my childhood bedroom, of course, makes me feel like being a teen again, in summer holidays when I had nothing to do and nowhere to be – in the best possible way.

Looking at the mountains again, I take a picture to send to Eddie, who replies, Looks gorgeous. Talk this evening?

I reply with a smiley-face emoji. I'm about to put my phone away again, when I notice that I got a message earlier from a number I don't recognize at first. Hi Celeste. I'm going for a swim in UCD, which I think is near your folks' house? I will be out around eleven, if you wanted to meet for a coffee or something.

It's from Patrick; and it's now ten past eleven. I'm surprised that he's gone to the University College Dublin campus for a swim, as it's not close to Dalkey, but they have an Olympic pool, and it is indeed just down the road from me. Feeling madly spontaneous, I press the call button.

'Celeste? Hi! How's it going?'

He sounds completely normal, as if we're old friends. It's a little surprising but I'm glad that his odd mood, or whatever it was, back in Vik's house seems to have subsided.

'Are you still in UCD?' I ask.

'Yeah, I just got out of the pool. Do you want to meet for a coffee?'

I think for a minute. We could go to the Union Café, which is a favourite haunt. But there's something about this weather that makes me want to see the sea.

'Give me twenty minutes, I'll pick you up outside the pool,' I say.

I pull up outside the UCD pool in Mum's Volkswagen Golf exactly nineteen minutes later. Patrick is outside, wearing jeans, a white T-shirt and trainers. He throws his sports bag in the back and gets in.

'Why don't you spread your swimmers out to dry?' I suggest. 'It's such a hot day; they'll be dry in minutes.'

'Are you serious? I've never even met your mom. I don't want to spread my smalls all over her car.'

'I just meant on the back ledge thingy above the boot, but whatever. It's up to you.' I start laughing; it's pretty odd that we're discussing his smalls but it doesn't seem to bother either of us today.

'Well, I will if you are sure she wouldn't mind.' He goes to the back and rearranges everything neatly on the car's back shelf. 'I like your outfit by the way.'

'I didn't really pack for the hot weather. So I dipped into my old clothes – the archive.' I'm wearing a black cotton slip dress that last saw action circa 2002, over a white T-shirt, and my ancient navy Converse. I'm a bit of mess, but at least I have my own sunglasses.

'It's a fabulous day, isn't it?' he says, as I turn the car around and set off down the drive. 'I wanted to get some lengths in, hence the pool.'

'Nice. Why don't I drive you back towards Dalkey, and we can get coffee somewhere along the way?'

'That would be cool, if you're sure it's not out of your way?'

'I'm sure. Let's take the coast road.'

Patrick laughs. 'Is that what you call it? It's not the Pacific Coast Highway.'

'True. But it's still a coast,' I say, as I cross the dual carriageway and set off down Woodbine Road. I turn on the radio, which I set to Sunshine 106.8 earlier; they're playing Hothouse Flowers' 'Don't Go'. I love this song, which just means summer holidays, freedom and driving somewhere – who knows where – so I turn the radio up.

'Great song,' Patrick says.

'Yeah, it is.' I don't know if it's the fact that we're both on holiday, or that we're in our home town, but any awkwardness has dissolved as we slip into friendly chat as easily as I find fourth gear. I even find myself singing along as I turn right on to Rock Road, towards the sea.

'You seem very upbeat,' Patrick says, smiling. 'Maybe this is a good day to show you the site. The site for the garden centre.'

'Sure, I'd love to see it. Did you say Monkstown village?

Parking is always a bitch there, but I know a place . . . the DART station,' I say, as he joins in in unison. 'Jinx,' I add, laughing.

We're speeding along the Rock Road now, past Black-rock Park. A glance to my left shows Dublin Bay, the water sparkling deep azure, splattered with the white sails of yachts. Across the bay, Howth Peninsula looks close enough to touch, patchworked in green and blue. You can even see Ireland's Eye, the island silhouetted behind Howth that only appears on the brightest, clearest days.

'Beautiful sailing day,' Patrick says, and I nod, though I don't sail. I don't know why I never have, considering I grew up right here; just one of those things.

'Are you going to join a yacht club?' I ask. I'm half joking, but I'm also not surprised when he replies, 'The George . . . I'm just waiting to have my membership approved.'

Soon we're driving along Seapoint Avenue with nothing but the sea on our left, with the white painted Georgian terraces unscrolling on our right, until we reach the DART station at Monkstown.

'Allow me,' says Patrick, nodding towards the parking machine, and I say, 'Cheers.' He tucks the ticket in the front dashboard and we walk up the hill towards the village.

'You know, no shade to Dalkey, but I think Monkstown is the prettiest village in Dublin,' I remark.

Patrick gasps and pretends to clutch his heart. 'Seriously? Actually, I kind of agree with you,' he adds. 'Especially in summer.'

We walk up the hill from the station and emerge on to Monkstown Crescent, a little arc of mews buildings, now housing boutiques, cafes and restaurants, all nestled behind granite walls with flower-filled gardens outside. The crescent is overlooked by the pepperpot church with its mock-Moorish architecture, and further along is another parade of Georgian buildings: a pub, a restaurant, a florist, all with outdoor seating beside a little area planted with palm trees. On a hot day like today it's positively Mediterranean. Everyone is marvelling at the weather; the tanned, wealthy-looking retirees and yummy mummies are all exchanging spontaneous remarks about it in the street.

'You'll certainly have the right kind of footfall,' I tell him.

'I know – recession, what recession?' he says. 'OK, this is it. Check it out.'

He's stopped outside a long low building on a corner, empty except for a bare counter and a few wooden crates.

'What was here before?' I ask, peering in the dusty window.

'It was a wine wholesalers. The owners retired to the south of France. They've left a few barrels behind them, which, of course, we'll use for planting.'

To my surprise he takes out a key and opens up. 'It's yours already?'

'Well, I'm renting it. I have to, to start the building work.'

I walk around, admiring the proportions and the light; it's deceptively big.

'But the best part is out the back – come and see.'

He leads me through the empty space to the back, where he unlocks a stiff wooden door that protests initially but then budges with a kick. It opens on to a long narrow yard sheltered by tall granite walls covered in greenery. There's nothing above the walls but deep blue sky. A wood pigeon coos from somewhere nearby; the air is hushed and cool after the heat of the streets.

'I had no idea that any of these places had so much space behind them,' I say, marvelling at it.

'They don't. This is a real gem.'

'You could have a little coffee spot even,' I say, looking around. 'Just half a dozen tables.'

'I think Monkstown might be at peak coffee, but it's an idea.' He looks at me. 'What do you think?'

'I think it's gorgeous, Patrick. It's the perfect place for a garden centre – I can't believe there isn't one here already.'

He exhales, looking pleased. 'I'll have a lot to learn. I have no retail experience, so I'll have to make some smart hires.'

'But why a garden centre then? I mean, why not stick to garden contracting – wouldn't that be more straight-forward?'

He leans back against the counter, running his hand along its wooden length. 'Good question. It might just be vanity, but I liked the idea of having somewhere to hang my hat. A place to be, and to stay and be part of the com-munity. Instead of just doing projects and piloting out.' He smiles and nods back at the dilapidated yard behind us. 'Plus, I love a fixer-up. As you might have guessed.'

'I might have,' I agree, smiling. 'Seriously – they'll be queuing out the doors.'

'Thanks.' He looks at his watch. 'Speaking of queuing – do you want to get lunch? Or do you want to go for a bit of a walk first?'

'It's such a gorgeous day; it seems a shame to waste it. Let's walk?'

'Good thinking,' he says. We set off down the crescent, out of the village and past the Purty Kitchen pub until we're beside the seafront and the marina of Dún Laoghaire Pier. I can hear the clanking of the yachts' masts, the cry of seagulls and the slap of the waves on the sides of the wharf. Though it's only a Friday the pier is thronged with walkers and joggers, and there's already a queue at the ice-cream van. I breathe in the sea air, feeling my blood pressure drop, as it always seems to in Dublin. In London I'm happy but I'm always on a very slight edge of alertness: amber or faint yellow. Whereas in Dublin I'm always on green. Strange.

'Where do you stand on ice cream?' Patrick says. 'Teddy's or Scrumdiddly's?'

'Teddy's all the way.'

'It's like that, is it?' he says. 'I'm not sure we can be friends after all.'

'Maybe we'll have to do a taste test,' I suggest.

We walk on towards Sandycove, where the James Joyce Tower overlooks the tiny beach, thronged with swimmers today. On the other side of the bay I see Dalkey Island, crowned with its Martello tower, shimmering in the haze.

'I saw Dervla last night,' Patrick says, referring to Hannah's mum.

'Oh, did you? Good for you,' I say, thinking that I must do the same.

'Yeah. She asked me a sort of favour . . . . Can I tell you about it?'

'Of course.'

'She wants Hannah's ashes to be scattered on Dalkey Island. She doesn't want to do it herself . . . I'm not sure why. So she's asked me to do it.'

'Oh gosh.' I take a minute to marshal my thoughts. One of which is that this seems a strange job for Patrick, who wasn't a family member. But Hannah had no siblings, and very little relationship with her father. It doesn't surprise me a bit that she asked Patrick to do this for her rather than me, for instance. He is obviously *that* boy, the neighbour you ask for help when you need it. And, of course, the island is on their doorstep, so to speak.

'What do you think?' Patrick asks.

'I think it's a nice idea,' I say finally. 'It's appropriate. She loved that place.'

'I think so too. I was surprised that she asked me, but it's – I don't know what the right word is. An honour, I suppose.'

'Yeah.'

He takes a breath. 'Would you want to do it with me?'

'Oh.' Again, words fail me for a minute. Then I say, 'We should ask Vik.'

'I did. He's OK with it.'

'Let's check with Dervla too. But in principle, yes. Thanks for asking. When does she want you to do it?'

'She's not ready to give them to me just yet. She'll tell me when she is, she said.'

I nod, thinking of what Peter the astrologer said, of Hannah's death being like a stone, casting its ripples forever – and for so many people. We pause for a minute to lean on the railing and look out at the island, and I think of Hannah arriving there on New Year's Day, 2000, with no idea what was in store for her. Not that we ever know, of course.

I look back up at Patrick, suddenly thinking of something. 'I'm sorry about you and Angelika by the way,' I say. 'I should have said.'

'That's OK.' He looks off into the distance. 'It was complicated, as you probably were able to tell.'

'Well . . .' It's hard to disagree.

'I kept telling myself she'd just had a bad week at work . . . but then I realized it was always going to be a bad week at work. Or a fight with her family. Or something. And it wasn't good for me to be supporting her though these endless crises.'

I'm tempted to ask what on earth the attraction was, but, of course, that's not something I can say. To my surprise he adds, 'What can I say? Being needed is a powerful drug.'

I'm still absorbing this when he says, with a change of tone, 'On a different note.'

'Yes,' I say, happy to change the subject.

'Fish Shack?'

'What?' I almost laugh before I realize he's talking about lunch. 'Yes. Sure.'

Patrick leads me back across the road to a little place I've never noticed before. It's perched on the side of the road opposite the sea, with wood-panelled walls, fishing nets hanging from the ceiling and a tank full of lobsters. It's already pretty busy, but luckily we score the last table outside.

'How did I not know this was here?' I ask, and he just shakes his head.

We order beers – non-alcoholic for me as I'm driving – and Dublin Bay prawns for me and fish tacos for Patrick. My prawns are delicious, sweet-fleshed and delicate, but the fish tacos also look so good that Patrick lets me have a bite. Seafood, beer, fresh air and sunshine; I feel as if I'm on a beach holiday. I stretch my feet out, and breathe the sea air in again.

'It's not the worst place in the world, is it?' Patrick asks, dragging his chip through mayonnaise.

'I never said it was,' I say, smiling.

'But you still couldn't imagine living here?' he asks.

We're interrupted at this point by the owner, who turns out to be a buddy of Patrick's from sailing and has come out to say hello. As we all smile and chat, I wait to feel the claustrophobia that sometimes descends on me in Dublin – the feeling that everyone knows your business, the small-town attitude. But it doesn't come. Instead I feel a sense of space, and peace and security, but also what is that odd feeling? Freedom.

'To answer your question,' I say, once the friend has gone. 'Yes, I probably could.'

'Yeah?' he asks, and I nod.

This surprises me, but the answer came up as easily as a bubble in the water. Not now, of course, with my work – and Eddie. But some day.

'Do you have time for one more detour?' Patrick asks, when we've finished our lunch.

'Sure,' I say, surprised. We split the bill and retrace our steps up the road and away from the sea until we've reached one of the back streets of downtown Dún

Laoghaire. We walk uphill to a pretty row of terraced cottages, one of which has a sign saying UNDER OFFER. It has what looks like an original Georgian front door, sadly peeling now under its fanlight, and two sash windows overlooking a small gravelled area behind railings.

'You?' I ask.

He nods. 'It used to belong to a boatbuilder,' he says. 'That was his yard –' he points to the right, to a small garage. 'When the boats were built they would be wheeled straight down to the harbour. This was about a hundred years ago. But one of his boats is still sailing out of Howth.'

I follow his gaze down to the bay, a blue glimpse at the bottom of the hill. You can hear the seagulls, smell the sea. 'That's lovely. What, um, state is it in, though?' I can see some missing tiles on the roof and, in one grimy corner of the window, a sign saying DO NOT ENTER. This looks even worse than Vik's place.

'Well, it's another project,' Patrick says. 'But it's got potential. It's a Tardis – a hundred square metres. The best thing about it is the yard. I can't show it to you but it's like the one in the garden centre. Much bigger than you'd expect and completely sheltered with the granite walls.'

'I'm sure you'll make it beautiful,' I tell him sincerely, though renovating a place like this would be high on my list of worst nightmares. Then I can't resist adding, 'But, Patrick, what happened to the cottage in Wicklow?'

He smiles. 'OK. No need to gloat, but I realized that actually I don't want to live all *that* remotely. I want to be able to walk to the pub, or the cinema or the library. Or to work, or to the sailing club. I'm not ready to retire to the country like Vik.'

'Good decision.' I grin at him. 'Now, how about an ice cream?'

'After that lunch? You'll have to roll *me* down the hill,' he says. 'But sure.'

We stroll down the hill, past the little parade of shops; I'm surprised to see, alongside the old-timey shops, a Korean street-food place and a very appealing-looking Italian called Zero Zero Pizza. Patrick, seeing a hardware store, wants to go inside for some widget or wodget, so I tell him I'll stay outside to enjoy the sunshine.

I've just found a little bench to sit down on when I hear a voice. 'Celeste? Oh my God! Hi!'

I look up. She looks older, but my first thought is that her hair is a big improvement released from its tight pony-tail. It's my old school friend Bronagh, pushing a buggy with shopping bags in one hand.

'Hi, Bronagh,' I say, taking off my sunglasses. 'How are you?'

'I'm grand! Just out doing some shopping . . . Are you living here now?'

We exchange five minutes of slightly sticky small talk (yes, I'm still in London; no, no plans to move back) and I admire the baby – Fiadh, nine months, the youngest of three, Bronagh says. Then she walks off – she's here for Baby Pilates apparently – leaving me to reflect that for all the sunshine and sea air there are downsides to Dublin and this is one of them.

Then she turns around again and walks back towards me. 'Celeste?'

'Yes?'

'I just meant to say – look, I'm really sorry for what happened. At the end of school. We had our differences but we shouldn't have . . . dropped you the way we did. We weren't nice. I see it now and I'm sorry.'

'Oh,' I say, startled and touched. 'It's OK. It was a long time ago.'

'I mean it, though. And, listen, if you're ever back and wanted to meet up, I'd love to meet you for a coffee. Oh, hi.' Now it's her turn to look startled, for Patrick has just emerged from the hardware store and greeted us both. I see him through Bronagh's eyes – golden and tanned and almost startlingly handsome in the dark little street – and I can't help but feel this isn't the worst timing ever.

Introductions made and small talk done, I tell Bronagh it was nice to see her and we stroll back down towards Marine Road. *That was nice of her*, I think. *It was a long time ago. And I was probably a bit of a pain myself.*

'I have a feeling there was a story there – was there?' Patrick says, as we pass St Michael's Church and head down towards the town hall.

'You know they say you should never meet your heroes? Well . . . meeting your villains is probably not a bad idea,' I tell him. 'They're not so bad after a few years go by.'

'I get you,' Patrick says. 'People mellow.'

I nod, because I certainly have. I'm still feeling that holiday feeling; I'm feeling relaxed, with nothing more to worry about than remembering where I parked the car.

'Oh, God, the car!' I say suddenly. 'Patrick, how much parking did you pay for?'

'Don't worry . . . I splashed out and did the whole day,' he says, smiling. 'Was that too optimistic?'

'No,' I say, relaxing. 'That was perfect.'

A day's parking wasn't optimistic; it was just right, because it's late in the evening, with the golden light mellowing and shadows lengthening, when I drop Patrick back to Dalkey and drive myself home, humming the Hothouse Flowers. We walked the pier; we got ice creams at Scrumdiddly's – I tried their new Scrum Fiteroles – and we sat in the People's Park for hours, chatting and watching the kids playing in front of the fountain, before going to the Purty Kitchen for mussels and chips. It was a perfect day.

'You've caught the sun,' Mum says, looking at me in surprise. 'What kept you out all day? I hope you had a nice time.'

'I did. I was with, um, a friend. Patrick Lacey? He's a friend of Vik's. Sorry I didn't text when I was coming home – my phone died.'

Mum looks intrigued, but all she says is, 'Great stuff. Would you like to come and watch *The Late Late Show* with me, if you don't have exciting plans? With a glass of white wine maybe? Your dad is out still with the golfers.'

'Sounds great, thanks, Mum.' I run upstairs to plug in my phone, noticing my glowing face in the mirror; I'm probably going to be peeling tomorrow even though I reapplied sunscreen like a maniac. I've got two messages from Mel, one from Sibéal and one from – oh dear – Eddie. Hope your weekend is going well. Want to chat tonight? It was sent hours ago.

I reply to Eddie right away, and try calling him, but there's no reply.

I type back, Hey, just got this. Was out all day – will tell you all about it when we talk xx

Sitting on my bed, I start to feel uneasy, and guilty. Was it bad that I spent such an idyllic day hanging out with Patrick and barely thought about Eddie until this evening? And will Eddie think it's weird that I spent all day with a man and forgot to text him to boot? But then I tell myself not to be so neurotic. Patrick is just a friend, and the reason it was an idyllic day was all down to the sea, the heatwave and the holiday. It was nice to see him, and see his plans take place, but in terms of Eddie I have nothing to feel worried about. I take my charger and go back downstairs to Mum, figuring that I can charge my phone while we watch TV together. I'll tell her about my encounter with Bronagh, and once we've finished with that I'm going to tell her about Eddie too. I know she'll be really pleased.

27

September

My return to London, a week later, seemed to bring with it the first signs of autumn. I noticed that the chestnut trees in the local park were tinged with orange, and the shops were full of back-to-school merchandise. I'm sad to think that the summer is over, but the evenings drawing in makes me think of other pleasures: crisp autumn leaves, roaring fires, pub lunches where you go in at twelve and come out at dusk, and also hot yoga, which I plan to return to as soon as the nights draw in. Or maybe I'm just happy because of Eddie. My temporary wobble in Dublin was just that. We're still seeing each other two or three times a week, including at least one weekend night. And it's been months since I even thought about his spending habits; that now seems like a thing of the past.

'I think I'm especially happy because . . . it makes me feel like I didn't get things so wrong with him,' I admit to Mel one Friday evening when she comes to my flat for dinner. 'It took me so long to trust my judgement afterwards. But now I feel I wasn't wrong about him.' I smile. 'Maybe he has changed in some ways. He's taking me to the ballet next week.'

'So romantic!' she says. 'Wait. Isn't that a resolution?

Celeste, this is huge! He's doing the resolutions with you – that's much bigger than meeting the parents, I know.'

'Well, he's already met my parents,' I say, laughing. 'But, yeah, I told him that was next on the list, and . . . he just booked it.'

'That's wonderful,' she says. 'You know, you've changed too, Celeste. You're so much more relaxed these days. You seem much happier.' She smiles. 'Important question: what are you going to wear?'

'I think cocktail wear,' I say. 'I have this green dress that I got with my personal shopper.'

Mel starts asking me about accessories, and I try to reply but my thoughts are distracted by what she said about me seeming much happier now. I can't understand why it bothers me at first, before I realize it's Hannah. If I'm so much happier now – a year and a half after her death – what does that say about me? That my best friend died and I've taken it as a lovely opportunity to embrace new hobbies and live my best life? It just seems wrong.

'What's the matter?' Mel asks, and I try to explain haltingly, though I'm not sure if it's making sense. 'It makes me feel sad. And guilty,' I finish.

Mel just shakes her head. Then she says, 'I know what you mean. It's complicated, isn't it? But . . . regardless of what you do, she's gone, right?' There are tears in her eyes, as there are in mine. 'I suppose you just have to live for both of you now.'

'I never thought of it quite like that before.' I take a deep breath and wipe my eyes. 'Thanks, Mel. Oh no, I don't want to make you cry too.'

We're both trying to hold it together, and Mel suggests that we change the topic back to accessories, offering to lend me one of her hair flowers.

'No, no! That's your thing. You know what, though? I would love your advice on layering necklaces.' It's just occurred to me that she's exactly the person to ask about this.

'Layering necklaces?' she repeats blankly. 'You just wear different ones together.'

'I know, but I think it looks wrong on me. I always get them tangled up. And I've got two bees now, and I can't figure out how to combine them . . .'

Mel, seeing that remedial help is needed, explains the basics to me and puts her own chains on to show me. 'I generally choose three that are different widths as well as lengths. But I'd keep them all the same colour, personally. Oh! And you can get these little things that clasp at the back to stop them from tangling.'

'Are you serious?' How did nobody ever tell me this?

'As for the bees, I just don't think you can wear them together to be honest. Not when they're the same length. You could put one on a longer chain, of course. Or just choose the gold or the silver, depending on your outfit . . . or how you feel.' She leans back and shows me my reflection in the mirror. 'See? Layers.'

'This is genuinely life-changing information,' I tell her, and she laughs. But I'm being serious. Of all the things I've learned this year, this is one of the most transformative. I look back in the mirror, and think, *I'm not just a one-pendant person any more. I've got layers.*

*

A week later, I go to meet Eddie at the Royal Opera House, where we've got tickets to see *Romeo and Juliet*. I must have passed this building dozens of times if not more on my way to go shopping in Long Acre or to meet friends in the covered market in Covent Garden Piazza – but I have never actually been inside. Once again, I wonder if I really have been living in London all this time, or just in a little *Matrix*-style simulacrum inside my head.

Eddie is waiting for me on the steps; he's picked up the tickets as arranged, and has booked somewhere for dinner. I presume that he's gone for somewhere cheap and cheerful among the many chain restaurants that abound around here, or even over in Chinatown – that would be fun. But instead he leads me round the corner, past the tube station down King Street, to a small building painted a dark wine colour. Inside I glimpse small round tables covered in snowy-white tablecloths and, most magical of all, a huge spreading cherry blossom tree, with lights threaded through its branches. It's Clos Maggiore, where we went on our first 'anniversary' of getting together.

'Oh, Eddie,' I say, turning to him with a smile.

'You like it? Phew. I'm so glad,' he says, beaming. 'Come on – let's go in.'

It's exactly as I remember it: the same relaxed, intimate atmosphere. A hostess leads us to our table, which is right in the back under the tree itself; he must have called in advance to book it. She pulls out my chair for me and I sit down, smiling at him.

'It's not too same old, same old?' he asks.

'Not at all,' I say warmly. 'It's lovely.'

The menu looks as delicious as ever and I spend a while

deliberating before choosing their most famous dish, rabbit with mustard, which I actually had last time. After checking if I mind, Eddie chooses the same. Then we start talking about veganism, and how we'd like to try it but we would miss cheese too much. Eddie asks me, 'Did I ever tell you about the time my little brother brought home eight friends from uni to stay – four vegans and three smokers? Poor Joy nearly died.'

'You did,' I say, laughing.

It's a good story, even though I've heard it before. It has to be said that a lot of his stories are ones I've heard before. And it occurs to me suddenly how much of our conversation tends to hark back to the old days. But then I tell myself that of course this happens when you have a history with someone. That's what makes it so nice. I look up, thinking how pretty it is here. The blossoms on the indoor cherry tree remind me of the trees I planted with Patrick. Though this one is artificial obviously.

'Ed, you got the ballet tickets. Let me get this.' I say, when the bill arrives.

'It's OK, Celeste. I've got it.' He glances up and I know he understands the significance of his words. He can get dinner and a show, and I don't have to worry about it.

'I know you do,' I say, smiling. 'Thank you.'

The Royal Opera House is beautiful inside, but we're in such a hurry to find our seats that I barely have time to get more than a quick impression of red-carpeted stairs, enormous chandeliers of pale champagne-coloured crystal and white marble everywhere. The crowd is very middle-aged and middle-class but there is a range of clothing styles. Some people are in jeans and trench coats, some in evening dress like us; one woman even seems to have a tiara, which I am very much here for.

We're in the front row of one of the balconies, and when we sit down I exclaim at how perfect our view is: I can see the whole set, with its beautiful pastel-coloured rendering of Verona's streets. I look down at my programme, admiring the photos of the leads dressed in their medieval pageantry – all doublets and hose, silk bodices and headdresses. It's pure romantic escapism, and I love it.

'I love that it's such a period look,' I murmur to Eddie. 'I hate it when they try to "update" things to, like, 1970s Finland or what have you.'

Eddie laughs. 'Yes. Tried and tested works best.'

'Yes,' I say, though that wasn't exactly what I meant.

The orchestra have finished tuning up now. They play the overture, and I reflect on how sad it is that 'Montagues and Capulets' now makes me think of *The Apprentice* and people trying to sell fish at a covered market and getting funding for their business idea called Energen. Then it's time for the first dancers to make their entrance. I gaze at them, wondering as ever how they can possibly do what they do with their bodies; it's athleticism and artistry all at once, literal poetry in motion. How Hannah would have loved this. I send up a thought to her. *Look, Hannah. I came here for you.* And a minute later: *Thank you for sending me. Thank you for giving me this.*

Of course I have Eddie to thank as well. I glance at him and find that his eyes are fixed on mine. I smile at him, and he reaches down to squeeze my hand.

And for the first time since we kissed after the ceilidh I feel – nothing.

I look down again, as surprised as I would feel at a car not starting or my computer not turning on. There hasn't been any problem in that arena lately; it's been great. So I don't know what's caused this sudden cold spot.

It's probably normal – just me getting in my own head again. I decide to put it out of my mind and watch the dancers. Juliet is doing a pas de deux with Paris, the man her parents have chosen for her. The choreography is so clever, because it's the same dance she just did with Romeo. The moves are all the same, but you can see that she's just going through the motions, her eyes elsewhere. *Like you and Eddie*, a voice says in my ear. I give myself a shake, thinking: where did *that* come from? It's not how I feel at all. Or is it? Will it be? I try to focus on the story, which soon draws me back in completely.

It's strange, because when I've seen *Romeo and Juliet* before I've always felt frustrated with their impetuous dash towards tragedy. 'Why didn't they just communicate better?' I remember saying to Hannah, only half joking, after we watched the Baz Luhrmann film on TV. 'Instead of rushing to assume the worst.' But something inside me has cracked open, and I get the story now, in a way I never did before.

It's such a beautiful production. Every scene is like a Renaissance pageant, and it's a feast for the ears as well, with the orchestra and the sound of the pointe shoes on the stage floor. But I can't take my eyes off the two principals, right up to the very end and the curtain call. Both of them are new to the role, and there's something so moving in the way they stand close together, holding hands and exchanging glances as if they can't believe what just happened. The tears are sliding down my cheeks as I applaud.

Eddie looks at me in surprise but he doesn't say anything, which surprises me too.

'What would you like to do now?' he asks, as we walk out of the auditorium. 'Shall we get a drink – or do you need to get home?'

I tell him a drink sounds nice, and we find a little table at the Paul Hamlyn Hall champagne bar, which overlooks Covent Garden Piazza. I tell him that these drinks are on me, and he accepts graciously. 'I'll grab us a table,' he says, squeezing my hand again.

I look down again; nothing. Oh, God. Is there something genuinely wrong here? Or is it me overthinking again?

As I queue at the bar for our drinks, I look at my ticket. The price of it is even higher than I'd imagined, and when I mentally add it to the bill for dinner, it does seem like a lot. I trust Eddie now, but should I feel bad that it was so expensive? *No*, I tell myself. *He's paid off his debt, and he can budget for special evenings like tonight.* If I thought he was maxing out his cards again, then, of course, I'd have cause to worry. Then I have a truly terrible thought. That it would be easier, in a way, if I thought he was getting back into debt, because then I would have a good reason to have cold feet.

'What would you like?' the barman asks me.

A very good question, I think, as I reply, 'Two white wines, please.'

I remember the feeling I had when Eddie squeezed my hand. Or lack of feeling, rather. Should I just ignore it or face it now? Can I say, in all honesty, that he's still the person I want to be with more than anyone else, the one I want to spend my life with? I thought I was sure, but now I'm not sure at all. And if that's the case, it's not fair to him either to ignore it.

I come back from the bar with two glasses of white wine, and we resume chatting: about the show, about other things coming up this winter and our travel plans. Ed's friend with the cottage in Northumberland can lend it to us for a weekend, he says, and the group might go back over in October half-term when Eddie's friend's kids are off school.

'There was even talk of going there for New Year's Eve,' he says, before adding, 'If you want to, of course.'

And then I know. I know because my reaction to the idea of spending New Year's with him is an instant, instinctive no – not because of Hannah, not even because of Vik, if he has another house party, but because it's just not what I want any more. I was right that he's changed. But I've changed too. I've changed too much, and though it breaks my heart I just don't feel the same any more.

'What is it, Celeste?'

I look at him with my heart in my mouth. 'I just . . .' But I stop; I can't do it to him now; I don't know how I'm ever going to do it to him.

'Are you worried about the bill for tonight?' he asks earnestly. 'It's fine – as I said, I've got it.'

I shake my head. 'No, I trust you. It's not that.'

He looks at me, and I look at him. And he knows. He

knows because he knows me so well. I know him too. And there's a lot of affection there, but it's not enough.

'Ed . . .' I say. 'I am sorry. I wish it could be different.'

'No, it's all right,' he says, his face unreadable. 'It's that thing about not being able to step into the same river twice, isn't it? Or something like that.'

'Something like that,' I say. 'I have had a good time with you. I just . . . I don't feel the same way any more. I'm so sorry.' I want to tell him more – that I know he's going to make someone else very happy, that I'm proud of him for battling his demons – but I know it's not my place so I just say, 'And thank you for tonight. I had a wonderful evening. Really.'

'That's good.' He nods to himself, looking oddly businesslike; I know he's trying to put a brave face on things. He looks around at the beautiful surroundings – the vaulted glass ceilings like a giant conservatory, the well-heeled crowd – then he adds, breaking my heart just a little bit more, 'It was worth a try.'

28

October

In the weeks following my trip to the ballet with Eddie I feel consumed with sadness, and guilt. Especially that he spent so much money on our last evening together; it's probably the least of his worries but it just seems like the final cruel twist of the knife. So much for fate bringing us back together. If seeing him outside the yoga place was an omen, it was a really bad one for Eddie.

'This is why I'd almost rather be dumped than be the one who has to do the dumping,' I confide in Vik, when he phones me one evening. 'I just feel so awful about it all. I wish I had never gone there in the first place.'

'You wanted to give it a chance,' he says. 'That's a good thing. And anyway, Celeste, he was the one who caused you guys to break up in the first instance. That's not on you. It sounds like the break-up was the thing that caused him to get help. So: silver lining.'

'Thanks, Vik. I know you've been through so much worse . . .'

'No Sadness Olympics here,' he says. We change the subject and catch up on each other's news briefly, before he says, 'What's next?'

'What's next?' I repeat, wondering if he means Eddie's love life, mine or my life in general.

'Next on your list.'

'Oh. Canal boat trip.'

'Can I come?'

'Oh, that would be fabulous!' I say, cheering up at the idea.

'I could ask Patrick along too? If you want.'

'Sure,' I say. I haven't seen Patrick since Dublin, and I have thought about contacting him, but something – I'm not sure what – has prevented me. 'I'll ask Mel too?'

'Great,' says Vik.

The London Waterbus Company runs boats from Camden Lock to Little Venice, and since we're all closer to Camden it makes sense to meet there. I haven't been to Camden in years and years either, possibly not since Hannah and I first made a pilgrimage here, hoping to find the epicentre of London cool and maybe even spot Jarvis Cocker. It doesn't seem to have changed a bit; there are still the same stalls selling trainers and novelty T-shirts, incense sticks and other tat, and still the same food market jostling a million different smells – though I'm pretty sure there wasn't poke or bao buns on offer back then.

Patrick's the first to arrive – wearing the same wool coat he had on the first time I met him, though it's still fairly mild for October. I hope I haven't been over-optimistic with my trench coat.

'How's it going?' I ask, raising my sunglasses. 'Thanks for coming aboard.'

'Not at all,' he says. 'I've climbed a wall, I've danced incomprehensible Scottish dances – this is nothing.' He smiles.

I smile too, though his words somehow make me feel a little sad, because he's reminded me that the list is coming to an end. There're only two more after this – visit a Christmas market and help someone in need – and then it's over. And Patrick is leaving. We're silent for a minute, all the camaraderie of our Dublin day out gone again.

'Are you –' I ask

'I heard –' he says at the same time.

Luckily Mel and Vik arrive the next minute and so I don't have to wonder if he was about to ask me about Eddie.

The canal boat moves into the lock, looking very low in the water. It's called the *Lady Luck*, which I hope is a good omen. We all pile in and squeeze ourselves into the tiny wooden seats, which remind me of the reclaimed school seats that you see in trendy bars. There are only a few other passengers aside from us – a family with a small boy, a couple, and two female friends. I look at them a little enviously. They're obviously on a girls' day out and full of high spirits, laughing and taking photos of each other. But I'm used, by now, of everything making me think of Hannah; and I have friends too.

And then we're setting off; chugging along the canal with its canopies of trees overhead, all just touched with autumn colours. People are jogging along the towpath, moving along in little boats; we even pass a small group of kayakers.

'This is fun – I don't know why I never thought of doing this before,' says Mel.

'You don't, do you?' says Vik. 'When things are right under your nose.'

The guide, Maureen, gives us a running commentary, covering the history of the canal from its glory days when it was the main way of transporting goods to now. The warehouses that were once used to house gin or spices are now fancy apartments; the boats once pulled by horses are now engine-powered; and the clip-clop of hooves on the towpath has been replaced by the slap of Nikes and Adidas. Everything changes.

'That reminds me,' says Vik. 'How are you transporting all your stuff, Pat?'

Patrick starts talking about his shipping and what he's doing with all his plants.

'I'm leaving them there for the landlord . . . unless any of you guys want any?'

'Maybe,' I say. I look at the willow trees, trailing their leaves into the water, and the chestnut trees that are turning golden, and feel a deep sense of melancholy for some reason.

'What's your final leaving date?' asks Mel. 'Not that we're rushing you away, of course.'

'No worries . . . Yeah, I'll head back on the twenty-first, I think it is, for Christmas and that will be me done.'

'But you'll be back at my place I hope – for New Year's? I'm planning on having another party. Consider yourselves all invited,' Vik says.

'Wouldn't miss it,' says Patrick. 'It's just a short hop from Stansted.'

'Sounds great,' says Vik, and he and Mel start making plans to visit Dublin next spring. I listen and watch as the boat passes London Zoo, where Maureen shows us their little landing dock, where the zoo authorities have an alarm light that flashes in the event of an escaped animal. Then we pass by the beautiful villas of Primrose Hill, with their gardens running right down to the water. We must be near where we went to the ceilidh – and where I kissed Eddie. I shiver in my trench coat, realizing I should have worn my winter coat; it's time.

Before long we're chugging towards the end of the journey, and the canal widens out into the beautiful waterway of Little Venice, with its triangular island trailed with more willow trees and occupied by swans. The boat berths and I see, with horror, that everyone else is giving Maureen a tip. Luckily Mel has a fiver, so we don't feel totally ashamed of ourselves as we disembark. The others all get out, and I'm last; I'm watching the little boy, who's been given the chance to ring the bell at the end, wondering if he's brave enough. I look up to see Patrick holding out his hand to me.

I don't need it but I take it anyway, as I step up out of the boat. And I don't quite know why, but the shock of solid ground, after nearly an hour of gentle rocking, takes me by surprise and I find myself stumbling. He catches me. I look up into his eyes, and what I see there makes me look away quickly in an effort to slow my racing heartbeat.

'You guys OK?' Vik calls after us.

'Yes!' I say quickly. I walk past Patrick on the pretext of asking Mel something, and we make our way to the pub.

I'm walking and talking, about what I don't even know. What just happened there? I felt something that I've never felt before – not for Eddie, not for anyone. If Eddie holding my hand was like a computer failing to switch on, this was like the moment when the gas fire finally ignites, making you jump back so as not to get singed. And I can't be sure but I think that it wasn't just me. But he's leaving in a few weeks; what am I supposed to do about it?

The others are all keen on a pub lunch, so we make our way to the Prince Alfred, which is a real old Victorian jewel, with fabulously ornate plastered ceilings and little snugs partitioned by engraved glass panels, plus a roaring fire. It's all a bit wasted on me in my distracted state, though I do welcome the red wine that Mel orders, draining half my glass within minutes.

'Ah. Red wine, cosy sweaters, crackling fire,' says Vik happily. 'I love autumn. I can't wait to Instagram my pumpkin spice lattes.'

Mel laughs and they all start talking about their favourite things to do in winter. I don't say much but focus on making the odd comment and ordering something off the menu almost at random, which is not at all like me. I can't meet Patrick's eye.

But then, as the food arrives and we all continue chatting, I feel a bit calmer and better able to rationalize. It was just a passing flicker of physical attraction – nothing more, nothing less. My body was reacting to him, maybe because it sensed a new possibility now that things with Eddie are over. But that doesn't mean that my mind or heart are involved. He's about to leave the country, which is probably what prompted that little flicker – like when they announce last orders at the bar and you think you probably could do with a chaser, even when it's actually the last thing you need.

'What's next on your list, Celeste?' Mel asks me.

'Um . . . visit a Christmas market. That should be easy enough, there's one on the South Bank . . .' I add tentatively, 'Anybody interested?'

'Sure,' says Mel promptly, making me think yet again what a great friend she is. 'How about the end of November – say the twenty-second?'

'That's my birthday,' says Patrick, smiling.

'Oh!' I say. 'Well, you probably have more exciting plans.'

He shakes his head. 'Not yet. A Christmas market could be a nice change . . . I mean, a bit of glühwein and gingerbread, what's not to like?'

I feel relieved that he's being so relaxed about it all, and I like the idea of having him along for the finish – since he was there from the start. Then he'll be back to Dublin, and we will be back on our normal footing, as just two friends among a group. With that thought I'm able to focus more on the conversation, which has moved on to the swan and how much calmer and happier he seems now under the influence of the chickens.

'It turns out he didn't need a new mate . . . He just needed mates,' says Vik, showing us a picture of them all pecking amiably at some seed together. 'He does still steal their food, though.'

I decide this is the perfect omen for me, or the perfect metaphor, for Patrick and me. We are best off as friends. It must just be that I've grown used to having him around. For anyone to leave is sad, after all.

Now Vik is talking about his plans to start opening the house and garden up to the local community. He's got to know a local youth theatre that works with teens in difficult circumstances, and thinks they could use the house for retreats and maybe even a show. Vik seems extremely taken with the group, and with their director, Megan. This seems to be the same Megan who's featured in a few of his anecdotes today.

'She's really quite amazing,' says Vik, when I ask him about her. 'She's actually had similar experiences to some of the kids – she was a care leaver and all sorts, and now she's doing this incredible work in the community.' He smiles. 'You should see her with the kids – she's five foot nothing, but when she talks to them you could hear a pin drop.'

'She sounds great,' says Mel solemnly. She catches my eye, and I think we're both thinking the same thing, that it would be nice for Vik to meet someone nice. I think a year ago this would have been a tough idea for me to accept, but now I can imagine being really happy for him. As for me, I'm done with romance; all I want for Christmas this year is to be happily single.

29

November

Hannah and I didn't ever really argue, but one thing we used to debate was the important question of when you can start feeling Christmassy. I always used to feel that you should hold out for December, but Hannah used to say that any time after her birthday – 5 November – was fair game. Either way her birthday always used to signal the start of the party season, with the nights drawing in.

This year, of course, 5 November has a different significance. But it hasn't been bad. Mel and I celebrate with Kir royales, in Hannah's honour, watching the fireworks from her top-floor flat. We exchange texts with Shib and Vik, who had some friends round to his place. And then we both receive a message from Patrick. Re Christmas market, what about a day trip to Ghent?

I'm startled by this bold suggestion, but the others seem well up for it; Mel says 'Cool!' and replies instantly with train emojis, and Vik sends multiple thumbs-up. I reply with a more cautious 'Sounds great' and Patrick says that he'll book Eurostar tickets for us all. I'm a little uneasy at the idea that I'll be spending all day with him. But there will be safety in numbers at least.

*

On the morning before we're due to meet, though, the plans start to fall apart. It starts with Mel messaging to say that she has a severe throat infection; she can't even speak apparently. And then Vik suddenly has an urgent appointment with a builder; his roof, or 'one of the roofs', is leaking.

It's a real shame that everyone is dropping out. And I can't help but feel terrified that we're now facing a two-some trip. However, it is his birthday, and one of my absolute golden life rules is that I never, ever cancel on someone's birthday. Plus, of course, it's a resolution so needs must. And even if it wasn't . . . a reckless part of me is thinking: *Might it actually be quite nice? To be alone again?*

My phone buzzes and I almost drop it when I see it's a text from Patrick himself. Are you free for a quick call?

I dial his number right away before I can chicken out. 'Sorry about all the drop-outs,' I tell him.

'Yeah, it sucks, doesn't it? I'm pretty used to it, though – it's just a birthday hazard if you're born in November . . .' He pauses. 'I just wanted to say, really, that if you want to take a rain check, I don't mind. I know it's a busy weekend for most people.'

'No – it's your birthday! I'm not going to cancel.' Then an unwelcome thought hits me. 'Unless you'd prefer to rain check? If you've got another option . . .'

'No.' I can hear him smiling. 'OK. I'll see you at the station tomorrow.'

'See you then.'

I hang up, feeling equal parts pleased and scared. What if this crush, or whatever it was that I felt on the boat, pops back up while we're away? But if it does, I'll just remind myself of the facts: he's leaving London, and we're friends. This trip is going to be about glühwein, gingerbread and – I try to think of a third G – good clean fun. In fact, maybe I'd better stick to hot chocolate instead of glühwein.

The next day, I arrive at St Pancras station a good twenty minutes early, so I browse in L'Occitane for a bit before I mooch along to our appointed waiting place outside Benugo. Patrick is there already, wearing the same navy coat that he had on the canal boat, with his Aran sweater underneath.

'Happy birthday!' I say, giving him a wave. The station is really hot, and I catch a glimpse of myself looking very dishevelled in my black wool trench, and a red sweater that's clashing with my face. I suddenly feel ridiculously shy as it hits me afresh that we're about to hop on a train together for a trip abroad. Is this a good idea? Maybe I should have cancelled when he gave me a chance. But he looks so pleased to see me that I immediately feel glad that I came.

'Birthday breakfast?' I suggest. He protests but I insist, so we go inside to get him a chocolate croissant and coffee with an extra shot.

'Only if you have the same,' he says.

'It would be rude not to,' I say. I ping the waistband of my trousers and add, 'I've got my eating trousers on!' Then I cringe at myself; it's fair enough to keep things on a friendly footing, but do I have to sound like an animal?

But Patrick looks amused. 'Good woman,' he says. Lifting his coffee, he says, 'Thanks for the birthday present!'

'Oh, you're welcome.' That's not actually his present; I

have another one, but maybe I'll hold it back till later. Otherwise it's all a bit too intense for this hour of the morning.

'So, Celeste,' Patrick says to me, as we settle back in our seats on the Eurostar, 'before we get there . . . I need to know how you feel about something.'

'God, OK. What?' My heart starts thumping at the serious look in his eyes. We're sitting opposite each other, with the fields of Kent rolling by. Patrick seems in high spirits; maybe he's on a sugar high.

'Chips with mayo.'

'Chips with mayo?' I repeat. 'Oh, no, no. I mean, ketchup, yes, obviously; barbeque sauce at a pinch. But mayonnaise? That's ungodly.'

'OK, they may not let you in,' he says. 'I mean, that's just one of the things that make Belgium, Belgium. Along with chocolates, medieval art and a great football team. And the bitter political and linguistic divide, of course.'

'Yes . . . I've never really got to grips with that one,' I admit. 'What's the story?'

Patrick explains about the contentious relationship between the Flemish population of Belgium and the French-speaking Walloons. Ghent is a Flemish-speaking city, which I hadn't grasped either.

'God, I actually didn't realize,' I say, feeling embarrassed. 'I've been practising my French phases, so I'm glad you told me.' I normally spend a lot more time researching for a trip; I've just been so busy at work that I haven't done the due diligence I usually would. And we're only here for a day.

'It's OK. I didn't realize either, until I lived in Antwerp for a year.'

'Gosh, I forgot you lived here.' I look at him, considering how much I still don't know about him. 'What's your favourite, of all the places you've lived?'

'South Africa,' he says promptly. 'It's got its problems, but I've never been anywhere more beautiful. So is Switzerland.' He smiles. 'Though actually, after this year – London is sneaking into third place.'

'Third place! High praise,' I say, raising my eyebrows. 'I'll take it.' I know it's silly but I can't help but wonder whether I've got anything to do with it rising in the ranks.

After changing in Brussels, we arrive in Ghent at lunchtime. I'm very glad that I brought my sunglasses, because it's brilliantly sunny but freezing; I can see my breath hanging in the frosty air – the perfect weather, really, for exploring. I get a nice impression of Ghent. It reminds me of Bruges, with the same medieval buildings, narrow, winding, cobbled streets and canals spanned by little arched bridges and guild buildings that look like miniature castles. But it's quieter and feels less touristy. As we wander towards the Christmas market, I spy sustainable fashion boutiques and lots of vintage shops and adorable old-timey bakeries, all lit up with festive lights and decorations.

Then we round a corner to the Christmas market itself, at the end of the Korenmarkt. The big cobbled square is lined with tall stately Flemish buildings with zigzag gables. Nestled beneath them are dozens of little stalls and huts, selling hot chocolate, beer and mulled wine. Christmas trees are strung with lights, already glowing in the dusky air, and there's a Ferris wheel turning slowly over the whole thing. It's the quaintest festive market I've ever seen.

'Hot chocolate?' Patrick asks me.

'That would be delightful.'

'Whipped cream, or marshmallows?'

'Oh.' My immediate response would be that I don't strictly speaking need either, but then I throw caution to the wind. 'Cream, please.'

He goes off to queue at one of the little wooden huts, and I wander a few doors down to check out some candy canes. They look they've come straight from the North Pole, with the most exquisite whirls on them, red and pink and white striped: far too pretty to eat.

'Seen something you like?' Patrick asks me, joining me and handing me a hot chocolate.

'Thanks. Just these – they're so pretty, but obviously not really an essential item.' I half turn away, but he ignores me, addressing the stallholder in what sounds like fluent Flemish. Then he hands me half a dozen candy canes.

'Patrick!' I protest, laughing, so he slips them straight into my pocket. 'I didn't need these. And since when do you speak Flemish?'

'I can count to ten and say please – that's not speaking exactly. Just take them. You can always give them to some rosy-cheeked orphan.'

'Well, thank you, kind sir. I will,' I say, tucking them into my bag.

We wander past more food stalls: handmade chocolates with tiny elaborate designs, exquisite little cakes and pastries, Turkish delight glowing like jewels under their soft coating of powder, and rows and rows of gingerbread men, iced with the most elaborate costumes complete with Christmas hats.

'Do you need any gingerbread men?' I ask.

'God, yes. You should always stock up when you can. Have you ever tried these?' he asks, as I pay the stallholder.

He's holding up a sample from the stall; it looks like gingerbread but wafer-thin. I've got my hands full of gingerbread men, so I lean forward to take a bite straight from his hand. It's buttery, biscuity and rich with cinnamon. 'Oh my God,' I say closing my eyes. 'That's so good. What are they?'

'Belgian thins, I think they are in English. Not very well named.' He's looking at me. 'You have a little – hang on.' He brushes his thumb across my face, right under my lip. I look at him, feeling dazzled by the halo of Christmas lights behind him. 'Just a crumb,' he says, looking away. 'Oh, look. Handmade lace.'

'Oh, great!' I say, trying to sound casual, though I can still feel the contact of his thumb for a good ten minutes afterwards.

The next stalls we come to are displaying the loveliest range of Christmas ornaments, from little carved nativity figures to painted angels. I decide they would make great Christmas presents and buy red felted hearts for all my friends and family. Then I notice some beautiful glass baubles – they look like little snow globes, complete with miniature scenes: two children on a toboggan, or a couple sitting on a bench in the snow.

'These are just gorgeous, aren't they?' I say to Patrick. 'But I don't know if they'd survive the train journey.'

'I can wrap them,' the man running the stall says, holding up a sheet of bubble wrap.

'Just get them,' Patrick says. 'You obviously like them . . . They should be fine if you're careful. And if they smash, they smash. You won't have lost anything except –' he looks at the price – 'fifteen euro for three. Bargain.'

I throw caution to the wind and get three of the prettiest ones. To my surprise Patrick buys the same ones, and we watch as the man wraps them in two separate extra-safe packages.

'What?' he says, smiling at me. 'Guys can have nice things too.'

Two hours and three toffee waffles later, we've exhausted the delights of the Christmas market. We're standing under the Ferris wheel, which is playing 'All I Want for Christmas'.

'What do you think?' he says.

'I mean . . . have you even been to the Christmas market if you don't go on the Ferris wheel?'

'No,' he agrees. 'You haven't.'

Soon we're in a little gondola on the Ferris wheel, slowly climbing the circle up towards the sky.

'Oh, wait – I don't want to go backwards,' I say, realizing too late as we start to ascend.

'Sit beside me then,' he says. I manage to wriggle over the barrier – safety be damned – and sit beside him, my heart thumping from the exertion. Or from something.

It's properly dusk now. Below us we can see all the little wooden huts, strung with white lights and red ribbon, and the gabled medieval buildings behind them, glowing with lights against the winter dusk. It's like a scene from a snow globe, impossibly pretty and miniature.

I turn to look at Patrick close beside me, then look away. I can feel his shoulder and thigh pressed against mine. It might be because the gondola is small, but it's not that small. I don't move and he doesn't move. And the feeling is just as dizzying as the ascent of the gondola. We've reached the top now, and every part of me is wanting something to happen; for him to turn to me and kiss me, or for me to reach for his hand, while we still have time. But then the moment goes and we're swinging back below to solid ground.

The ride tips us out and we stand unsteadily beside the Ferris wheel, my legs unsteady from the feel of solid ground again. *Calm down, Celeste*, I tell myself. It's just Christmas spirit. Or a sugar high. You've survived almost the whole day without doing or saying something embarrassing – don't mess it up now.

'You look a little pale,' Patrick says. 'Do you want to go inside somewhere – get a bite to eat?' He looks at his watch. 'We've got just over an hour, I'd say.'

I nod. 'Good idea. I'm not sure I've had anything all day that wasn't chocolate or covered in cream.'

We start walking away from the market, and a side street leads us to a restaurant called Pain Perdu. It's a cute little place with reclaimed school-style furniture that clashes artily with the red-ribbon decorations and a multitude of delicately carved angel ornaments hanging from the ceiling. We order Flemish pizzas and 'Christmas beer', which turns out to be dark, sweet and spicy. I'm worried the beer will make me feel even more light-headed, but a sip seems to calm me down. I start to remember the original purpose of this trip: not to experience weird feelings but to celebrate Patrick's birthday *and* complete my resolution.

'Happy birthday,' I say, lifting my glass to his.

'Thank you,' he says. 'Happy resolution. Number eleven, right?'

'Yep. Lucky eleven. It's been one of the good ones, so thank you.'

He smiles at me, while I realize, in dismay, that he looks even more handsome by candlelight than he did in the light of the Christmas stalls outside. We're distracted by our Flemish pizzas arriving, and I fall on mine gratefully, though I find that after a few bites I seem to have lost my appetite again. What is wrong with me today?

'So . . . what do you think you've learned from your list?' he says.

'Learned?' I repeat, stalling for time as if I don't know what he means. Though of course I do.

The truth is I've learned a lot. From the hot yoga I learned to face my pain. With climbing I learned to face my fears. The appointment with the astrologer changed how I see myself on the inside. And the personal shopping appointment changed how I see myself on the outside.

'It's funny how they almost fell into season,' I tell him. 'The spring ones . . . they helped me with, I suppose, personal development? And the summer ones . . .' I think of the ceilidh, the afternoon tea, the outdoor swimming. 'Those just helped me connect with other people and have fun again honestly. So did the canal boat and – even this.' I gesture around the restaurant.

'Even this,' he says teasingly. 'Even this last dud item on the list.'

'Very funny,' I say. 'Anyway, that's enough about me. This is your birthday! Speaking of which . . .' I reach in my bag, where under my pile of impulse presents, I have his gift, wrapped in plain brown paper with a red ribbon.

'Is this for me?' he asks. 'You didn't have to.'

He opens it. It's an antique pocket compass in a brass case that attaches to a fob like a key ring. One trembling black arrow points to a red N. He lifts it slowly, and I watch the hand turn until it points to me.

'I must be north,' I say, joking. 'No wonder I've been so cold all day.'

He's quiet for a minute, then he says, 'You remembered.'

'You said you wanted to be able to tell where north was, so . . .' I trail off, feeling a little embarrassed. Is it too much? I bought it second-hand on eBay, and I thought it would be just right, lost in the general melee of other presents and cards. I didn't imagine gifting it to him across a white tablecloth, as if it's our silver anniversary dinner.

'I think it's the nicest present I've ever been given.'

'Gosh.' I feel the impulse to make a joke, about how rubbish his previous gifts must have been, but I resist. 'I am really glad you like it,' I say instead.

'That's something I remember Hannah saying about you. That you always gave the best presents.'

'Really?' I say, deeply touched. 'I do love giving presents.'

He nods. 'She said that. Also, that you were very reliable. You never cancelled ever, unless you were at death's door.'

'Oh.' I'm less enchanted by this. 'Well, that makes me sound like an old Volvo.'

'No, no.' He shakes his head. 'Quite the reverse. More like a comet. The mysterious Celeste. Would she agree to show up – or would she not? You never knew. But if you said you'd come, you would come.'

I look down at the tablecloth. 'Unless I've changed, right? With the whole list thing.'

'You have changed in some ways. In other ways I think you're just the same as you were when I first met you.' He smiles in a teasing, tender way that turns my knees to water.

'Can you even remember when that was?' I ask, suddenly wanting to know.

'Of course I do.' He takes a sip of his beer. 'New Year's Eve, 1999. Hannah had a party and you came. We took a boat to Dalkey Island the next morning. Isn't that right?'

'Yes,' I admit softly.

'But before then . . . you and I had a brief chat in the kitchen. About the *Titanic*. I remember it . . . Do you?'

I swallow, my mouth feeling suddenly dry. 'Yeah, I do.'

'You were wearing a sort of silvery top, I remember. Sleeveless. And your hair was long and parted in the middle. Just like it is now.'

Trying to keep my tone light, I say, 'I'm impressed you remember. That was a long time ago, and you only spoke to me for about two seconds.'

'Of course I did. You were my little sister's friend's friend . . . I was an old man of twenty, and you were, what, seventeen? Eighteen?'

'Eighteen.'

'Yeah.' He continues, 'Way too young for me to chat you up. Or kiss you at midnight.'

I look down at his hand on the tablecloth – strong and beautifully shaped. How can someone's hand – just their hand – be so attractive? It's excessive. Unreasonable.

'Anyway,' he says, 'thank you for the present. And for not flaking out today.' He sips his beer. 'I can't imagine you ever flaking on anything actually. Has that ever happened?'

'Well,' I say, 'you probably know that I was engaged once and I broke it off.' *And got back together with him, and dumped him again*, I think but don't add. 'Some might think that was flaky.'

'I think it was courageous.'

I'm totally flattened by the look in his eyes.

'Any coffee or desserts for you?' says a voice in English, making us both jump out of our skin.

'No thanks,' Patrick says at the same time as I say, 'Just the bill, please.'

This conversation has wandered down too many byways; we need some fresh air and a reality check, before I find myself going down a road I can't turn back from.

Leaving the restaurant, we walk slowly towards the station. It's properly dark now. We climb the bridge that leads away from the market and pause to look back again at the scene, which is like something from a fairy tale. I could almost imagine a host of medieval knights clattering over the cobblestones, their horses' tack jingling in the cold air. I can still hear Christmas music softly drifting across the square from the Ferris wheel; it's playing Mariah Carey again.

Then, out of nowhere, a massive bang erupts, seemingly in my ear. It's a firework, shedding its red and white lights over the dark waters of the canal. I'm so startled that it takes me a second to realize I've stepped backwards involuntarily – right into Patrick's arms. He takes a step back as I knock into him, then steadies himself.

He doesn't do anything, waiting perhaps to see if I'll move away. I don't move but stay close to him, while the crowd jostles around us, spreading out for a better view. After a second I feel his arm circling tighter around me. He rests his head on mine and I feel him exhale. I remain there, stock-still, while we watch the firework display burst its colours above our heads. My heart is beating louder than the explosions, and I'm frantically trying to decide what on earth I should do next.

Then I stop thinking, and just let myself feel this moment. The fireworks peter out and the crowd drifts off, leaving us standing on the bridge. I can't really register anything but his arms around me, his head on mine. I turn around and look up at him.

'Celeste,' he says. But I've already reached up and pulled his face to mine.

I've never felt weak at the knees during a kiss, and I always thought it was just an expression. But my knees do actually buckle briefly as I feel this kiss – this once-in-a-lifetime kiss. The fireworks display a minute ago was nothing compared to the explosions that are happening inside me right now. My hand strays up towards his hair, which is just as soft as I'd imagined. I slip my other hand under his coat to pull him towards me, feeling the strength and heat of him; I can't get him close enough.

327

After a minute we stop. His mouth close to my hair, he says, 'We're going to miss that train.' His voice is ragged, but I hear the smile in it too. Then he kisses me again, and I get so distracted that I almost forgot what he said until he reminds me gently.

'Fine. Let's miss it.'

'Are you serious?' He puts both his arms around me. He's looking down at me steadily, but I can feel his heart racing as fast as mine.

'Yep. We can get another one later – or tomorrow.' I look up at him so he knows exactly what I'm saying.

'And sleep out under the stars?'

'Sure.' I glance up at the night sky, which is brighter and clearer than the one in London. I see the winter constellations, Orion and the Plough, then I find Polaris. I remember the astrologer's words about it knocking me off course. Maybe this is it now, hitting me with something I never expected but want more than I've wanted anything before. There might be shocks and disasters to come, but I'll worry about those tomorrow.

30

We find a hotel near the market, which looks cute and quaint, with a swinging shield-shaped sign hanging from a beam outside. Inside, they're playing traditional Christmas carols, and there's a glass dish of miniature candy canes on the reception desk and a six-foot Christmas tree lit with white fairy lights.

'One double room?' asks the charming receptionist.

'Celeste?' Patrick looks at me to check. I'm not even going to go through the motions of considering an alternative; I just nod.

She leads us upstairs, round a crooked little flight of steps, to a room with exposed wooden beams and a four-poster bed, and wishes us a pleasant stay before leaving. I part the heavy velvet curtains and look out of the leaded window, admiring the quaint little street downstairs, the festive crowds going to and from the market laden down with festive treats and bags of Christmas shopping. Then Patrick comes up behind me, lifts my hair and kisses me on the back of my neck, and all thoughts of sightseeing go out of my head.

'Did you imagine that anything like this was going to happen?' I ask him, breathless.

'Not in my wildest dreams,' he says, and he bends to kiss the gap of skin just over my waistband. I look up at the ceiling and sigh aloud as he runs a hand around my back, under the edge of my sweater, and up to my bra strap. And I thank the good angels who inspired me to put on my prettiest underwear this morning and shave my legs.

I murmur in his ear, 'What is this hotel called again? I've forgotten.'

'Me neither. Doesn't matter.' He pauses in between kisses. 'Or does it? I don't want to rush you.'

'Oh, you're not rushing me,' I reply. 'We can find out tomorrow.'

When I wake up, it's just starting to get light. I didn't imagine it; Patrick and I really are in a hotel room in Ghent. I look at his face on the pillow beside me, sleeping peacefully, and I try to imprint every detail of it on my memory, along with all of last night. It's twenty-four hours since everyone cancelled but it feels like a lifetime.

'Oh good,' he says, opening his eyes. 'It wasn't a dream.' He wraps an arm around me and we kiss again, slow and lazy. It might not have been a dream, but it certainly feels like one.

'So . . . what do you want to do today?' I ask him after a minute.

He looks at me and I can feel my insides dissolve.

'What a question,' he says, grinning, and pulls me towards him. Then he looks past me at the window. 'Hey, look at the light.'

'What?' I turn my head and behind me I see what he means. The little leaded window is muffled with snow. 'Oh, snow!' I scramble of out bed, slipping his shirt on as I go and crouch down beside the window to look out. 'It's so gorgeous – come and see.'

He comes over and looks out of the window, leaning a hand on my shoulder. 'That is gorgeous. Do you want to go out and see it now, while it's fresh?'

With any other man I would have said yes immediately, but with Patrick I'm torn. Snow is rare and precious, but so is our time alone together; I don't want to miss a minute of it. He looks down at me as though he's thinking the same thing.

'We've got plenty of time. Come on,' he says.

We wrap up in our warmest layers and go downstairs, and outside into a fairy tale. The sky is a deep, keen blue and the air is crystalline, cold and fresh. There's perfect icing-sugar snow as far as the eye can see, muffling all the roofs and gables of the pretty little street. In the distance I can see the blue line of the canal carved out against the white banks and bridges. It's early and completely quiet. One man and his little boy go by, dragging a toboggan; they give us a wave and a good morning, and we wave back. The boy looks as ecstatically happy as I remember being as a kid when it snowed, as happy as I am now.

We walk down the little street, its windows and doors all shuttered, until we find a bakery open which sells us steaming-hot coffees in red paper cups printed with snowflakes. These keep out the cold as we walk towards the nearest bridge, where we have a fuller view of the canal. Weeping willows, Flemish houses and medieval towers are hooded in pure white, and the whole is reflected in the pristine mirror of the still water. It's like standing in a seventeenth-century oil painting. Despite my freezing feet, I could stay here all day, just gazing.

'I've honestly never seen anything so pretty,' I say to

Patrick, who's just come back from putting our empty paper cups in a bin. 'I want to take photos, but I know it won't do it justice.'

'True. But I'll try anyway,' he says, and snaps a picture of me with his phone.

'Very funny,' I say, punching him lightly on his arm, but who am I kidding? I'm also basking in his open admiration.

'Let's take one of the two of us.' He puts his arm around me and takes a picture, our faces close together.

'And send it to the others?' I suggest. 'Give them a surprise?'

'We can if you want to,' he says immediately. 'Why not? Vik's been texting, asking how it went . . .'

'Oh no – I was joking.' I shake my head, not quite able to analyse the instinct that makes me want to keep all of this under wraps for now. 'Let's just keep it to ourselves for now. Just me and you. Until we have to leave.'

He doesn't say anything for a minute but puts his gloved hands on my face and bends down to kiss me. I press as close to him as I can, despite our bulky winter clothes, and feel the shivers that I seem to get every time he touches me. Suddenly I remember the ballet. This is it. It's the pas de deux, all the same moves I've been through before with other men – but as different as night and day, sun and snow.

'Who said we have to leave?' he says. 'I don't know about you, but I don't work weekends. Why don't we stay another night?'

'Just like that?' I ask, laughing.

'Yes, just like that. It is still my birthday after all.'

'Is it?' I gaze up at him, wanting to say yes with all my

332

heart but also mindful of practicalities, not least that I don't have anything with me, or any clothes except the ones I'm standing up in. He continues, 'Didn't you know the rule? For every person who cancels on your birthday, you get an extra day's celebrations. So Vik and Mel have just given me . . . till Sunday evening.'

'I don't even have a toothbrush with me,' I say, smiling. 'Do you?'

'I'll buy you one. Early Christmas present.'

'OK then.' I slip my hand into his. 'Since it's the rules.'

'Great.' He looks, so happy, as happy as I feel, and I can't believe I even considered saying no. He says, 'Let's stroll a bit further, then go back to the hotel, have our breakfast . . . see if they have toothbrushes, and if not, we'll go shopping.'

'That sounds perfect,' I say.

The rest of the weekend goes by in a snow-bound dream. We wander around the whitened streets with their icy cobblestones, and dip in and out of the cafes along the medieval Korenlei and Graslei quays where we eat waterzooi, a delicate chicken stew, and drink cherry beer while huddled knee to knee in cosy booths. And when the snow falls again, on Sunday morning, we agree that there's no point in rushing out, when there's a blizzard outside and our hotel room is so cosy. Until all too soon, it's time to take the last train home, on Sunday evening.

We sit side by side on the train, exhausted and happy, and I lean my cheek on Patrick's shoulder while he flicks through the Eurostar magazine, which features an article on Ghent and its many sights.

'My God,' I say, feeling a little guilty. 'There is so much we didn't see.'

He leans down to kiss the top of my head. 'I saw everything I wanted to.'

I look down at his hand entwined in mine, and at the package of baubles, which I'm carefully holding on my lap. This weekend has been an enchanted bubble, like one of those scenes, but now we're heading back to London, and our jobs and friends and reality. Not to mention, it's very nearly December – his last month in London before he moves to Dublin permanently.

'Hey,' he says, glancing at me, 'we can go back to Ghent another time, I promise. We'll see that altarpiece.'

'It's not the altarpiece,' I say, smiling. 'It's just – it's been nice, hasn't it?'

'"Nice" is one word,' he says with that expression that makes me dizzy.

'We've been in a little bubble.' I look out of the window at the dark Belgian landscape streaming by. 'But it's back to reality now, I suppose.'

He doesn't reply for a minute, but I think he understands that I'm not just talking about our return to London – but about him leaving next month.

'I've got an idea,' he says. 'Why don't we just stay in the bubble?'

'Stay in the bubble?'

'Yes. I mean, sure, I've got packing and stuff to do, over the next few weeks. But that's all the more reason to see as much as we can of each other . . . if you want to?'

I nod wordlessly.

'Good. And we can do all the nicest, most festive things

we can think of – and see who can plan the best ones. If London in the run-up to Christmas is all it's cracked up to be, we should be able to come up with some ideas.' He runs a finger down the side of my cheek. 'Does that sound like a reasonable plan?'

'Very reasonable,' I say.

'Good. Obviously we'll have work to do, and you have some resolution obligations possibly?'

'Not really. December's one is "Help someone in need".'

Patrick laughs. 'Well, I *need* to get my Christmas on. Think you can help me with that?'

I tell him I'll try, and as he leans down to kiss me again, I reflect that it might not be on the list exactly but making Patrick happy is one new thing I certainly want to try.

31

December

It's a law of economics, and of physics, that bubbles will invariably pop. But as November turns to December, ours holds steady. Patrick and I spend almost all our spare time together, trying to outdo each other by planning the most festive things we can think of. He starts off strong, with a visit to the Winter Wonderland in Hyde Park, followed by a drink in the Churchill Arms, the pub in Kensington whose Christmas lights are probably visible from space. I retaliate with a walk around Mayfair, which I think has the prettiest decorations in London, including Annabel's club, which is all done up to look like a gingerbread house, before heading to the Connaught for Irish coffees.

'Good effort,' he remarks, lifting his coffee glass to mine. 'But I've got something for next weekend that's going to blow you out of the water.'

He refuses to say what it is, but tells me to meet him the following Friday evening at the Coal Hole pub on the Strand, which I do.

As I push my way through the crowds, I reflect that there are few things more Christmassy than a pub in December. It's already gone hard with tinsel, plastic Santas and fairy lights, and they're playing Slade at such a volume that I almost don't hear Patrick behind me, calling 'Celeste!' I turn around to see him sitting with the *Evening Standard* and a pint. He's wearing an impeccable dark navy suit and a crisp white shirt, with no tie. I've never seen him wearing a suit before and I don't know if it's this that makes my heart dip, or the fact that he's waiting here just for me and has planned me a special surprise.

'Hi,' I say, bending down to kiss him. 'Oh, thanks.' He hands me a glass of mulled wine, steaming with cloves.

'I can get you something else if you want? But it might be good to have something warm first, before our evening's activity.'

'Oh, God don't tell me. Boat trip?' I smile, thinking that actually a trip down the Thames might not be so terrible: curled into his arm, watching the festive lights go past . . .

'I'm not saying,' says Patrick. 'Although . . . Hm, I probably should have checked if it was something you wanted to do. Or even could do.' He looks worried suddenly.

'Stop. I can't take the suspense. Horse riding? Bungee jumping?'

He pushes two tickets across the table at me and I take a look. It's for skating at Somerset House.

'Patrick! This is something I've wanted to do for literally years.'

He smiles. 'Really? So why haven't you? You've lived here, what, fifteen years?'

I shake my head, thinking what an excellent question this is. 'I suppose – when you can do something at any time, you put it off. Or I do.'

'Well, maybe time pressure has its uses then.'

Not wanting to talk about his impending departure, I

decide to change the subject. 'Are you OK to skate in your nice suit?' I ask, and he laughs. 'I'll just have to stay vertical.' Seeing that I've finished my mulled wine, he stands up, saying 'Come on. Time to get our skates on,' and I groan.

The skating rink is in the courtyard of Somerset House, a classical stone building off the Strand. It's overlooked by a thirty-foot Christmas tree decked out with red and gold baubles and white lights. The three wings of the eighteenth-century building are floodlit, and below them are pop-up bars where you can wrap up in blankets and fur rugs, and drink hot chocolate, Baileys or champagne, maybe depending on how traumatic the skating has been. As we queue to drop our bags and hire our skates, I decide that if I've forgotten how to do this and I keep falling flat, I'll just turn spectator with a nice festive drink.

But I haven't forgotten. Even though I haven't been since I was a teen, it all comes back to me, as I hold his hand and wobble across the ice, skidding at first but then more confidently until I am actually gliding. As we swirl around to music from *The Nutcracker*, I reflect that even without the white ice uplighting everyone's faces, I would be glowing from within.

'You OK?' he asks, as I come to a stop at the edge of the rink.

'Just catching my breath.' I look up at him, laughing. 'The last time I went skating was in Dolphin's Barn,' I add, referring to the old rink I went to in Dublin. 'And that's been closed for years, as you know.'

'Do you know the old joke? Americans have SeaWorld, we have Dolphin's Barn.'

This makes me laugh again, and I think how nice it is that he gets my cultural references, and that I understand his too. It looks like I was wrong about dating Irish men. I was wrong about a lot of things really.

'I'm glad it was a hit,' he says, smiling. 'Especially because I have one more suggestion for this weekend – and then I'm out of ideas.'

'What's that?' I ask.

'Well, it's not very exciting. But I've got some friends who are going to use my flat, over Christmas, till my tenancy ends. They've got a kid . . . so I thought it would be nice to decorate the place, or put up a tree at least.' He lifts his shoulders. 'I could do with some help if that's not too dull?'

'That's not dull at all. Of course I will. And it will be nice to hang out at your place.' I have been there by now, twice, but I can't say that I've been able to take in my surroundings very fully. 'When do they arrive – your friends?'

'Well, I leave on the twenty-second, and they arrive the next day – the twenty-third.' He looks around. 'Their little boy is eight, so I might book this for them. Do you think they'd like that?'

'Of course they would,' I say. I'm torn between two thoughts: how thoughtful he is, and also that he's leaving. On the twenty-second. That seemed an eternity away but now it's ten days. We stand quietly at the edge of the rink, looking at the other skaters gliding past, all bundled up, with flushed cheeks under their winter hats, all under the glow of the Christmas tree.

'It's not the worst place in the world, is it?' I ask, just as he asked me in Dublin.

'I never said it was,' he says – which was my reply then.

He looks down, and puts his arm around me. 'We'll have to go skating in Dublin,' he says. 'And then . . . I'm coming over to Vik's for New Year's . . .'

'You're not suggesting we skate on his pond, are you?' I say, trying to smile, because I don't want to think about the future when he's gone.

'Now there's an idea,' he says. 'You know what I mean, though. We'll figure it out – right?'

I nod, smiling up at him and heartened by his words. We will figure it out, and meanwhile we're wasting valuable skating time.

'Come on,' I say, pushing off into an unsteady glide. 'Last one round buys the drinks.'

It's the day of the office Christmas party, and I'm in work, reflecting on how much has changed since last year. I've just been to the very Pret where they offered me my free lunch, a year ago to the day. Except that this year, I took fifteen minutes to eat my lunch with no distractions, and I'm actually going to go to the office party instead of working. I did have my Pret Christmas sandwich, though. Some things are too good to change.

I've just sat back down at my desk to tackle my afternoon's to-do list, when Swati and Dasha bustle up, both in secret squirrel mode.

'What's up, ladies?' I ask, thinking how nice it is to see them together; they're not quite as joined at the hip as they once were, but they're friends again, which makes me feel surprisingly emotional.

'We have a message for you,' says Swati in a low voice.

I'm assuming this is something to do with this afternoon's Secret Santa, so I'm astonished when Dasha continues, 'From a party that wanted to contact you without using your work contact details,' explains Dasha.

I have no idea what this is about, but I take the card that Dasha proffered. It belongs to Kemi McLaughlin, the CEO of Effie.

'Thanks, guys. I'll call her.'

I haven't heard from Kemi since our last piece of work

for her back in October, and my first thought is that something must have gone wrong, either with our advice or with their execution of it. I don't know why she's reaching out in this odd way, but I'm sufficiently worried about it that I call her right away, barricading myself in the nearest empty meeting room I can find.

But Kemi doesn't sound upset, but rather excited. 'Celeste? Thanks so much for calling!'

'Not at all,' I say, sitting down on the edge of a desk. 'How can I help?'

'Well, I'm sitting here with Orla – you're on speakerphone by the way.'

'Hi, Celeste!' Orla sounds equally excited.

'Hi, Orla,' I say, relieved but also confused at her joyful tone. Maybe they've won some award or something, but why the cloak and dagger?

'We hope you know how happy we are with all your work and advice this year,' says Kemi. 'Consulting you was a big stretch for us financially, but we've made it back in spades. We've got a further two million pounds in VC funding, and the app's just reached 1.2 million downloads.'

'That's wonderful!'

'Which is all to say that we're expanding, and we're looking for a new chief financial officer. And we wondered if you would be interested in the role?'

There's a silence, expectant on their end and on mine simply stunned. 'Me? As your CFO?'

'Yes. We can offer exactly the pay package that you recommended for that role,' says Kemi. 'Including the share options and the performance bonus. This is all coming to you in writing by the way.'

I manage to say, 'And where would the role be based?'

'In Dublin. We've just signed a new lease for our building, in Silicon Docks.'

'Wow,' is all I can say. 'I am extremely flattered, and really honoured that you've considered me. Could I have some time to think about it?'

'Yes, of course,' says Kemi. 'We know it involves relocation, and that's a big ask. But we would love to have you on board, Celeste. Have a think about it. Obviously it's nearly Christmas so you could let us know afterwards, maybe the first week in January?'

'Perfect. I will. Thanks so much, Kemi. I really appreciate the offer.'

We hang up and I walk to the glass window of the meeting room, pressing my cold hands and hot forehead against the glass and looking down, hundreds of metres, to the wintry street below. I've heard of consultants being poached by clients, of course. I've had offers too, but not for a job at CFO level. I wasn't lying when I told Kemi I was flattered – I'm super flattered that a company this innovative and exciting wants my talent, especially in the C-suite.

And yet. They're such a new venture and their future's not guaranteed. Two million pounds in funding is not the same as two million pounds in profits. The share options they're offering would be a big asset if the company's profitable, or they could turn out to be worthless if the company goes belly up – which is possible. I don't think it will, but I don't have a crystal ball either. Do I really have the appetite for that kind of risk?

I sit down and face the obvious point that I've been

avoiding thus far. This isn't just any job offer; it's an offer to move to Dublin. A year ago I would have ruled it out automatically because I felt London was home. But my sense of home has shifted. I want to be close to my parents and my brother. And, of course, there's Patrick. If I'm being honest, right now that feels like the biggest draw of all. The timing of this job offer couldn't be more perfect. No painful decisions or death by long-distance. It's like a sign.

Except that I don't believe in signs. I tried to; I thought that bumping into Eddie outside that yoga class could be a sign, and look how well that turned out. There are no magical signs or portents that can solve my dilemmas for me, just cold hard reality and lists of pros and cons. This job offer has plenty of pros: the salary for a start, which is more than I already earn. But the con – of joining a brand-new company that could flourish or go bust within eighteen months – is one that I just can't ignore.

'Celeste? I've booked this room, sorry,' says Marcus, with a self-important rap on the door. I nod, and he bustles inside, moustaches bristling. For a minute I reflect on how nice it would be to tell him that I'm leaving to become a CFO at a start-up. But Marcus isn't stupid, and he would know that a fancy title and wage fillip is worth nothing next to job security and a decent pension.

I'm still chewing over the whole thing when I arrive at Patrick's place the following evening. He lives in one of the new apartment buildings that overlook the reservoir near Clissold Park. It's modern and fairly featureless, but his flat has an exposed brick wall and a beautiful view of

'I do. But that's very different from trusting my whole future with them.' There's another silence, and I ask, 'No?'

'Sure, except it's not your whole future,' he says. 'At the very worst, you spend a year there and they go bust. Leaving you to step into another job with some valuable experience under your belt. Right?'

'Or leaving me unable to get another job because I'm associated with a failed project, living with my parents and getting into debt.'

Patrick smiles, and for the first time in a long time I'm reminded of how smug I found him when we went to Vik's last New Year's. 'Hardly,' he says, in a tone that I think is meant to sound reasonable but is just patronizing. 'I'm just going to take a wild guess here, but is it possible that you've built up three months' living expenses in savings?'

'Six,' I admit. 'But it's not just about that. Think of the costs of relocation – that's not nothing.'

'I know,' he says. 'Look, it's your call obviously. But just know that if you did decide to take a risk, I would have your back.'

'In what sense?' I ask, suddenly wrong-footed by this change of tack.

'In every sense,' he says simply. 'Practical, emotional, financial even. Whatever you needed.' He smiles, looking more like my Patrick again. 'I realize I'm not giving you very impartial advice. But the idea of having you in Dublin is very appealing. It's selfish, I know.'

Now he's being so nice, I'm feeling guilty – which makes me a lot more defensive than I would be normally.

'I'm sorry I'm not jumping at the chance to take this

job, just so I can move to Dublin,' I say, hoping I don't sound as agitated as I feel. 'It's not just the risk; it's everything I would be giving up here. Like my job – and all my chances of promotion.'

'Didn't you say that you felt like the promotion was never going to happen?' he asks. 'You told me about the award they gave you back in the summer – how you thought that was a bad sign, sort of a consolation prize.'

God, he's relentless. And his memory for all this work stuff is extremely inconvenient. 'Yes, but I don't know that for sure. I was just sore at the time.'

'That's fair enough,' he says. He stands back, looking at the tree in its entirety. 'What do you think? Are the lights even?'

I don't really like the way he's changing the subject, almost as if he thinks it's not worth trying to discuss it with me.

'Do you think I'm wrong to turn down the job? You can say so.'

'Of course you're not wrong,' he says in that reasonable tone of voice that I find so irksome. 'It's your career, your decision . . . Not everyone is suited to that kind of risk.'

I was just starting to calm down before he said that last part. 'You must think I'm such a stick in the mud.'

'I don't! Celeste, I feel I can't win here. You're right: the job is risky. That's not for you, so you're turning it down. End of story.'

'Yes,' I say. But I still feel judged, and the mood of the whole evening has soured. Especially with Patrick's next remark, which is, 'I suppose your whole resolution project hasn't changed you that much.' He's smiling, as if it's some kind of joke but to me it's not funny at all.

'What is *that* supposed to mean?' I ask quietly.

His face changes. 'You're right. I am sorry. That was a shitty thing to say. Can you forget that I said it?'

I stare at him, wondering how he expects me to forget something so horrible.

'You know,' I say, 'the point of me doing the list of resolutions wasn't to change me. It was to honour my friend's memory.'

'I know that! That's why I helped you with it.'

'*Helped* me? How did you help me exactly?'

'By encouraging you, coming climbing with you – why? What have I said?'

I don't know exactly how to put it into words. But I'm remembering what Vik said, long ago, about Patrick wanting to fix women.

He tried to fix Ivana, with her drinking problem. He tried to fix Angelika, with her work stress and assorted crises. Did he want to fix me next? Maybe he thought he would work his magic on me and end up with someone who was open to anything. Including giving up my career and moving with him to Dublin on a whim, to work at a risky new start-up without a care in the world because life's an adventure.

'So, when I went to Belgium with you, were you helping me then?'

'Of course not,' he says. 'But, OK, I'll be completely honest. I have been worried about this happening.'

'What?'

'About this exact situation. You finding reasons to stay

349

in London, because you don't want to commit to a big change. And yes, I know I'm being a hypocrite, because I don't want to change my plans either. And I know it's way too soon to bring it up. But I can't not say it, because if you're never going to leave London, I'd prefer to know now.'

'Well,' I say, when I can keep my voice steady, 'I would hate for you to waste any more time than you have already. So maybe we should call it quits.' I stand up and start pulling on my coat and walking towards the door.

'Celeste . . .'

He looks troubled, but he's not grabbing my arm or pulling me back down to my seat. He's just told me that he doesn't want to waste his time, which tells me exactly what kind of priority I am for him. I suppose I should be glad that he's been honest.

'It's OK, Patrick. I think you're right.' I look back at him. 'Long-distance relationships don't work.'

I try not to see the scene I'm leaving behind: the tree twinkling with lights; the paper chains ready to hang on the wall; the bottle of wine, still half full – or half empty. The record player is urging me to have myself a merry little Christmas. All I want to do is to get out of here. I grab my bag, which was lying on the kitchen counter, and then I hear a crack. A glass bauble has smashed on the tiled floor; one of the ones he bought in Belgium. I kneel down and try to pick the pieces up, my hands trembling.

'Celeste . . . Leave it! You'll hurt yourself.' He grabs a dustpan and brush, and kneels down beside me. 'Honestly, leave it. It's fine.'

I watch him sweep up the shards. The symbolism is just

too perfect. Our bubble hasn't just popped; it's smashed into a hundred pieces that he'll be finding on the floor for weeks to come.

'I'm sorry,' I say, my voice unsteady. And I am sorry that I broke it, but it was his fault, as much as mine.

But he doesn't say it's OK or take me in his arms or ask me to stay. Instead he says, 'Will you let me know you got home safely?'

'Sure,' I say, before turning around and walking out, blinking back tears. That I can do. But I am not going to Vik's place for New Year's. And ideally I won't see Patrick again for a long, long time.

33

It turns out there are no limits to my paranoia and my urge to self-sabotage. I was supposed to be flying back to Dublin on the same day as Patrick from the same airport, but I can't face the very real possibility of running into him, so I buy a cheap ticket to the train and ferry instead. That's more eco-friendly, and it gives me more time to look out of my window and think, and ponder the mess I've made of things.

Was it all my fault, though? I didn't imagine the impatient tone in his voice, or his irritation that I wasn't springing forward into the future on his approved time scale. If he does want to fix women, I can see why he was attracted to me. I was vulnerable and broken when he met me. Then he felt like he played an instrumental part in my 'recovery'. And now he wants to reap the rewards. But it doesn't work like that. A relationship has to be reciprocal, and I don't want to be with someone who has such a clear vision of what he wants me to be.

Something is preying on me, though, as I travel. Patrick, clearly, thinks I haven't changed at all, or not enough. But I keep thinking of what Hannah said on that last New Year's – when I asked her if I was old-fashioned for wearing silver, as opposed to trendy gold. *You're silver and heels, and you always will be. Never change, Celeste.*

Obviously it's not as if she's looking down disapprovingly

from heaven, wagging her finger and wanting me to undo all the experiences of the past year. That's not her style for a start. But as I watch the soft green fields of Wales unroll from my train window, I identify the feeling that's predominating in my unhappily muddled mind. It's guilt. I feel guilty for changing, for having new experiences. Because Hannah can no longer have those. And more than that: if I change so fundamentally that she really would be surprised – even if I just move on with my life and do things that she will never know about – then that means that she's really gone.

The winter landscape dissolves as the tears start sliding down my cheeks. I press a tissue against them and fish out my sunglasses, glad of the brief appearance of a pale sun.

I take out my book but find myself watching all the people – families with children tearing around, people travelling alone, and one couple in particular sitting near me, doing the crossword together. They look so relaxed and happy together; the woman keeps laughing, and twining one of her long chestnut curls around her finger. They're obviously a new couple – or are they friends? It's hard to tell. But it makes me think that of everything I'll miss about Patrick, our friendship will be high up there. I can almost picture a parallel life where I take the job in Dublin, and Patrick and I stay together, in love. The word shocks me a little, but then I realize it's true; I was falling in love with him. I remember my idea about a relationship feeling as remote as a trip to Australia. Well, now I want Australia – I want to move there, relocate permanently. And I can't.

By the time we arrive at Dublin Port I'm in a deep, dark emotional hole such as I've never experienced and never want to experience again. The Christmas atmosphere makes it worse: the carols playing softly as we wait to disembark, and all the families and couples. I didn't ask my parents to meet me as I know they find it a stressful drive; last time my mum attempted to come out to the port, she ended up in Clontarf. I said I'd just get a taxi. But I do regret it slightly as I see all the people being met, the family reunions, the parents and grandparents and the home-made signs. There's a giant SANTA STOP HERE sign with candy-cane decorations, reminding me of the ones Patrick stuffed into my pocket in Belgium. How on earth am I going to get through the whole charade of Christmas without a complete breakdown? Then the carols change. They're playing Hothouse Flowers' 'Don't Go'. Great. Now I have another song that makes me cry.

But just as I'm sinking deeper into self-pity I spot a familiar face in the crowd.

'Hey, Celeste.' An arm is raised in my direction. I let out a shriek of joy and surprise and bound over towards him.

'Hugh! What are you doing here?' I surprise us both by leaping into his arms, giving him a huge hug that almost knocks him sideways.

'Careful now,' he says, laughing. 'I was working out this way – thought you might want a lift.' He picks up my bag. 'Let's hustle – I'm parked where I shouldn't be.'

We run out into the night air, all my gloom forgotten briefly in the pleasure of having my brother pick me up. I'm so touched, and I also notice that something is different about him. He seems lighter – joyful, almost. And his car is bearing a Rudolph red nose and antlers, which he's always derided before as ridiculously tacky.

'Grab a euro for the toll there,' he instructs me, swinging out on to the exit road. 'One twenty I think it is. Daylight robbery.'

I obediently sort through coins, using up as much small change as I can. We zip through the toll bridge and then we're heading south past the cottages of Ringsend and on to Strand Road, with the lights of Howth twinkling at us across the bay.

'How's tricks? How's London?' he asks.

'Um, you know. Good. The usual.' I'm very glad that I didn't mention Patrick to any of my family yet; they've barely recovered from Eddie the Second. 'How are you, Hugh? Any news?'

'Ah, not much. You know yourself. Though I will say, I'm feeling fairly *positive* these days.'

'Oh. Great.' He sounds very wink-wink but I don't get it – it's probably a reference to some local scandal I haven't been following, like the TD who fell out of a swing.

'Nessa's feeling *positive* too,' he says.

And then the penny finally drops. I am so unbelievably dense. 'Oh, Hugh,' I say. 'Really?'

He indicates left and swings into one of the car parks on Strand Road, seriously annoying the driver behind him who gives a mild hoot, which is a sign of great displeasure in South County Dublin.

'I was going to wait and tell you once I got you back to the house but . . . I've waited long enough. Here you go.' He reaches in the dashboard and takes out an ultrasound scan picture. 'She's sixteen plus two. That means sixteen weeks plus two days. Pregnant.'

'I know,' I say softly, looking at the picture. I've seen so many of these on social media and they've never held that much personal significance to me before but now I'm looking at my niece – or nephew. A new life and an end to their suffering. 'Oh Hugh, Hugh. I'm just delighted for you. For both of you.' I reach over and give him a big hug. *Sixteen weeks*, I think. *That's well on the way – thank God.* There will be the twenty-week scan, but it's so far and so very good.

'Yeah. We're pretty happy. Come on.' He reverses back out of the car park, and we wait to leave it again – always a lengthy wait on Strand Road. This would normally drive him round the bend, but he just whistles a tune as he waits for the endless stream of southbound traffic to pause, and waves in a jaunty way to the driver who lets him out.

'How's Nessa feeling?' I ask.

'Ah, she's OK. She was pretty wrecked for the first twelve weeks, but now she's back on form and nesting away . . . She's on a mad decluttering kick. I had a hundred and thirty-one T-shirts, which I didn't know.'

'Well, that is a fair number.' I smile, thinking it's been so long since I saw him so excited. 'Are Mum and Dad delighted?'

'They are! Though they're pretty busy with the dog. And with the personal trainer, as you know. Dad's still at it. She has him doing crunches.'

I laugh aloud. 'Crunches? My God. Dad's going to have better abs than me at this rate.'

'I know. It's good times,' he says. 'Just . . . do me a favour, will you? If you know anyone who's struggling in the same way – don't tell them about us. Or not unless they ask you. Sometimes you want to hear those miracle stories, and sometimes you just don't.'

'I won't,' I promise.

We've passed the Merrion Gates now, and I look to my left and see the DART train, whistling towards Dalkey, where I caught the train so many times to Hannah's house. But we're turning right, away from the coast, up Booterstown Avenue towards my parents' place.

Hannah. The resolutions. 'Oh no!' I say suddenly.

'What?'

'My December resolution. I totally forgot to do it,' I reply in blank horror. How on earth could I have forgotten? I suppose it was all down to the excitement with the job offer – and Patrick.

It takes a second to catch Hugh up and explain that for December I had to help someone in need.

'I wouldn't worry,' he says. 'I think you're covered.'

'How so?'

'Well, you've been helping your pal Vik with his garden. And then there was your mad colleague – the junior one, who fell out with her friend? No?'

'Oh yeah,' I say, having forgotten that I'd told him about Dasha.

'And me,' he adds. 'Honestly, you offering to lend us the money for our treatment, the way you did – it meant a lot.'

I'm so touched at this, I can't really think of a reply except to punch him lightly on the arm, which I think he understands. Maybe he's right and I'm off the hook. Or maybe I'll still have the chance to help someone in need before the month is out.

'Oh,' Hugh says. 'I forgot to say. We're doing a brunch on Stephen's Day. For all Nessa's rellies – and you and the folks obviously if you're free.'

357

'Yeah, I'm free. Brunch, though? Really?' I know the brunch craze is unstoppable but to have one on 26 December seems mildly sacrilegious.

'Yes, really. We do have brunch in Dublin, you know.'

'Is Nessa up to cooking, though?'

'Who said anything about Nessa?' he says. 'I'm cooking. Turkey hash browns and smoked salmon brioche. It's a Neven Maguire recipe. Vegan option: bagels with homemade white bean dip, with a touch of sumac.'

'My God,' I say.

'Get with the programme, sis,' Hugh says serenely, waving another car past.

It is so good to be back. The Christmas tree is twinkling from its usual place in the front window. The O'Briens, two doors down, have their usual tacky multicoloured display complete with flying Santa: a holy show, as my dad always says. Our front door, with its holly wreath, opens and I'm home.

'Happy Christmas, darling.' My mum embraces me, and my dad comes forward and does the same. I feel the consolation of home and the warmth of my family. Even the dog consents to wag her tail softly, peeking her long shy nose out at me.

'Have you seen the madness two doors down?' Dad asks, as we all sit down.

'A holy show,' we all say in unison, and Hugh says, 'But maybe that's what Baby Jesus wants.' The same joke he makes every year. But then: something new.

'Have you heard the news?' Mum asks me, her eyes brimming, and I nod.

Mum and Dad open a bottle of Prosecco to toast Hugh

and his news, and we go over all the details again; sixteen plus two, they don't know if it's a boy or girl, happy with either, Nessa's fine now but was tired earlier. Due date: 19 May. Hospital of choice: the Mater. None of us will get tired of rehearsing all these details, which are now passing into family folklore. The dog looks anxiously at us all, obviously unable to account for all the mad excitement on top of the brightly decorated Christmas tree with its weird white lights.

'It's all right,' I tell her, stroking her ears. 'Babies are noisy but she won't harm you.'

'She?' repeats everyone.

'Yeah, I have a feeling,' I say, laughing. I also saw the scan picture; I'm no radiographer but I made a guess.

'We'll be very happy with either,' Hugh says for the tenth time. I can't get over the transformation in him, how radiant he looks. I realize how much our family needed this – needed a change. It didn't have to be a new baby; the new dog had a similar effect. Looking at all the happy faces, I understand that change is life. And I'm not scared of change, whatever Patrick might have thought. *Are you sure?* says a voice, the same one I heard during the ballet. I ignore it, though I'm pretty sure I know who it is by now.

The next day, the twenty-third, a freak snowstorm hits Dublin. I sleep through the storm itself, but I wake up to find a world muffled in white, as far as the eye can see. It covers the streets and hedges and drives with a white veil so that everything is magical, transformed. Even the snow, though, doesn't cheer me, reminding me as it does, of Patrick.

Mum and I go for our customary walk on Dún Laoghaire Pier anyway, with the dog wrapped up in the warmest tartan coat. The wind has dropped after today, and we have a bright blue sky and winter sun to whip the roses into our cheeks as Mum says. Looking over the clinking masts of the few yachts that are still out, I wonder if Patrick's membership has been approved. Then I hope to God that I don't see him – though it's probably inevitable at some point, Dublin being what it is. At least I know he'll be safely in Suffolk for New Year's. I haven't told Vik yet that I'm not coming; I'm too scared that he'll try to persuade me, and maybe even be successful.

'Are you OK, Celeste?' Mum asks gently, pressing my arm.

'I'm fine, Mum. Why?' I must be looking gloomy, so I put on a smile.

Mum says, 'It must be hard. Your younger brother . . .'

'Oh, the baby? No, Mum, not at all, honestly. I'm delighted for Hugh. Really. And for you and Dad.' I squeeze her arm. 'He's let me off the hook!' I add, trying to lighten the mood.

Now Mum looks upset. 'You were never on the hook, Celeste. We just want you to be happy.'

'I know, Mum. Sorry. I didn't mean it like that. You've never put any pressure on me, and I do appreciate it.' I put my arm around her. 'It's not the baby, honestly. I was – seeing someone, that's all. And it didn't work out.'

'What do you mean someone? Eddie, surely?'

'No! Someone else.' Now I feel even worse putting Mum through two heartbreaks.

'Oh, I'm sorry,' she says. 'That's awfully disappointing when that happens.'

I'm about to wave away her words, say it's all fine, but then I catch myself. 'It is. It's really sad.' I let out a long breath. 'We just wanted different things I think. He wanted to . . . fix me, I suppose. Change me.' I feel slightly uneasy as I say that last sentence, wondering if it is completely true.

'Change you? That's no good,' says Mum. After a pause she says, 'Helping you, though – that's another matter. Everyone needs help.'

'I suppose.' I exhale, wondering if I'll ever be rid of this piercing sadness. But then I think of the new baby coming. 'Hugh will certainly need your help, won't he? And Nessa. I'm so happy for them, and for all of us, Mum, honestly. It's brilliant. I'm going to be an aunt!'

Mum's eyes fill up with tears, as if my words have given her permission to let out her true feelings. 'It's the answer to all my prayers,' she says.

'Oh, Mum,' I say, giving her another hug.

We've reached the end of the pier now, where the mandolin player is strumming away as he does in all weathers. People are gazing at the view, from Howth to Dalkey and then north to the city centre, all to the sound of the waves lapping against the rocks. We turn back and look at Dún Laoghaire Harbour all lit up for Christmas, the Dublin Mountains behind whitened out after the dramatic snowstorm yesterday. The whole city seems to be holding its breath before tomorrow's festivities. Or am I the one holding my breath?

I think of what things would be like here if I weren't

sailing back next week. I think of walks on the pier with my mum and the dog; going to the Pavilion Theatre to see films with my dad; going for runs beside the sea and driving into the mountains on a whim; catching up with old friends over Irish coffees in hotel bars. I know that I have a rosy view of life here from only ever seeing it on holiday. I've never had to commute or pay taxes in Dublin; never had to sit in traffic on a freezing January morning in a damp bus. But it's still true that life is more peaceful here. The skies are wider, the pace is slower; people are friendlier. I breathe in the sea air, fresh and salty; it's like nothing else on earth, especially at Christmas.

Then I think of London – the rush, the buzz, the constant sense of something new round the corner, the whole world in one city. I could certainly be happy there too, continuing as I am, with – hopefully – new friends and new adventures. But maybe the biggest adventure of all would be coming back home. The job that I've been offered is a great opportunity – that's clear. And, yes, it's riskier, but I have built up the resources to ride the storm if I have to. The uneasy thought comes to me that this was exactly what Patrick was trying to say to me – but then I dismiss it; it's so much easier to think straight without him pressuring me. How do I know, though? How will I ever know if it's the right thing to do?

'What's that noise?' says Mum. 'Oh, Celeste, would you look at that! A bee! How did that get here?' She stares after it, adjusting her scarf. 'A bee in December, on Dún Laoghaire Pier. Poor thing is a long way from home.'

I stare after it, a half-formed smile on my lips. I watch the tiny speck zigzagging over the rocks and back, heading,

I presume, towards the People's Park. A bee. Hannah's words come back to me when I asked her about the Suffolk move. *How do you know?* I said. And she said, *I don't really. Sometimes you just have to hold your nose and jump.*

I find myself smiling properly now because I know what I'm going to do. And it's not just because I saw a bee. The bee reminded me of Hannah, but I'm the one who decides what it means. It means hold your nose and jump. If the job goes wrong, I can get another one, and if I don't enjoy living in Dublin – well, I can always move back. Though somehow, I don't think I will want to.

'Will we head back? It's perishing,' says Mum. 'How about tea at the Royal Marine? They allow dogs.'

'That sounds lovely,' I say, smiling.

'That's just reminded me,' she says. 'You know I told you I ran into Dervla Golden at Mass? Well, we've become quite pally. She's joined my walking group, and we've been for tea at the Royal Marine a few times too.'

'Oh, really, Mum? I'm so glad.' The idea of Hannah's mum and mine becoming friends genuinely warms my frozen heart.

'She's a very interesting person. We're very different, of course,' Mum comments. 'But those can be the best friendships, sometimes.'

I can't help it; the tears are welling over now and I put my fist to my mouth to choke a sob. But I'm smiling too.

'Oh, pet,' Mum says, all concern again.

'No, it's OK,' I say. 'They're happy tears. I'm really pleased, Mum. I think she could do with a friend like you.'

We turn around, arm in arm, and start walking back towards the pier. I could tell her now about the job, but I think I'll wait. I'll wait until we have our tea and scones, in the cosy drawing room of the Royal Marine Hotel, with its chandeliers and tall Christmas tree. I'll pour for her, or let her pour for me, and as we drink the tea that never tastes the same in London, I'll tell her that I'm moving back home. I want to savour this moment, which I'm only now realizing has been so long overdue. I know how happy she will be, and Dad and Hugh and Nessa. It's a good reminder that even though things didn't work out with Patrick I still have a lot of love in my life.

34

I might have a lot of love in my life, but I still feel a gloom descending on me at various stages of the Christmas festivities. Like on the following night, Christmas Eve, when Mum has me light the candle in the window, as the youngest member of the household now that Hugh's not here. Or on Christmas morning, when I wake up in my childhood bedroom, still with the same *Romeo and Juliet* poster on the wall that now reminds me of the ballet and my failed romance with Eddie – as well as Patrick. Two in one year – a personal best. I hope next year doesn't bring the hat trick.

Then I remember the astrologer's prediction, about November being a time of romance. And his ominous words about 'the rule of three'. Of course: Hannah, Eddie – and now Patrick. I hope that's it for me. Certainly, as far as romance goes, I'm done.

The aftermath of a break-up is never fun, even when it's a brand-new relationship, especially when you have to answer questions about your single status over your newly expecting brother's turkey hash brown and brioche brunch. But then again, I tell myself, maybe it's the fact that it was such a new relationship that makes the ending of it so painful. Patrick and I weren't together long enough for me to get sick of his anecdotes or the way he drives, or his refusal to go out on Sunday evenings, say. I don't even know what his policy on Sunday evening outings is. And now I never will.

As New Year's approaches, my feelings of sadness intensify. I don't receive any invitations. Hugh and Nessa are watching a film at home with a takeaway, and Mum and Dad are doing the same at home with me – and the dog. In honour of the occasion I change into my thickest fleece-lined tracksuit bottoms and my most unflattering old hoodie, which is part of my Dublin wardrobe from college days, still housed in my old bedroom. Then I flip through social media, looking at pictures Vik has posted, obviously of the gang at his house. There's Patrick in yet another woollen jumper, laughing and chopping wood. And sharing his saw – ugh – is some gorgeous dark-haired girl I don't recognize. I'm so glad I skipped that invitation. I sent a cowardly text to Vik yesterday; he hasn't replied yet, but I hope he will understand.

Perhaps I'm being too cynical; I don't even know any more. Hugh certainly thought so when I told him the other evening while I was driving him home from Mum and Dad's.

'Wait a minute,' he said. 'So you're having a great time, he's declared himself and all is roses except he has to leave to go to Dublin. To pursue his dream of a career change, which he's been working on for months. And you tell him you've been offered a job in Dublin, but you're not going to take it because, hmm, too risky. What's he supposed to say to that? I would have been disappointed too.'

'Huh,' I said, acknowledging that there was, maybe, a grain of truth to that.

Before I can chicken out of it, I get out my phone and send him a text. After pondering several versions, the best I can think of is, Hi Patrick. Happy New Year. I hope it's a good year for you. Cx.

There we go. He can make of it what he will. I flip through the rest of my feed, thinking that the flood of engagement rings has peaked from a few years ago; now it's all birth announcements, baby pictures, first teeth, first days at school. It's not what I long for myself, but it does give me a pang or a pause, as I see how my friends' lives are changing while mine is still the same.

Not quite the same, though. I do have an international house move to plan for, plus a new job. Trying to pep myself up, I go back downstairs, and get out the ingredients for a little pick-me-up: condensed milk, cream, a touch of cocoa and, of course, whiskey. I whisk together the cream and condensed milk, add the cocoa and whiskey, and pour it into three glasses with ice, carrying them through on a tray to Mum and Dad. They're in the Good Room, as the rarely used living room is called, as a concession to the evening. Their faces light up when they see what I've made: my home-made Baileys, like every year.

'Fantastic. This is the real deal,' says Dad, lifting his glass and toasting me.

'I've tried to make it,' says Mum, 'but nobody has your touch, Celeste.'

'Thanks, guys.' I smile at how they ooh and aah, treating my very basic cocktail as if it's been crafted by the head mixologist at the Ritz. It's nice to be around people who make me feel so good about myself, and I remind myself for the millionth time how lucky I am to have them. 'Cheers. Happy New Year, ladies,' says Dad, and Mum and I join in.

'Oh, that'll be the man from the Spice Pantry,' says Mum, hearing the doorbell. 'Thanks, lovey. Will you tip him? I have five euros.' Mum and Dad are still doubtful about the whole concept of delivery, still believing that 'takeaway' should mean literally that you take the stuff away.

I go out to the hall, checking the hall table is free just in case I don't have enough arm space for the feast that's been ordered, and open up.

But it's not the Spice Pantry. It's Patrick.

He clears his throat. 'Hi – Happy New Year,' he says.

'Happy New Year,' I say, unable to compute. Isn't he meant to be hundreds of miles away in the wilds of Suffolk?

'I was just –'

'What's wrong, Celeste?' Mum calls from behind me. 'Do you need more money?'

'No, no. It's a friend.' I take a step outside, closing the door over behind me.

'I just got your text,' he says. 'And . . . look, can I talk to you? I have my car . . .'

I could just tell him that whatever he has to say can be said in front of my parents, and the dog and maybe even the man from the Spice Pantry. But I don't want to do that, so I just put my head round the door, tell them I'm going out for a bit and pull on my coat, following Patrick down the drive. It's a serious breach of good manners to let a visitor come and go without the requisite fifteen-minute chat with Mum and Dad, but I can't handle that until I know why he's here and what he's got to say.

He opens his car and we sit inside it. It's warm, and it smells faintly of that aftershave of his.

'So,' he says, 'it turns out . . .' He tries to smile. 'It turns out that there is something you can't get in Dublin after all.'

I don't want to talk in riddles, so I just say, 'What do you mean, Patrick?'

'Just that I'm sorry,' he says. 'When you told me you were turning down the job in Dublin, I was gutted. It just felt as if you were telling me about it to prove some kind of point. So I overreacted and said some things I shouldn't.'

'Like that I'm stuck in the past?'

'I didn't say it like that,' he pleads. 'But, OK, I shouldn't have said anything at all. I was disappointed, but I shouldn't have taken it out on you. I just want to be with you – in whatever way we can work out. Even if it means me giving up on the place here.'

I look up at him, my pulse pounding in my ears. I can't believe that he's here and telling me this. It's like a dream, except that the hand that's holding mine now is solid and warm. I curl my fingers around his. He looks down at me, his eyes bright with emotion, and he says, 'You don't need to be fixed, Celeste. You just need love. And, honestly, so do I.'

I reach up to kiss him, and one word floats into my mind: blessing. A blessing, dropping from the sky like the unexpected snowfall the other night. His hair, his face under my fingers, his arms around mine: I never thought I'd feel these sensations again or feel this happy ever. Not just content or coping or fine, but floating with bliss.

'I'm sorry too. And I'm taking the job,' I tell him, as soon we pause for breath.

He looks as me as if he can't take it all in; he looks just as radiant and transformed as I must too.

'Don't joke with me,' he says.

'I'm not, I'm not,' I assure him, as if I would do that. I'm so happy to see him looking so happy.

'Seriously? You're taking it?'

'I can't call them today obviously. But I will on the second.'

He shakes his head repeatedly as if – in Mum's phrase – all his Christmases had come at once. 'Congratulations,' he says. 'That makes me so happy.'

'Me too.' I gaze at him for a minute before my head starts to swim again, as I wonder how on earth he can be here, when I've just seen photos of him at Vik's.

'But why aren't you in Suffolk? Where were you . . . when you got my text?'

'I was down the road in the M1,' he says.

I'm completely befuddled – does he mean the motorway in England? But then I realize he's referring to a nearby pub called the Merrion Inn, which for reasons unknown is often called the M1.

'I was with some buddies. Feeling pretty depressed. But then I got a text that gave me hope. Not a guarantee, but a glimmer of hope that you might accept an apology. And so I abandoned them and hightailed it up here. Vik gave me your address,' he adds, anticipating what was going to be my next question.

'What about that photo? And the girl in it?' I ask suddenly. 'Sharing a saw with you.'

'Sharing a what? Oh. That's the famous Megan,' he says, raising his eyebrows. 'Vik's new friend. That must have been taken a few weeks back. You know he's always late with his social media. It's funny, he didn't push me that hard when I said I wasn't coming to Suffolk. He might have been a few steps ahead of us.'

'Oh,' I say, finally out of questions.

'Celeste,' he says, and his eyes are glimmering with humour now as well as love and relief. 'Don't you think I want someone to spend New Year's with too?'

I curl my arms around him tighter and kiss him again, revelling in the feeling, even more so because I know that it's not a diminishing resource, like it was before Christmas, but a renewable heat source that's going to stay firing for as long as we both want it to.

'What now?' he asks, when we next pause. 'I don't want your parents to think I've kidnapped you.'

'We could go for a drink or something. But first why don't you come inside and say hello? They'd love to meet you. Unless that's too soon?' I add doubtfully.

'It's not too soon,' he says instantly. 'And thank God it's not too late either.'

I resist kissing him again; if I start now, we'll never get out of the car.

'It's not too late,' I say. 'We've still got four hours until midnight. You can be the first-footer.'

'Isn't that supposed to be a tall dark stranger?'

'Two out of three,' I say.

Epilogue

January

At eight o'clock the next morning, we both leave Patrick's house in Dalkey, where we spent the night. Luckily for me his mum and sister were both out when we got in; I think we've had enough family introductions for one night – or one year.

The sun is just coming up outside and it's freezing. I'm wrapped up in rubber boots borrowed from his sister and a fur hat and gloves that I think belong to his mother. We walk down his road through the slush, treading carefully to avoid icy patches. We pass Hannah's house, the lights all out, and I send a farewell in its direction. The granite walls and hedges are all edged and bowed down by snow. Every house glimpsed through a snowy gap is a Christmas card; every window reveals a Christmas tree. Then a bend in the road reveals the tiny storybook Bullock Castle, and the sea, and another turn takes us past the last row of cottages to Bullock Harbour.

'Give me a hand?' says Patrick. He's lifting a tarpaulin, heavy with snow, off a small motor which is berthed beside the short pier. We clamber aboard, me feeling very glad she was already in the water and we didn't have to push her down the slip and jump in as we did last time.

After a few revs, the engine finally roars into life and we putter slowly out of the little harbour and up the short coast. There's a keen wind whipping our cheeks, and I shiver and pull my borrowed hat tighter on to my head. A deep pink is growing from the eastern horizon now, spreading up towards the gold and pale blue of the sky. White horses dot the dark navy waves, and between us and the sunrise is our destination, Dalkey Island. I've never seen it covered in snow before and it looks almost unreal; topped with its round tower and touched with rays of gold and peach, it's like a castle in the air.

We skim along the waves to the long jetty that stretches to the left-hand side of the island. Patrick stills the engine, throws a rope and ties it to a metal hook. 'Not my best-ever cleat hitch but she'll do,' he says, smiling at me.

We climb on to the pier, the solid ground already feeling strange after the short boat journey. And then we're on the island proper. It hasn't changed in the twenty years since I first came; it's just a short stretch of land between a ruined early Christian church and a Martello tower that dates from the Napoleonic wars. Without discussing it, we walk slowly up the path, climbing the gentle hill towards the Martello tower.

The wind rises as we climb the hill, an east wind whistling straight at us across the water from Wales. All of Dublin is asleep across the bay from us, and behind the city are the mountains capped with snow and catching the light from the sunrise.

'Are you ready?' Patrick asks, when we've come to the highest point. I nod. He unscrews the canister, which he's been carrying in his inside coat pocket. He's about to open it but then he hands it to me. I feel a moment of fear, of what it will look like and how it will feel, but when I open it, it's just a fine grey mist that flies with the wind across the bay, until it's gone.

'There's a poem too, as I said.' He takes out a piece of paper. He starts reading, and I realize it's the same one that was read at her funeral. I hated the sentiment then. But now I feel the truth of it, and I feel that she really is present in the beauties of nature, the wind and the snow, because these things will always make me think of her. When Patrick finishes reading, he hands me the piece of paper and without thinking I let it fly too, the wind whipping and whirling it far above our heads towards the sea, until it's lost as well. And Hannah's resolutions are done too, the last item completed – to help someone in need. It's a day late, of course, but I don't think Hannah would mind; she was rarely on time after all.

The sun has properly risen now, and it's beginning to warm our faces with the first rays of the new year. Patrick shades his eyes. 'See you on the other side,' I hear him say.

His words remind me of last New Year's but also our very first conversation, nearly twenty years ago to the day. My first celebration with Hannah. It occurs to me that she always will be with me at New Year's in a sense. And if I'm very lucky, Patrick will be too.

He clasps an arm around my shoulders and I feel him exhale. We scan the horizon for a moment, and I wonder if we might see a sign of some kind, a bee or a seal or perhaps even a dolphin; they've been seen here, though rarely.

But there's nothing, just the steady wash of the waves and the occasional cry of a seagull.

'Come on,' he says. 'Let's go back to the house. You can meet my mum and my sister, and I'll make you breakfast.'

I nod, and we set off back across the snow, to where the boat is waiting to take us home.

Acknowledgements

Thank you to the first person I told this story to; the same person I sent my first ever novel to: my amazing agent Rowan Lawton. Thanks also to Eleanor Lawlor and all at the Soho Agency. Thank you to dream editor Rebecca Hilsdon for everything, and to her and Clare Bowron for bringing out the best in my writing and tactfully querying the other bits. Huge thanks to all at Michael Joseph including Sriya Varadharajan, Kallie Townsend, Hanifa Frederick, Lucy Upton and Nick Lowndes.

Thank you to my dear friend Helen and family, who welcomed me into their house in Suffolk – thank you, Helen, for the insightful editorial feedback and advice on gardens and swans.

I'm grateful to Dr Ghee Bowman for checking my references to the Indian Army in the Second World War. Thank you also to Dr Diya Gupta and to Urvi Khaitan for helping to put me in touch with Dr Bowman. Thanks to Jo Pugh for taking the time to advise me on the Eighth Army's campaigns in Italy. Any errors are all my own and I welcome any corrections.

Patrick Geary was my consultant astrologer and helped guide Celeste through her celestial journey – you can reach him at stillwaters.space. Again, any bloopers are mine.

Last and biggest hugs and thanks go to Alex, who makes it all possible, and to Stella, the brightest star in my sky.